CAPTAIN
NEMO

THE FANTASTIC ADVENTURES
OF A DARK GENIUS

CAPTAIN NEMO

THE FANTASTIC ADVENTURES OF A DARK GENIUS

KEVIN J. ANDERSON

"WHAT ONE MAN CAN IMAGINE, ANOTHER CAN ACHIEVE."
—JULES VERNE

TITAN BOOKS

CAPTAIN NEMO

Print edition ISBN: 9780857683427
E-book ISBN: 9780857686183

Published by
Titan Books
A division of Titan Publishing Group Ltd
144 Southwark St
London
SE1 0UP

First edition: September 2011
1 3 5 7 9 10 8 6 4 2

© 2011 WordFire, Inc.

Visit our website:
www.titanbooks.com

What did you think of this book? We love to hear from our readers. Please email us at: readerfeedback@titanemail.com, or write to us at the above address.

To receive advance information, news, competitions, and exclusive offers online, please sign up for the Titan newsletter on our website: www.titanbooks.com

A CIP catalogue record for this title is available from the British Library.

Printed in the USA.

This book is for CATHERINE,
who has been an intelligent, insightful, hard-working, and
all-round delightful companion on many of my fictional
"extraordinary voyages."

Jules Verne's characters could not have hoped
for a better fellow adventurer.

PROLOGUE

Amiens, France
February, 1873

Damp winter clung to northern France, but a fire warmed Jules Verne's writing study. Sultry smoke, orange light, and dreams.

Verne had composed many of his best stories in this isolated tower room, where narrow latticed windows looked out upon the leaden Amiens sky. The bleak view reminded him of the polar wastelands in *Captain Hatteras*, or the Icelandic volcano in *A Journey to the Centre of the Earth*. Though he chose not to venture far from his study, imagination had taken him to many places, both real and unreal.

Elms graced the flagstoned courtyard of the author's house on rue Charles-Dubois. Thick vines climbed the brick walls like ratlines on a sailing ship. How could he not think of the three-masted *Coralie*, on which a young and ambitious Jules had almost taken a voyage around the world?

Almost. At the last minute, Verne's stern father had snatched him from that real-life adventure, then punished him for "boyhood foolishness."

It had fallen to his friend André Nemo to go on the voyage without him. "A world of adventure is waiting for us," Nemo always said, imagining the excitement the two would experience. But he had been forced to do it all alone.

Though he was much older now, and wealthy because of his skill at crafting fanciful extraordinary voyages, Verne knew in his marrow that nothing was holding him back anymore. He promised himself he would go out and see exotic lands and have exciting adventures, just like Nemo. *One day.*

At the age of forty-five, Jules Verne was a world-renowned writer, bursting with ideas and an ever-growing readership around the world. Persistent gray strands streaked his unruly reddish hair, and his long beard lent him the appearance of a wise philosopher. Often depicted in the French press, Verne had watched his fame grow with each successive novel. Lionized for his brilliant imagination, he was a man to whom the world turned for exotic, titillating thrills, a breadth of astonishing experiences that the average man could never hope to have.

And I deserve none of it.

His "inventiveness" was a sham. *Nemo* was the one who had experienced all the real adventures, survived the trials, explored the unknown. Verne was nothing more than an armchair adventurer, living a vicarious life through another man's exploits.

No matter. Nemo wouldn't want the applause or the fame anyway.

In the tower study, Verne's maplewood shelves groaned with reference books, atlases, explorers' journals, newspaper clippings – information compiled by others, artifacts kept by a poseur. He had no other way to achieve verisimilitude in his fiction, and so far he hadn't been caught. Verne had been everywhere on the planet, but only in his mind. His life was safer that way, after all – more comfortable, and not so much of a bother.

Verne picked at the plate of strong Camembert his quiet and frumpy wife had brought him hours earlier. He smeared the soft cheese on a piece of brown bread and ate, chewing slowly, deep in thought. Trying to concoct another story.

Nemo had once said to him, "There are two types of men in this world, Jules – those who *do* things, and those who wish they did."

Oh, how Verne envied him . . . rhetorically speaking.

Ten years ago, his first novel, *Five Weeks in a Balloon*, had established him as a popular writer, and his subsequent "Extraordinary Voyages" had made him a fortune.

Despite the fame, Verne envied his old friend Nemo, the experiences he'd had, the opportunities he'd seized. Nemo had loved and lost, had come close to death countless times, had suffered tremendous hardships – and triumphed. Such an exciting life . . . if one wanted that sort of thing. Nervous perspiration broke out on Verne's forehead. *What is it about the man?*

Verne had followed *Five Weeks* with *A Journey to the Centre of the Earth*, which explored exotic regions underground, and then *Captain Hatteras* about a dramatic quest for the North Pole. Next came *From the Earth to the Moon, The Children of Captain Grant*, and *20,000 Leagues Under the Sea*, all published in the years before the Franco-Prussian War devastated the French countryside.

Ignoring the gray sleet and the skeletal elm branches outside his window, Verne added another length of wood to the fire. He closed the shutters, increasing the gloom in the study. There, better for concentration.

Downstairs, the family's big black dog barked, and his ten-year-old son, Michel, squealed. The rambunctious boy had an impish face, chestnut hair, and the soul of a demon. The dog barked again, and Michel shouted, chasing it around the house. Outside, when the regular train from Amiens to Paris clattered by, the engineer took malicious delight in tooting its whistle.

So much clamor and disruption was enough to drive a man mad. *Adventures enough for me*, he thought.

The latest novel, *Around the World in 80 Days*, had taken Verne beyond success into genuine celebrity. Installments published in newspapers generated more excitement than actual news. Chapters were telegraphed around the globe; men made wagers as to whether the intrepid Phileas Fogg would succeed in his quest to circumnavigate the globe. Already, Verne had begun talks with a well-known playwright to create a stage production with real cannons and a live elephant. Very exciting.

It was yet another idea he owed to Nemo's real-life exploits.

What is it about the man?

Of all Verne's novels, the popular favorite by far remained the undersea adventure of the *Nautilus* and its enigmatic captain who had isolated himself from humanity, a man who had declared war on war itself. To Verne's surprise, the dark and mysterious villain had captured the public's imagination. *Nemo, Nemo, Nemo!* No one guessed the man was based on a real person.

Verne thought he'd ended Nemo's story by sinking the submarine boat in a maelstrom off Norway. The fictional Captain Nemo had perished in that vortex of waves, while the erstwhile Professor Aronnax, his manservant Conseil, and the harpooner Ned Land barely escaped with their lives.

Verne hadn't really believed Nemo would stay down, though – not even after his literary death.

He pushed the tea and cheese away, then stared down at the thick ledger book in which he wrote his manuscript. This massive new novel would be a challenge to his heart as well as to his storytelling abilities.

Verne had never intended to write about his friend again. He had begun this new novel, a shipwreck story, back in 1870 during the horrors of the Prussian war. Buildings had burned, and desperate citizens had eaten zoo animals and sewer rats just to stay alive. And in the midst of that turmoil Verne had lost his beloved Caroline forever.

But now, two years later, the world had returned to order. The trains ran on schedule, and once more Verne was expected to release his "Extraordinary Voyages" like clockwork.

He hated to reopen old wounds, but he would force himself to tell the rest of Nemo's story. He knew the real André Nemo better than any man alive, the passions that drove him, the ordeals he faced. Future generations would remember Nemo's life the way *Verne* chose to portray it, rather than what had actually transpired. He would concoct a fitting background for the dark captain. The "truth" posed no undue restrictions: Monsieur Verne was a *fiction* writer, after all.

He opened a fresh inkwell and dipped the sharp nib of his pen, then scratched the blackened tip across the paper. Beginning a new story, a long story: *The Mysterious Island.*

He could finally lay Captain Nemo to rest and then live his own life, seek out his own adventures. One of these days. . .

What is it about the man? Over the years, the jealousy had grown to rivalry, and then to something even darker.

The words began to flow, as they always did.

Part I
EXTRAORDINARY VOYAGES

I

Île Feydeau, Nantes, France
July, 1840

In their younger years, Jules Verne and André Nemo were the best of friends.

Walking together on damp ground that sloped down to the bank of the Loire, the boys each ate a sweet banana that had been carried on one of the trading clippers that had just arrived from the East Indies. Thick cumulus clouds hung like unexplored islands in the sun-washed sky.

Nemo led the way. "By the quays, Jules. I want to be close to the ships when I submerge myself." With his new apparatus, the dark-haired young man had made up his mind that he could walk and breathe *underwater*. And Nemo was so insistent that Verne actually believed him.

Growing up near one of France's largest shipyards, both young men had an abiding love for the sea. Sailors from Batz unloaded a cargo of salt onto the dock. The fish market, its air thick with the stench of day-old catch, sweltered in the July humidity. The fishwives teased each other in loud voices, using colorful language that would have brought a blush to the cheeks of Verne's strict father, a local lawyer.

Even forty miles inland, the broad Loire River was sluggish as it drained toward the Atlantic. A century earlier, through dredgings and diversions, engineers had created an artificial island, Île Feydeau, separated by a shallow canal on one side and the deep river channel on the other. The swollen waters of annual spring floods still reached up to the first floors of the row houses, and many families kept small boats tied up in their courtyards, just in case.

Île Feydeau was shaped like a boat, and Verne and Nemo often pretended the entire island would detach and float down the river – village and all – to the coast of France. From there, they could drift across the Atlantic and explore the world. . .

Now, the two boys made their way past the barrels, crates, and lumber piles to where they had stowed their equipment. *Walking underwater.* Verne found his friend's plan incredible – but his fiery-eyed and determined companion might succeed where no one else could. Nemo did not believe in the impossible.

Preparing for the underwater experiment, Nemo carried his equipment over one shoulder. Verne hurried after him with the remaining items. Soon enough, they'd find out whether the invention would work. Though he wouldn't try the apparatus himself, Verne planned to write a chronicle of his friend's underwater adventures, provided Nemo ever went anyplace more interesting than the Loire channel.

Half a century before, Nantes had prospered from the "ebony trade," shipping slaves from Africa to the West Indies. Merchants used the money raised in the Caribbean to buy sugar cane, which they brought back to France and resold at a high profit. With the decline of the slave trade, however, Nantes had faded as a major port, and when local sugar beets replaced expensive imported cane, the city became dependent on its shipbuilding industry. The shipyard forest held frameworks and dry docks for clippers, schooners, and packet ships.

A nearly completed vessel floated in the deep channel just ahead of them, a ship named the *Cynthia*. In the hot afternoon, men chanted as they swung heavy mallets, pounding deck boards together, hammering iron eyes. Pulleys rattled as thick ropes were hauled up to the tops of the three masts. On deck, cauldrons of bubbling tar gave off a harsh chemical stench that overwhelmed the aroma of old fish. Painters covered the outer hull with traditional black, then added a sleek white stripe from bow to stern.

Nemo shaded his eyes, trying to discern a familiar silhouette among the workers. His father Jacques worked as a carpenter and finisher aboard the *Cynthia*. The wiry, good-natured man had been a seaman in his early years and now used his expertise to construct the tall ships. Verne and Nemo often listened to Jacques's tales of glorious days at sea.

It seemed strange that the son of a conservative lawyer would be such a close friend to the child of a widowed shipbuilder, but the two shared a fascination for far-off lands and the mysteries of the earth. They had the same favorite books: Defoe's *Robinson Crusoe* and Wyss's *Swiss Family Robinson*, which they collectively called their "Robinsons."

Though both boys were dreamers, they were different in appearance and temperament. Jules Verne had blue eyes and tousled reddish hair, freckles on his pale skin, and a plodding sort of persistence; André Nemo had deep brown eyes that held an undeniable spark of optimism. Corsican blood from his long-dead mother had given him an olive complexion, straight dark hair, and an independent spirit.

Reaching the docks they had chosen, the boys dropped their bundles in the mud beside the thick pilings. Nemo removed a flexible bladder that had once been a wine skin, which he'd altered by inserting a wide reed through a hole and cementing a narrow rectangle of thick glass fashioned from a broken pane. Near the mouth area he had added a one-way flap valve so he could exhale his used air. After the modifications, he had closed the skin with tight little stitches covered in gutta-percha for a watertight seal.

Helping him, Verne fiddled with the tube that protruded from the bladder hood. Earlier in the summer, he and Nemo had taken hollow reeds and dunked their heads under the Loire, wading around just below the surface like clever American Indians they had read about in the adventures by James Fenimore Cooper. But this experiment was much more complex.

The preparations finished, Nemo extended the modified bladder helmet toward Verne. "We are in this together, my friend. You have as much right to be first as I do. Here."

Verne backed away, shaking his head. "I wouldn't dream of it, André. I'll just stay here and help feed the tubes. You . . . you try it first."

Not surprised, Nemo strapped a belt of heavy stones around his waist, then thrust a dagger into the sheath at his hip. In an emergency he could cut the weights free and rise to the surface.

Nemo tugged the bladder over his dark hair, adjusting it from side to side until he could see through the rectangle of glass. The flexible sides fit tight against his ears and temples, and it smelled of sour wine. He slathered his neck and the edge of the bladder with thick grease, then cinched a leather belt to seal the helmet against his skin to prevent air loss, though not tight enough to strangle him. Both boys knew this was risky – but Nemo refused to hold back with such an opportunity at hand.

Nemo adjusted the breathing reed and the exhale flap. When he tried to speak, the bladder muffled his words, so he turned to meet Verne's eyes through the viewing plate. Verne clasped his friend's hand and wished him good luck, as if he were a businessman about to embark on a journey.

Verne uncovered a pot of sun-warmed pitch and arranged the hollow reeds on the ground beside him. With quick hands, he dipped one end into the pitch and inserted it into the tube that protruded from Nemo's helmet, thereby extending the air line.

Nemo stepped into the water, moving slowly so as not to strain the connected reeds. Verne picked up a third reed, smeared the seam with pitch, and sealed it to the second segment. Nemo sank waist-deep and kept going until his shoulders disappeared beneath the greenish-brown river.

Just as his covered head entered the water, he took a careful breath, then exhaled through the exhaust valve. Everything seemed to be working. With one more step, he was submerged, his bare feet walking along the silty riverbottom.

KEVIN J. ANDERSON

17

Verne attached reed after reed, careful to keep the pipes clear, feeling a tremendous responsibility. His friend might drown if the experiment failed. The line of joined reeds disappeared under the water like a long straw. He could see Nemo making his way toward the *Cynthia*'s construction quay and envied him – but only in a theoretical sense. Personally, he was glad to be safe and dry on shore.

Taking a break now that he was several reeds ahead of Nemo's progress, Verne looked around to see if anyone was watching them. Steep terraced gardens made a splash of green and wildflower colors by the facade of the Church of St Martin. Seagulls spun overhead, dived down to snatch garbage from the water, and then splattered bridges and rooftops with gray-white runnels.

Then he saw a straight-backed girl with strawberry-blond hair tucked under a wide-brimmed hat. She walked along the cobblestone path above the riverbank, coming toward him. Her afternoon dress was blue moiré silk with a high-waisted bodice, trimmed with row upon row of white fringe, bows, and roses to conceal the restrictive stays beneath. Her leg-of-mutton sleeves looked long and hot in the bright river sunshine. She wore the dress as if it were an unpleasant uniform.

Startled to see her, Verne dropped the sticky end of a reed into the dirt, then spluttered at the clumsy mess he had made. When Caroline Aronnax approached, he wanted to look impressive and dashing, not like a clod.

She had already noticed him, seen his blunder, and he blushed crimson. Caroline shaded her eyes and called out, "Jules Verne, what are you doing down there?"

With a glance to ensure that no one of sufficient social station was watching her, the proper young woman hopped off the cobblestone path, lifted her ankle-length skirt, and hurried across the mud to join him by the dock pilings. Even fine clothes could not disguise her tomboy nature or her fascination with all manner of things her exasperated mother considered "unseemly for a young lady."

"Up to something interesting, I hope? It is not often I see you without

André. Where is he?"

Verne swallowed hard. As always when he was around Caroline, the words caught in his throat, and his sharp wit and intelligence faded into a confusion of stutters. "He . . . I . . . André's *there*." He pointed to the line of reeds. "He's exploring under the water. I'm in charge of keeping his air line clear. It's a very important job."

Caroline bent down, careful not to muddy her dress, and looked out at the river. Verne regarded her pointed nose and slender neck. In an impassioned love letter he'd once written, Verne had described her hair as "honey caught on fire," but, as with so many things, he'd never found the nerve to send the letter – though she could not be blind to his attraction. Or André Nemo's.

Caroline's eyes were cornflower blue, and her skin, though fair, was vibrant instead of pale and translucent, as was most valued by French high society. Madame Aronnax constantly scolded her daughter for going outside into the sun and tried to reign in her outgoing ways.

Caroline's father was a wealthy merchant, one of the last to have made a fortune in the sugar cane trade of the West Indies. Of late, he had become an importer of rum and North American rice, as well as exotic cargoes from Asia and the East Indies. Monsieur Aronnax adored his daughter and had taught her how to read maps and charts, told her about places his shipping fleet visited, and discussed with her how the tea crop in Ceylon might affect the price of cowhides from California. Her mother could not understand what Caroline would ever do with such useless knowledge, and hired a music tutor for her instead.

Caroline learned to play the harpsichord and the pianoforte, became proficient in the works of Bach, Handel, and Mozart. But when she was alone, Caroline composed her own fugues and concertos, delighting in the creative process. When asked, though, she credited the original compositions to a mythical 18th-century French composer named "Passepartout," since Mme Aronnax would have been horrified to learn of her daughter's creative ambitions.

Caroline also dabbled in traditional art to keep her mother happy, sketching the shipyards at sunset or still lifes of fruit and flowers (as well as secret drawings of distant ports and strange creatures described by sailors aboard her father's merchant ships).

Both Verne and Nemo were infatuated with Caroline, and both did everything possible to impress her. André Nemo was the free-spirited son of a shipbuilder, and Jules Verne was the child of a dull country lawyer. Neither had a chance to win her hand, if Madame Aronnax had any say in the matter.

Caroline shaded her eyes against the sunlight and looked ready to wade in after Nemo. "How long has André been down there?" Verne realized that he needed to add another reed or his friend would drag the end of the breathing tube underwater.

"I don't know, my – my lovely lady." Verne stumbled over his words even as he tried to be as debonair as the heroes in dramas he had seen in the Nantes playhouse. "When you come near me, all time seems to stop."

Caroline endured the flattery with patient grace. "Then perhaps you had better consult your pocket watch." She raised her eyebrows and indicated the end of the breathing reed, which tottered close to being submerged.

Embarrassed, Verne splashed into the water to seal on the next tube, getting sticky gum on his fingers.

As she stood beside Verne, watching the breathing tubes disappear beneath the river, a smile emerged at the corners of her graceful mouth. Seeing Nemo's preposterous scheme of walking beneath the water, Caroline said, "It is wonderful to see impossible dreams come to fruition."

Verne nodded as he stood up to his ankles in the water. "André never believes it when people tell him about difficulties. He makes up his own mind and does things as he sees fit."

"And I admire him for it."

While he chattered about plans he and Nemo had made for exploring the hidden undersea world, Verne couldn't help but see that she was more interested in what Nemo was actually doing than in the fictional stories he made up.

II

Underwater, Nemo felt the river current around him like a thick wind. His feet sank into the bottom, meeting smooth rocks, slick mud, and loose sand. The shimmering surface high above him filtered the sunlight as if it came through stained glass. The belt of rock weights around his waist kept him submerged, as deep as he wanted to go.

Each breath required all the strength of his diaphragm to fill his lungs, and it was an effort to exhale as well, pushing the used air back through the exhaust flap valve. Though the wine-sour helmet became stifling, he continued through the murky Loire. Sweat ran like tears down his temples and cheeks. In front of him, he could discern shadowy, barnacle-encrusted pilings. River weeds curled like peacock feathers around boulders that floods had tossed downstream.

As he trudged ahead, Nemo thought of Captain Cook journeying to uncharted islands, Lewis and Clark forging their way across North America, Willem Barents trapped all winter long in a wooden hut high in the Arctic. All of them explorers of unknown places.

And here he was, André Nemo, treading another new realm . . . a place where visitors to drowned Atlantis might have felt at home. He wished Jules could have joined him. It would have been simple enough to make two sets of the breathing apparatus, though he suspected his friend would find some excuse to stay on shore. Jules Verne's imagination had always been greater than his desire for true adventure.

Determined, Nemo pushed on and fought to take breaths as he went deeper, as the hollow tube stretched farther from fresh air. The current turned colder and darker, but he pressed on. Overhead, the curved gray shapes of ships' hulls were like the shadows of floating whales. He could hear booming vibrations through the water – the pounding sounds of heavy work above.

He saw what must have been the underbelly of the *Cynthia*, flat-bottomed to increase the size of her hold. Her timbers were well caulked, the exterior waxed to deter barnacles and weeds. Above the waterline, the bow was rounded and the stern squared for added stability on the stormy Atlantic; but underneath, the bow had a sharp edge to cut through the water. By the dropping of the stones at his waist, Nemo could have floated up to the bottom keel, and only a few hull planks would have separated him from his father at work. How astonished the man would be to hear someone knocking from the bottom of the hull!

It had become too difficult to breathe, though. Over the distance, the air line had begun to kink, and some of his seals had developed slow leaks. Droplets of water spat into his helmet with each heavy breath he drew.

Before Nemo could turn back toward shore, the stifling air in his helmet forced him to drop his belt stones. Fighting back his instinctive alarm, he rose to the surface, fumbling to undo the greased seal at his neck. Steam fogged the window glass.

As his head and shoulders bobbed to the river surface, Nemo tore off the bladder helmet, drew in a huge gulp of air, and blinked in the sunlight. Despite his sense of urgency, he was proud he hadn't used his knife to cut it off, and so he could use the apparatus again for further exploration.

Today André Nemo had accomplished an amazing thing. He would return beneath the water, of course, but he would have to make modifications to the helmet, widen the breathing hole to improve air circulation. The world beneath the surface remained a grand mystery to him. . .

He searched the shore and spotted Jules waving at him, then noticed the lovely Caroline Aronnax beside his red-headed friend. Grinning and feeling just a bit cocky, Nemo waved back.

III

The shops and merchant stalls on Île Feydeau carried every imaginable item from every imaginable place: pearls and tropical birds from the Sandwich Islands; bananas, breadfruits, and papayas from Tahiti; wooden drums from the Congo; scrimshaw walrus tusks made by Eskimos in the Arctic. Pot-bellied merchants strolled beside ladies carrying parasols. The smells of outdoor cooking curled like fog through the air, pungent, sweet, or savory.

Rue Kervégan, the main avenue in Île Feydeau, stretched away from the bustling wharves, lined with elms and flanked by the offices of businessmen and tradesmen. Cafes and restaurants served coffee from Sumatra, *chocolat chaud* from Mexico, and black tea from India.

While walking with the two young men who fawned over her, Caroline admired coral necklaces brought back from the South Sea islands. Both Verne and Nemo stumbled over themselves, promising to obtain fabulous coral trinkets for her in the adventures they planned to have.

She laughed at their enthusiasm. "Monsieurs, I will believe that promise as soon as I can hold it in my hand. My mother warned me not to heed the sweet words of ambitious young men."

"But you never listen to your mother," Nemo said, and Caroline returned his smile. Confident and happy, she left them and hurried off for her daily pianoforte lesson.

At the Nantes shipyards, Verne and Nemo watched workers string a cat's cradle of rigging on the new vessel. The *Cynthia* was a "packet" ship, designed to make good speed across the Atlantic, carrying passengers, mail, and cargo. Previously, cargo ships would depart whenever they had a full load, and not before; a packet ship, however, set sail on a specified date to New York harbor or Chesapeake Bay, regardless of whether her cargo hold was full or all of her passenger cabins inhabited – and she also returned on a set schedule. A trip to North America took five weeks fighting the westerly winds, while the return journey required only three to four.

As Verne and Nemo walked down the quays, a figure on the new ship's deck waved to them. Jacques Nemo rapped a quick pattern with his hammer, a little rhythm he and his son had developed to signal each other, because it was easier than shouting across the din. André Nemo's dark hair and Verne's tousled red locks made the boys a distinctive enough pair even from a distance. Nemo waved back at his father before the man went belowdecks.

"He's gilding the aft passenger cabins today. *Gilding!*" Nemo shook his head. "Considering the sailing stories we've heard, I never imagined passengers would be so pampered."

"Like a royal carriage," Verne said, not that he'd ever ridden in one. *Someday*, he promised himself.

Muscular sailors used a rattling block and tackle to lower cannons through the hatches. On the gun decks below, engineers rolled the cannons out to the open ports, then chocked the wheels. Though northern Atlantic waters were civilized, pirates roamed the Caribbean and the south-eastern coast of America.

A horse-drawn wagon brought kegs of gunpowder to the dock, where a line of workers passed the barrels down to a pallet on deck. Straining at the main capstan and winch, sailors lowered the pallet and stored the kegs below in the powder magazine.

A month earlier, the *Cynthia* had been launched from dry dock, then tied afloat so the masts could be fitted and the rigging run. The flag of the French Republic already flew high and proud from her main mast.

Nemo stared at the ship's lines. "Last night when we were playing cards, my father said that you and I are invited to the christening ceremony. We can be standing close enough to watch the mayor of Nantes break a bottle of champagne across the bow." He looked over at Jules, eyes shining. "Tomorrow night at sunset. You'd better be there."

For the past few months, Verne and Nemo had made impromptu lunches of bread, cheese, and cold meat aboard the *Cynthia*, where they could listen as the shipbuilders chatted with one another. The men sweated hard and labored from dawn until dusk, but Jacques Nemo snatched a few idle moments with his son. Even around the boys, the ship's carpenters told bawdy stories that Verne wouldn't dare repeat to his family, though he couldn't help enjoying the yarns.

Now that he thought about it, Verne couldn't recall that he'd ever seen his father smile with amusement. Certainly, Pierre Verne did not let himself laugh with easy abandon the way Monsieur Nemo did.

"I can't go to the christening." Jules let out an embarrassed sigh. "I've got my studies, and my family will go to a late Mass." Nemo did not look surprised.

Some wagging tongues around Île Feydeau scolded Jacques Nemo for letting his son run wild in the streets, but Jules thought his friend was better adjusted to survival in the world than most of the spoiled residents of Nantes. Once, in an angry outburst, Nemo had bloodied a would-be tough who had sneered at him and insulted his father.

Nemo's grandfather had been a sailor lost in a typhoon off the China Sea, and his father had grown up aboard tall ships, until he'd married and settled down in Nantes to build the vessels he loved so much. Nemo's mother, from whom he had gotten his dusky skin, was long in her grave, which forged a tighter bond between father and son.

The two played cards each evening; they laughed and sang; they read to each other. Nemo's father told him stories by firelight, while Nemo did the household work. Though poor, the two never seemed unhappy. Jules often wished that he and his own father got along half as well. Since they did not, however, Jules contented himself with sharing the Nemos' warmth and comradeship.

Walking down to the docks where the boats unloaded cargo, Verne and Nemo saw toothless men with wiry muscles. The old faces were weathered from salt wind and tropical sunlight; many bore scars from badly healed cutlass slashes. The sailors loved to sit on crates and throw stories at any listeners while they munched on overripe fruit that couldn't be sold in the market.

In front of a weather-beaten barge that had come up the estuary from Paimboeuf, the seaport at the mouth of the Loire, the two spotted a veteran with six tattoos on his arm, one for each time he had crossed the equator. Though most of the sailor's scraggly gray hair had fallen out, he'd tied a few strands into a limp braid like the tail of a wharf rat. His eyes gleamed as he leaned forward, pointing at the boys.

Verne drew back, noting that two of the man's fingers were gone. The sailor cackled and held up his hand to display the jagged stumps. "'Twere bitten off by a shark. And a shipmate o' mine was swallowed whole. Reached down the monster's gullet, I did, to pull 'im back ou', but them jaws, they clamped shut and gobbled up me mate. Lucky I only lost this much."

Behind them at the barge, men hauled on hemp ropes to raise crates of animal skins, botanical specimens, and mineralogical samples.

The old man continued, knowing he had their full attention. "We sailed down and up the Ivory Coast o' Africa, the Gold Coast to the Bight o' Benin, saw men there blacker 'n coal, with fangs as long as yer fingers. Aye, it's true! Those demons'll strike ye dead just by looking at ye – and then they'll rush up and chew the flesh off yer bones. Cannibals!"

"If they could strike you dead just by looking at you, then how did you see them and survive?" Nemo asked with a skeptical frown. He crossed his arms over his chest.

"Pah! Tweren't hungry that day." The old sailor spoke in a rough but convincing voice, waving his three-fingered hand for emphasis. He told them stories about Prester John's kingdom, with its fountain of youth and a throne cut from an enormous diamond that had been coughed out of the gullet of a giant whale.

Verne and Nemo soaked up details about colorful lands, fabulous treasures, strange peoples. They learned about New Zealand, the Canary Islands, even Tierra del Fuego at the tip of South America. They heard of bloodthirsty pirates, whirlpools big enough to swallow four-masted barks, and sea monsters that could rip the hull out of even the largest ships.

Before the man could finish his tale, though, an explosion echoed through the shipyards like a cannon salute for the king. Everyone on the docks turned to look. Black smoke gushed like a geyser from the *Cynthia*.

Nemo let out a cry as he leaped to his feet. "My father!"

The fingerless sailor swore out loud. "One o' them tar-pot fires must 'a caught 'n the powder magazine."

The explosion had blasted out the starboard side of the new ship's hull. The *Cynthia*, once a cathedral of masts, rigging, and furled sails, now shuddered and twisted, its backbone broken. Buckets of varnish and turpentine blazed hot, spreading fires across the deck.

A second explosion rumbled as more powder kegs caught fire. Pots of boiling tar sprayed liquid like black blood. Carpenters and sailors dived overboard into the river, some with their breeches on fire.

Nemo raced down the dock, dodging crates and excited onlookers. A crowd clogged the narrow ways so that even firemen could not get through. He shouldered aside two ladies dressed in enormous crinoline gowns, ignoring their indignant glares. Following him, Verne made hurried excuses for his friend and wormed his way through the crowd to the water's edge.

Scorched or smeared with soot, shipbuilders climbed out of the river, panting and trembling on the bank. All turned in horrified awe to watch the *Cynthia* groan and tip. The bow rolled over on its side, while the stern upended itself before plunging into the water. As if drowning, the painted figurehead – "Cynthia" herself – stared skyward before rolling into the oily current.

"Where is my father?" Nemo said to anyone who looked at him. "Jacques

Nemo. Where is he?" The hubbub, accompanied by the crackling inferno of the doomed ship, was so loud that no one heard his words. As several spectators hauled an exhausted man onto a dock, Nemo recognized him and rushed forward. "My father! Did he get off? Where is he?"

The survivor's wild eyes focused on the dark-haired young man. "André?" He put his soggy arm around Nemo in an awkward embrace. "Jacques . . . your father . . . trapped in one of the passenger cabins belowdecks." The man pointed a big hand at the flaming wreck as the stern sank into the deep channel. He shook his head. "Underwater by now."

Nemo yanked hard on Verne's arm. "Come on." Seeing the determination on the young man's flushed face, the crowd parted as Nemo elbowed his way out, dragging Jules Verne behind him. The two slipped and slid down a muddy bank beneath the docks until they reached where they had stored the bladder helmet, breathing tubes, and reeds.

"I have to go out there. If my father's underwater, maybe the room was sealed. He may still have air." Seeing his friend's desperate hope, Verne didn't voice his doubts.

Nemo dug muddy rocks out of the riverbank and thrust them into his pockets for weight while Verne connected the breathing reeds. Nemo secured his dagger, tugged the bladder over his head, and adjusted the viewing glass so he could see. "Hurry, Jules!"

Not far away, the *Cynthia* smoldered and groaned. Its timbers cracked like thunder as it sank. The crowd continued to gather, both horrified and curious. Firemen threw water on the flames, but they knew the ship was doomed, and no one could do anything about it.

Before Verne finished attaching three reeds to Nemo's helmet, the dark-haired young man had cinched the bladder against his neck. He strode into the river without hesitation until he had submerged himself. Verne hurried, but the cold pitch did not seal well. He grabbed another reed and tried to attach it while he moved, rather than yelling for his friend to wait. Nemo did not dare move any slower.

Fighting the current's resistance, Nemo pushed toward the roiling disaster, picturing his father's panic, his need for rescue. The rocks in his pockets held him to the soft riverbottom. Bubbles and orange reflections of flame flickered from the wreckage; he could see it through the water.

Scarecrowish bodies drifted about. One nudged him. He pushed the corpse away, relieved that it wasn't his father. Nemo didn't remember the man's name, but thought he recognized him as someone who'd played a squeeze box, squeaking out impromptu melodies while the sailors danced and pounded their heels on the deck boards. . .

Nemo didn't have time to mourn, intent on only one thing. He forced his way forward, trying to breathe against the growing ache and dread in his chest as he saw the stern of the *Cynthia* completely submerged, the poop deck underwater. Through filtered light from above, he discerned cracked boards and gaping holes near what would have been the passenger cabins.

His faceplate steamed up, and a few dribbles of water leaked in through the breathing tube. He hoped Jules could keep up with him on the bank, that the connected reeds would remain sealed. His heart pounded, his lungs felt hot. Nemo struggled forward through the muck, but didn't for a moment consider turning back.

The young man struggled across the splintered stumps of the *Cynthia's* masts. The logs floated on the river surface, while rigging, pulleys, and tackle dangled beneath like a giant spider's web. Fish swam about like underwater spectators in a drama they could not understand.

As he made his way to the lower deck aft, Nemo passed ornately paneled chambers. Open doors flopped in the current, showing walls of exotic wood embellished with gold leaf for first-class passengers; now only river fish would enjoy the lavish accommodations. He found another body wedged in a door jamb, but saw the man's wooden peg leg and dismissed him . . . not the person he sought. He wished he could call out.

Nemo drew his knife and tugged against the restraining air tube that trailed behind him. He wheezed and sucked in a deep breath, angry at fate. He'd never intended to go this far. He couldn't get enough oxygen, couldn't force a breath over such a distance, but even dizzy as he was, he continued.

His father might be dying down here.

Muffled booming and rumbling sounds surged through the water as the *Cynthia* continued her death throes. A few chambers remained sealed, their doors shut, and Nemo clung to hope. He could see bubbles trickling from one of the closed rooms. As the ship continued to sink and twist and shift, the door opened a crack, and air boiled out.

Nemo swam there, trying to see if his father had found refuge inside, but no one came out as he yanked the door open. He thumped at the second sealed door but heard no response from his father, no pounding, no return vibration. *Where?* The underwater dimness made details and options murky around him.

Quickly he moved to a third stateroom door, which had a heavy beam wedged across it. A line of bubbles frothed and surged from the bottom of the door, where water must be flooding into the small room.

Nemo hammered with the hilt of the dagger, hoping to detect something through the water. Just when he was about to give up, he heard a slap, a flat palm thudding against the wall.

Nemo pounded four times, and the other slapped back four more times – the code rhythm Jacques Nemo used to signal his son – then hammered repeatedly to get out. Half afloat and half balanced, Nemo wrenched at the thick beam that jammed the opening, but dizzy from lack of air, he could not budge it.

The air bubbles continued to creep higher along the jamb as the chamber filled. The pounding sounds inside the sealed room became more frantic.

His blood burning with desperation, Nemo dug with the point of his dagger, wedging it like a crowbar. With a great twist, he tried to lever a board free, but the dagger snapped in half. He screamed in dismay, but no one could hear him through his helmet. He went wild, hammering and pounding on the wood with his fists, shouting for his father, but utterly helpless. As he jerked his head and shoulders, one of the hollow reeds loosened, and river water dribbled into his bladder helmet. He began to choke as his helmet filled.

Jamming the broken dagger back into his belt, Nemo wrestled with the door as he used the last air in his lungs. His vision turned red, but he refused to back away. He could hold his breath for a few moments longer, though now he didn't know if he could last long enough to reach the surface.

Under his continued onslaught, a crack opened in the wood, and air bubbles spurted out with greater velocity. Water poured inside.

Nemo pounded and pummeled. Foul river water leaked inside his helmet and spilled past his chin into his lips, and he could inhale only thin breaths through his nose. But he didn't give up. He wrestled until he broke part of the board free – but it was nowhere near wide enough for his father to get through.

Bubbles surged to the top of the door as the stateroom filled completely. The man inside struggled and tugged. Finally, all Jacques Nemo could do was push his fingers through the small hole.

Nemo grasped his father's hand. As the last air escaped from the submerged room, the trapped man struggled and thrashed. But somehow he kept his grip on his son's hand, love passing between them.

And then water filled Nemo's bladderhood. He couldn't breathe anymore. The leaking water covered his nose, and he had already emptied his lungs. Blackness floated around him. He would drown, too, down here beside his father. He wanted to scream, but he had no more air.

His father's fingers clenched one more time and then fell slack. Unable even to sob or cry out because of the water in his helmet, Nemo struggled away from the sunken ship. He realized how close he was to death, and a candle flame of survival burned brighter even than his grief.

But the heavy stones in his pockets held him down, as leaden as his heart. He couldn't surface, now that he wanted to. With jerking fingers Nemo yanked most of the rocks out of his pockets. He couldn't see because his vision was dimmed, but also because river water now covered the inside of the viewing plate.

With a violent wrench he tore the breathing tube from his helmet and snapped it in his hands, since it hindered his freedom of movement. His lungs burned, his chest ached – and his heart was ready to explode with anger and despair. But still he wanted to live, to breathe fresh air again, to feel the sunlight on his skin. He tore at the belt sealed around his neck, and finally used the broken end of his dagger to slash the bladder free and tear it from his head.

As he swam toward the surface, fighting and kicking, letting his own buoyancy lift him, greenish light beckoned like angels from above. Rigging ropes and pulleys dangled around him like a poacher's net, but he fought his way through them.

Nemo choked in a mouthful of water, as if hoping he could breathe like a fish, but his body convulsed. He couldn't last for a second longer – but he would not let himself be defeated.

His head burst above the river surface like a champagne cork. Wooden debris from the *Cynthia* drifted all around him. Barely conscious, he grasped one of the floating cross-stays and sucked in huge breaths of air, sobbing and coughing. But he could not clear the water from his eyes, because his tears blinded him.

Below, the *Cynthia* came to its final rest, taking Nemo's father and his own future along with it.

IV

Inside the house, the lawyer Pierre Verne kept a telescope pointed through an upstairs window toward the clock face of the distant monastery, so he could always know what time it was. Precision was important to him.

The family Verne lived in the heart of Île Feydeau's old town, the most desirable section of Nantes. Their narrow four-story house stood on rue Olivier de Clisson, named after a 14th-century French commander who had fought against the English in the Hundred Years War.

The low tables in their sitting room displayed the weekly Parisian publication *Le Magasin Pittoresque*. The elder Verne encouraged his two sons to read illustrated geographical stories about foreign places and explanatory articles on scientific subjects. As a Christmas gift, Jules had even received a model telegraph, a toy that was all the rage across France.

When the family gathered for the formal evening dinner, Pierre Verne insisted on proper etiquette. Both of Jules's sisters changed into lacy silk and *chiné* dresses complete with constricting whalebone corsets, while Jules himself wore an embroidered waistcoat and cravat, as did his ten-year-old brother Paul. They sat at a long, dark table made in a style that imitated the great French masters. Meals were served on fine china that had been part of his mother's dowry when she'd married Pierre.

Several days had passed since the tragedy of the *Cynthia*, and Jules found this particular dinner and this particular conversation more maddening than usual. His mother had broiled small squabs for each of them, accompanied by buttered peas and delightful onion pastries (a secret family recipe she had tried to teach Jules, though thus far he had mastered only her special omelet).

With linen napkins folded in their laps, the family solemnly murmured the traditional prayer, and then Pierre Verne opened the bottle of Bordeaux, poured a goblet for himself and for his wife, before watering some wine for each of the children. Pierre was a gaunt man with long sideburns and dark hair; he hadn't the slightest twinkle in his eye or an appreciation of the humor his elder son often displayed.

They ate under an imposed silence broken only by the sound of silverware clinking against china, the gurgle of wine as his father refilled his goblet, the delicate chewing and prying of meat from small pigeon carcasses.

Verne and his siblings waited for their father to begin the evening's conversation, usually when he was half finished with his main course, always before the dessert. As a lawyer, Pierre Verne was a man of rigid habits who adhered to schedules, written and unwritten. Sometimes he would challenge his children with word games or round-robin poetry, having each of them make up verses – a pastime at which Jules excelled. Other evenings, they waited until after the meal, when his sisters would demonstrate their prowess on the heirloom pianoforte.

Tonight, however, with grim face and ill-temper, the lawyer chose Jules's least favorite activity: a discussion of current events and local matters. Pierre Verne held strong opinions; thus, the family did not have a dinner discussion so much as a lecture, during which Pierre instructed his family on what they should think about the matters of the day.

Before his father spoke, Jules already knew the issue that concerned him. "Since the burning of the *Cynthia*, there'll be work coming into the office. When you get older, Jules, I intend to have you as my assistant, but for now I must hire help to draw up papers, submit forms and claims. It is an unconscionable mess."

The lawyer drew a deep breath as if this all made him very important. He dabbed the corner of his mouth with a napkin. "Lawsuits will be filed on behalf of the ship's investors. The carpenter who caused the disaster lost his life in the explosion, unfortunately, so there can be no seeking restitution from him."

"And not against his family, I hope," Verne's mother, Sophie, said.

"Family?" The lawyer frowned. "The man was a sailor and shipbuilder," he said, as if the profession were an insult. "It hardly seemed worthwhile to go looking for any family." Jules was stung by his father's callous dismissal of everyone like André Nemo, whose father had also died in the wreck.

Reading her son's distress, Sophie Verne looked at him with compassion. "Do you know what your friend will do now, Jules?"

He hadn't realized his mother knew the extent of his friendship with Nemo. "I suppose he'll be able to survive for a while. André is a very resourceful young man."

"He's going to have to be." Pierre Verne looked up in surprise, interrupted in his thoughts. "That young man's father had no money. He was bankrupt. All wasted on gambling and liquor, no doubt."

"Pierre!" Sophie snapped, but her husband didn't back down.

"What do you mean he has no money?" Jules said. "Monsieur Nemo just finished building a ship and had a bonus coming. He worked every day."

"The man left no inheritance for his son, mark my words. I've already seen repossession paperwork come through. That young man is in trouble."

Jules could barely speak, daunted by his father's lack of sympathy. "But what . . . what is he going to do?"

"He'll be thrown into the streets, I expect."

Jules looked across his dinner plate and for the first time assessed Pierre Verne as a person, not simply as his ever-present father. The man took care of local matters in his tedious law practice, though he had never spoken with eloquence at a dramatic trial, never even set foot in court as far as Jules knew. Pierre handled little more than property deeds and standard contracts. Only at a time like this, after a horrible tragedy, did he show any excitement in picking up the pieces.

"Perhaps André can go into an orphanage," Sophie said.

"Too old," Pierre answered with a dismissive wave of his left hand, which still clutched the now soiled napkin. "No orphanage would take a young man of working age. Maybe we should hope those idiots in Paris get us into another war, and then Nemo can join the fighting and take a soldier's pay."

Sophie spoke in an artificially sweet voice. "And which idiots are those, dear? The monarchists, the Republicans, or the Bonapartists? I can't remember which ones are the idiots this week."

"I shall let you know after I read tonight's paper," her husband said. Then he looked over at his son, as if expecting his words to carry some kind of comfort. "You're lucky you aren't in that young man's situation, Jules. You have prospects, a secure place in town, and a job with me in the law office."

Sick to his stomach, Jules pushed himself away from the table. "I need to be excused, Father." He hurried up the narrow stairs to the room he shared with his younger brother.

He opened the shutters to let in the moist air. Outside his window, the tall masts of sailing ships in port rose like towering trees. Jules felt trapped at home. He looked out toward the empty dock that had held the unfinished *Cynthia*, but nothing remained except a few protruding boards from her sunken hull, burn marks, and soot.

Despite his father's confidence, Verne's life appeared to be a dead-end path. He would never leave France, never have adventures and explore the world as his fictional heroes did. And now, André Nemo – who had always shared his enthusiasm, creativity, and energy – had lost everything. Where would he go? How would his friend survive?

Jules could sneak him food and clothes for a time, and Nemo would certainly find his own solution before long. Jules just hoped he himself could be part of it. Together, they had dreamed and imagined so much, but prison doors were now slamming shut around them.

It was the dark edge of twilight, and Paul hadn't come upstairs to bed yet. Jules threw himself on the blankets and lay wide awake, smelling the river fog, listening to the ship bells and groaning timbers and creaking ropes. The water and the ships called to him like a distant siren song.

From the fourth-story window, he had an unobscured view of the masts. Any one of those vessels could take him away from this sedentary place. In his imagination, Jules had climbed into their riggings many times, raised himself to their crow's nests, gripped the yardarms to hear the tug and flap of wind-stretched sails. Did he have the nerve to make those dreams real?

Ships came and went at all times, departing for far-off lands and returning with exotic treasures. But Jules had to stay in Nantes, confined in his little room in his family's narrow house in a tiny provincial town.

Didn't he?

Miserable, he managed to fall asleep before his brother came up to join him.

V

Nemo needed her help, more than ever in his life. Caroline Aronnax vowed to do everything in her power to assist the young man who had made her imagination blossom and given her dreams of her own. She had to keep his dreams alive.

Before she'd met André Nemo and Jules Verne, Caroline had never imagined spending time with two young men of such different social stations, but from the moment they first spoke in the market, she'd been captivated by both of them.

Two months ago, all three had bumped into each other in front of a silversmith's shop, listening to the shrunken old man dicker with a sailor for coral chunks to use in new jewelry. Her maidservant Marie had been dealing with a potter for a new vase, and Caroline overheard Nemo and Verne discussing far-flung ports and island chains, eyeing the sailor's coral as if it were splinters of the True Cross.

Since her father had a merchant fleet, Caroline knew all about the Canary Islands and ports in India, Madagascar, Ceylon. She stepped up to the boys and corrected their misconceptions, surprising both of them. The three of them had talked for a full hour while Marie flirted with the potter.

Nemo had sensed a kindred spirit in the strawberry-blond young woman and boldly invited her to join them in a night-time escapade, exploring backstreets and quays where no one else could see. He whispered that they might even creep aboard an empty ship on the Loire docks. With a daring glance to her maidservant, Caroline had promised to join them at the appointed time. . .

Marie, skeptical but bright-eyed to assist her mistress in this little intrigue (after Caroline reminded Marie of her own secret activities), helped the young woman slip out of the row house owned by M. Aronnax. After nightfall, Caroline hurried through the streets, strange byways that took on an entirely different character in the dark. She was anxious to find Verne and Nemo, concerned they might think she had gone back on her word.

They were to meet in a shadowy backstreet behind the smelly fish cleaners' stalls, then they would scamper about in the alleyways near the docks, maybe even go aboard one of the tall ships.

She pushed aside the unthinkable ramifications of being found out, hurried around a corner – and caught her breath. This was no playground, no garden party. Offending smells struck her hard, as did the presence of a drunken dockhand sprawled across her path. *What am I doing here?*

As her courage was about to fail her, Nemo and Verne approached from the opposite alley. Caroline's unease melted in an instant, and she spun around with a swish of her watered silk gown. Nemo grasped her right hand and smiled that broad white grin. "A world of adventure is waiting," he said, while Verne hurried to take her other hand. Delighted and filled with wonder, they had dashed together toward the creaking ships tied up to the docks.

As the stars wheeled toward midnight, the three spent hours play-acting scenes of pirates and swagmen. Nemo fell into the role of brave hero, proud to rescue the fair maiden from the clutches of Jules Verne, who relished playing the villain – though, whenever Nemo came at him with even a mock sword, Jules fled. Caroline's heart fluttered as Nemo swept her into his arms and protected her from the imagined cut-throat. Earlier, she had dismissed tales of damsels in distress as mere feminine nonsense, but the swashbuckling young man made it seem so real. *What was it about him?*

That night, months ago, had been all she'd hoped for, and more. Caroline still clung to the memory of climbing, laughing, jumping, even swinging from a real sailor's rope. Far from sitting still with proper manners, they had danced in the alleyways of Nantes. Later, they had spun tales of adventure, casting themselves in the most outrageous of roles.

Two hours before dawn, as they had paused to catch their breath, Jules grew nervous and agitated. "I need to get back into my home." He pulled out a thick brass key for his front door. "My little brother sometimes wakes up in the middle of the night. What if he finds me gone?"

Sad that their adventures had to end, Caroline was also aware of how terrible it would be if she were caught outside. Nemo stood beside her. "I will see that Caroline arrives home safely, Jules. Run back to your house, and step quietly up your stairs."

With a fumbled goodbye, a confused gesture that seemed to be an attempt to kiss her goodnight that was withdrawn at the last instant, Jules ran down the streets with long legs and clomping feet.

As Nemo walked beside her, though, Caroline's sense of urgency faded. "I would never let anything happen to you," he said, and she believed him completely. Caroline did not concern herself with fears of highwaymen or cutpurses or kidnappers – after all, had she not just seen how the swashbuckling André Nemo could deal with any foe?

When they arrived back at the merchant's house, Caroline slipped around to the servants' entrance – and was astonished to find the door locked. "Marie was supposed to leave it open for me! She knew I was coming in late." Caroline bunched her small fists.

"Maybe you're out too late even for her to forgive," Nemo said in a rich, understanding voice.

Caroline shook her head. "No. She's gone out on a rendezvous of her own, probably with that pottery seller."

With good grace, Nemo took her arm. "Then we'll just have to find a comfortable place to wait. She will be back before dawn, won't she?"

Staring at the locked door, Caroline tried to open it with sheer force of will, but gave up. "After all the times I turned a blind eye to her secret meetings, why should she have to ruin mine?"

With a smile, Nemo had led her toward the Church of St Martin. "I wouldn't say she's entirely ruined it." They sat together in the deserted courtyard of the old church, resting under the sweet-smelling magnolias.

Caroline talked about her own dreams – and he listened, without once suggesting that, because she was a woman, she could not achieve her goals. Nemo had shared some of his hopes, too, brash enough to believe he would succeed in everything. "I want to see the world, beat the odds, become something *I* choose." He stared up at the endless sky between the fluttering, dark-green leaves of the magnolia. "And I will."

He surprised her by stealing a kiss. It was the first time she had ever been kissed by a man, and she responded awkwardly – but insisted on practicing until she got it right. . .

There in the churchyard, all alone except for God and the midnight stars, they promised each other they would do the impossible, beat the odds. Though still young, Caroline understood the importance of her words when she said, "My heart will always be yours, André."

"My heart belonged to you the moment I saw you in front of the silversmith's shop." Somehow, they both understood they would keep this moment between themselves, would not even tell Jules Verne about it.

The pastel colors of dawn came much too soon, and Nemo escorted her back to her house, where a frantic Marie waited for Caroline beside the half-open servant's entrance. "My lady! I thought you'd been murdered, or kidnapped! You could have been robbed, killed –"

Caroline had given Nemo a warm glance. "I have never felt safer than tonight, being with André." Then she chided her maidservant, "And *you* should pay more attention to the time and keep the door unlocked, as you promised." Marie ushered her inside in a flurry of clothes, ready to hurry Caroline into bed before anyone noticed.

Just as the door had closed, Caroline flashed a last glance at Nemo, already eager to see him again. . . .

But that was all before the disaster of the *Cynthia*. Now, penniless and fatherless, André Nemo and his enthusiastic future had been cut off at the root. Unless Caroline could talk with her father and secure an alternative for him.

VI

The landlord waited several days, giving the young man time to grieve – but Nemo knew the squint-eyed man would soon come to insist on payment.

All morning long Nemo ransacked the two rooms his father had rented, gathering scrimshaw combs and snuffboxes, colorful seashells, and exotic trinkets Jacques Nemo had collected as a sailor. Unfortunately, with the death of his wife and the raising of his son, Jacques had already sold any valuable items, keeping only sentimental ones.

Dry-eyed but sick at heart, Nemo stared at the worn deck of playing cards that he and his father had used on long candlelit evenings. On a shelf sat a wooden ship model the two of them had made together. Building the model had taught him the basic structure of the vessels tied to the docks of Île Feydeau. But the model was worthless, other than the memories it held.

Two days after the *Cynthia* disaster, Nemo had awakened at dawn to find a small basket wedged against his doorstep, a package filled with hard bread, cheese, boiled eggs, and flowers. Even without smelling the faint trace of her perfume, he knew that Caroline Aronnax had stolen these items from her family's kitchen and sent her maidservant Marie through the midnight streets to deliver it, unseen.

"I will talk to my father, André," she had written in a note tucked into the basket. "Perhaps I can help."

Nemo felt a lump in his throat. She had hidden her friendship with the streetwise young man, much as she had kept her own musical compositions secret. Nemo could not ask Monsieur Aronnax for work in his shipping offices, or even at one of the local docks, unloading and inventorying cargoes arrived from far-off lands. He had to find some other way to pay his living expenses.

Breathing hard with resentment, he used a rock and a long chisel to smash the padlock that secured his father's sea trunk. He didn't know where the key might be, since he hadn't seen his father open the chest in years.

Nemo rummaged through the documents and keepsakes, and found an old engraving of his mysterious, dusky-skinned mother. The chest also contained dried flowers, a book written in a language he couldn't read, a set of cups, a dusty bottle of wine that Jacques must have kept for some anticipated celebration he would now never witness. Perhaps his son's marriage? Nemo couldn't venture a guess. And hidden behind the false back of one divider in the trunk, he discovered a handful of coins. . .

The next day, by selling some of the trinkets to a vendor of eccentric items, Nemo scraped together enough money to have a funeral Mass read for his father at the Church of St Martin. Hearing the priest speak Jacques's name aloud, though, Nemo felt no particular honor, no special consolation.

Neither he nor his father were devout Catholics, but sometimes, when a teary-eyed Jacques had had too much wine or just seemed sad with life, he would recall the promise he'd made to Nemo's mother on her deathbed, that he would give their boy a proper upbringing. . .

Alone in the empty room, Nemo slept on a straw-stuffed tick that served as a mattress. He continued, one day at a time, not looking beyond the following morning . . . until he realized he had to plan for his future. Nemo always had plans, but they were too many and too unrealistic. Now he didn't know what he would do.

Four days after the disaster, the squint-eyed landlord and a pair of burly companions pulled open the door without knocking. Nemo sat at the rickety table on which he ate and where he had learned his letters and arithmetic. The two hirelings stood together, a barricade of muscle and flesh.

The landlord stepped forward, a small-statured man with one eye larger than the other. His seamed face displayed a heartfelt sorrow, belied by his stern voice. "You'll have to move out, boy. Got no choice. Sorry." The landlord frowned at the two toughs, as if dismayed by the necessity of bringing them along. "And I'll take any possessions as part of the payment for which your father was in arrears."

Nemo, though, would not be bluffed. "You're lying. How could my father be in arrears?" He stood from the table, arms loose at his sides, ready to throw himself on the thugs if they harassed him. "He had a job. He paid you every month."

"No, he *promised* to pay me every month. He was two months behind." The landlord's drooping eye squinted, and he shook his head sadly. "I gave him credit because I knew he'd get a bonus when the *Cynthia* was christened."

"And dead men don't get paid," one of the hirelings said.

The landlord nodded. "Even as his son, you have no claim on his back wages. Sorry, boy."

"I'll find some way to pay you." Nemo gripped the side of the chair with a white-knuckled hand. He felt hot, angry at this second joke Fate had played upon him. "Let me stay here until I can come up with a job."

"A job?" One of the henchmen laughed.

Nemo bristled. "Never underestimate me." His voice carried such a low threat that the thug flinched.

The landlord tugged at his waistcoat to straighten it, uncomfortable. "Be realistic, boy. Are you going to work fifteen hours a day in one of the garment factories? That'll only bring you thirty sous a week. You'll never have enough to pay me what your father owed. I've already done the arithmetic."

Nemo took deep, heavy breaths, trying to calm the rising anger in his gut. "Then I'll sell some of my father's artifacts." This brought another round of laughter from the henchmen.

"He'll rob the citizens of Nantes, more like," one of the big men said.

"I'll not have a thief renting one of my houses," the landlord said with increasing sternness. His smaller eye twitched with a nervous tic.

"I am *not* a thief." Nemo's dark eyes flashed, and he stepped forward. Though he was much younger than the other man, his look of determination drove the landlord back a pace. The two muscular men closed in, ready to pound him – but Nemo looked as if he just might best both of them, then go after the landlord. He would be in jail before the day was done.

"It's only a matter of time, boy. You've no prospects, and there are good families in need of a dwelling like this," the landlord said from behind the broad shoulders of his two companions. "If you're not gone tomorrow, I'll have my friends carry you into the streets."

"They can try," Nemo said in low fury.

The landlord squinted once more. The men looked as if they wanted to break something, but the landlord marched them out. In an unexpected show of courtesy, the small-statured man closed the door behind himself.

Some time later, Nemo went to the doorway. He looked between buildings down toward the river and the shipyards where the masts stood tall. He could hear the sounds of workers on the docks as vessels prepared to set sail with the outgoing tide, and he recalled the tales his father had told of his days at sea.

VII

Caroline Aronnax arranged to meet him at the rue Kervégan flower market, where she often went with Marie to gather fresh bouquets. The Aronnax household was well known for its sweet scents and colorful blossoms.

Nemo watched the intelligent and independent Caroline, but he could no longer allow himself to dream of a future with her. He remembered their night under the magnolia trees, when they had spoken foolish promises. Now an invisible chasm separated him from the young woman he loved. . .

Rather than let the landlord take his father's belongings, Nemo sold every scrap and trinket that might bring him a few sous, even the sea chest. He kept only the engraving of his long-dead mother. With her dark and mysterious features, her large black eyes, and a smile that seemed just for him, Nemo had always gauged feminine beauty by her standard. But Caroline Aronnax set a standard all her own.

He had lost his mother before he'd ever got a chance to know her. Now it looked as if he would lose any hope of Caroline. Maybe that was for the best, even though his heart would ache for the rest of his life.

In the afternoon sunshine, Caroline moved with flowing grace, despite the frilly clothes she wore and the high society airs her mother urged her to imitate. Although Madame Aronnax made her daughter cater to fashion, Caroline's burnished hair and blue eyes announced to anyone that she was her own young woman. The delicate freckles on her face would probably fade with age, or with a deeper tan, if – to her mother's chagrin – Caroline continued to spend time out in the sun. She would never grow up to be a quiet, gossiping socialite; no doubt she would be quite a challenge for her future husband.

Nemo thought she was magnificent.

Caroline drifted through the flower market, humming the melody of one of her secret compositions. Nemo recognized it, since he often lingered in the street outside her home, just listening to her play the pianoforte as the town sounds dwindled with the gathering dusk.

Late at night, he and Caroline had held long, but hushed, conversations from her window. He had encouraged her to nurture her creativity. "You can do anything you set your mind to, Caroline, whether it be writing music, traveling the world, or running a shipping company."

"But everyone says it's impossible," she had said, leaning over the windowsill.

"Those who believe in impossibilities prove themselves correct every day," Nemo said. "You know better than that." In those stolen hours and secret conversations, Nemo and Caroline had both dared to believe – just a little – in their waking dreams.

But now, for him, those dreams were crushed under the boot heel of reality. All of his promises and reassurances to Caroline seemed as empty and implausible as an old sailor's stories about sea monsters.

Now in the flower market, he watched her sort through roses and magnolias, pansies and chrysanthemums, sniffing a few, shaking her head at others. Her maidservant was captivated by simple blossoms, daisies and hollyhocks. The two young women chatted, easy in each other's company now that they were away from home.

Sensing his gaze, Caroline looked up, and her eyes met his. She flashed a sudden smile that quickly shifted to a look of concern. Nemo stepped forward, paying no heed to the people in the market, not hearing the bartering voices, not smelling the heady perfume of flowers. Caroline was as much beauty as he could handle at one time.

"André, I am so sorry about your father! But I believe I have good news for you." She reached out to touch his arm with her delicate hand. "I found a way to help."

"I don't want your money, Caroline. Just your . . ." He stopped at the word "love." He swallowed his pride. "I just want you to think about me."

"Of course I will think about you. I remember the promises we made, under the trees –"

Nemo looked away. "Too much has changed. I won't hold you to unwise words spoken in haste."

Caroline sniffed. At another time, she might have teased him. "I intend to do what I said, sir, and I expect you to do the same."

Marie looked up in warning. "Your mother would not like you to be seen talking with him, mademoiselle. And I know from experience that a young man's promises aren't strong enough to hold a snowflake."

Caroline rolled her eyes. "Then you should choose your young men with better care. My mother wouldn't approve of *your* liaisons, either. I thought we had an understanding?" Her voice had a firm edge of command, and Nemo could see that someday she would indeed be able to run a shipping company with as much verve and vision as any man could.

She took Nemo's arm in her own and nudged him to the left. "André and I are going to have some *chocolats chauds* in the cafe over there. You will be able to see us at all times, but we must have a private conversation."

With her other hand, she touched the sleeve of Marie's dress. "Go choose some flowers, but make certain to buy bouquets that *I* would select, so my mother believes we bought them together." Caroline's smile turned mischievous. "And perhaps you should also pick a carnation for whichever of your gentlemen friends kept you out until near dawn Tuesday last."

Without waiting for Marie to agree or even to argue, she guided Nemo toward the small tables under colorful parasols. Dizzy with the warmth and the nearness of her, he pretended to lead the way. Nemo held the chair for her, and she signaled a waiter. "Two *chocolats chauds*, please. And some croissants. Do you have fresh marmalade?"

The waiter brought the two frothing cups made from steamed milk mixed with a bitter but delicious Mexican cocoa. Knowing that Nemo had no spare money, she withdrew a few sous and paid the waiter.

"I cannot bear the thought of you in a pauper's prison, André." Caroline smeared a croissant with marmalade from a porcelain jar, then nudged the plate closer to him. He chose one of the flaky croissants for himself and bit into it; he hadn't eaten a decent meal in a day. Frustrated and uneasy, Nemo sipped the rich, dark drink.

"And so," Caroline continued, "I have found a way for you to sign onto a ship."

Surprised, Nemo sat up. "But I've already talked with the men down on the docks. The crews are filled –"

"My father says you wouldn't want to ship out with those captains anyway. But he has found an alternative, provided you can leave tomorrow."

He looked into her uncertain gaze. He was excited by the prospect, though the consequences made it bittersweet. "Leave? Where? On which ship?"

"My father has offered to sign you aboard a three-masted brig, the *Coralie*. It is an English research and trading vessel – and you would be paid." She drew in a long breath. "It is your chance to see the world, to do the things we talked and dreamed about. You will find adventure, sail the seas, go to exotic ports. . . I am only saddened that, in order to help you, I must send you away from me. It is the last thing I want." She touched his hand, then quickly withdrew. "If you are interested in going, that is?"

Nemo looked at her, stricken; he knew he had no other choice. "I – of course I'll go." Then he repeated what he had said to her on their secret night outing. "A world of adventure is waiting."

Caroline continued in a rush of words. "You will be the personal cabin boy to Captain Grant. My father says Captain Grant is a kind and intelligent man, and the captain was pleased to hear about your curiosity and your studies. He even offered to continue teaching you while you are on-board."

Nemo sat up, trying to absorb everything she was telling him. "Where is the *Coralie* bound? With what cargo? Does she sail for 'Aronnax, Merchant'? With an English captain?" His excitement drove back the looming dejection and helplessness he had felt during the past several days.

"Captain Grant wishes to explore the world. He owns his own ship, with only a few investors for the cargo. In fact, he reminds me of you, André, with the same passion, the same curiosity, the same refusal to believe in the impossible. He doesn't care whether you are French or English – only that you are eager to learn."

In her father's office Caroline had studied the maps and learned the route by heart. "You will sail down the African coast, around the Cape of Good Hope, and up to India, where the *Coralie* will take on a load of spices. Then south again through the Indian Ocean to the South China Sea and New Zealand."

"New Zealand? I heard the Maori people tattoo themselves black and file their teeth to sharp points." He couldn't wait to tell Jules Verne about it.

"Then the *Coralie* will cross the Pacific to San Francisco before going south again. Captain Grant wants to see the Galapagos Islands, which are supposedly full of strange fauna. Then down around Cape Horn and Tierra del Fuego, and finally back to France."

"It sounds like I'll be gone forever." As he said it, though, Nemo realized there was nothing to keep him here in Nantes. Nothing but Caroline.

"Two or three years, maybe more." She looked away. "I will miss you very much."

Nemo felt bright hope once more. "I'll only be gone long enough to make something of myself." He finished his *chocolat chaud* and brashly ate another croissant. "When I come back, Caroline, I'll have my fortune – and you will be old enough to be . . . to be betrothed?" Nemo lowered his eyes, afraid to say anything more. He remembered the things they had whispered to each other, and the things they'd left unsaid.

Caroline looked up at him, startled. She opened her mouth, about to say something. Always before, they'd had all the time in the world, all the flexibility and imagination – until real life had intruded.

"Ah, André, there you are!" Jules Verne rushed across the flower market in a tangle of long arms and legs, interrupting Caroline and Nemo. His hair was tousled, eyes bright, skin flushed. "I've heard what you're going to do – and I want to go with you."

Caroline and Nemo often spoke of their fondness for the red-headed young man, but they also knew that he didn't completely comprehend them. Nevertheless, Jules missed no opportunity to try to impress her.

Nemo looked at his friend skeptically. "Why would you want to go with me? I have nothing to lose here. But you . . . you have –"

"*Prospects*," Jules said with sarcasm. "I know. I am expected to stay here for the rest of my life and take over my father's practice and become a boring lawyer and never leave France." He shook his head. "You and I, André, we have too much excitement destined for us. I belong with you on that ship." He puffed out his chest. "We'll write letters home. And you, Caroline –" He raised his eyebrows. "I plan to bring you the largest coral necklace I can find, just as I promised. I'll barter with the natives, and it'll be worth a fortune."

Jules crossed his arms over his narrow chest, but Caroline, considering the overblown promise, giggled. "You are my friend. I don't want you to have any regrets about this." Nemo thought of all the times that Jules had intended to do a dramatic act, and then backed out at the last minute. Nemo had always been the instigator and Jules the naysayer. But he sighed and accepted his friend's excitement.

Caroline pushed herself away from the table, uneasy now and sad at the opportunity she'd been forced to offer to Nemo, his only chance. "The *Coralie* sails tomorrow at dawn with the tide, Jules. Captain Grant may take you aboard along with André – but I want you to think about this for the rest of the day. No regrets."

"There won't be," Jules said.

Nemo gave a brisk nod. "Very well. We'll meet at midnight at one of the inns – L'Homme aux Trois Malices. Caroline, may we stop by late tonight? So you can bid us bon voyage?"

Tears shone in her eyes. "Of course you may."

With Jules's eager eyes on them, Nemo and Caroline remained circumspect, but they touched hands under the table and shared a knowing glance before they rose from their chairs.

The three split up. Caroline went back to Marie and her bouquets of flowers, and Jules went off to begin packing in secret.

VIII

Though his stomach was knotted and his pulse raced with growing anxiety, Jules Verne made every effort to eat a large evening meal, knowing full well that this might be his last home-cooked food for some time. He'd read stories of moldy, weevil-infested biscuits and rotten meat that sailors had to eat on long sea voyages. When his mother remarked on his appetite, Jules claimed that her cooking was especially good (though an hour after leaving the table he could scarcely remember what the main dish had been).

Jules was determined to make good on his promise, for once. He would not back out of this adventure at the last minute. He would share his friend's desperate situation, though he could not compare his own dull life with Nemo's helpless straits.

Before he went upstairs to his room, Jules embraced his parents, terrified that they would notice his maudlin attentions. Fortunately, his father was so focused on the newspaper that he wouldn't have noticed a placard fastened to Jules's chest. Sophie, sharp-eyed and attuned to her son's moods, might have detected something in his manner, but she did not comment on it.

His brother Paul mercifully fell asleep. As the boy snored, Jules crept about the room in the moonlight, gathering the possessions he insisted on taking with him: copies of *Swiss Family Robinson, Robinson Crusoe, Last of the Mohicans*, as well as *Ivanhoe* and *The Pirate*. Over the past two years, Jules and Nemo had shared those novels, since Jacques Nemo had not been able to afford books.

Jules took a bound, blank journal along with several lead pencils so that he could record his experiences and observations. Someday they might be useful to him when he was a respected chronicler of his own adventures. . .

As the hours crawled by, he tossed and turned, eager but also terrified. That afternoon he had marched down to the docks to look at the *Coralie*, a fine and magnificent ship. The brig had a full crew and a full cargo hold. Captain Grant had been on many extended ocean voyages before. All things considered, Jules had nothing to worry about.

Long after his parents were abed, he crept down the flight of stairs, wearing only his nightshirt. He tiptoed to the window where his father kept the telescope pointed toward the clock face of the distant monastery. Jules peered into the eyepiece, focused, and waited for the moon to emerge from behind a gauzy cloud so that he could read the hands on the dial.

Jules still had an hour to get dressed and make his way down to L'Homme aux Trois Malices. Stumbling about, tripping on his shoelaces, he dressed without lighting a candle or turning up the gas. Paul continued to sleep with little-boy snores, suspecting nothing. Jules's heart strings tugged at him, and he thought again of how much he was leaving behind, but he raised his chin and counted the wonderful things he would experience instead.

Aboard the *Coralie* he would find a new life, and he couldn't wait for that adventure to begin. . .

Jules tiptoed along the evening-moist streets, carrying his sack of belongings over one shoulder. Wharf rats scuttled away from him into the dank alleys, where he heard women giggling and men grunting. He must have looked like a cutpurse creeping along. He was afraid he would be arrested as a vagrant or malicious prankster.

The *Coralie* would depart with the outgoing tide and travel some thirty miles down the Loire to Paimboeuf on the sea coast. There, she would take on more crew and exchange some of her cargo before Captain Grant pointed the bowsprit out into the wild Atlantic.

Ahead, L'Homme aux Trois Malices welcomed travelers with a glow of orange light from half-shuttered windows. A droning hum of laughter and music came from inside. Jules looked up at the sign hanging above the inn door, depicting a well-dressed man surrounded by a woman, a monkey, and a parrot. It was like no place his father had ever taken him, too noisy, too smelly.

As he hesitated at the door, Nemo stepped out of the shadows. "I wondered if you would come, Jules."

"I told you I would." Jules swallowed a defensive tone. "I promised."

"I know – but still, I wasn't sure you'd come," Nemo said with a smile. "Come on, I've talked to the innkeeper. My father used to know him, and as a good-luck gesture, he's buying us each a flagon of Breton ale. I bet you've never had any of that in a goblet at your dinner table. Let's go have a toast."

Uncertain, Jules followed his friend into the smoky room full of strangers and odd human odors, greasy cooking and sour old drink. The thick rafters were stained with soot. Someone was playing a squeeze box and singing off-key. Others howled and laughed, pounding on tables. Some played cards. A few, dead drunk, snored in their chairs.

Seeing Nemo and his red-headed friend, the innkeeper filled two ceramic tankards from a keg behind the counter. Nemo took them and handed one to his friend. They clanked their flagons together. The Verne family drank only French wine, usually diluted – and the yeasty, hoppy taste weighed on his unsettled stomach.

The innkeeper gave a cheer as the boys slurped the foam. "To two lads about to make their fortunes off at sea." The innkeeper drank from his own mug, then patted his belly. A few others at the bar raised their tankards in the toast, but didn't seem to realize – or care – what they were celebrating. Around them, the noise continued unabated.

"I thought our going was supposed to be a secret." Jules hunched away from the myriad bloodshot stares directed at him. He didn't dare let his father find out.

"The ship sails at dawn," Nemo said. "By the time word can get to your house and wake anybody up, it'll be too late."

Jules took a reflexive swallow of the bitter beer and felt its effects rush to his head. For years, the two of them had concocted schemes to explore the world and go to the exotic places they read about in books and in illustrated Parisian magazines. But now it was real – *too* real and too soon.

Panic began to rise within Jules, and he wanted to kick himself. Nemo rested a hand on his friend's forearm. "I told you, you don't have to go."

"I do. Yes, I have to go." Jules repeated it as if to reassure himself. "I have to go . . . just in case you need rescuing."

"All right, then." Nemo drained his flagon and stood up. He knew that his red-haired friend would never finish his ale. "We have an appointment to say goodbye to Caroline."

IX

Generations of successful French merchants and shipbuilders had built row houses along the main avenues of Île Feydeau. With Nantes's fading prominence as a great seaport, however, the waterside houses now canted like drunken sailors as foundations settled into the watery soil, although scrolled facades, brick patterns, and ironwork balconies struggled to maintain the illusion of splendor.

Nemo pointed up at a set of shutters high on the whitewashed bricks. "Third floor. Second window over."

"Are you sure?" Jules said, then rounded on his friend. "How do you know?"

"I listen to her play the piano sometimes," he said casually, not admitting how often he came to talk with Caroline. Nemo bent over to choose a small pebble and tossed it up at the window. Jules did the same, but his stone missed, clinking against the stone walls.

With a flurry at the curtains, Caroline opened the sash and leaned out, dressed in her nightgown. Seeing the two furtive young men waving at her from the street below, she signaled back and closed the double windows.

Jules hovered next to Nemo, away from the street lamp's blue-yellow gaslight. He was afraid someone might see them, afraid Caroline's father would chase them away, and he didn't want to lose his chance of saying farewell to her.

When the tall, gold-inlaid door creaked open, Caroline stood there, her honey-on-fire hair tied back with a few colorful ribbons, a hastily donned cashmere robe cinched at her waist. A forced smile covered her sad expression.

And in the shadows behind her, her maidservant fussed about, trying to make the young lady look presentable while scolding her for unacceptable nocturnal activities. Marie thought her mistress should have been looking ahead to a good marriage and fine prospects; with the significant dowry Monsieur Aronnax could provide, Caroline would have her pick of suitable young men in Nantes.

Caroline shushed the maidservant and stepped out onto the tiled porch, pulling the door shut behind her and leaving Marie inside. She looked searchingly at Nemo, then over at the other young man in outright surprise. "So you're truly going, Jules? I hope you are not just doing this as a lark."

"We might not be back for three years." Jules's voice was raw, as if he could barely believe it himself. He squared his shoulders.

She sighed and looked at Nemo. "André, I wish there was some other way to help you. I just could not think of –" Her voice broke as, leaning toward him, she whispered, "You must come back home."

"Caroline, you have saved my life. You've given me a chance – and I promise I will come back to you."

"So will I!" Jules said.

"I will remember you," Caroline said, fighting back tears. "Both of you. That is a promise." She embraced Jules and then Nemo – perhaps for just a little longer – and stepped back to take a long look at them, as if she were making a daguerreotype in her mind. On impulse, she snatched two ribbons from her hair. "Take these and think of me." She handed a red one to Nemo, a green one to Jules. "I wish I had thought of something else to give you."

Nemo accepted his and kissed her on the cheek, feeling his lips burn; she moved, wanting more, but then Jules also tried to be gallant, taking her hand like a fancy lord and kissing it as he blushed.

"Be safe, both of you, and watch over each other." As if it required the last of her composure, she forced a smile. "Remember, you promised me a coral necklace." Caroline hurried back inside her house before sorrow overwhelmed her.

Nemo and Jules stood disconcerted for several minutes before they walked together toward the docks. Each tied the precious hair ribbon around his wrist, where he could see it every day. Jules sniffed it, trying to catch a scent of Caroline's perfume.

Passing the dock guard and stating their business, they crossed a creaking gangplank onto the deck of the ship that would be their world for the next several years.

At dawn the *Coralie* weighed anchor, cast off her mooring ropes, and sailed down the Loire toward the ocean.

X

Pierre Verne awoke as usual, breakfasted on croissants, berries, and soft cheese served by his wife, and then strode off with a long-legged gait to his business offices. Every day the same, all of life in its place.

At mid morning, though, his son Paul came running through town with an urgent message from Sophie Verne. Jules had disappeared. Pierre threw himself into the problem with all the forthrightness he reserved for his daily routine, his legal challenges, and any other business he conducted.

At first, he believed that Jules had simply got some crazy notion into his head. The young man was irresponsible and full of fancies; he would have to buckle down and get serious if ever he was to become an attorney. Today, Jules must have climbed out of bed at dawn and gone to follow his imagination without bothering to let anyone know. The boy often skipped his breakfast.

Upon further consideration, Pierre convinced himself the scheme must be some unwise idea concocted by that shipbuilder's son. Despite Pierre Verne's obvious disapproval, the two young men remained incomprehensibly attached to each other, and it made even less sense why the daughter of Monsieur Aronnax would choose to associate with such a pair. Jules, at least, came from a respectable home – but that Nemo boy . . .

With a scowl and a sigh, he shut and locked the doors of his law offices, though he still had much to do, thanks to the legal matters attending the *Cynthia* disaster. Pierre suspected he would be back within an hour, after dragging Jules home from his absent-minded truancy and punishing the boy for his own good. His wife would be calm again, and all would return to normal.

Scowling, he marched along the docks, brusquely interrogating sailors from one ship and another, asking if they had seen a red-headed young man, perhaps accompanied by a dark-haired boy of the same age. The friends often played down here among the noise and the dirt and the smells.

Pierre shook his head as he strode along. Such activities might make perfect sense for André Nemo, since his father had been a shipbuilder and the boy could hope for nothing better in his life; for Jules, though, there could be no benefit in understanding ships if he intended to practice law in Nantes.

Shielding his eyes from the hot sun and wrinkling his nose at the smell of fish and river water, he saw one of the sailors whose papers he had filed after the *Cynthia* disaster. This man had worked with Nemo's father; perhaps he had seen the two. Pierre strode up and introduced himself briskly, while the sailor continued to repair frayed rope and lash heavy cords into knots.

"I remember ye," the sailor said.

"And you certainly knew Jacques Nemo, who died aboard the *Cynthia*."

"Aye. A good man, he was."

"And his son. Do you know his son André, as well? André Nemo?"

The sailor turned his head, scratching tangled gray hair on a sunburned scalp, then he reached into his belt to withdraw a long dagger with which he trimmed the rope's frayed end. "O' course. I was there when André climbed his first ratlines, right to the top o' the mast. Boy has spunk and a good head about 'im. Even with the world against him, he'll still make his way, that one. I wish 'im all the best, now that he's gone."

"Gone?" The elder Verne stiffened. "Where did he go?"

Surprised, the sailor set the rope in his lap. "Why, he set sail this mornin', sir. Off to sea. Cabin boy for Captain Grant's explorin' ship, the *Coralie*."

Pierre frowned. He didn't recall the ship, but then so many came and went in the port. "What about my son Jules?" He frowned at the sailor as he tugged on his own grayish sideburns, trying not to show his uneasiness. "A red-headed young man who often plays with the Nemo boy?"

The sailor blinked at him in perplexity. "Ye mean ye don't know, sir?"

"Know? Know what?"

"Shipped out together as mates, they did. The two lads sailed off at dawn."

Pierre Verne gave a strangled cry. The sailor bent back to work on the rope to hide a smug grin over this supercilious man's look of horror.

Madame Aronnax could not understand why Monsieur Verne, a local lawyer, would be pounding on their door at noon, or why he would insist on speaking with her young daughter. But Caroline answered the summons, straight-backed, her mouth a firm line, dressed in the daily finery her mother demanded.

"My son Jules is gone." Pierre looked into the girl's blue eyes, shattering the porcelain composure of her expression. "Did you know that he boarded an English ship, the *Coralie*?"

Caroline drew a deep breath. "It is possible, monsieur. My father arranged for André Nemo to take passage aboard Captain Grant's ship, and I believe your son joined him. They told me their intentions last night."

"And you didn't think to inform *me*, his own father? You could have written a message, sent out one of your servants –"

"It is not my place to tell you, monsieur." She used all the hauteur her mother had taught her. "It was a matter given to me in confidence."

An appalled Madame Aronnax looked on, but Caroline held her ground. "Your son and André Nemo talk a great deal and have big ideas. Jules Verne is known for the stories he likes to tell." She sniffed. "Should I come running to you each time they make up a wild scheme, monsieur? I would be at your doorstep every afternoon."

Pierre seethed, but he could not take out his anger on the daughter of a wealthy and politically powerful merchant in Nantes. "Do you know where this ship is going? When does it come back?"

Madame Aronnax gave a stern glance to her daughter, and Caroline's lips trembled. "The *Coralie* is sailing around the world to a hundred exotic places. She is not expected back for three years, perhaps." Her voice cracked.

"Three years . . . around the world?" Pierre shot up from the chair that Madame Aronnax had politely offered him.

"The ship went down the river to Paimboeuf." Caroline remembered the schedules she had studied in her father's shipping offices. "She will tie up for the day, making final preparations, and will set off again at dusk with the tide."

"Paimboeuf," Pierre said, suddenly intent. "Thirty miles from here." Then he marched to the door of the Aronnax home. "I must find a carriage."

XI

While the three-masted ship traveled downriver into the wide estuary, Jules and Nemo stood on the scrubbed deck in exhilaration. They whistled to people on shore; some waved back, but most had seen so many ships go along the Loire that they found nothing special about it anymore.

The night before, in the deep darkness before dawn, the two had caught a few hours sleep on the *Coralie*'s deck, and they awoke feeling stiff and sore. But their excitement at setting out from Nantes filled them with energy. Jules couldn't believe they were underway, plying the winds and currents. Each moment, he grew farther from his family and home as the breeze freshened and the sails strained like the belly of a gluttonous man.

After the bustle of early morning duties, Captain Grant came to introduce himself, shaking Jules's hand and giving him an assessing look. The English captain had close-cropped brown hair, broad shoulders, and thin and wiry arms. His wide-set eyes were surrounded by a deep set of crow's feet, as if he had spent most of his life gazing into sunrises and sunsets. He wore a mustache in the English style and spoke stilted French with a strong accent, though Jules and Nemo could understand him well enough.

"I warrant we'll spend plenty of time together while we sail. 'Tisn't often I'm called upon to educate such fine young men to be cabin boys." He patted the two on their bony shoulders. "I've got no children of my own, so you two will have to substitute on this voyage." Grant's voice was gentle and intelligent, but when he barked orders at his sailors, the long-practiced tone of command invited no questions.

When the ship tied up at Paimboeuf just past noon, some sailors went ashore to procure last-minute supplies, while another part of the crew worked on-board. Here on the Atlantic coast of France, the ships were larger. Some of the huge four-masters boasted spacious cargo holds larger than the *Cynthia* and the *Coralie* combined.

Captain Grant pointed to the new cabin boys. "You two better go ashore while you're still able. Mark the feel of solid ground under your feet. I warrant it'll be some time before you do it again." He marched down the creaking gangplank. "See that you return in an hour, lads, and be ready to sail." The captain tipped his hat at three young ladies strolling by, then headed for the harbor master's offices to fill out final paperwork and enter his logs.

As they departed from the ship, Jules thought of his mother's cooking and smiled at the memory of how his sisters played the pianoforte, how he often recited poetry or made up impromptu verses after dinner.

Then his thoughts turned to exotic countries, strange animals, and mysterious cultures. He wanted to see them all. In time, he knew his family would get over their shock at his departure, and he would become a man, more well-rounded than he could ever be if he spent his life on Île Feydeau.

Jules vowed never to regret his decision. Even though Nemo's father had been killed, and Jules was leaving his own father behind, the two young men could now become surrogate sons, children of Captain Grant.

He followed Nemo through the dockside markets, wandering down the rows of carts where women sold fresh shellfish. Merchants tallied colorful bolts of silk from China, tusks of ivory from Africa, jaguar pelts from Central America, monkeys in cages, parrots with brilliant plumage, dried shark fins, drinking cups made of rhinoceros horn (guaranteed to shatter at the touch of poison). Though they had little money, he and Nemo moved from stall to stall, eyeing the wares with fascination. Jules kept his eyes open for something special to bring back for Caroline, even though they hadn't even left France yet.

He fingered the green ribbon tied at his wrist, which only last night had held back the lush hair of Caroline Aronnax. He recalled the tinkling melodies she composed in secret and wondered whether, by the time he returned, Caroline could compose an entire symphony to celebrate their triumphs. . .

XII

Though the driver was not a man to hurry his horses, he cracked his whip when Pierre Verne promised him a gold piece if they made it to Paimboeuf before the *Coralie* sailed. The brougham rattled down the river road, bouncing on rocks and splashing through mud.

Any other time, Monsieur Verne would have complained about the rough ride and the lack of padding on the carriage seats. Today, he didn't care.

Up ahead, a lad no older than Jules, wearing a floppy hat and carrying a willow frond three feet taller than himself, shooed seven sheep along the road. The driver hollered while urging his horses ahead, and the lad scattered his sheep out of the way before they could be run down.

Six miles farther along, the path drove into steep highlands above the river estuary where the road was blocked by a cart with a broken wheel. An old farmer sat next to the sagging wagon, watching his mule munch on a sack of grain. He seemed unconcerned that he had stalled all travel while waiting for someone to help him replace the wheel.

The carriage driver leaned back and called to Monsieur Verne, "If you want to move ahead, we'll have to help him change his wheel."

"All right. Be quick about it," Pierre said impatiently.

The wagon owner and his mule appeared to be in no hurry, but Pierre scolded both drivers until they set to the task. So great was Pierre's urgency that even he, dressed in fine business clothes, knelt in the mud and helped use a lever and boulders to lift the cart and replace the wheel. Then, before the farmer could casually pull in front of the brougham, Pierre shouted for the driver to hurry. The horses got up to a gallop again, and the carriage thundered past the rickety cart.

The sun lowered toward the horizon, spilling golden rays in an Atlantic sunset. Other carts and horses and wagons began to fill the road as they approached Paimboeuf. Monsieur Verne saw dozens of ships on the docks. He didn't know how he would ever find the *Coralie* among them. It might take an hour to talk to the harbor-masters and study docking records – and by that time the ship would have sailed with the outgoing tide.

Instead, he instructed the driver to take the brougham down to the quays. The impatient attorney leaned out the window, questioning sailors. "Where's the *Coralie*?" He asked seven times until finally he added, "She's about to sail. Which one is the *Coralie*?"

A young seaman with tanned skin and a wispy beard sat on a crate munching an apple. He looked up, oblivious to Monsieur Verne's urgency, and gestured down the docks. "Fourth one. You'd better hurry. They're casting off."

The driver whipped his horses. People on the docks scattered, much as the sheep had scattered on the highland road. The carriage rattled across the boardwalk, iron-shod wheels thundering like drumbeats. At last, Pierre caught sight of a three-masted ship with her sails unfurled to catch the wind and the outgoing tide. He saw the markings, the name *Coralie*, and – with horror – realized that sailors were already working to untie the brig from the pier.

With a rattling clangor, the heavy chains were drawn up into the hawse holes. The sailors raised the anchor.

XIII

Because Jules and Nemo were both good with figures and arithmetic, Captain Grant had sent them down into the cargo hold with ledger sheets. After their brief respite that afternoon, the two young men spent hours marking the inventory of everything the *Coralie* would take to circumnavigate the globe.

The larder was filled with forty-five fresh hams, sixty slabs of bacon, seventy-one wax-covered cheeses, and sacks and sacks of flour, cornmeal, coffee beans, sugar, and potatoes. The diet of salt meats and ship's biscuits would be relieved by fresh eggs from caged chickens, as well as milk (so long as the cow didn't go dry from seasickness). Pigs and goats – which would eat all sorts of refuse including wood shavings, dirty straw, and even old newspapers – would also provide occasional fresh meat.

Experienced sailors worked hard with the ropes, lashing crates into spaces and storing barrels of water, beer, and black powder. Heavy cannon barrels were tied in the lowest decks for ballast, spares in case a cannon should explode during firing.

Some of the crew had already noticed that the two cabin boys were favorites of the captain. Jules hoped the special treatment wouldn't cause problems later, since he expected to put in his share of hard work. In theory, at least. He already dreaded the uncomfortable conditions he would have to endure from storm-churned seas or long hot passages through tropic doldrums.

With the outflowing tide at sunset, the crew prepared to set off from Paimboeuf and head out to sea at last. A full moon would light their way, laying a path like molten silver across the calm Atlantic. Jules had seen the big wall chart in Captain Grant's quarters. How many of those places had the captain seen? How many did he intend to visit during this voyage? Jules wanted to do it all. He just hoped there weren't too many storms.

Just as he and Nemo finished their last check, the ship's bell sounded, signaling departure. With heavy thumping steps, the ship's quartermaster climbed down the ladder into the cargo hold.

The quartermaster was a broad-shouldered Upper Canadian named Ned Land, who had sailed with the English captain on other journeys. His chest was as broad and as hard as one of the kegs in the larder, and his curly blond hair looked disheveled no matter how often he wetted or greased it down. His striped shirt had been painstakingly mended with Ned's own sewing skills during long hours aboard ship.

In his rough and salty accent, Ned Land had claimed he could bring down seagulls with his rifle when they were only black specks in the sky. Jules didn't ask why Ned would want to shoot at seagulls, but he and Nemo expressed appropriate admiration of the man's marksmanship.

In addition to his duties as quartermaster, Ned served as the boatswain, sailing master, and Captain Grant's first lieutenant. The big Canadian had a blustery good humor and the uncomfortable habit of clapping both Nemo and Jules on the back hard enough to make them think one of the cargo chests had dropped on them.

"Hark, Jules! Boy, yer wanted up to the bridge," Ned bellowed. "Come too, André Nemo."

Puzzled, Jules hoped the captain meant to let them watch as the local pilot guided the *Coralie* out of the harbor and into the open Atlantic. They scrambled up the ladders into the last rays of the sunset. The anchors had been drawn up, but the ropes were still tied to the quay and the gangplank remained in place. A few seamen stood by the sail ropes and looked oddly at the two, but Jules didn't pause. He and Nemo trotted up the wooden stairs to the quarterdeck and the captain's cabin.

Inside, Captain Grant sat in the large chair, staring across his tiny bureau at Pierre Verne. Seeing his father, Jules's heart turned to stone and sank to his stomach. Nemo stopped beside him at the doorway, but didn't say a word.

Pierre Verne gazed at his son, and his peppery sideburns bristled. Jules could read behind the man's gray eyes that a terrible storm brewed inside.

Captain Grant looked at Jules with a sad smile and pulled out one of the single sheets of paper each recruit had signed. "It is my sad duty to rescind your contract, sir." With a flourish, he tore the paper in half. "In normal times, 'twould not be this easy for a cabin boy to get out of his term of service, but your father and I have reached an agreement."

He offered the scraps of the contract to Jules, but Pierre Verne snatched them away and stuffed them into the pocket of his jacket. Tears of shame filled Jules's eyes, and he looked over at Nemo. "You'll have to go alone after all. But I *would* have come this time. I really meant to."

"I know, Jules," Nemo said.

"We will go home now," Pierre Verne said, his voice as gritty and cold as the last block of ice stored in sawdust after winter. "Your mother is waiting."

Jules turned to Nemo, remembering the possessions beside his assigned hammock belowdecks. "Keep my books, André. Think of me when you read them. And the journal – write down what happens, so that when we see each other again I can read everything you did, since I can't be there with you."

"I'll write everything down," Nemo said. "I promise."

Pierre Verne placed a strong hand like a vice on his son's shoulder, but Jules broke away and embraced his friend. "I'll see you in two years, three at the most."

But it would be a great many more years before they laid eyes on each other again. . .

XIV

When Jules returned home to his concerned siblings and a tearful mother, Pierre Verne gave him the worst caning in his life. He was exiled to his room and locked inside, as if he might attempt to escape.

For three days Jules received only bread and water. Worse, his father did not even lecture him, and the silence was far harder to endure. The young man had no opportunity to explain himself, could not say what he was feeling. No one gave him a chance.

At times he sensed his mother just outside the closed door, but she refused to comfort him. Then the stairs would creak softly as she went back down to the lower levels of the house. Instead, Jules sat alone staring at Caroline's colorful green hair ribbon tied around his wrist.

After an interminable time, his father opened the door and stood there, looking deathly solemn. He stared at his son while Jules sat on his bed in terror, still bruised and aching from the whipping he'd endured days before.

"I want your vow, your solemn vow, and then I'll let you out of this room," Monsieur Verne said.

Jules swallowed hard, but he could endure his imprisonment no longer. He knew what the older man was asking of him.

As if he were ripping his own soul out of his chest and handing it to his father, Jules Verne said, "From now on, I promise to travel only in my imagination."

PART II
CAPTAIN GRANT

I

Brig Coralie
October, 1841

The winch creaked as sailors raised a dripping net out of the water. A hoarse-voiced man chanted a work tune, and Ned Land stood on the quarterdeck, directing operations with his brawny arms. With a shout, the men released the catch and the bulging net spilled open. Strange fish rained flopping onto the deck.

"'Tis a big haul!" Ned bellowed. "These waters be filled with fish."

With long-practiced ease, a barefoot Nemo ran forward with his fellow crew members to grab the slippery prizes. His hands and clothes already smelled like old fish and fresh tar. After more than a year aboard the brig, he knew every knot in every rope, every splinter on the top deck boards, every minute of the daily routine.

Like the rest of the crew, he wore a checked shirt and a black-varnished tarpaulin hat. Duck trousers fit snug around the hips and loose about the feet in wide bell-bottoms that could be rolled up in a flash. Seasoned sailors walked the deck with their hands half open and fingers curled, ready to grasp a rope in an instant at a rigger's barked command.

The cook already had his pots and barrels ready for the fresh haul of fish, while Captain Grant – who was not afraid to get dirty and slimy himself – stood amidst the mess and called for Nemo to grab any unusual fish that he could preserve in his bottles of alcohol.

The English captain, a naturalist and explorer, kept shelves full of specimens in his cabin and maintained careful records in a massive scientific logbook. He had taken Nemo under his wing, instructing the young man in the English language, as well as mathematics, nautical arts, and sciences. On calm evenings, Nemo helped the captain sketch some of the stranger species they had caught. As he made his drawings, he couldn't help thinking of Caroline's artistic aspirations; he toyed with the now-frayed hair ribbon on his wrist, thinking of Île Feydeau and Jules Verne. . .

After Captain Grant made his selections from the wriggling catch, the cook grabbed what he wanted for the stewpot. The remaining fish were dumped back overboard, and then under the beating sun, Nemo and his crew mates set to work swabbing fish guts and scales from the deck. Fourteen months at sea had made his olive skin brown and his muscles as strong as capstan knots. For Nemo, this ship already felt like home.

When the *Coralie* had first set sail, every seaman knew what to do – except Nemo. Unintelligible orders were barked and followed without question. Nemo tried to help, but found himself more often in the way. He did his best to stand clear as the sailors intuitively worked the ropes and sails.

"I warrant there's no more helpless and pitiable an object as a landsman beginning a sailor's life," Captain Grant had said from the quarterdeck, his voice warm and understanding. "Don't fret, lad. Within a month, ye'll be scurrying about to follow orders without a second thought. Best enjoy these first days on deck, because there'll be little enough time for sentiment once we get under way."

Indeed, it hadn't taken long for the change to occur in Nemo. As the ship voyaged southward, the salty breezes and sun-glared blue expanse called to him like a mermaid's song. During the day, trade winds stretched the sails taut and made the rigging hum. The layers of canvas pulled the three-masted brig along as if by the finger of God.

In the lower decks, the port and starboard watches shared bunks or hammocks. Open hatches let in sunshine and fresh air; lanterns hung from the rafters, providing the only light in the hold when sailors sealed the hatches against stormy weather.

Each man had a kit of meager possessions and a few changes of clothes that would last him for two years on-board the *Coralie*. When not on watch, the crew made themselves comfortable amongst the coils of rigging rope, spare sails, and patch cloth. On quiet evenings, older seamen told stories, topping each tale with another adventure even more outrageous than the previous. The thick air was redolent of old sweat and sour salt water. Nemo swung in his hammock and listened to their lore with a contented smile.

The *Coralie*'s deck fittings were painted light gray so the ship would be visible on moonless nights; the white deck houses stood out smartly against a rich oiled deck. And on the night watch, a blizzard of stars in the dark sky shone down like nothing Nemo had ever seen from Nantes. . .

After leaving Paimbeouf, the *Coralie* had sailed south along the coast of France and around the Iberian Peninsula with a four-day stop in Lisbon, where Captain Grant had once spent several years learning his trade from a Portuguese mentor. The Portuguese were themselves great explorers of the oceans, and revered their long-ago monarch, Prince Henry the Navigator, as a patron saint.

Lisbon was a city that looked like a staircase. The streets and whitewashed buildings stumbled down from the surrounding summer-brown hills. The crowded houses stood in successive layers, their narrow windows bedecked with flower boxes. Level after level led down to the Tagus River, which spilled into a calm, sheltered harbor at its mouth. The air was heavy with screaming gulls and the salty dampness of the sea.

Departing from Portugal, the brig continued south to Casablanca in Morocco. The *Coralie* sat at anchor across where the sea turned a jewel blue against the curve of sandy shore. Five times each day, the muezzins stood atop the elegant spires of minarets, summoning the faithful into mosques for prayer. Their warbling voices sang out across the crowded and haphazard streets, echoing along the walls of white-limed houses.

After putting ashore again for resupply on the Canary Islands, they cut across the hot and moist doldrums of the Tropic of Cancer, then rounded the western elbow of Africa, Cape Bojador, which had once been considered the edge of the world.

Standing on deck, Nemo saw bleak deserts that poked into the ocean, turning the water a dirty brown with suspended sand. The *Coralie* sailed past barren cliffs of naked sandstone, where the burning sun baked the rock so that not even a weed grew in the crannies.

Captain Grant guided them south along the Gold Coast, the Ivory Coast, the Ebony Coast, until the brig reached the wide mouth of the Congo River. They stopped at a Belgian outpost, trading a few items from the hold to stock up on fresh fruit and meat.

Now, as they reached the Cape of Good Hope, the haze of southern Africa filled the horizon. More than a century before, the Swedish naturalist Carl Peter Thunberg had filled volumes with specimens obtained from South African shores. Thunberg had tramped across the wilds, heedless of predators, collecting samples from unexplored cliffsides and rugged valleys. He wore out three pairs of shoes in a single expedition. Captain Grant had told Nemo the story.

Now, looking at the coastline, the captain mused aloud, "'Tis sad so little remains in all the world to discover, lad. But whatever remains, we shall find it."

All travelers were welcome here at the southern tip of the world, and any ship received permission to drop anchor in the harbor, provided it was non-hostile. The Dutch had established Cape Colony, raising vegetables to sell to passing ships that rounded the tip of Africa en route to the Orient. In the past decade, the town had grown substantially, spreading from the beach up the surrounding hills. Now Cape Town had three hospitals, a military parade ground, and six chapels and churches that served various faiths.

The *Coralie* lay at anchor while Nemo rode with Ned Land in a skiff dispatched to negotiate docking privileges at Cape Town. As the skiff approached the shore, Ned stood at the prow and pointed with a callused hand. "Look there, scamp – that be Table Mountain, and there be the Lion's Head." The quartermaster winked at Nemo. "Or, if ye want more civilized sights, in town ye'll see elegant houses, the likes o' which ye'd find in London, Glasgow, or Paris."

The Canadian was eager to be ashore, because once on dry land he could smoke tobacco again. On-board the ship, smoking was forbidden because of the fire danger; instead, the sailors chewed plugs of tobacco and spit brown streams over the sides. Ned pulled his clay pipe from a shirt pocket, holding it with anticipation. Maybe, Nemo thought, the Upper Canadian could also get a new striped shirt. . .

The *Coralie* remained at the Cape of Good Hope for a fortnight while her crew cleaned the hull and hold, restocked supplies, refitted and repaired any components that needed it. Nemo composed a long letter to Caroline Aronnax and left it to be posted on the next ship heading back to Europe. Though it had been such a long time since he'd seen her, he still remembered the way her hair shone in the sun, the scent of her perfume, the feel of her parting embrace – all as if it were yesterday. He hummed the melody of some of her illicit musical compositions.

Nemo also tore out the pages of his journal describing the voyage thus far and packaged them to be sent back to Jules Verne, so that his friend could read a detailed account of his year aboard ship. Though he wished Jules had been able to accompany him, Nemo had no regrets.

Captain Grant did not approve of his crew's wild impulses in the city known as the "Tavern of the Seas," but he would rather they let off steam under the watchful eyes of Cape Town's magistrates instead of aboard his ship.

When they returned aboard, exhausted and penniless, the *Coralie*'s crew was ready to set off for the Indian Ocean. . .

II

"Time for your Sunday lessons, lad," Captain Grant said, interrupting Nemo from another afternoon of swabbing the sun-washed deck. Naturally, the young man didn't complain.

At sea, the ship was its own country. On-board, the captain became peacemaker and disciplinarian, judge and jury, physician, expert seaman, and businessman. For an eager pupil like Nemo, Captain Grant had become a teacher as well.

Inside his spacious, specimen-crowded quarters, the captain hauled out his favorite volumes – copies of Leonardo da Vinci's notebooks, filled with drawings and musings and ideas. "Leonardo lived three and a half centuries ago, yet his inventions remain marvelous today." Captain Grant stared at the pages with wistful eyes. "I purchased these copies in Milan – crude reproductions of the originals, but the magic remains."

He pointed to sketches of contraptions that looked impossible, yet intriguing. "Leonardo lived in troubled times, lad, when Italian city states warred against one another. Because he believed knowledge must be based on observation, Leonardo drew studies of plants, architecture, human anatomy. He developed theories of mechanics and mathematics, and applied them to engineering."

Nemo could not decipher the writing on the pages. "I don't speak Italian, sir." By now he had learned passable English aboard the ship, but had not yet managed any other languages.

Captain Grant chuckled. "'Twould be of no help to you, lad. Leonardo was left-handed, so he taught himself to write backward. One must hold the letters in a reflecting glass to understand." He turned a ragged page. "Feast your eyes on the drawings alone and let your imagination translate."

An architectural plan of a cathedral, the cross-section of a human skull, designs for strange weapons. . . Nemo pored over plans for a gigantic crossbow, a chariot with revolving scythe blades to mow down infantrymen like weeds, and a four-wheeled car armored with wooden planking. The brilliant inventor had also drawn designs for flying craft, mechanical flapping wings, a flying screw, and a broad kite large enough to let a man soar on the winds like a falcon.

Most intriguing to Nemo, though, was a small boat designed to travel *underwater* while keeping a man safe and protected. "Are these ideas possible, sir? Or just fanciful visions from an impractical man?"

Captain Grant looked at the cabin boy, amused, then closed the book. He replaced it in a revered place on his shelf. "Anything is possible, lad – given enough imagination, a little bit of engineering knowledge, and a lot of persistence."

III

In the shark-infested Indian Ocean, the ship traveled around Madagascar off the eastern coast of Africa. They put ashore several parties to collect colorful specimens of *Lepidoptera*, the Latin name for butterflies.

Under Captain Grant's guidance, the *Coralie* sailed north-east to the southern tip of India and the island of Ceylon, where they took on a load of black tea, saffron, and cardamom, which they hoped would keep fresh until the ship returned to the trading ports of Europe.

At dawn after a long night watch, Ned Land stood beside a bleary-eyed Nemo. They watched a purplish-maroon sunrise brighten into a wash of scarlet before full daylight came. The muscular Canadian turned to the cabin boy. "Red sky at morning, sailor take warning. Aye – know that, don't ye, scamp? Means a bad storm is coming." Ned sniffed the wind. "Mark my words." The sailors on deck flashed knowing looks, and within half an hour, Captain Grant ordered the sails to be trimmed.

By afternoon Nemo found himself scaling the tarred ratlines with bare feet and callused hands to reach the topgallant sail on the foremast and yank ropes to furl it against a devastating wind. The ropes were slippery, and the squall-drenched cotton canvas sails were heavy as wet clay.

In a team effort, the sailors worked the deck ends of the lift lines while Nemo and the younger crewmen stepped into foot ropes, clinging to the horizontal yardarms high above the deck and the roiling sea. The ship lurched like a wild horse – and the sway was much more pronounced high on the masts. But Nemo had no fear of falling, no loss of balance. He felt like a *sailor*, at home even on the frothing seas.

After calling all hands, Captain Grant stood on the quarterdeck. The first and second mates yelled orders, which were sometimes lost in the wind. Rather than riding atop the heavy swells, the brig's sharp prow cut through them, which brought huge surges over the deck.

From his high vantage, Nemo looked into the foaming waves and wondered how quiet it must be just a fathom beneath the surface. He recalled da Vinci's speculative drawings of a boat that could travel underwater, safe from the reach of bad weather.

Then the storm took all his attention again. . .

When the weather died down, the crew worked through the day to put the *Coralie* back in order. Exhausted and dripping, Nemo changed into his second set of dry clothes so he wouldn't catch cold, nor get water spots on Captain Grant's precious notebooks.

At the captain's table the two ate cold meat and boiled eggs. "I prefer my food solid and immobile," Grant said as the ship continued to rock and sway. "'Tis not weather for soup, lad, not if ye want to keep any in your bowl."

Nemo ate in silence, until finally he asked, "In the da Vinci notebooks, the drawings you showed me, I keep thinking of that underwater vessel. Do you really think it could be built someday?"

The captain smiled at him, brushing down his trim mustache. During the voyage he had let his brown hair grow longer. "Aye, lad, I've heard of schemes to use sealed boats underwater. In the Year of Our Lord 1620, the court engineer for King James I – a man named Cornelius Drebbel – constructed a 'submarine boat' and demonstrated it in the Thames River. To maneuver he used oars sealed at the locks with leather gaskets. Alas, it did not prove practical."

Nemo tried to picture the spectacle in his mind, with the finely dressed English king and his court waiting on stands at the riverbank. The court engineer submerged his awkward boat by admitting water into the hull, and rose to the surface again by pumping it out, using a contraption like a blacksmith's bellows.

"Then, lad, during the American rebellion in 1776, a Yankee named Bushnell built a sealed ship he called the *Turtle*, barely large enough to hold one occupant. 'Twas driven by two hand-cranked screw propellers, one for vertical movement, one to go forward. Sergeant Ezra Lee took the *Turtle* underwater toward the loyal British flagship *Eagle* anchored in New York harbor. He carried an explosive charge to attach to the hull plate. Fortunately for the British, he couldn't maneuver at all and got lost. He never did manage to sink our ship."

Nemo peeled a cold egg. "So no one has made a functional submarine boat?"

Captain Grant dipped his knife into a small pot and smeared mustard onto a slice of gray-brown salt beef. "Robert Fulton, the American who invented the steamboat, came close to succeeding at the turn of this century. He journeyed to France in 1797 and your Napoleon Bonaparte granted him funding to build a functional vessel twenty-five feet long. 'Twas metal and streamlined like a fish, could hold three or four men in its belly, and used inclined diving planes to submerge. Compressed-air tanks augmented the oxygen supply. In theory, the vessel could stay underwater for six hours."

"Six hours?" Nemo remembered his experiment with the bladder helmet and reed-breathing tubes in the Loire. "And did it work?"

"Aye, but Napoleon decided that underwater ships had no military potential. Fulton couldn't rally any support from the British or American governments, either, so he abandoned his lovely submarine in 1806."

Nemo, his imagination captivated now, met his mentor's eyes. "Did Fulton's submarine boat have a name?"

Grant rummaged through his notebooks, confident that he could lay his hands on the information. "Aye, he christened it the *Nautilus*."

IV

The Straits of Malacca, a narrow trench between Malaysia on the north and Sumatra on the south, were known to be haunted by seafaring bandits. As the *Coralie* navigated the narrows, Captain Grant maintained full crews at the cannon, powder magazines, and crow's nests.

"We stop at Borneo, perhaps Java, then continue to the Philippines before we strike across the Pacific to the Sandwich Islands." Grant indicated the specific islands on the large nautical chart mounted under glass in the navigation room. "I warrant we'll see San Francisco before Christmas next."

Days after the three-masted brig emerged into the island-cluttered waters of Indonesia, Nemo sat at the bow, cradling in his lap one of the books Jules Verne had left for him, a worn copy of Defoe's *Robinson Crusoe*. He and his friend had sat at the edge of the Loire, imagining what they might do if ever marooned on a deserted island.

Engrossed in the story, Nemo did not hear the captain's footfalls above the groan of the rigging ropes and the whisper of tight sails. Captain Grant saw what his cabin boy was reading. "Crusoe, eh? You know the account Defoe used for his inspiration?"

Nemo looked up at the captain. "*Robinson Crusoe* is a true tale, sir?"

"Not exactly," Captain Grant replied with a smile. "'Twas told by the pirate William Dampier, who was also a naturalist and meticulous observer. One of his men, a Scottish sailor named Alexander Selkirk, demanded to be put ashore after a disastrous raid against the Spaniards. Dampier left him off the coast of South America, then sailed away."

"So he was marooned?" Nemo asked.

"By his own choice, lad. Four and a half years later, when William Dampier came around Cape Horn again – this time commissioned as the navigator on a legitimate ship, not a privateer – the crew spotted a strange light on the coast. When they stopped to investigate, they found a bedraggled Selkirk, who had built a huge fire to attract them. The poor man had not seen another living soul for four long years."

Seeing Nemo's fascination, Captain Grant said, "I have Dampier's book in my cabin, lad. You can read it tonight by lamplight, if you wish." The captain then pointed a scolding finger. "But first, 'tis your turn at watch. Go climb the ratlines and spend your hours up in the crow's nest."

V

Sitting alone atop the mast for hour after hour, Nemo imagined himself in another world. Far below, the *Coralie* held the smells and stains from the long voyage, despite vigorous daily scrubbings. He'd grown accustomed to the crowded and unpleasant conditions, but he preferred to be up high, where the breezes danced around the topmost spire. Here, his thoughts could roam.

The sails laughed with each gust of wind. In the South China Sea, islands, reefs, and peninsulas dotted the charts in Captain Grant's stateroom. At the moment, all Nemo could see was the hazy, curved plane of metal-blue water, a calm sea with just enough of a breeze to keep the sails filled and the ship moving on course.

Sunlight glinted across the stippled waves, fragmenting and reflecting back at him, though he no longer felt the baking heat upon his bronzed skin. Nemo stared, looking for any interruption in the quiet sea that would indicate an island, an approaching storm, or another ship. The world was so vast, so full of possibilities. No birds were visible, which could mean the ship was far from land. He took a moment to retie the faded red hair ribbon Caroline had given him, which sparked a wash of memories of Nantes. With the chance Caroline had offered him, asking her father to arrange for his spot on the *Coralie*'s crew, Nemo had indeed made something of himself.

In the crow's nest he had carried the thick leather-bound journal Jules had given him. Now he wrote with a lead pencil, scratching out thoughts and recollections, adding details of the past two days. Jules, who had been forbidden to take this journey himself, would want to know everything.

Nemo glanced up again and scanned the sea, startled to see a black speck on the horizon riding the wind toward the *Coralie*. He took out his spyglass and placed the warm brass eyepiece against his face. Through the lens he could make out a sailing ship, though he could determine no specifics. "Ship ahoy! East by north-east."

The sailors on the *Coralie* looked up at him, then out to sea. From his place at the wheel, the helmsman signaled that he had heard. Nemo glanced again at the distant craft, then returned to his writing.

Over the next hour or so, the other ship came closer while the *Coralie* tacked at an angle to the wind. The stranger – a large, sturdy sloop – chose a course bound to intercept them, moving with the breezes. As the distance between the two vessels closed, Nemo periodically checked with the spyglass.

Captain Grant's sailors continued to adjust the rigging, pulling the *Coralie*'s sails to snatch every breath of wind. Some gathered at the rail to look at the oncoming ship. It had been some time since the crew had encountered another vessel, but this was a high traffic sailing lane in the South China Sea, so encountering another sail was not unusual.

Nemo could have finished his shift, scuttled down the shroud ropes, and asked to look at the Crusoe-inspiring books Captain Grant had promised him. But with another ship coming closer, he wanted to remain in the crow's nest where he could be the first to see.

Using the spyglass, he finally made out the flag atop the foremast of the sloop. "She's British. Flying the Union Jack."

The other sailors milled about on deck, some shading their eyes and trying to see. The sloop picked up speed, coming closer. Nemo finished writing another page in the journal and stuffed the heavy book inside his shirt, tight against his chest.

Captain Grant stood on the raised quarterdeck, using his spyglass to observe the approaching ship. The sloop clearly intended to rendezvous with the *Coralie*. The captain went into his cabin and emerged wearing a new jacket with bright brass buttons.

Nemo made out the details of the sloop, a black hull with a line of tan at the waterline, six gun ports on a side, and a single tall mast with long booms that kept the gaff-rigged mainsail extended. Two square sails had also been hoisted to give her greater speed to run before the wind. A well-dressed man stood at the tiller – a British captain? – and others strutted across the deck wearing finery. Some appeared to be ladies in colorful gowns made of oriental silk. They waved cordially at the *Coralie*.

Nemo knew that British ships were common in the South China Sea. Perhaps it was an opium trader; more likely, this sloop carried a group of ambassadors or colonists out on a pleasure cruise among the islands.

Captain Grant signaled the sloop and called all hands on deck to prepare for a meeting at sea, where they could exchange news and mail. Nemo waited, breathless with anticipation, wondering what tidings the sloop might bring from the territories in South-East Asia.

Unexpectedly, two of the women in bright dresses went to the mast and tugged ropes to draw down the Union Jack. Nemo squinted through the spyglass, trying to see what they meant to do. As the flag was lowered, two of the sailors on the *Coralie*'s deck yelled a warning.

Another flag ran up the sloop's main mast – a black banner sporting a crudely stitched skeleton and a bloody sword.

The sloop's six gun ports opened up, and the ominous snouts of cannons protruded. Nemo saw flashes of light and puffs of smoke as three cannons fired in successive, overloud drumbeats.

The pirates' first cannonball ripped through the *Coralie*'s mainsail, leaving a smoldering hole. The second ball crashed into the hull above the waterline, blasting one side of the upper cargo hold. "They've heated the balls red hot!" a sailor shouted. The technique was devastating against wooden ships, easily starting the victim vessel on fire. The crew quickly filled buckets to extinguish any sparks.

The third cannon blast was the worst. Its load contained chains and mauls, rods of metal that spun like saw blades, tearing into the rigging, severing ropes. The sails flapped free. One of the ratlines dangled like an amputated arm. Fires began to burn on the *Coralie*'s deck.

The men belowdecks started to scream and shout. When another blast splintered the side of the mizzen mast, Nemo knew he had to get down from his vulnerable position. His heart pounded, and he thought quickly. So far, the voyage had been marvelous and breathtaking, but now he wondered about the difference between adventure and danger.

The sloop full of pirates narrowed the distance as the *Coralie* wallowed, unable to flee. The crew shouted, preparing to fight for their lives. Nemo swallowed hard and went to join them.

Down below, Captain Grant's weapons master managed to fire two of the starboard cannons, but the pirates' rapid approach made the range difficult to determine. The cannonballs sailed past their target, only one of them tearing a hole through the pirates' triangular foresail.

Nemo used his spyglass again and saw the men aboard the sloop shedding their disguises, fine women's dresses worn by younger pirates to lull the unsuspecting *Coralie*.

One of the raiders stood up, displaying gaudy clothes, a scarlet sash, and a striking black tricorne hat – obviously the captain. The pirate leader's nose and ears had been sliced off, giving him a cadaverous appearance that made Nemo's heart freeze. He had heard of pirate justice, how a man caught stealing or grabbing more than his share of booty would be thus disfigured with the grotesque markings of his crime. But this noseless captain had acquired a vessel and a crew of vicious cut-throats. He raised a long cutlass high in challenge.

Flushed and breathless, Nemo scrambled down from the crow's nest, grabbed a swinging rope, and made his way from yardarm to ratline. His mind raced, trying to think of defenses the *Coralie* could mount against the pirates . . . but surely Captain Grant already had a plan.

He needed to descend to the deck, where he could join in the imminent fighting. He had an odd memory of play-acting late at night with Jules

Verne and Caroline Aronnax, when he had pretended to be the brave hero fighting against a bloodthirsty pirate king, but somehow he doubted these real raiders would flee in panic as easily as Jules had done.

Standing on the *Coralie*'s deck, quartermaster Ned Land removed his long rifle and loaded it. His disheveled blond hair was damp with sweat. The blustery Canadian had bragged about his shooting accuracy, able to pick off seagulls when they were mere flyspecks in the sky. Now, his face red with anger but his expression cool and focused, Ned lay the weapon across the railing, took aim, and fired at the approaching ship.

Nemo saw one of the pirates stumble backward and fall dead to the deck.

With a howl of rage, the marauders tossed the body overboard. They began to fire their pistols at random, striking the *Coralie* with a barrage of unaimed bullets. But the pirates had their own sharpshooters and a more vicious agenda. Captain Noseless barked an order, and several rifles fired from the deck of the sloop. They picked off the *Coralie*'s helmsman and then two deckhands who were wrestling to bring the flapping sails under control.

Now the *Coralie* lay helpless and burning, unable to use her sails or her helm. Captain Grant shouted to rally his crew. Without waiting for the key, one of the older seamen scrambled down the deck ladders to smash open the armory. The English sailors distributed swords and pistols and powder. Below, the weapons master recalculated his aim and fired another cannon blast. The shrieking ball struck the bow of the sloop and splintered the masthead.

Just as Nemo managed to land barefoot on the deck, the enemy sloop came alongside the *Coralie*. The marauders threw grappling hooks and boarding ladders across the gap between the ships. Nemo felt numb but not fearless, and stood with his shipmates to face the enemy, no matter what.

The pirates had painted their bodies with brilliant colors and coated their skin with thick grease to help deflect edged weapons during hand-to-hand combat. They scrambled aboard with knives in their teeth, boarding axes in their hands, and murder in their eyes. The shouts and smells were horrific: sweat, blood, gunpowder, and rancid grease.

His tattered striped shirt stained with soot, Ned Land continued to shoot his rifle. With every blast, another pirate fell, but the quartermaster had neither enough shot nor enough powder to save them all. Nemo both dreaded and anticipated when he could take part in the fighting.

Running to help the other grim sailors who were rattling their swords and tapping their pistols, Nemo seized a firearm of his own, loaded it, then thrust a second one into his belt. He looked around for a sword and settled on a long knife, though he had no training with either. He would have to learn as soon as the fighting began. And Nemo had always been a good learner.

The pirates swarmed aboard like a plague of rats. Many wore bandannas around their heads; some had lost fingers, hands, or feet – but none of those deficiencies slowed them down. Captain Grant's men engaged them with a clang of steel and a blast of shot. Struck down, bodies squirmed and twisted, screaming in pain and in defiance.

Wounded men fell overboard. Crates and barrels began to tumble into the water from a hole blasted in the *Coralie*'s cargo deck. Adding to the chaos, a few chickens, pigs, and even a cow had got loose from their pens and now milled about belowdecks.

Feeling like a dust mote in a whirlwind, Nemo stood his ground as Captain Noseless strode aboard, sweeping his long cutlass from side to side like a harvester cutting grain. *Coralie* sailors fell with their heads lopped off or a sword point thrust into their bowels.

Ned Land shot five more times, but at close quarters his rifle proved useless. He swore in French and English; the pirates were not bothered by either language.

Toward the rear of the ship, against the raised quarterdeck, Captain Grant used a sword with his right hand and fired a pistol with his left. Three dead pirates lay in front of him, their blood and entrails smearing the boards. The captain glanced over at Nemo, and the young man's heart swelled. Their eyes met for an instant, then both went back to fighting. Nemo's knees were watery with terror, his stomach knotted . . . but a crimson fringe of anger flared around the edges of his vision. He had no qualms about killing these bestial men. He let out a loud yell, and it felt good.

Nemo fired his first pistol and wounded one of the pirates, a man with a shaved head and crooked yellow teeth. The bald pirate snarled at him, clutching his wounded shoulder, and strode forward, sword in hand, until an English sailor struck him down from behind. This was no duel with rules or honor; this was a fight for survival against ruthless pirates. His head buzzing, Nemo shouted in confused triumph and chose another pirate to attack.

Fires continued to lick along the deck, the rigging, and the sails. A few *Coralie* men threw buckets of seawater, trying to douse the flames, but the pirates shot those men dead, and their dropped buckets of water mixed with the blood on the deck.

The disfigured pirate leader strolled through the melee, making his way toward Captain Grant.

Seeing the threat to his mentor, Nemo dodged sword thrusts, jabbed with his long knife, and worked his way to the quarterdeck. He had to defend Captain Grant! Reckless but outraged to see what the pirates were doing to his ship and his mates, Nemo ran forward, yelling – and suddenly found himself face to face with Captain Noseless. His bare feet skidded to a halt on the deck.

Nemo had little chance – a young man on his first voyage against a brutal cut-throat who had no doubt slain hundreds of men – but he could not let the villain coolly march forward and murder Captain Grant. His lips curled back from his teeth in defiance.

Nemo yanked the second pistol out of his belt and pointed it at the scarred pirate. When Captain Noseless grinned at him, his face looked even more like a skull. Nemo pointed the pistol at the pirate's chest and pulled the trigger, feeling no remorse. "Die!"

The hammer clicked against the flint. Nemo's stomach turned to ice as he recognized his mistake: when he had grabbed the two pistols, he had not loaded the second one. The pirate knew it.

With a brutal thrust, Captain Noseless jabbed his cutlass hard into the young man's chest. Nemo felt the point of the sword slam just below his sternum. The pirate thrust, hard, and the force of the blow drove Nemo backward.

The next thing he knew, he lay senseless on his back, reeling, unable to breathe, trying to scream, unable to believe what had just happened to him . . . expecting to die. But he wasn't dead. Despite the pirate's murderous intent, the cutlass had bit into the leather-bound journal that Jules Verne had given him. Nemo had stuffed it into his shirt before climbing down from the crow's nest. The steel point had poked through half of the pages and hammered him backward, but the book had saved his life.

Another pirate bounded toward Nemo as he struggled back to his feet. A flame-red beard protruded like a shovel from his chin. Astonished to see the young man still alive after the sword thrust, Redbeard intended to finish the job.

Nemo backed away, crouching and looking dangerous. He couldn't catch his breath, or focus his thoughts. The deafening sounds of battle faded to a mere background hum as he concentrated on staying alive. Nemo took out his long knife to defend himself against the bearded pirate.

His own two pistols were spent, so he threw them like metal cudgels at the pirate's face, but Redbeard ducked from one side to the other, grinning. Nemo breathed hard, inhaling fire with each breath, hating the pirates, hating their thirst for mayhem and slaughter. He wanted to kill them all. When he tripped on a fallen sword, he bent to pick it up.

Near the bow, Ned Land fired a final shot from his rifle, blowing a pirate completely off the deck. Then the burly quartermaster grabbed the long barrel and flailed the rifle like a steel club. The oak stock splintered as he brought it down on the face of a pirate, smashing the man's nose. A spray of blood, mucus, and teeth spewed from the pirate's broken head.

Ned Land thrashed the rifle from side to side, biceps bulging, until the splintered wooden stock broke off . . . and a swarm of angry pirates converged on him. With dismay, Nemo saw the Canadian quartermaster go down under a flurry of long knives and sword thrusts.

Concentrating on his bearded attacker, Nemo backed against the deck rail with nowhere to go but the debris-filled ocean. Intent on venting his anger against this one opponent, dismayed at what had just happened to Ned Land, he shoved his sword toward Redbeard, but the pirate clashed his own blade hard against it. The jarring impact numbed the young man's arm all the way up to the elbow, and the sword clattered from his throbbing grip. Now Nemo had only the long dagger in the other hand.

Redbeard raised his sword for the killing blow. Nemo glared at him, ready to jump and fight with his teeth and fingernails, if necessary. He wouldn't give up, certainly not now.

Then a singularly loud pistol shot cracked over the din. Crimson splashed from a new hole beneath the bearded pirate's breast. The marauder grunted and stopped, holding his sword high, still preparing for the thrust.

Nemo looked wildly to see that Captain Grant had fired his last shot. The captain had aimed and hit the murderous pirate to save the life of his cabin boy.

Before Nemo could react, the noseless pirate leader strode up to Captain Grant and brought the pommel of his dripping cutlass down on the captain's head, driving him to the deck. A gasp of shame and despair rose like a banshee's cry from the survivors of the *Coralie*.

"No!" Nemo cried.

Mortally wounded, Redbeard took one more staggering step forward, as if in death he meant to embrace the young man. He collapsed like an avalanche on top of Nemo, knocking him into the rail, which shattered. Both of them tumbled backward into the waves.

In the water, Nemo struggled to take refuge in the scattered wreckage. A fan of red murk oozed from Redbeard's body, and Nemo kicked his way free, pushing against the pirate's lifeless body. Already the marauder sloop and the damaged *Coralie* were drifting away. Out in the open sea, a dazed Nemo had to tread water before trying to swim back toward the ships.

All the remaining pirates had swarmed from the sloop over to the *Coralie*.

With the battle won, some went about extinguishing fires and minimizing further damage to the brig.

Nemo looked up from the water. At the tall quarterdeck, he watched the disfigured pirate leader haul Captain Grant to his feet. Noseless marched the stunned man to the tallest point, where everyone could see. By now, many of the *Coralie* survivors were surrendering to whatever fate awaited them.

With his ringing ears, Nemo couldn't make out the exact words Noseless spoke – but he knew the speech was about Captain Grant, who stood reeling and barely conscious, struggling to maintain his dignity. Nemo felt helpless, desperate to do something, and he swam harder, stroking toward the ships that continued to drift farther and farther away.

Then the pirate leader pointed a pistol at Captain Grant's chest and fired. The blast knocked the captain to the deck. Nemo gave a wordless shout that went unheard in the remaining din of the takeover. He choked on water that splashed into his gasping mouth. He swam harder, tears stinging his eyes with the salt water from the sea.

Without ceremony, a pair of pirates picked up the captain's body, swung him twice, then heaved him overboard. The man who had shown him the ways of the sea and the ways of science fell dead into the water, among the other floating debris.

The pirates had taken complete control of the *Coralie*, retying sails, regaining the brig's maneuverability. Because it was far more powerful and more impressive than their sloop, they would no doubt repair the *Coralie* and make it one of their own vessels.

As the ships sailed away from him, Nemo knew he could never catch up, no matter how fast he swam. Still reeling from the horror he had seen but not yet acknowledging the even worse straits in which he now found himself, Nemo clung to the wreckage that had spilled from the *Coralie*'s cargo hold.

He screamed after the pirates, but they either did not hear him, or ignored his pitiful shouts. Captain Grant had taught him to be resourceful, however, and Nemo looked around at the splintered wood, the broken spars, and the few casks and crates of supplies. Perhaps he could construct some sort of a temporary raft. But he had to act quickly, for every moment the flotsam dispersed more and more. He could not lose vital resources now. Every scrap might make the difference between his survival or his death.

All around, spilled blood stained the water purple. Corpses floated face down like tiny islands, their gaping wounds washed clean by sea water. Somewhere in the distance, the body of Captain Grant lay among them.

The two ships dwindled to tiny specks, until there was nothing else but the sea. Nemo was adrift and alone, lost and helpless.

Soon, the sharks would come.

VI

Even before the still-smoking *Coralie* and the pirates' sloop disappeared over the horizon, Nemo realized how alone he was out in the ocean. To have even the slimmest chance of surviving, he'd have to rely on his own wits. He thought of Captain Grant, Jules Verne, and Caroline Aronnax, and he strove for some way to keep himself alive.

Alert for the circling razor fins of sharks, Nemo paddled toward the nearest crate. If he could assemble the drifting junk, he might find enough worthwhile components. Kicking hard with sore and exhausted legs, he pushed it closer to one of the others. Then, with the tangled end of a burned rigging line, he lashed them together into a crude raft. Breathless but refusing to think about his exhaustion or fear, he swam over to fetch a barrel that bobbed in the waves. Hoping it would contain water or beer, he was dismayed to find that the keg held only damp black powder.

He did retrieve a dead chicken, drowned inside its cage, which he knew he'd appreciate when he grew hungry enough. Not knowing how long he might remain adrift, or what items he might require, he grabbed a waterlogged scrap of canvas from a torn sail, a long piece of wooden rail with a splintered end, a tangled mass of rigging rope, and someone's bloodstained shirt. He still had the waterlogged journal that had saved his life from the sword thrust, and he even kept the battered chicken cage. Anything might prove invaluable.

Soon, he saw dark fins cutting the surface, circling and approaching the floating bodies. Many of the fresh corpses were slain pirates, and Nemo wanted nothing more than to see them devoured by sharks. But other human forms floating here – like Captain Grant himself – had been his mates aboard the *Coralie*. These brave men, his friends, his teachers, were now nothing more than fish food. . . .

With so many sharks in the water, he didn't dare leave his meager refuge on the tilted crates. Using a broken slat of wood, he paddled his cumbersome raft away from the scene of carnage. For hours, he watched the voracious sharks fight over the floating bodies. Standing above the water, he shouted his rage and helplessness at them, but they ignored him. . . .

All that night Nemo huddled on the raft, knees drawn up against his chest in a sky filled with the southern constellations Captain Grant had taught him. He heard only the sounds of water lapping against his crates, and the ferocious tearing and splashing of sharks as they devoured the last scraps of human meat.

He sat and listened and thought about his boyhood in Nantes, his days of imaginary adventuring with young Jules Verne . . . and flirting with Caroline Aronnax. Nemo kept seeing the face of kindly Captain Grant, thinking of how the man had used his last pistol shot to save *him* before falling prey to Captain Noseless.

Nemo spent the night wide awake in grief and despair. He faced the overwhelming fear, and by dawn he had come through the worst of it. After much contemplation, Nemo decided to live. Somehow.

During the worst heat of the afternoon, Nemo curled up under the wet canvas. Sometime during the second day he devoured the dead chicken raw. Before long, the meat would rot and do him no good, so he sucked every drop of moisture from the flesh and chewed the fat for every scrap of energy it could provide.

Finished, he made the mistake of tossing the entrails over the side, which attracted the sharks again. One persistent shark circled, sensing more food atop the lashed crates. Its fin traced a spiral, coming closer and closer. Looking into the water, Nemo could see its sleek torpedo form, and he thought of what Captain Grant had told him about Robert Fulton's submarine boat, designed to move underwater like an armor-plated fish.

The shark finally grew impatient and rammed Nemo's rickety raft. Hastily knotted ropes strained as the crates lurched. The impact nearly threw Nemo overboard, but he grabbed the rough ropes to keep his balance. His left foot splashed into the water, but he yanked it back out. The shark returned for another lunge, its soulless black eyes filled with dull hunger.

The shark rammed again, cracking some of the boards. Knowing the crates wouldn't last long under such an onslaught, Nemo spread his feet apart for balance and snatched up the splintered wooden pole. It wasn't much of a spear, but it was the only weapon he had.

On the *Coralie* Ned Land had caught several sharks along the coast of Madagascar. Nemo knew that such a fish had tough hide, reminiscent of chain mail armor with overlapping scales. He also knew that the shark's most sensitive spot was the snout.

As the killer fish came at him again, Nemo braced himself and jabbed with the spear. The jagged point scraped the shark's head, missed the sensitive nose, and slid off the hard scales between its eyes. Startled, the fast-moving creature swerved, missed the crates, and dived deep before it could cause further damage to the raft. Nemo withdrew his spear, held it tighter . . . waiting.

The shark came up from below and rammed the crates. They creaked, but held. Nemo hoped the bottoms of the boxes hadn't burst, or he would lose whatever resources he had managed to salvage.

Again, the shark returned. Its head and snout protruded from the water, jaws wide open like a two-man saw wrapped into a circle. Seeing the sharp teeth and wet, red mouth, Nemo fought off disorientation. One slip could send him head first into that maw.

Marshalling his strength, Nemo raised the splintered end of his spear – and jabbed. The sharp wooden point stabbed deep into the fish's nose and gouged a jagged wound.

The shark thrashed, tearing the weapon from Nemo's grip. Splinters sliced open the young man's slick palms, but he felt no pain. Not yet. The wooden rod clattered onto the crates, and he scrabbled for it, but the spear bounced off into the sea.

Without thinking, heedless of the blood on his own hand, Nemo dropped to his belly and snatched the wooden pole back out of the water. He dared not lose his only weapon. The wounded shark flailed about, bleeding into the water, and the other sharks converged on it, sensing more food. Smelling fresh blood.

Shuddering with adrenaline and exhaustion, Nemo watched five of the predators tear the wounded shark into strips of meat, devouring it alive. Nemo huddled on the raft without moving, clutching his spear as if it were a religious artifact. Even with his ordeal, though, he had enough presence of mind to press part of his torn shirt against the cuts on his palm, slowing the blood to keep it from dripping into the water. He sat for so long his joints seized up and his muscles cramped until the turmoil in the reddened water faded away.

He didn't move for the rest of that afternoon. After many drawn-out hours, the ocean became quiet and empty again. The sharks had gone, every scrap of food consumed.

And Nemo was more alone than ever.

The vast blue sea stretched forever around him, for days and miles. He had no maps, no idea of his position. The nearest land could be just over the horizon, or it could be a thousand miles away. Nemo had no way of knowing.

The sun went down, and the sky was as empty as the sea. Curling his fingers in the water, Nemo caught a few scraps of floating seaweed. He chewed on it, but the leaves tasted bitter. Later, he endured abdominal cramps that could have come from the seaweed, or just from deep hunger.

He thought of how the sharks had fed and wished that he had managed to rip some scraps of meat from the shark he had injured. He deserved some of the spoils of his hunt, but the other predators had consumed the entire carcass.

Nemo looked in vain over the edge of his raft. He trailed the empty chicken cage like a sieve, trying to catch an unlucky, curious fish. He ended up with only a few more strips of seaweed and one tiny crab, which he ate in the blink of an eye, crunching the shell and swallowing before he could taste anything.

Desperately thirsty, still huddled under the canvas, he finally spotted a line of clouds at the horizon. He sat up sluggishly, shading his eyes. Over hours, he realized this was no illusion, that he was indeed seeing a blurry line. A circling bird high overhead reassured him that he must indeed be close to land.

His weary heart swelled with a glimmer of hope. He realized he had to set course for this distant patch of ground. He planted his wooden spear in the crack between the crates and threaded the tattered canvas onto the pole like a crude sail. He tugged on one side, using his weight and shifting position until he managed to catch a few breaths of wind. Though he couldn't see any change in his position, Nemo knew he had begun to move – toward the island, he hoped. He tilted the makeshift raft, used the sail to tack in the proper direction, and aimed for the misty gray clouds and the land that seemed infinitely far away.

Now that he had a goal, he could focus. Nemo lost all sense of time. The sun passed in a parabola overhead from an undistinguished horizon in the east, hovering overhead with pounding rays, and then falling toward the west. All the while, Nemo grasped the shreds of the sail in his raw fingers and rode the raft driven by whatever power the wind could give him.

The clouds thickened, rising taller in the air. At first, Nemo took delight in recognizing that he was moving closer to the land mass. Then he also realized that the clouds were getting larger. Darker.

Before long, the wind began gusting, and the sea grew choppier. With the sky so dark, he could no longer see the distant island. When the clouds finally burst, Nemo stared into the downpour, turning his face toward the sky in ecstasy as cool water poured onto his cracked lips, filling his parched throat. He swallowed every drop as if it were a pearl, lapping the little bit that managed to pool in the cracks on the crates, and turned his face up to drink more. He took off his shirt, wrung the moisture into his mouth, and tried to sop up every drop of rain.

Before he had his fill, though, before he could enjoy the sensation of being satisfied, the storm grew worse. The squall turned cold and violent, spinning the raft around so that Nemo had no idea which direction to sail. The waves heaved him up and down, battering him worse than the persistent shark had. The rain revived him from his daze – just in time for him to realize the danger he faced.

The frayed rope holding his raft together creaked, half rotted through. The small keg of wet gunpowder bobbed and clattered against the wooden crates. A gust tore the sailcloth out of Nemo's hands, so that the tattered canvas flapped like a banner in the wind. He clutched the fabric in a desperate attempt to steer, but the wind yanked the sail from his trembling fingers a second time. Nemo let it go as the raft rode up and crashed down in a surge of whitecaps.

Drenched and choking, he grabbed the crates with his last strength. He could do nothing more than hold on. Rain pounded on his skin like tiny nails. The wind moaned with the cries of sailors lost at sea. Nemo clung as the waves crashed against him from all sides.

Minute by minute the storm grew worse.

When Nemo awoke again he found himself cast upon a rocky, jagged beach. The splintered remains of his crates had been tossed high up on the shingle, and the blue waters of the lagoon behind him were calm as a mirror now, a taunting apology for the storm.

He blinked, amazed to be alive even on this forbidding shore. The island's coastline spread out on either side of him, covered with rocks and sand. In the center of the land mass towered the steep cone of a smoldering volcano.

Nemo got to his feet, brushed sand and broken shells from his skin, and looked around. As the sun rose he took an inventory of his resources.

He could see forests and streams inland, so he knew he could survive here.

Water and then food would be his immediate priorities. Nemo swallowed a lump in his still-parched throat and began to explore the mysterious island. This would be his home until he could find a way to rescue himself.

PART III
THE MYSTERIOUS ISLAND

I

Nantes, 1842

As he stood on the uneven dock, Jules Verne couldn't guess the last time anyone had taken the weathered sailboat out onto the river. His reddish hair purposely unkempt (to look more worldly wise and savvy than his lanky frame implied), he lifted his eyebrows and appraised the vessel's chipped gray wood.

He said to the boat's pot-bellied owner, "I'm not convinced, monsieur. She doesn't look entirely . . . seaworthy."

The plump owner leaned against the moss-grown retaining wall. "She's only one franc, boy." He spat out the chewed end of a grass stem, and his smile showed gapped brown teeth. "Go on, take her for the day. You look like an adventurous boy. I used to have a lot of fun with her when I was your age."

Verne didn't want to think about how long ago that had been.

Considering the single patched sail on the boat's short mast, Verne wondered how far this vessel could manage to go downriver. He pointed an accusing finger at the craft, as if trying to talk himself out of the escapade. "She doesn't even have a keel."

The old man shrugged. "Never bothered me."

A scum of algae marked the sailboat's hull at the water line. Larger boats went by on their business down the Loire, stopping at Nantes or continuing to Paimboeuf and the sea. His friend Nemo had been gone for two years after riding the *Coralie* out into the wide world, but Verne was still stuck in Nantes and waiting to make something of himself.

Verne had never stopped dreaming about a life of travels to exotic lands. He longed for when he'd been able to share those hopes with Nemo, and Caroline too. Perhaps this sailboat was the best he could do for now. A river outing on this ramshackle rented boat might be just what he needed.

In his pocket, his fingers rubbed a franc coin. He pretended to be more concerned about the money than about taking the boat by himself without telling his father. But at his age, he should be making his own choices, whatever the consequences. It wasn't so much money, really. Not for a grand adventure.

The old owner scratched his bulging belly, in no hurry for Verne to make a decision. Flies buzzed by, and the water smelled of fish and drying weeds. Some might have found the smells unpleasant, but Verne had lived on the riverfront all his life. To him, the Loire carried the scents of distant countries, treasures and trinkets, rich spices and unusual cuisine.

Right now, he supposed Nemo was having a fine time sailing the seven seas. Had he already made it around the world? Both Verne and Caroline had received a few dated letters from Nemo, although not in some time. He was anxious to hear news, but it did not occur to him to worry, since messages sent across such great distances were often delayed or lost.

Verne looked again at the small, forlorn boat. Though his friend lived a life of excitement, he would have to content himself with drifting downriver in a leaky sailboat. He looked at the questionable craft, then at the pot-bellied man, and yanked the coin out of his pocket. "I'll take her for the day."

With agonizing slowness the old man extended his hand to take the money. "Ride out with the descending tide, and then come back with the flood tide a few hours later. You can't get lost. Just follow the river."

Verne worked at the damp knots of the frayed tether rope. "I'm not worried, monsieur. I have faced danger before."

* * *

Earlier, after Nemo's silence had stretched for eighteen months, Verne had screwed up his courage and gone to see Caroline Aronnax. He met her in the outdoor cafe where they stole a bit of conversation over gooseberry pastries and cups of *chocolat chaud*.

When he looked at Caroline, Verne felt the confusion of youthful love. Stranded here in Nantes while Nemo went around the world, he felt as if he had let Caroline down. "I'm sorry I couldn't be there to take care of André, as I promised to do."

She dismissed his concern. "I'm sure he can take care of himself."

Verne shared his stories and poems with her, glowing every time she laughed at one of his clever plot twists. He needed to show her that the son of a dull attorney was worthy of her love. Monsieur Aronnax was a friendly enough sort, though Caroline's mother always sniffed in disapproval whenever Verne came asking after her daughter. . .

Hands trembling around the delicate porcelain cup in the outdoor cafe, he tried to meet Caroline's bright blue eyes. Verne noted how beautiful she looked in a lilac dress and a hat trimmed with fine lace from Chantilly. She kept nudging the lace aside, as if it made her itch. "So, what did you want to see me about, Jules? Another new adventure story?" She laughed in anticipation. "Pirates on the high seas? Explorers in Amazon jungles?"

"Not a story this time, Caroline, though I did write you a . . . poem. But I, uh, forgot to bring it with me." He flushed, remembering the heartfelt and embarrassing expressions of undying love he had written. He didn't dare let her read them, however. "I . . . you must be aware of my . . . feelings for you." He cleared his throat. "I'd like you to consider –" He drew a deep breath.

All the words drained out of his head: the beautiful speech, the lyrical love letters and passionate sonnets he had penned but never sent. "I mean, would you *wait for me*? I realize you miss Nemo, but he's been gone for a long time."

Caroline looked up, startled. At least she didn't laugh at him. Instead, she clasped his hand. "Oh, Jules – you dear, sweet, optimistic boy." He felt as if his heart might catch on fire. He hadn't dared to hope that she might say *Yes*.

Then Caroline's face clouded. "You cannot think *I* have any choice in the man I marry? Whether it is you, or Nemo – or anybody else? There was a time when I had hoped . . . but that no longer matters." She tried to soften the blow. "Jules, my father is a wealthy merchant, already negotiating with other families to secure a proper husband for me. My mother began making plans years ago."

Caroline hadn't said outright that he wasn't good enough for her, hadn't said that she still clung to a hope that André Nemo would return with chests full of gold and jewels from ports on the other side of the world. She didn't need to. Verne understood it all too well.

He would have died for her touch at any other time, but now he withdrew his hand. "I thank you for hearing me out, mademoiselle." He sounded much too formal.

Her expression fell. "Wait, Jules. Will you not stay a while and tell me one of your stories?"

With a slow shake of his head, he stood, tossed a few coins on the table without even counting them, and marched off in search of a place where he could be alone with his wounded pride.

Now, trying to find a comfortable spot on the old sailboat's splintered seat, Verne paddled into the current and set the patched sail to catch a breeze. The pot-bellied man, who had not lifted a finger to help, plucked a fresh stalk of grass and stood chewing, still leaning against the stone wall. Verne was glad to sail out of sight so he no longer needed to pretend to know what he was doing.

Several times Verne nearly capsized, from either a misguided shove at the helm, a botched maneuver, or an ill-advised tug on the sail rope when a swell ruffled the Loire. It was truly dangerous.

He was having the time of his life.

In the doldrums of summer, the low water was treacherous because of occasional sandbars. The sailboat handled sluggishly, catching a breeze in its threadbare sail and lumbering about like a blinded ox. He shaded his eyes against the bright sun, hugging the shore as he enviously watched pleasure yachts skim past him. Someday, he wanted to purchase a boat like that.

The outgoing tide was strong and the current swift, and many miles of riverbank passed by. Two years ago, while leaving home on the *Coralie*, he had felt himself a brave sailor on a tall ship cruising toward distant adventures. *I really would have gone along!* This was much different, of course. Verne navigated around sandbars and islands covered with willows and reeds despite periodic dunkings from seasonal high waters. He would never get far in this old hulk.

But still, it was something.

Engrossed in this journey, he didn't notice the seeping water at his feet until it sloshed around his ankles. He scowled at the rising puddle, wondering if the old owner had duped him, or if the man had just overestimated the seaworthiness of his boat.

By now, Verne was many miles from home. Using his heel, he pushed down on the sideboard to determine the extent of the leak. With an alarming crack, one of the planks split. He placed his hands over his mouth in horror, then bent down, trying to hold the rotted wood together. But water gushed through the broken hull like wet fingers, prying the weakened boards apart.

Verne grabbed the sail as if he could turn the skiff around and flit homeward. The old boat, however, began to break apart, riding lower in the water, splitting at the sides. He waved and called for help, but saw no one to assist him, not even any pleasure yachts. His collapsing vessel sank deeper, until the water was up to his knees in the little boat. Not much better than being in the river itself.

He tugged the sail again, trying to angle the waterlogged craft toward a low, wooded island that protruded from the Loire. When the skiff broke apart completely, Verne abandoned ship and plunged into the warm, waist-deep water. He slogged through mud to the solid ground of the islet. He had no supplies, no resources – and he was stranded.

On shore, he trudged through clawing willow branches to find a sunny spot where he could dry himself. "Hello, is anyone else here?" He raised his voice again, but already he knew this would be a deserted island, a small refuge in the middle of the wide estuary.

No one lived here. He was alone . . . on an uninhabited island.

Verne sat down on a fallen tree, wondering what he should do, indignant that the rented sailboat had fallen into pieces on him. He certainly didn't intend to pay the old man for the damages. His father was a lawyer, after all – in fact, the pot-bellied owner's blatant disregard for a young man's safety would look very bad in a court of law.

But Verne didn't want to think what his father would say about the whole misadventure. How would he get rescued? Would he ever see his home again? His loving mother, his sisters, his young brother Paul?

Around him, he found an unexplored world of trees and grass. This was the closest he'd ever been to re-enacting his beloved "Robinson" stories. He allowed himself a wan smile . . . and then his imagination took over.

In clothes still wet and uncomfortable, Verne pushed his way through the clumps of willows, knocking aside gnarled branches that scratched his face. As his soggy shoes sank into the river grass that covered the ground, he thought that perhaps he might be the first person ever to walk here. These footprints – like the footprints the man Friday had left on Crusoe's beach – might be the first mark a human soul had ever made on this untamed land.

He studied the loose rocks piled by spring floodwaters and imagined firepits with blackened bones from cannibal feasts. But he found nothing more than a rat's nest and a worm-eaten plank washed up from some old ship.

His heart thumped, and a foolish grin crossed his face. This might be similar to some of the ordeals Nemo was enduring on his worldwide explorations. He couldn't wait to tell his friend about it.

Before long, Verne was sweaty, sunburned, and miserable. As any true castaway would have done, he salvaged the sail from his sunken boat where it had caught on shore weeds. Then he raised a lean-to shelter of weathered sticks to protect him from wind and storms, hurricanes or snow. Curled on the prickly ground, he imagined he could live here for a while, isolated from the world. Perhaps he'd even keep a journal of his daily struggles, scratch words on smooth bark. There was no telling how long he might remain lost on his little island. . . .

Exhausted in the afternoon and at a loss for what else to do, he tried to nap, troubled by thoughts of tropical storms or pirate ships on the prowl. The ground was uncomfortable, and his shelter let in the biting flies so prevalent during summer along the sluggish river.

Within an hour, Verne began to consider how he might signal for help. He thought of piling dry branches and lighting a bonfire so that passing ships could see the smoke and send rowboats to investigate. But as Verne gathered sticks from the shore, he realized he had no matches and no other way of lighting the blaze. Glum, he sat with his chin in his hands.

He had absorbed the wilderness adventures of James Fenimore Cooper, tales of wild Indians, Hawkeye and Chinganook, *The Last of the Mohicans*, *The Deerslayer*, and *Drums Along the Mohawk* by Walter D. Edmonds. He had learned about survival in an untamed new world.

But though he furiously rubbed sticks together, he got no smoke or sparks – only blisters.

Frustrated, Verne knocked apart his pile of firewood and scanned the islet again. His stomach knotted with the first pangs of hunger, and he wondered what he might eat, since he had packed no lunch. Could he perhaps fashion a stone knife or maybe a throwing ax to kill some wild animal? He would skin it and roast its haunch over a crackling fire.

But again, he had no fire, no weapons, and he'd never killed anything in his life. He couldn't recall seeing any animals other than a few sparrows on this whole islet. He doubted he could even catch fish in the river without net or line.

How could anyone survive like this?

Before the afternoon was out, Verne was miserable. When he went back to the shore, he found that the broken boat lay high on a hummock of wet silt. The tide had gone out, draining the estuary and leaving an expanse of glistening mud flats. With a sinking feeling, he realized he could simply walk to the main shore.

Verne sloshed through brown, ankle-deep muck and lost one of his shoes in the sucking mire. The mud flats stank of old weeds and refuse and belly-up fish. Verne's sunburned face was streaked with tears and mud spatters by the time he dragged himself up the bank of the Loire, then to the road back to Nantes.

Aching and weary, a one-shoed Verne stumbled toward Île Feydeau. Fortunately, the driver of a passing horse cart took pity on him and let the young man climb into the back and ride the rest of the way along the bumpy road.

With his clothes torn and dirty, his red hair disheveled, Verne made it back home just in time for supper.

II

Shipwrecked. Marooned on a desert island.

Nemo collected himself, wet, bedraggled, and hungry on the stony beach. He would have to work hard here, but he had his wits, his resourcefulness, and his sheer stamina. He was better equipped than most people would have been.

His time on board the *Coralie* had toughened him, given him the skills and strength to endure much adversity. He had always been a clever young man, and Captain Grant had taught him many things. He would survive.

One step at a time. After drinking his fill from a thin silver stream that ran to the beach, Nemo looked around himself, listening to the roar of the sea as he concentrated, deciding where to begin. Waves curled against black reefs that sheltered the lagoon. With forced optimism, he decided that eking out a living here day by day probably wouldn't be much more difficult than being a penniless orphan in France. . .

As his first order of business, he dragged the battered crates, the torn sail cloth, and other bits of wreckage higher up the beach to where a line of dunes met a pitted rock wall. A shallow overhang formed enough shelter for Nemo to make camp.

He cracked open the two crates and separated out the items he could use. With care, he unknotted the lashing rope, knowing it might be one of his most valuable possessions until he could weave cords of his own. From his shirt, he removed the waterlogged and cutlass-scarred journal that Verne had given him.

From the first crate he set out a few bolts of cloth to dry in the sun, a magnifying glass, a sewing kit with four needles and two spools of thread, a thin dagger (better suited as a letter-opener), and a set of silverware, engraved and obviously intended as someone's dining set. Nemo could use the utensils for cutting and carving other items he would need. Next to them he set the small keg of black powder, which might yet be of some value to him. In the back of his mind he was already formulating plans, considering options.

It was a start.

At times, he felt suddenly overwhelmed as the immensity of the problem raised itself before him. But he took a deep breath and focused his thoughts, getting back to the task at hand.

In the second crate he found a tortoiseshell comb, a lady's mirror, two bottles of brandy, a shoehorn, one black leather boot, whalebone stays for a corset, and a perfumed sachet that now smelled more of fish than flower blossoms. He had no idea how he would make use of these items, but he didn't dare throw anything away. He might be on this island for a long, long time.

Nemo could see a curl of smoke rising from the volcanic crater, as if it slumbered uneasily. Girdling the central volcano, lush jungles covered the island. He assumed he could find edible fruits and wild game there. He might even be able to trap fish in the lagoon.

He could pound the fibers of vines and make them into rope or twine. He could fashion snares, weave baskets. It would be difficult, but he would manage. He concentrated on the possibilities, rather than the overwhelming problems.

As gulls and albatrosses screamed overhead, Nemo remembered how glad he'd been to see the birds when he was lost and adrift. Now he studied the cliffs and the fallen rocks on the beach. Most of the stones were black lava rock, but he recognized several chunks of flint. An excellent find indeed.

Now he could get down to the next order of business.

Nemo gathered a pile of dry driftwood from high on the beach, then struck the steel dagger against a lump of flint. He worked for half an hour until his arms and fingers ached, but finally he struck a spark that caught on a wad of dried seaweed. Soon he had a smoky, foul-smelling fire crackling against the dunes. The first step of civilization.

The flames cheered Nemo's heart. He sat staring into the burning driftwood, thinking of his circumstances and trying to decide how he should proceed next. Once he had a plan, he could see things improving. He had the power of his imagination.

At the moment, however, his stomach was knotted in agonized hunger. After days with almost nothing to eat, he wasn't sure he had the strength to forge a path through dense foliage in search of coconuts or breadfruit. Instead, he waded into the lagoon and secured handfuls of mussels that clung to the rocks. He used the dagger to pry open the black shells and, though their flesh was bitter, he swallowed each morsel. Next, he tried rinsing and chewing some of the seaweed. Despite the strange, salty taste and stringy texture, it provided some substance for his digestive system.

He slept on the sand in the shelter of the rocky overhang, hunched against repeated stomach cramps. He must have derived some nourishment from the food, though, because the next morning Nemo awoke feeling much stronger. Curious and alert, he set out into the jungle to explore his new world. . .

It didn't take him long to locate coconut palms, papayas, mangoes, and sweet berries. As he had hoped, he also found thin vines and made plans to cut them. Using pieces of flint from the beach cliffs, he could, with some effort, fashion stone knives or axes.

His initial exploration continued for days. He spent several nights in tree branches, always careful to keep track of the way back to his initial camp down on the beach. At night he heard wild boars rooting through the undergrowth and sensed the slithering rustle of snakes through the branches above.

As he climbed up the slopes of the volcano to get a vantage on his surroundings, the ground became rockier. Nemo discovered several hot springs. In a warm mineral pool, he took a long bath, reveling in the tingle of his aching muscles and the luxurious sensation of being clean again. His imagination began working again, deciding how best to use this new discovery.

Halfway up the steep mountainside, he encountered a grassy, tree-dotted plateau just at the edge of the jungles. Nemo looked out from the top of the plateau to where the rockface dropped off in a sheer cliff. Far below, the sheltered lagoon lay placid against the beach where he had washed ashore. Partway down the cliff, large natural caves peered out like eye sockets.

Now he decided on the next thing to do. Once he fashioned a sturdy rope, Nemo could secure the line to one of the tree trunks and descend the cliff face to explore the caves.

High on the plateau edge, he recognized the potential of such a shelter. From there, he would be able to see passing ships, and he could build a large signal fire on the plateau overlooking the sea. His thoughts grew more ambitious – and why not, if he had sufficient time? By using pulleys and vine-fiber ropes, he could set up a counter-weighted elevator system to get him up and down the cliff side, while keeping him safe from the island's predators.

He looked around, mentally keeping a tally. When he returned to the beach, he would scratch his lists and plans inside the blank, water-stained journal Jules Verne had given him. Nemo didn't want to forget any of his ideas.

A stream that ran across the meadow would provide fresh water. The volcanic hot springs were also near. With hollowed-out bamboo piping, he could run water from both the stream and the hot springs down into the caves so that he could wash, cook, or even heat a bath if he wished. And no landlord to throw him out, no matter what he did.

Nemo grew excited at the possibilities. He had much to do.

He would soon grow tired of coconut and breadfruit supplemented by seaweed and mussels. He would need to make spears for himself, as well as bows and arrows for hunting, nets for fishing. He had seen goats running wild on the grassy meadows; in time, he might build a corral and domesticate the animals, so he could have a supply of meat and milk.

Nemo paused, still haunted by thoughts of everything he had lost because of the pirate attack and the circling sharks. He missed Captain Grant, not to mention Jules Verne and Caroline Aronnax (he still kept her frayed and faded hair ribbon knotted around his wrist).

It might be years and years until he saw them again. If ever.

Back on the beach, Nemo found a broad stream that drained into the ocean. While wading in it, holding a stick for balance, he discovered good sticky clay on the river bottom. Each time he found a new resource such as this, he immediately realized how he might use it. With his hands he scooped out piles of the clay, which he formed into crude bricks. He set them out on the beach to dry hard in the sun.

But that was only a first step, not good enough for what Nemo had in mind. After two days he stacked the bricks and, using more fresh clay as mortar, built a hollow beehive structure with air holes on top: *a kiln.*

Though many of the salvage items from the crates were proving valuable, he needed to make bowls, jugs, even a plate, since he didn't want to eat off a slab of rough bark all the time. Since simple dried clay would not be durable enough, he built a low-banked fire of green wood inside the kiln. Next, he shaped more clay into a small pot and a bowl, which he dried, then thrust into the heat and baked over the fire all day long. . .

Listening to the surf, Nemo crouched at his old beach camp, thinking of how to fix up his new cliff-side house. On a wrinkled page from the bound journal, he drew notes and sketches, planning ahead. The beach camp had always been a temporary solution. Now Nemo began to think in a longer term. If he must remain on this island, he wanted a place that would be his *home.*

When he removed the still-hot bowl and pot from the kiln, he saw that, although his creations lacked finesse and artistic merit, they would serve their purpose well enough. This was merely the first of many accomplishments he was sure to make. Water, food, fire, a home, now clay utensils. Allowing himself a satisfied smile, Nemo reconsidered his situation.

Yes, he could survive on the island for as long as necessary. With enough optimism and imagination, life here might not be so terrible after all.

III

On a cool morning, Pierre Verne summoned Jules to his law offices, instructing his red-headed son to wait while he finished transcribing a legal document. Two low-paid clerks scribbled in ledgers, transcribing contracts and detailing lists of assets. The sounds of the shipyards drifted through a half-open window, along with an annoying breeze that fluttered documents held down by paperweights.

Verne had no idea why his father had called him here and expected to be scolded for some act of omission or negligence. Inwardly, he groaned. As Jules grew older, Monsieur Verne often brought him into the offices to do small jobs and learn the intricacies of being a country attorney.

Finally, Pierre Verne looked up across his mahogany desk. "I have news for you, Jules." He took out some recently arrived sheets of paper on which shipping lists had been printed. "Look here." He pointed to the name of a three-masted brig on the sheet – the *Coralie*.

Verne's heart sank when he saw the heading of the column: Vessels Lost at Sea. Since the *Coralie* was a British-registered ship and had not originated from Nantes, news of her fate had taken two full years to reach France.

"No known survivors. Since only a few vagrant dockhands signed aboard from our docks, it's doubtful anyone we know will file for damages against Captain Grant's heirs or the shipping company."

Verne read and reread the printed letters, hoping he had misunderstood. But there was no mistaking the stark words: *Lost with all hands.*

"Now, son, are you not glad I withdrew you from your foolish venture? You would be dead now, sunk by a storm or some enemy attack, just like that Nemo boy."

But Verne, with a leaden feeling in the pit of his stomach, only mumbled, "All hands lost." The words swam before his eyes.

"Yes, you'd be at the bottom of the ocean. And *I'd* be training your brother Paul to carry on my practice."

"Thank you . . . for letting me know, Father." Verne walked away on rigid legs, barely able to restrain himself from galloping out of the office. With his long legs and big feet, he'd probably trip and fall on his face. He left the door wide open as he staggered into the bright sunlight.

Caroline . . . he had to find Caroline. *Nemo dead*?

When he told her the news, standing without ceremony on the doorstep of Monsieur Aronnax's row house, she wept bitterly. Her father would no doubt bring her the same message when he returned from his merchant offices. After all, he had recommended Captain Grant, had arranged for Nemo to be taken aboard as a cabin boy.

The stricken look on her heart-shaped face told him how much she had been waiting and hoping for Nemo's return. He caught at her hands. "I'll be here, Caroline. I'll take care of you. I . . . I'll always love you."

"Ah, poor André!" She pulled away, blinking in shock. "Nothing will ever be the same."

"I just want –" he said.

"Please, Jules. I need to be alone now." Fresh tears ran unchecked from her beautiful eyes as she closed the door softly in his face.

IV

Inside the completed cave dwelling – which he called Granite House – Nemo sat in the dim light of goat-tallow candles and listened to the winter storm outside. He had called this place home for two years now. The comfortable wicker chair, painstakingly woven from cane, reeds, and grasses, creaked under his weight as he sat pondering at the driftwood writing table.

He had done everything by himself, thinking up ideas, designing the pieces, and implementing them. When a concept failed, sometimes disastrously, Nemo went back to his ruminations, his scrawled plans, and refigured the math and the engineering. Captain Grant had taught him the fundamentals, and Nemo had learned the rest by trial and error. Luckily, he had lived through the errors. . .

He opened his weathered journal and smoothed down the central cut made by the noseless pirate captain's cutlass. He glanced over the pages of densely written words that documented his time marooned on the island, his schemes, his failures. Nemo had lived through storms, earthquakes from the restless volcano, attacks from wild animals, even a lightning-sparked forest fire that had raged across a section of the island.

Now he dipped the sharpened end of a quill feather (from an albatross he'd shot with a handmade arrow) into a baked clay pot of ink (made from the distilled excretions of certain shellfish). He kept the record for his own sanity. Every day seemed so much the same, week after week, month after month. . .

Because he didn't know how many blurry days he had been cast adrift from the *Coralie*, Nemo was no longer sure of the exact date. He had, however, come up with a close approximation by making his own instruments and using pebbles and shadows on the beach to mark the sun's passage along the ecliptic. Thus, he had determined the summer and winter solstices, and by measuring the angle of the Southern Cross in the sky, he had derived an estimate of his latitude, not that it did him any good. He had no charts and could not pinpoint where the mysterious island might lie in the South China Sea, though he must be far from any well-traveled shipping lanes.

Now the wind howled past the cave opening on the cliff face. Rain lashed down, pelting the rocks and filling Nemo's cisterns out on the plateau. Stray gusts made the candle flames flicker, but a roaring fire in the natural chimney at the back of the main grotto, as well as the steaming gurgle from the hot springs he piped in from the thermal area, kept Granite House cozy throughout the worst of winter.

Like a genuine home, with every necessity, every amenity made by his own hands.

During the first months of his island sojourn, Nemo had built a hut of branches and deadfall in the lowlands as a place to store supplies and sleep while he worked on the permanent and defensible home inside the cliff. The effort had taught him much about the practicalities of construction, which he applied to his more permanent cliff dwelling. Though the rock face looked sheer and solid, Nemo had found it to be riddled with passages and steam vents.

Though the volcano appeared dormant, the ground often trembled and the crater belched forth plumes of dark smoke in fits of geological indigestion. But Granite House seemed solid enough, and Nemo was quite proud of what he had accomplished during his years of isolation.

He had created a showcase of primitive technology that even Wyss's *Swiss Family Robinson* would have envied. Using charcoal on the cave floor, along with makeshift geometrical devices, he had drawn up plans for his complex ideas, much like the ones he had seen in the notebooks of Leonardo da Vinci.

He built a pulley-driven pair of wooden cages that served as elevators, taking him up and down the cliff. He piped in hot and cold water. He'd erected lookout towers so he could keep watch for any passing ship, though after so much time, Nemo began to lose hope.

He maintained mounds of tinder, grasses, and dry branches, ready to be set ablaze as signal bonfires. But so far he'd had no reason to do so, and the volcano smoke would be seen much farther away than any signal he could make himself.

His original clothes from the *Coralie* had tattered and split, and now he wore garments cut and stitched together from the bolts of cloth he'd salvaged from his crates or from hides he tanned using bark distillations. Moccasins made of cured seal hide protected his feet. Caroline's old hair ribbon, long since fallen into threads, lay in a hollow in the rock wall, where he could look at it.

He confined eighteen goats within a crude stockade on the grassy plateau, using the animals mainly for milk or a thin cheese. Out of the goats' reach, he had planted a vegetable garden with squash, wild onions, and other herbs and roots he'd transplanted from elsewhere on the island.

Now, after so much hard living, Nemo was more muscular and able to withstand the adversities of his solitary island. He ate fresh fish, mussels, and oysters from the sea, game and fowl that he hunted in the forests. A month's supply of smoked meats hung in the cave's cool alcoves.

Nemo diligently wrote down even the most monotonous events in his journal as he struggled with knowing that in all likelihood no one would ever read the account. Hardest of all was simply learning how to be *alone*.

V

During the breezy days of spring, Nemo worked up enough nerve to test his glider. Using scraps of old sailcloth stretched tightly over a framework of lightweight bamboo, he had constructed a kite-like contraption, based on designs he'd seen in da Vinci's sketchbooks, a lifetime ago in Captain Grant's cabin.

The concept seemed simple enough. One time on Île Feydeau, Nemo, Verne, and Caroline, all together, had flown kites up over the river. They'd run along the riverbank and watched their colorful paper constructions dance at the ends of their tethers, trying to keep them from becoming entangled.

But this enormous glider kite would have no tether, and Nemo could only hope it would hold his body aloft. He did not know his exact weight, since he had grown while stranded on the island; instead, he had constructed a clever balance on a fulcrum, using stones to approximate his weight. Then, using those same stones lashed together into a wicker framework to simulate his body, Nemo had tested his glider, making sure it would stay airborne long enough. More trial and error, which entailed frequent wild pursuits along the island's coast, chasing down the glider as it drifted along.

Now, he hoped he had it right. He could think of no other way to explore his island so quickly, or thoroughly.

Judging from how hard the wind tugged on the broad frame, as if impatient to be off, Nemo decided the glider wings should be sufficient to hold his weight aloft. Ocean winds whipped around the high plateau above the cliffs of Granite House. He prayed that a cross breeze wouldn't slam him back against the sheer rockface.

He had investigated his island as much as possible on foot, but areas of dense jungle and parts of the rocky shoreline remained inaccessible. The thought of looking down like a seagull from above fired his imagination.

As he strapped himself into the kite framework, the huge wings spread like a hawk's against an updraft. He had already walked underwater near the Nantes shipyards; the air would offer him an entirely different perspective. From a fish to a bird.

Despite his tests and checks, he knew he was taking a grave risk. With a capricious downdraft, he could well be dashed against the rocks. Even if he received only a common injury – a broken leg or a shoulder twisted out of its socket – Nemo had no one to tend him, no one to help. He would be on his own. But he steeled himself – he was accustomed to that.

The wind stung his eyes, and he wished Caroline could be there to watch him, to cheer him on. Determined, he took two running steps to the abrupt cliff and jumped out into the open air . . . and kept going.

The brisk wind caught the giant kite and jerked Nemo up so sharply that his head struck the bamboo framework. His flight steadied, and the breezes took him where they would, an invisible and gentle escort. The cloth creaked against the framework, taut, and he seemed to be completely motionless, just hanging high above the ground.

After recovering his breath, Nemo laughed with delight.

He tilted his arms, banking the glider to test his degree of control. Only by looking at landmarks on the ground could he determine how fast and how far he was moving. His feet dangled, and he had a sickening sense of vertigo, just suspended high in the air, but then the excitement captured him once more, and he stared with wide, hungry eyes.

Circling around again, he flew back toward the meadow where he looked down at his corralled goats and the skewed square of his vegetable garden. From there, Nemo soared above the densest jungles where he spotted new streams, a breathtaking sheltered waterfall, and small ponds he hadn't known existed (and which might contain good freshwater fish).

As he glided along, he calculated his rate of descent, surprised at the amount of time he could remain aloft. Breezes caught him again, and he spiraled higher in the updraft. He ranged even farther, over a spit of land that formed another cove on the mostly inaccessible south end of the island.

To his astonishment, he saw a cleared area at the crook of the long promontory – as well as the weathered skeleton of an overturned rowboat and a collapsed lean-to shelter. Someone else had been shipwrecked here! His heart pounded at the discovery. Could anyone still be alive? He had to see, had to determine how long ago these visitors had been there. Maybe he wasn't alone on this island after all.

Nemo tilted his glider wings and angled toward the spot. Once he landed, it would be a painstaking process to detach the cloth from the framework and disassemble it – and a long walk back to Granite House – but it would be worth the effort if he received an answer to his question.

He landed hard on the beach, wrenching his ankle and ran like an albatross, trying to come to rest. He unfastened his arms from the glider and let go, rolling on his back as the breezes blew the framework against the hummocks of dunes. Limping on his sore ankle, Nemo ran after the glider wings and caught them. He used his knife to cut the lashing and removed the fabric, folding it up and weighting it down with rocks.

With curiosity and hope thrumming in his ears, he made his way along the shoreline. He wanted to shout, to call out a greeting, but his voice sounded strange in his ears. He climbed over shallow reefs that would be submerged at high tide, until he reached the site of the settlement.

His heart sank when he saw the collapsed hut and the overgrown clearing. No one had lived here for years. But perhaps he might find some supplies . . . or at least a clue as to who this strange castaway had been.

The crude hut was empty, and the broken rowboat rotten and worm-eaten. When he found a few corroded buckles and some lead shot on the ground, he pocketed the precious bits of metal. Then he moved to the remains of a firepit at the edge of the clearing.

He froze as soon as he saw the skeletons.

A rusted spade with a broken handle protruded from a sandy pile of dirt. One of the human skulls had been bashed in. The other skeleton lay face down with a pitted cutlass thrust through its empty ribcage. Some of the bones were fire-blackened.

Nemo imagined poor prisoners forced to dig their own graves, then murdered and left exposed for the scavengers. He had seen barbarism to match this only one other time. *Pirates.* He knew it in his heart. His jaws ached from his clenched teeth as rage boiled up again behind his eyes.

Had they come here only once? Or was this deserted island a regular stopping point? He took a deep breath, remembering Captain Noseless and his murderous crew. These waters were infested with brigands.

Taking the old cutlass, Nemo backed away from the abandoned encampment, wondering when the pirates might return . . . how soon they would come here to find *him.*

VI

☼

A note came for Jules Verne at the law offices, hand-delivered by afternoon post. Standing in the sunlight by a window, he opened the card, already recognizing the flowery script. Caroline's stationery smelled of lilacs, the perfume she often wore. Giddy, he sniffed the envelope, imagining the touch of her fingers against the paper, as if she might be holding his hand.

Now nineteen, he worked as a clerk in his father's offices. Though three years had passed since he'd learned of Nemo's death, he had never forgotten his friend . . . and his life had got no more exciting. Verne had a small, tidy desk in the front office, while his father sat in a separate room to deal with important cases. Verne did little more than file papers and recopy documents in his own hand. He had never yet found a way to leave France . . . or even Nantes.

The routine was tedious, and he found little to interest him, day after day. His imagination wandered, and he often stole a few moments to scribble verses he invented. Poetry had been his family pastime, and now he turned his talents to writing occasional love sonnets for Caroline. He never dared to send them, though; he left them safely hidden in his notebooks. At least it was practice.

But now she had sent *him* a card. So long after the shock of Nemo's loss, it was possible she had changed her mind about him. Perhaps her mother had relented in trying to arrange a marriage for her headstrong daughter. . . He could never give up hope.

Verne glanced up to see his father deep in thought over a curled document. Framed by gray-frosted sideburns, a frown creased Pierre Verne's face. The elder man had not noted the postal delivery, since messages came at all times of the day. Real estate deeds and wills provided all the entertainment his father needed, but Verne never ceased to want *more*.

Turning his back for a bit of privacy, fingers shaking with anticipation, Verne broke the dollop of red sealing wax. He peeled open the envelope and withdrew the note inside, eyes widening with pleasant surprise and disbelief.

"My dearest Jules, please come to my home at your earliest possible opportunity. We must discuss my future. I wish to speak with you in person, for you must hear of these matters from my own lips."

Verne read the note again. He didn't know what they meant. "Father, I have an important errand. I will be back within the hour." He straightened the papers on his desk out of habit, arranging them alphabetically in neat piles.

"Very well, if you must." His gruff tone indicated no interest in the nature of his son's "errand." Without looking up, Pierre Verne raised one impatient finger. Verne froze, waiting for him to finish scribbling a comment in the margin. The attorney crossed out a line like a hunter securing a prize, then dropped the quill pen back into its inkwell. He deigned to glance at his red-headed son. "When you return I have a matter I wish to discuss with you."

Verne gave a quick acknowledgment and hurried out of the law offices. As soon as he was around the corner, away from where his father could see him, he stopped to dust imaginary lint from his waistcoat, straighten his cravat, and brush his unruly hair. Then he ran onward.

In recent years he had grown tall, with awkwardly long arms and legs. He was intelligent, even rather handsome, according to what some young ladies said, though few saw him as a marriageable prospect. They said he was too flighty, too unsettled – and his vivid imagination alarmed them. No matter, he thought petulantly, since their dullness alarmed *him*.

But Caroline Aronnax was different. And now she wanted to speak with him regarding *her future*.

Several times in the past year, heady with her closeness, he had walked beside her under the lime trees in the courtyard of the Church of St Martin, or the two had smelled the magnolias at the quai de la Fosse. They never spoke of love, but he knew she valued his friendship. Could it be that her parents had finally agreed to let Caroline choose her own husband? Strange things did indeed happen in the world. . .

He swallowed a lump in his throat and strode off, chin high. Humming, he made his way down the narrow streets toward her tall house in the merchants' section of town. He felt very different from the time when he and Nemo had slunk through the dark streets to tap on her window. Now Verne almost looked respectable, an actual gentleman caller.

It seemed like a scene out of a story to him, a story he himself might write someday, and he wondered how this tale would end. In the past year he had become more and more interested in literary pursuits beyond exchanging verses across the dinner table as a family pastime.

Verne had read the magnificent works of Victor Hugo, France's most important literary hero, the spearhead of the Romantic movement. He was proud to live at a time when such writers came from his own country. He'd read *The Hunchback of Notre-Dame* and the plays *Cromwell* and *Hernani*, in addition to Hugo's Romantic verse, all of which made a profound impression on him, perhaps even more than the boyhood adventure stories he and André Nemo had devoured.

In his notebooks Verne had drafted two plays of his own (both heavily influenced by Hugo). His first, *Alexandre VI: 1503*, was a romantic drama in verse, five acts long, about the Borgia Pope – a villain if there ever was one. Next, even more ambitious, he had written *The Gunpowder Plot*, about Guy Fawkes. He had showed the work to Caroline, and she had expressed her encouragement and delight. "You have such a gift for telling stories, Jules. I am certain that someday you will be successful."

With light footsteps he danced along the streets, letting the fantasy carry him. Nantes had a respectable playhouse on place Graslin, modeled after the Paris Odéon. If ever he got up his nerve, he would investigate any connections his father might have to get his plays performed on stage. And, if he actually married Caroline Aronnax, even more doors would open for him.

Verne imagined how wonderful it would be if *The Gunpowder Plot* were to be performed there. Dressed in his finest suit, he would sit in the author's box and watch the players take their bows. He hoped Caroline might be beside him, cheering along with the audience. "Author! Author!"

Grinning, Verne strode up the brick steps to the ornate façade of Caroline's house and rang the bell. The maidservant Marie, looking awkward and embarrassed, opened the door and allowed the young redhead into the foyer. "I shall let Mademoiselle Caroline know you have come. Please wait here."

Marie hurried off with a whisper of her crinoline petticoat. A pendulum clock ticked in the main drawing room, and Verne waited. Feet planted, he looked at the many odd items that M. Aronnax had acquired over the years – trophies brought by his merchant ships from their voyages around the world.

A pink conch shell sat on a glass tabletop, surrounded by delicate shells from the South Sea islands. A carved elephant tusk sat on a black lacquer stand. Around the corner, in shadow, stood an airtight case that contained a dark mass that just might have been a shrunken human head. . .

Marie returned from the back room and gestured toward a pair of folding French doors that led out to an enclosed flower garden. "Mademoiselle Caroline awaits you in the courtyard. She has requested *chocolat chaud* for the two of you." She hurried off.

A cast-iron table, painted white, stood on the patio flanked by two chairs. Caroline, wearing a lavender chintz dress with full sleeves and lace collars, sat in the sun without a hat or parasol, staring listlessly at a cluster of scarlet blossoms. Her back was to Verne, though she must have heard him arrive. A sketchpad lay on her lap, its top page covered with a quick drawing of a face. Nemo's?

Gathering courage, he stepped forward. Caroline folded her sketchpad and turned. Her heart-shaped face was achingly beautiful as she smiled at him. "Please sit, Jules."

He almost tripped over his own feet as he hurried to take the scrolled-iron chair opposite her. Verne's heart fluttered as if it were pumping air bubbles instead of the red blood of a young man in love. He rested his elbow on the table, before remembering his manners. He sat up again, straight and proper.

Through the interior windows, Verne caught a flash of Madame Aronnax pacing in the sitting room, a distant chaperone. Verne berated himself for not thinking to bring a bouquet of flowers. He still had a lot to learn about love.

"It can be no news to you that I reached marriageable age some time ago, Jules," Caroline said, and he caught his breath. "My parents have received many offers from suitors attracted by my social standing."

And also by your beauty, Verne thought, but did not dare say it aloud.

With a resigned and confused expression, she forced out the next words. "My mother has completed all the necessary arrangements for me to marry. He is an older man, a well-respected sea captain. My father concurs, and so the decision has been made."

Verne felt as if he would shatter from despair if he moved even a fraction of an inch. Her news struck him like an avalanche.

"Captain Hatteras has sailed my father's ships with great success. I . . . looked over his records. His profits have always been excellent. The captain is an ambitious man who wishes to become an explorer." Caroline continued rapidly but without emotion, as if she had memorized her speech.

"He has recently financed a new expedition to seek an alternate passage to Asia. He will go north-west, up around Greenland and North America, hoping to discover a route through the Arctic Sea and back down to China and Japan. Such a route could bring vast fortunes to my family." She toyed with a ruffle on her sleeve. "And it is time for me to stop waiting." He could hear the unspoken message in her words. *With Nemo gone, I can ask for no better husband.*

Verne swallowed hard, tried to articulate any objections that came to mind. "But . . . but that's so dangerous. Around the Arctic Circle? It's never been done."

He thought of the Dutch explorer Willem Barents, who in the 17th century had sailed around Norway and upper Russia until his ship became ice-locked and crushed. Barents and his crew were forced to build wooden huts on the no-man's-island of Novaya Zemlya. During the spring thaw, the survivors braved the Arctic Sea in open boats. Barents himself died, as did many of the crew, before anyone reached civilization.

Caroline intended to marry a man who would attempt a similar passage.

She sat straight and proper in her wrought-iron chair. "M. Hatteras is a brave man. If anyone can do it, my captain can. Our marriage is already scheduled, as is his expedition. We will be wed very shortly, before he departs."

Caroline looked directly at him. Verne knew that his face must be pale, his freckles prominent, his expression stricken. Given the wording of her note, had she not guessed what he might think?

"I know this is a disappointment to you, Jules, but I wanted you to hear it from me, rather than from gossip." She took his hand again. "I want you to come to the wedding. You must remain my friend, and keep telling me your stories. When M. Hatteras departs, I will have no one to talk to – certainly no one with such imagination."

Numb, Verne climbed to his feet again just as Marie arrived with a pot of steaming *chocolat*. He didn't even see her, didn't want any refreshment – and he could not endure staying here any longer. Bees thrummed among the courtyard flowers, and birds sang from the hedges – but for Jules Verne, this place held only the deepest shadows.

Moving like a man in the final stages of consumption, he managed a bow to Caroline. "Accept my best wishes for your health and happiness. I . . . I'm certain your parents have made the proper decision for you."

He forced himself not to run as his hopes crumbled around him. He wanted to hurry home, though the work day was not yet over. Caroline called after him. "Wait, Jules! Can you not make a joke for me to remember? Tell me another amusing story? Please, you are my only true friend."

Verne didn't dare let his feelings out, lest the emotions crack his invisible armor. "Am I a friend, or a court jester? A jongleur to tell stories? Caroline, I'm sure your betrothed must have a wit and imagination that far outshines mine. After all, I've never even left France."

He walked back to his father's law offices, where he hoped to sit alone at his desk and bury himself in the tedious work of copying and certifying documents. There seemed to be nothing else in store for him in life.

But when Verne seated himself and set a new stack of papers before him, his father called. "Jules, I must speak with you."

The young man moved like a clockwork machine. His father would no doubt give him instructions for a fresh set of documents or perhaps ask him to deliver a sealed testament. Pierre Verne saved money by using his son rather than hiring the local courier boys.

Verne stood in front of his father's desk, wearing his formal frock coat and vest rather than play clothes. The elder Verne did not invite him to take a seat. "I have already made arrangements for you."

Wondering what his father could mean, Verne blinked. After his conversation with Caroline, what else could go wrong this day? "What arrangements, Father?"

"It's time you were certified, Jules. You have worked as a law clerk in my office for nearly a year, and you must proceed with your instruction. I am sending you to Paris so that you can enroll in a well-respected school." The older man tugged on his sideburns and met Verne's gaze. "You will pass the entrance examination for the Paris Faculty of Law, and then your future will be bright. You need have no worries."

Verne reeled. He had never liked the profession, did not intend to become a lawyer for the rest of his life – yet he was the eldest son. And while his brother Paul had already failed his application to enter the Naval Academy, the younger boy had received his father's permission to sign aboard as an apprentice shipmate . . . much the way Verne had wanted to do when he'd run away from home with Nemo.

"You will take the train, son. Pack lightly, but bring enough clothes so you can be presentable at all times. One never knows when an opportunity might arise. You will visit the Faculty of Law, see the school, and return here to help me in the office during the summer pause in classes. In autumn, I expect you to return to Paris to work toward your law degree. It will take you several years, but you'll be well rewarded in the end."

Verne could not answer, but discipline and his strict upbringing had taught him not to challenge his father's wishes. At least he would have an excuse to be away from Nantes during Caroline's wedding. He could not endure seeing her take marriage vows to another man.

He had heard much about Paris, though: the opera, literary salons, coffee shops, and theaters. Perhaps in the City of Light, he would find a home near to his heart, a place that would sing to his creative spirit. Perhaps there, he could forget his misery over Caroline. . .

The next week passed in a blur as he prepared to go to the capital city. Barely nineteen and still wide-eyed with innocence, Jules Verne went to the largest city in France – a hotbed of discontent – on the eve of the bloody and violent revolutions of 1848.

VII

○

By any measure, Nemo was a man now, twenty years old according to his careful reckoning with the solar calendar and daily journal. His hair had grown to his shoulders, though he hacked it off with a flint knife; his cheeks and chin were covered with a thickening dark beard.

Dragging out the glider wings once again, he stood near the plateau cliff and looked behind him at the cone of the volcano. For months, the earthquakes had been growing worse, striking with greater frequency. At unpredictable times the ground heaved and bucked as if a subterranean beast were stirring in its sleep. Something mysterious and unknown lay beneath his island, and Nemo wasn't sure he wanted to know what it was.

Now, as he reattached the fabric to the glider frame, winds gusted up the slopes. Another fine day for flying. After the first risky test of the kite wings, Nemo had modified and improved his design. He'd added a small rudder, flaps, and cords to control his flight. The craft allowed him to continue exploring the island's wild parts, but he also enjoyed the pure exhilaration of flight. Even after years ashore, Nemo had never allowed himself to become complacent.

The sky was clear to the ocean horizon. Nemo had spent so many years in solitude that he no longer even *thought* about rescue. Once he'd stopped tormenting himself with thoughts of Caroline and Jules, his misery decreased.

He'd left Nantes so long ago, yet he could still remember the smell of the

Loire in summer, the bustling docks, the coarse bread and pungent cheese he and his father had shared during lunches together, their late-night card games.

He wondered if Verne had gone on to become a success. His red-headed friend would be a lawyer by now. Had Caroline married? Probably. She'd had such good prospects for a rich and well-connected husband. Could she and Verne have married each other?

Rather than think of such things, Nemo finished the tight lashings on the glider kite. Out of habit he gazed across the boundless sea – and stood bolt upright. He saw the distant silhouette of a large vessel with three masts approaching his island.

A ship!

Nemo weighted his glider down so the winds would not blow it away, then scrambled pell-mell along jungled paths until he reached the meadow overlooking the sheltered lagoon. Here, he'd long ago piled mounds of dry wood for a signal fire.

Though the ship would still take hours to reach the island, he hurried, breathless and flushed with excitement. Expert now, Nemo used his flint and steel to strike sparks, and within minutes, the bonfire was ablaze, a dazzling signal that raised smoke into the sky. The ship *had* to see him. He was saved!

For the first time in years, Nemo thought of rescue, of fellow human beings. The young man didn't even know if regular society would accept him anymore. Some poor wretches – such as William Dampier, the original inspiration for *Robinson Crusoe* – had become more like animals than men after being stranded on desert islands.

But Nemo could learn again. He had the imagination and the drive. Once back to civilization, he could be cleaned up and dressed in finery. He could return to France, give speeches, wave at the crowds, an adventurer and hero. He would see Caroline again, and Jules. Nemo hurried down the counter-weighted elevator into Granite House. Oh, the stories he would tell!

Then the waiting began. Hour after hour. He found it agonizing. All day,

Nemo continued to feed his blazing bonfire in an unmistakable call for help.

By late afternoon, the strange ship had grown close, angling in from the west. In the orange-tinted sky of sunset, the details of her three-masted form were clear enough in silhouette.

Nemo stared through his rockface window, using a crude spyglass he had constructed out of bamboo tubes, the lens from his magnifying glass and a second lens painstakingly ground from the bottom of a salvaged brandy bottle he'd found in the original jetsam that had washed ashore. Now he realized with a growing cold sensation in his chest that he knew this ship. Knew it too well.

The *Coralie*.

Nemo could never forget the vessel on which he had become a seaman, where he'd learned the ways of rigging and sails and the currents of the seven seas. There could be no mistake. Led by the hideous Captain Noseless, the brigands must have taken the *Coralie* as their own, killing all crew aboard who refused to join them. For years now, the marauders had used Captain Grant's brig as if it were their own.

And now that pirate crew had arrived at the island. *His* island.

Thanks to the signal fire, they would know that some poor castaway lived here. Now the pirates would come after *him* and take everything he'd managed to hoard for his survival. Then they would delight in killing him.

Swallowing hard, knowing the enemy would come in with the morning tide, Nemo set about preparing his defenses. This would be his chance to avenge what the pirates had done to him, to the *Coralie* crew, and to Captain Grant.

Maybe it would be worth all the suffering.

VIII

On the clearing above the cliffs, he let his bonfire fade to embers, but it was already too late.

Engrossed in the slim possibility of rescue, he had never planned or built military defenses. Even from the shelter of Granite House, Nemo had no way to drive back a hundred armed and bloodthirsty pirates. He'd already seen how these men fought, how they killed without compunction. Not even Captain Grant, the brawny Ned Land, and the seasoned English sailors aboard the *Coralie* had been able to drive them back.

And Nemo was just one man. How could he possibly succeed where the others had failed?

But he had time, and resources, and ingenuity on his side. He would never run and hide. He had to protect what he could and inflict all possible damage – if only in honor of Captain Grant's memory.

During the night he returned to the plateau and loosed his goats from the corral. The pirates would slaughter any animals they found and take the meat back to their ship. Bleating, the goats ran into the forest, where at least they had a chance to escape. If he got through this, Nemo could round up most of them again. He could not save his vegetable garden, nor the outdoor huts where he stored the supplies he'd accumulated over the years.

Nemo secured himself inside Granite House. He drew up the ladders, severed the baskets of his elevator, and set fire to his bamboo stairway so that it fell off the cliff side in smoking cinders. Safely isolated, he ate and drank his fill, then tried to doze. He would need all of his energy the following day.

He meant to kill as many pirates as possible. For Captain Grant.

A long passage in the rear of Granite House led through winding caves up to the mountainside. The entire island was honeycombed with underground tunnels, covered by jungle-overgrown openings. If forced to run, Nemo could hide in the wilderness. . . but if the pirates decided to set up a permanent base, he would have a long battle ahead of him. Sooner or later, he intended to wipe them out. They all deserved to die.

At dawn, he went to the cave opening and looked out to sea. The *Coralie* had sailed into the lagoon with the tide and had anchored not far from shore. Squinting through his spyglass, Nemo could just make out the hideous Captain Noseless standing on the quarterdeck and watching his crew. Already, two longboats filled with men were being lowered over the sides. Once in the water, the pirates rowed toward the base of the cliff where he had set his bonfire.

Anger simmered within Nemo as he remembered how this ferocious pirate had coldly executed Captain Grant. Now he'd dispatched his henchmen to explore while he remained safe aboard the *Coralie*. Apparently, Noseless would not venture into danger until he discovered who waited for them on this island.

The longboats came ashore where Nemo hoped they would, and he loosed his first desperate defense before the marauders expected anything. For just a moment, he had the advantage of surprise.

Eight pirates climbed from each longboat and stood on the shore. Two brigands pointed at the signs of habitation on the cliff side. The men made their way toward a slope of broken rock jarred loose by recent seismic tremors.

From his southernmost window opening, Nemo pushed several boulders he had lined up. The heavy rocks tumbled down the cliffs, striking more boulders on the steep slope, ricocheting and gaining momentum, carrying others along with them in a building avalanche.

The pirate shore party looked up as countless chunks of stone fell and bounced with a cracking, roaring sound. The brigands scattered on the beach. One boulder crushed a pirate like a cockroach under a boot heel; the rest of the rockfall plunged down the cliff, across the beach, and into the sea. Several large stones splintered and sank one of the longboats.

Nemo had struck the first blow, and he found it very satisfying.

He looked over to see the *Coralie's* gun ports opening up. So, the pirate captain had been watching. He retreated deep into his caves as Captain Noseless launched a full broadside from the ship. An instant after he heard the boom, cannonballs pounded the cliff side. The front of Granite House splintered, and the main chamber filled with smoke and rock dust. As the air cleared, Nemo saw that the cliff face had been blasted away, leaving him vulnerable.

Below, the shore party cheered, then ran howling as debris rained down from the cliffs above. Noseless would be preparing a second broadside, and so Nemo ducked deeper into the back tunnels heading for escape onto the plateau.

The landing party, frustrated because Nemo had destroyed his stairs and ladders, ran along the beach, searching for a different way up. From the *Coralie*, Noseless launched a third longboat, and more brigands swarmed ashore.

Panting, smeared with smoke and rock dust, Nemo tried to plan what to do next. He was running for his life.

IX

The raiding parties landed at different points on the coast and crawled upland. The marauders, enraged by his first attack, drew their cutlasses as they climbed the steep slopes, fought through the jungles – and searched for Nemo.

He knew it had been years since this band had come to the island. Did they know the terrain, or was this just an occasional stopping point? Though jungle thickets might have hidden him better, he fled higher up the volcano's slope. He preferred room to move, a vantage from which he could see his enemies coming. He had to outsmart them.

Breathing hard, Nemo worked his way up the rugged hillside toward the heights of the crater, careful to stay hidden among the boulders. From time to time he looked down at the *Coralie* still anchored in the lagoon. More longboats came ashore. When he saw smoke curling into the sky from the vicinity of his home, he realized they had set fire to his corral and his storage sheds. By now the pirates would have lowered themselves with ropes into Granite House. They would smash his handmade furniture and destroy his belongings. More destruction, more loss.

Yes, they all deserved to die. Rage simmered within him. He had hidden some supplies, and he could always rebuild . . . but he hadn't anticipated the extent of damage Captain Noseless and his men would inflict. Nemo vowed to stop them, to strike back in every way he could.

When he saw seven men climbing up from the plateau, Nemo moved behind tall rocks, where he could observe the invaders and yet be out of their line of sight. The pirates wove back and forth, searching for his trail. He raised his head to get a better view, secure in the shelter the rocks afforded him –

He heard the crack of a flintlock pistol, and a ball shattered with a white starburst against the stone a yard to his left. Four more pirates charged toward him from the opposite side of the slope. He hadn't even noticed them coming.

Nemo ducked as one of the men jerked a pistol from his belt and fired a wild shot, which drew the attention of the first party of seven. He ran as both groups charged toward him from opposite directions. He could never fight them all.

Three more pistol shots rang out, though the balls each missed him by an arm's length. Nemo took heart from the wasted shots, since the pursuing pirates would have no time for the tedious muzzle-reloading process. And Nemo didn't intend to let them get close enough to use cutlasses. The pirates might have been murderous, but they were not smart.

Unfortunately, the gunfire might rally the other brigands on the island, and Nemo could find himself trapped before long. But he knew exactly where to run. It wasn't far.

Nemo had survived by his wits for years, and he wouldn't give up now. He scrambled down a slope, threading his way through a labyrinth of rocks. As he neared the thermal areas, the ground felt hot through the soles of his seal-hide moccasins.

Soon he reached the most perilous part of his flight: a stony clearing where sulfurous steam hissed from fumaroles in the ground. He had very little cover, and if the pirates had kept any of their pistols loaded, a lead ball could catch him in the back.

Hearing the pursuers behind him, he put on a burst of speed, wishing he could fight them face to face, one at a time. But before he could go far, the ground bucked and shook with a heavy tremor that jarred the mountainside in the most powerful earthquake Nemo had yet experienced. He stumbled and sprawled on his face, cutting palms, arms, and chin on the sharp lava rock. The raiders shouted, terrified by what was happening.

Then with a tearing sound and a rumble from deep beneath the surface, part of the steep hillside caved in. The crust of the mountain dropped away and rocks sloughed aside, leaving a yawning black door – the entrance to a cave that had been sealed until the quake shattered it open. Humid, swampy smells came from the new cave, as if an entire subterranean world were hidden within the mountain. A pallid glow of eerie phosphorescence leaked out of the dark hole.

Nemo scrambled backward as he heard something deep in the cavern: footsteps like mallets pounding against rock, an explosive exhalation of breath, a loud and hungry snort.

The pirates, however, had no interest in the phenomenon. Their only concern was killing him. Intent on their victim, the men passed the broad cave mouth. Their shadows fell across the sunlit opening.

The noises from within grew louder . . . hungrier.

Nemo staggered to a halt as he saw a reptilian shape emerge from the cave. The pirates backed up and shrieked as the enormous beast lumbered out. Its hide was covered with scales, and it had huge, muscular back legs, a lashing tail, and a head barely large enough to contain its yawning rack of jaws. Scarlet, glittering eyes fastened on its prey.

When reading the science magazines Verne had shared in Nantes, Nemo had become familiar with paleontology debates, the remarkable discoveries of the French naturalist Baron Georges Cuvier and the meticulous restorations of the American paleontologist Othniel Charles Marsh. He had seen sketches of enormous skeletons on display in museums, as well as artists' renderings of how the beasts might have looked before some catastrophe had made them extinct.

Dinosaurs, they had been called.

"It's a dragon!" one of the pirates screamed.

Nemo sprinted across the sulfurous clearing toward the distant rocks. As the marauding party scrambled for cover, the predatory dinosaur moved clumsily after them, sniffing and squinting in the bright island sunshine. The creature's nostrils flared as it scented fresh meat. It opened its mouth and emitted a honking roar – then set out after the prey.

Though its front claws looked small and delicate, the monster snagged the red-and-white striped shirt of the closest pirate. Before the man could even scream, the beast tucked him inside its gigantic shovel-shaped maw, bit down with a crunch of bone, and swallowed the morsel in a spray of blood.

Nemo disregarded the pirates, hoping they would all be slain. He had to get down off this rugged slope to the grassy plateau above the lagoon. The screaming men fled after him, as if hoping Nemo might lead them to safety.

Two scrawny, blue-shirted men ran pell-mell next to each other; with a wild look, the man on the right reached over and shoved his companion, who stumbled and sprawled on his face. When the dinosaur paused to gobble up the unfortunate man, the first raced ahead – but the monster caught up with him in a moment, and soon two torn and bloodied blue shirts dangled in shreds from its long fangs.

One bearded pirate turned, braced his legs, and pointed his flintlock pistol. He pulled the trigger, a spark flared the powder, and the ball flew – but the bullet made only a red mark on the dinosaur's hide. The beast noticed the shot no more than a buzzing gnat. The bearded pirate fired a second pistol shot, but the dinosaur responded by devouring him with two swift crunches.

A one-eyed brute stopped running and turned about, wielding a curved cutlass in each hand. With greasy sweat glistening on his bald pate, he turned to face the dinosaur. His scarlet silk pantaloons rippled in the breeze.

As the monster advanced, he screamed a counterpoint yell to the dinosaur's roar and slashed with both blades, nicking the armored hide. The gigantic reptile bent forward to grab him. The bald pirate continued to stab and slash the tender meat inside the monster's mouth even as the jaws crushed him. Two bloody swords clattered to the rocky ground.

Roaring so that the sky trembled and Nemo's ears ached, the dinosaur threw the mangled swordsman down without even eating him. It stomped the corpse of the bald man into a mess with one huge hind foot, then charged forward on a more furious rampage.

Nemo dropped down the steep hill until he reached the grassy plateau. Without pausing, he made for the rocks at the edge of the cliff. Foolishly, the pirates followed, seeing hope light up Nemo's face.

The dinosaur sprang forward with its muscular back legs, using its tail as a counterweight so that it landed, completely balanced, on the meadow below. The pirates threw knives, stones, and empty pistols at it, but nothing slowed down the monster.

Nemo rushed to the sheer drop-off where he had weighted down his glider the day before. He uprooted the ropes, grabbed the kite-wing handholds, and took a running start. He didn't have time to tie himself in. He leaped out into open space, clinging to his glider supports as the winds pulled him up and away from the mountainside.

The doomed pirates staggered to a halt, howling with surprise as he left them behind. Now they were trapped, with no hope of escape. The cliff dropped to foam-battered rocks far below. Nemo soared away, feeling no pity for these vicious men. If only Captain Noseless could have been among them. . .

The dinosaur stomped toward its cornered prey. Some of the pirates drew their swords, making a stand, while others hurled themselves off the cliff rather than be devoured by the dinosaur. When the last victims could not make up their minds, the beast chose for them.

Flying on the winds, Nemo watched the hapless victims, remembering how they themselves had slaughtered the good men aboard the *Coralie*.

Nemo banked and drifted over the thick jungles, eluding pursuit. He landed out in the inaccessible wilderness, where he intended to hide until he could hurt the pirates again. These vile men would no longer take him lightly.

X

For the next day, taking advantage of whatever cover he could find, Nemo crept through the jungles to the shoreline. He knew this island well enough to take back paths to the sheltered lagoon where the *Coralie* had anchored.

Nemo didn't know how many men Captain Noseless had kept on-board while raiding parties scoured the island. Fewer and fewer of the roaming brigands survived, though, as the dinosaur continued to hunt through the night. And Nemo hunted too, looking for means to harm the pirates.

He stood shin-deep in a mangrove swamp, watching for snakes, but more interested in keeping himself hidden from view as he spied on the three-masted brig. The pirate ship was just across the dark waters of the lagoon. Anger and hatred simmered within his heart.

The scarred captain paced the quarterdeck. His remaining men talked amongst themselves, subdued with fear. Nemo fixed his gaze on Noseless, despising the pirate. As the sun sank into the west, painting the sky tangerine and scarlet, Noseless glanced toward the swamps, as if he could sense the young man glaring at him from the deepening shadows.

Nemo wracked his brain for a way to strike at the pirates who had twice destroyed his life. How he hated them! As dusk settled in, accompanied by the night songs of insects, the stillness began to lull Nemo into complacency.

All at once the island grew ominously silent.

The dinosaur's roar split the gloom. The beast crashed through trees, just behind the closer yells of men. Two of the surviving brigands howled in panic as they broke out of the jungle cover by the lagoon. "Help, help!"

On board the *Coralie*, pirates began to mill about. The men on shore shouted toward the anchored ship, but Noseless just stood on the quarterdeck, hands on hips. His face looked more cadaverous than ever, cold and calculating.

As the terrified pirates stumbled across the beach, the trees behind them bent aside. The bloodstained dinosaur pushed its way into the clearing, and its scarlet gaze locked onto the men crossing the swatch of sand. The pirates beckoned for their captain to send help, to launch another longboat, but Noseless made no move to assist them.

One of the pirates fell to his knees in an abject expression of prayerful penitence, while the other raced out into the shallow water, sloshing up to his knees and then his waist, as if he could swim out to the *Coralie* in time.

The dinosaur stepped over the huddled form of the praying man, batting him to the sand with a powerful sweep of its tail, then lunged into the water and scooped down like a pelican catching a fish. The swimming pirate wailed, only to fall abruptly silent as the creature crunched its jaws. Next, the monster turned back to the beach, where it daintily bit the praying man in half.

Nemo watched from his hiding place, stunned by the cold-blooded attitude of Captain Noseless on-board the ship. Dozens of pirates remained on the *Coralie*, and all had refused to help their comrades. The young man's nostrils flared, and he grew angrier by the moment.

From the beach, the dinosaur stared at the ship, defiant, as if its tiny brain knew that its main enemy lay out there. Its roar split the twilight.

In response, Captain Noseless's command echoed across the water. "Fire!"

The dinosaur roared again as a volley of blasts rang out. Every cannon on the port side of the pirate ship fired. Eight of the balls went wide, striking the rocks, the sand, or the jungle – but five hammered into the beast, blasting huge wounds in its massive body. The dinosaur was knocked backward, thrashing.

The remaining men on the *Coralie* surged to the port sides, cheering.

The monster staggered, wailing and honking. Blood poured in gouts from mangled holes in its hide. It clacked its huge shovel jaws together. Two more cannons fired, and both balls struck, shattering the dinosaur's spine and ribs.

At that moment Nemo saw his chance. While Noseless concentrated on his extravagant destruction, the young man slipped into the water. If ever he hoped for an opportunity to get aboard the ship, it was now while the pirates were cheering the dinosaur's death throes.

The dying beast twitched, thrashed, and collapsed onto the bloodied sands. Its monstrous primeval body had been ruined as easily as a defenseless cargo ship, another victim of the pirates.

As the tropical dusk darkened into night, Nemo stroked through the calm lagoon, crossing the distance without a splash. He approached opposite from the gathered pirates and clung to the *Coralie's* barnacled hull at the waterline.

Using the stealth and meticulous care he had developed as a hunter on the island, Nemo climbed the side of the ship, finding footholds on the rough hull planks, pulling himself up by portholes and the hinged starboard gun ports.

He hauled himself over the deck railing and crouched behind a tall coil of rope. Tense and completely alert, he knelt on a bloodied grating, over which the pirate captain must have flogged his poorly disciplined crew. A gunshot rang out, and Nemo ducked, sure that he'd been caught, ready to fight and make a full accounting of himself. But then he heard the hooting laughter of the pirates celebrating their victory.

Most of them must be up on deck, celebrating, now that the cannons had ceased firing. Without being seen, he scampered to a hatch and climbed down into the rank-smelling shadows. A satisfied and confident smile stole across Nemo's face as he calculated what he could do, how much damage he could cause. The pirates would rue this day.

Experiencing an eerie déjà vu, he hurried down the ladder into the main hold. He *knew* this ship, had lived aboard her for two years. The *Coralie* had been his home as much as Île Feydeau or his Granite House cave. He remembered where his bunk had been, as well as those of the first mate, the carpenters, and sailmakers. Most importantly, Nemo remembered where the gunpowder was stored, where kegs of explosive black powder were stacked in the heart of the ship, shielded from outside attack.

But the protected stores were not proof against an infiltrator like himself.

Saddened by what he found himself forced to do with Captain Grant's fine ship, he cracked open one of the casks and spilled the sharp-smelling black grains over the decking and then ran a trail around the other barrels, so that all the kegs would ignite simultaneously.

Noseless kept a full storeroom of explosives. With a bitter grimace, Nemo realized that a pirate ship needed to use its cannons far more often than a research vessel like Captain Grant's. The scarred captain's additional stockpile would bring about the pirates' doom.

He took a smaller cask of gunpowder and walked backward, leaving a long dark line all the way to the ladder. He could still hear the pirates reveling up on deck; apparently none of them felt any grief for the loss of their devoured comrades, nor did they leave the ship to investigate the dinosaur's carcass.

Kneeling, Nemo removed his flint and steel. When he struck them against each other, the clinking sound rang out – but the squeeze boxes and singing and laughter from three decks above were far too loud for any of the pirates to hear him. Finally, a spark flew from the dagger blade and landed in the black powder. Igniting with a fountain of gold flecks, the flame ate along the fuse line faster than a rapid walk.

Foregoing all pretense of caution or silence, Nemo scrambled up the ladder, past the second deck, then through the hatch into the open air. He burst out between two drunken pirates, who reeled backward with a cry of astonishment. Nemo took advantage of their disorientation and ducked past them, shoving with the flat of his hand. One of the pirates grabbed his arm, but he whirled like a cobra and sank his teeth into the man's knuckles like a vicious animal. The pirate yelped and released him.

Standing at the quarterdeck, Noseless saw the young man. "Get him!"

Only then did the brigand captain look over at the deck hatch, as if wondering what Nemo had been doing below, where a wisp of smoke curled up. His cadaverous face changed, and his scarred visage held a look of horror. "Down below! Get to the powder storeroom." But the pirates didn't understand his urgency.

As the raiders closed in, Nemo threw himself overboard. It was a long drop to the sea, but he didn't care. He tumbled, landing feet first with a splash and sinking deep. Then he swam underwater as far as he could; when he finally surfaced, several pirates stood on the deck, blasting with their pistols. But their aim was off in the dark, and lead balls splashed all around him in the lagoon.

Nemo swam desperately to get away, mentally counting down. He looked over his shoulder, wondering how much time remained. Noseless stood on the *Coralie*'s deck in the same spot where Nemo had last seen Captain Grant.

Then all the powder kegs exploded.

The shockwave punched him like a gigantic fist, hurling Nemo through the water toward the shore. The concussion knocked the wind out of him and made his ears ring, but still he thrashed closer to the shelter of the mangrove swamp.

Splintered wood showered the water like Roman candles. He heard the wails and screams of dying men. The *Coralie* burned, flames racing up the rigging and the sails – a complete inferno. The end of Captain Grant's abused ship, the end of the pirates.

Shaky, battered, and nearly deaf, Nemo made his way into the thick mangrove swamps. Panting as he held a knobby root, he watched the ship burn and sink. In the flickering orange firelight, he saw no survivors, no men swimming for shore or clinging to flotsam and groaning for help. The pirates had been taken by surprise, and they had paid the ultimate price.

The lack of mercy bothered Nemo not a bit.

He gradually got his breath back. He had protected his home and his island, but most of all he was proud to have avenged the murder of Captain Grant. For that, he was thankful.

XI

Over the following afternoon, Nemo assessed the damage the pirates had done to his home in only two days.

His storage sheds had been burned to the ground, the corral torn apart, his vegetable garden uprooted and trampled. Using green vines as crude ropes, he lowered himself down the cliff face into the ruins of Granite House. His caves had been gutted, everything breakable smashed to pieces. Malicious vandalism, not because the pirates wanted anything of his.

Where he had hidden it in an alcove, he found the journal he had so diligently kept during his isolation. With tears in his dark eyes, he flipped through the intact pages that described his daily tribulations. It had taken him years to put everything together here. . .

How he hated the pirates!

Later, Nemo sat by himself on the beach, knees drawn up to his chin. With the first dinosaur attack, Noseless had retrieved the longboats from the beach, stranding his own men on the island, and those boats had burned with the *Coralie*.

Nemo listened to the sighing water out by the sheltering reefs, and realized he simply did not have the heart to begin all over again. He clutched the logbook to his chest, remembering how it had saved him from a sword thrust long ago. The written words were all that remained of those years of his life, now that his home had been ruined.

Nemo retrieved enough food from his hidden supplies to make a meal for himself. Then he spent hours just smelling the bitter odor of smoke and listening to the lonely wind as he contemplated what to do.

The *Coralie* had been destroyed. He supposed a few surviving pirates might still be lost in the jungles, raiders who had survived the depredations of the dinosaur. If they came after him, Nemo would fight. But he would rather avoid the brigands altogether.

Once again, André Nemo was about to start clean with his life, just as when he had signed on aboard Captain Grant's ship after the death of his father. Now, though, without the driving juggernaut of vengeance in his heart, he felt empty, aimless. He could do anything he desired now, without being tied down. . .

The strange cavern that had opened up on the side of the volcano intrigued him. Numerous caves and passages riddled the island, extending deep into the earth – but the huge dinosaur had emerged from that place. What sort of subterranean world lurked beneath this island?

With the new morning, Nemo hiked up to the cave and stared at the wide opening. From inside wafted strange and lush smells, humid air with a taint of sulfur, mixed with the freshness of thick vegetation. Fog crept out of the cave mouth, and faint light came from a glow down the steep passage.

Nemo knew that he must investigate this place. It was what Captain Grant would have done, to see, to explore, to learn.

From the tales he and Jules Verne had told each other during their imaginative musings, the theories they had read, as well as discussions he'd had aboard the *Coralie*, Nemo was no stranger to the idea that the earth might be hollow, that a new world lay waiting to be explored beneath the crust. To explain the magnetic phenomena of the earth's poles, the renowned astronomer Edmond Halley had hypothesized a hollow world composed of concentric spheres rotating like a dynamo around a small central sun, and the American soldier John Cleves Symmes had recently repopularized the idea.

Now Nemo had a chance to test it for himself. He didn't know where these tunnels might take him, whether they led to passages extending beneath the ocean floor . . . or even to the center of the earth.

He did not undertake such a journey lightly. He secured every useful item he could bring, found a scrap of rope from the ship wreckage and even retrieved two cutlasses and a brace of pistols that the pirates had dropped during their flight from the dinosaur.

He stitched together a satchel made of burnt scraps of sailcloth that had washed ashore from the wreck of the *Coralie*. He would carry torches coated with sulfur and dried resin, though he could not bring enough to guide his way for long. He hoped that the greenish underground illumination would remain steady enough for him to find his way.

Nemo sliced flesh from the fallen dinosaur's carcass, cooked and tasted the meat. Although it was bitter, the flesh seemed nourishing enough and in plentiful supply. Anxious to go, he didn't want to take the time to hunt other game, so he built a green, smoky fire and cured strips of the reptile meat, which he wrapped in fresh leaves and packed in his satchel.

His final and most important task was to tear out the writing-covered pages from his journal. He rolled them into a tight tube, which he then inserted into the empty brandy bottle he had kept for so long. He added a note instructing whoever found this message to deliver it to his friend Jules Verne in Nantes, France. He sealed the bottle and went to the end of the lagoon.

When the strongest current of the tide went out, he gripped the bottle, knowing there was virtually no chance in all the vast oceans that this message would ever see its intended reader. But he had beaten the odds before.

He hurled the bottle into the waves, watched it bob on the surface for some minutes and float away. He hoped it would drift into the shipping lanes. For a long time he'd clung to nothing more than hope. . . but hope had served him well enough over the years.

Taking his satchel, Nemo climbed the volcanic slopes to the intriguing cave opening. He took one last look around him at the shores that had encompassed his world for so long, and then he turned toward the mystery ahead.

Nemo ventured into the cave, not knowing if he would ever come back.

Part IV
A JOURNEY TO THE CENTRE

I

Nantes, 1848

Caroline Aronnax stood at the head of the crowd on the docks, wearing her best silk gown, her finest lace cuffs, and her proudest expression. Her whalebone corset was laced up so that she stood as straight as the masts on the exploration ship about to depart. On the street beside the quays, a band played lively patriotic tunes. Spectators cheered and howled for Captain Hatteras.

"I am so happy for you, my dear," Madame Aronnax said, touching her daughter's shoulder. "You must be very proud of your captain."

Marie stood apart from Caroline in the crowd, craning her neck to get a better view; Madame Aronnax insisted it would be unseemly for a mere maid to wait too closely beside her mistress on this momentous occasion. Caroline had to wish her new husband farewell with all due decorum.

Tied up to the dock, the freshly painted *Forward* creaked in the afternoon breeze. Her copper-plated hull would provide greater durability for crashing through layers of polar ice. A gangplank extended to the dock, but the crew had already boarded. The previous days had been busy as deck workers loaded crates of supplies.

As was his custom, the Mayor of Nantes arrived in a spectacular carriage drawn by four white horses. White-clad coachmen drove the omnibus, and a postilion (also dressed in white) sat astride the front left horse. While rattling across the paving stones, the turning wheels actuated an internal music box that sent out tinkling chimes. These extravagant contraptions, called 'White Ladies,' reminded Caroline of something Jules Verne might have imagined for his amusing stories.

Investors and newspapermen stood beneath crepe streamers, lecturing on the potential of this voyage of discovery. Some voiced proud optimism that Captain Hatteras, of all men, would find the fabled Northwest Passage.

The uninspired but enthusiastic band played the French national anthem. Standing in the crowd, Caroline wished she were at her pianoforte instead, composing an original piece for the *Forward*'s departure, a grand explorers' march. At the moment, though, her job was simply to remain visible and look beautiful – nothing more. Once Hatteras departed, she could reshape her life and accomplish more than she'd been able to do under her mother's thumb.

She was the fresh young bride of the great captain. Her parents stood with her, the successful merchant and his wife, beaming with pride as they stared at the well-provisioned ship. Caroline had married her sea captain only the day before and had seen him for no more than ten minutes this entire morning. They had spent their wedding night together, and once again Caroline had performed to the expectations that others forced upon her, but she still did not know this man who was now her husband. She wouldn't miss Hatteras a hundredth as much as she missed her long-lost André Nemo.

Hatteras had graying hair, mutton chop whiskers, and a face weathered from years facing the salty wind – but worst of all, she did not *know* him. Other than her father's records of his business dealings, Caroline had discovered little about her new husband's past. According to M. Aronnax, the good captain's accomplishments and glories should have made any young woman proud. But Hatteras was twenty-five years her senior. He'd been married twice before, and both wives had died from fever while he was away at sea. She didn't know his sense of humor or his personality, had never even asked if the man liked *music*.

Caroline wouldn't get an opportunity to know him either, not for a long time. Hatteras would take his ship out with the afternoon's outgoing tide. Even given the most favorable winds and the best weather possible, she would not see her husband again for at least two years, probably more than that.

No doubt Captain Hatteras had women in other ports, as was traditional for seafarers who sailed around the world, but he seemed little interested in romance. His entire life focused upon finding a trade route around the North Pole. Perhaps his heart was as cold as the arctic seas he intended to explore.

Yet Caroline had married him. She had spoken the vows before God, and before witnesses. Years ago, she had made promises to Nemo, and she had meant them at the time – but Nemo was gone, and her life would never be the same. She had to accept his loss. Hatteras was her husband now.

She had slept with him in a strange bed, in a strange house. An unfamiliar man in the darkness, he had been businesslike and oddly passionless for a man with a new young bride. Caroline had closed her eyes, tried to imagine being with Nemo instead of Captain Hatteras, but that did not help. The feelings were disappointing, and she did not want to diminish the fantasy lover in her mind. And so she found their marriage consummated, herself no longer a virgin, the wife of a sea captain who would be gone for months or years at a time.

Caroline's path had been set, regardless of her private dreams and ambitions – impossible fantasies for a woman of her social standing in this place, in this time. She would be expected to remain home and while away the hours, as a good wife should. But she had other plans.

It would have made her miserable, had she meekly accepted society's expectations. But Caroline Aronnax had always made her own expectations, and she had learned from Nemo never to listen to the impossible. Nemo had insisted that she could do whatever she set her mind to.

Married, but with her husband far away, Caroline thought her new situation might offer her a freedom that she'd never experienced before. As wife and head of the household, she controlled the captain's finances – enough money to make her wealthy. She would live in Hatteras's home on rue Kervégan, where she could spend every day in her own pursuits. She'd hire private tutors, not only for music and art (neither of which would raise eyebrows), but also to study business. In particular, she wanted to learn about shipping manifests and accounting practices so she could help her overworked father at his merchant offices.

Yes, as far as she was concerned, Captain Hatteras could stay away from Nantes for as long as he wished. What could have become a trap for other women, Caroline considered to be an *opportunity*.

Cannons blasted as Captain Hatteras and his first mate strode in full naval attire down the docks and up the gangplank. The gruff captain waved to the assembled spectators before tipping his broad black hat toward where Caroline stood waiting for him. She even managed to show some tears, though they were not for Hatteras, but for a young man gone long ago . . . gone along with so many shared dreams. With an eerie sense of disorientation, she wondered if her husband even recognized who she was. . .

Caroline thought of her younger years, of the wild childhood dreams she had shared with André Nemo and Jules Verne . . . and especially of that special night that had changed her forever, the enthusiastic promises she and Nemo had exchanged. Together, the three of them had bolstered each other's optimism, made it seem that she truly could write her own music or run her father's shipping business, that Verne could become a famous writer, that Nemo could sail the uncharted seas.

But they had drifted apart, and they had each failed their own fantasies.

Though Caroline wished Jules Verne could have been here, the young redhead had already gone off to Paris to begin training for his law degree. She understood why the lovestruck young man had wanted to make himself scarce during her wedding. She felt sorry for Verne, and promised herself that she would do everything in her power to help him achieve his dreams. With Nemo lost at sea, Jules Verne was the only kindred spirit she had left. . .

The mayor of Nantes stepped up to a hastily erected podium and extended his ponderous congratulations and well wishes (as he had no doubt been paid to do by the *Forward*'s investors). Accompanied by more cheering, dock workers cast off the ropes, and the copper-plated *Forward* drifted into the current. Crew members pressed against the deck rails and waved back at the citizens of Nantes as the ship began to descend the Loire.

Caroline watched them, feeling strangely invisible. Streamers and confetti fell around her, clustering in damp wads on the dock planks or floating waterlogged in the river. The crowd jostled her, talking loudly, laughing. She dried her eyes.

Such a large ship. So many sailors. Caroline thought of all the warm clothes and supplies the men had squirreled away in the cargo holds. Before long, they would be facing a frozen white wasteland, searching for a passage that many other explorers had perished trying to find in the past. Did the *Forward* have any better chance of succeeding?

As the ship entered the current, she watched the silhouette of proud Captain Hatteras at the wheel, facing westward. Finally, as an afterthought, he turned toward her and gave a brief salute before returning to his duty.

Caroline waved farewell, but she never knew whether he had seen her.

II

Following his instincts and knowing he might never see daylight again, Nemo trudged downhill into the newly opened cave. The tunnels wound deep into the earth, knotted and twisted like malformed worm burrows.

And still he kept going.

The earth itself seemed to breathe, drawing air from above to fill the caverns below. Noting the direction of the torch flame, he followed the air currents. That was what Captain Grant would have done.

Many of the catacombs dead-ended. At times, the eerie light from glittering crystals and phosphorescent algaes faded inside the still passageways. He lit one of his precious torches and continued to explore, making marks on the walls at turning points with soft, chalky stones he picked up from the floor.

The existence of the predatory dinosaur that had emerged from the cave proved that some new world must lay hidden: a living, lush environment, separate from the mysterious island above. And if these tunnels did lead into the bowels of the earth, they might also let Nemo travel beneath the ocean's crust. He might emerge in a different place . . . perhaps one closer to civilization.

Nemo kept trudging downward, always downward.

When his first torch finally gave out, instead of lighting another, he realized that the phosphorescence now provided enough delicate illumination. Over the hours, his pupils widened to gather every scrap of light. He also became more adept at finding his way through the blurred shadows by listening to the echoes that came back to him as he walked.

When he was too tired to continue, Nemo sat down and drank a sip from his water skin, ate dried dinosaur meat, and then slept, his sleep haunted by questions and impossibilities, and memories of lost friends. When he awoke refreshed, he continued his plodding journey downward, ever deeper.

On the next "day," he found a trickling stream that emerged from a crack in the granite wall, a warm spring far beneath the earth's crust. When Nemo tasted it, the flavor was rich with minerals, and so he refilled his water skin. If he ate sparingly, the dried meat and other supplies in his pack would last him for many days. Though he had only two more torches, he continued long past the point where he could be confident of returning. Nemo had decided to risk everything and did not regret the direction he had taken.

He followed the stream as it chose the path of least resistance through the sloping stone floor until the warm water, joined by other springs and trickles, became a roiling creek that ran along one side of the tunnel.

Nemo jogged down the steepening slope, picking up speed until the stream hooked to the left and disappeared under a shoulder-high arch eroded through the stone wall. The water was like a heated bath on his feet. He splashed along, ducking under the low arch. After wading through, Nemo emerged into a chamber so vast that he windmilled his arms to maintain his balance.

The warm water gushed through the wall opening and plunged over a precipice into a thundering waterfall. Spray washed up, echoing within the vaulted grotto like music in the nave of a cathedral. The cavern reflected sound waves back at him with such intensity that he could not guess its boundaries. The bottomless pit in front of him was an open mouth greedily drinking of the water.

Nemo made his precarious way along a narrow rock ledge to a forest of dripping stalactites, which he grasped in order to steady himself. Removing one of the unlit torches from his pack, he worked with flint and steel to light it. He held his breath as the blaze took hold around the firebrand, then he raised it up.

Dancing light spread through a grotto filled with more wonders than he had ever imagined. Immense faceted crystals jutted from the stone walls, dripped like tears from the ceiling, and flashed in the firelight: a treasure more breathtaking than the combined wealth of Pirate Roberts, Captain Kidd, and Blackbeard. On the side nearest him, a waterfall of stone kept timeless pace with the pouring cascade of mineralized water that had led Nemo through the arch.

He shouted with delight, and the noise echoed back at him, refracted by the crystals and stalactites, so that it sounded as if an entire chorus of wide-eyed young men had expressed their amazement. If only Caroline could be here.

He drank in the splendor for minutes, until he remembered he had few torches remaining. Then he extinguished the fire and sat waiting until his eyes adjusted. A brighter patch of the pale glow appeared from below. He would use the staggered flow of stalactites as a staircase to reach the bottom of the pit.

Nemo made his way, grasping with both hands, feeling with his feet. The stalactites were slick and damp. Every inch was accomplished at the risk of falling to his death, but he continued, undaunted. He knew there must be an easier path somewhere, for the dinosaur could never have toiled up through this treacherous labyrinth. For Nemo, though, any path that continued to lead forward was as good as any other.

Halfway down, he found a wide ledge, where he curled up and slept again. Some hours later, he woke, drank some mineralized water that had pooled in a depression on one of the rocks, and set off once more.

When he reached the bottom, he fell to his knees on the cold, hard stone. After he caught his breath, he walked toward the brightening light. He emerged into a second grotto, even more vast than the first, and Nemo knew he had stepped into another world – a fairyland beyond even the wildest theories of modern science.

The ground was soft and crumbly, and the air smelled of mulch. All around him, as far as he could see, stood immense fungi, mushrooms as tall as trees. The mushroom caps were white, each ringed with a golden frill. Some were the size of dining chairs, others grew four times as tall as a man. Wreaths of mist crept around the gigantic toadstools, and dripping strands of moss clung to the rocks. A greenish, cold light filled the chamber as if it oozed from the rock walls.

Far in the distance, obscured by the humid air, Nemo heard a raucous cry from a bird whose species he could not determine. It sounded immense, louder and stranger than any bird he had encountered in his travels.

He walked into the forest of mushrooms like a lost wanderer and stood under them as if seeking refuge beneath Herculean garden umbrellas. They made him think of the parasols Caroline carried when she strolled out in the sun dressed in her finest clothes. Her mother had seen to it that she had the finest accouterments, but Caroline held them awkwardly, daydreaming, letting her parasol droop to the mud as her attention wandered to other things.

Nemo shook that thought from his mind and continued.

He rapped his knuckles against the stiff stem – or was it the trunk? – of a mushroom. It was softer than wood, but still firm and thick. When he pushed harder, a rain of dusty spores showered from the broad mushroom cap. They covered him like sawdust as he coughed and sneezed, but he laughed and knocked the mushroom again, setting off another shower. He ran through the mushroom forest, bumping the pallid stems and unleashing a torrent of spores.

He climbed one of the mushroom trunks and used his pirate cutlass to hack off a chunk of the soft fungus. He chewed on it, finding the delicate flesh a wonderful accompaniment to his preserved dinosaur meat.

Nemo wandered through the mushroom forest, always continuing toward the brightening light. When at last he passed beyond the mammoth toadstools, Nemo looked ahead into a steaming primeval jungle filled with prehistoric plant life. He could lose himself in its wonders and mystery for months without end.

Just then Nemo heard the ominous sounds of large creatures crashing toward him through the dense underbrush.

III

Paris, ah Paris!

Leaving his backwater town behind, Jules Verne felt as if he had stepped into a color-filled painting by one of the great masters. The buildings, cafes, cathedrals, street performers – the *culture* – were all so different from home. The Seine! The Louvre! Notre Dame! It was like a fantastic world from the stories of Marco Polo or the romances of Sir Walter Scott. Paris was indeed the center of France, its heart and its mind. And Verne reveled in being here.

He had at first been fearful of the political turmoil: bloody uprisings, gunfire in the streets, worker barricades, revolutionary fervor. His father had been concerned, and his mother had gnawed her fingernails in worry. Verne, though, wrote from his narrow room to reassure them that he was having a fine time. And, of course, learning much.

He reached Paris in July, just after a long string of violence that had plagued the capital since February. Though Pierre Verne was a staunch conservative and had raised his son to hold similar opinions, the younger Verne now found it confusing enough just to keep track of who was running which portion of the country during any given week. Politics made him dizzy.

Two years of bad wheat and potato harvests had sent prices soaring, and peasants began looting bakeries and food storehouses, demanding their due. When factories closed, unemployed workers took to the streets. The government refused to institute changes, and during a protest march in February, a frightened army patrol had fired into the crowd, triggering a riot.

The incident united the dissatisfied people behind barricades, and even the National Guard joined the rebels after ransacking armories for weapons. Within days they had ousted numerous officials from the government, then marched on King Louis-Philippe himself, who abdicated and fled to England. In his wake, the French people declared a new Republic. Elections were held on April 23, and in the following months the government struggled to assert itself. The bloodiest battles took place in June – the Archbishop of Paris had been killed while trying to negotiate peace with a pocket of rebels.

A month later, when Verne entered the city with little spending money and an avid curiosity, he explored the alleys and byways, careful to stay clear of any danger. He saw the cluttered barricades thrown up in the streets – carts, barrels, ladders, and crates stacked on top of furniture to block the military guard. He tried to imagine the bravery, the sacrifices, the heroes and traitors. It took his breath away . . . so long as he didn't have to be counted among the participants.

Some nights as he lay awake, he heard gunshots in the distance. Later, he spotted white starbursts where bullets had struck the brick walls and shattered windows. He could even see the path of a cannonball down a long street, tracing the wreckage through successive balconies, balustrades, and facades. Verne stood with his hands on his narrow hips and marveled at the sight.

Though others railed against the changing governments and charged off to join the continued fighting, Verne kept a low profile in Paris. It was a matter of common sense. He remained in his rooms far from the gunfire, cannon shots, or battle cries. He had no interest in seeing the excitement, did not want to place himself in danger's path.

His lost friend Nemo would probably have gone running in with a flag in one hand and a musket in the other, outraged at the injustice they were fighting. Verne had always admired the *idea* of doing the things Nemo did, but his personal safety took precedence.

He remained on the outskirts of politics, a mere bystander, risking nothing. Outside the Paris National Assembly, he watched revolutionaries celebrating their victory in April's elections. The shouting men wore cotton caps and raised thin sabers, no doubt stolen from fallen soldiers in the street fighting. Since February, the peasants in the militia had been allowed to carry their own weapons, and they did so with great fervor.

At times, surrounded by turmoil and chaos, strident voices and gunshots, celebrations and parades, he longed for quiet days on the peaceful docks of Île Feydeau. But then he would remember that Caroline was married to her sea captain, Nemo was lost at sea, and his own father wanted him to spend every hour in the dreary law offices. At least Paris was exciting, in its own way.

To him, there was no point in going home. Verne would rather stay here to feel the excitement in the air, the thrill of liberty – a vigor that could not be matched in a provincial city like Nantes. In Paris, the world had opened up to him. He discovered the marvels of the theater and the opera. In Nantes, staged dramas had been unusual events, but in Paris Verne grew dizzy trying to keep up with the performances scheduled for every night of the week.

Ah, if only he could afford them all! His father had given him a limited budget based upon what the country lawyer considered a fair cost of living. But the revolutions and the fighting had created extraordinary inflation in Paris, and the value of the franc had plummeted. Verne could buy barely half of what his father expected him to afford with his allowance. Meticulous Pierre Verne required his son to keep an itemized list to prove that he needed a larger monthly stipend.

Verne worked hard in his law classes, discussed the various lecturers with his fellow students, and knew how eccentric and facetious their grading systems could be. All of his prior legal knowledge had come from a provincial practice dealing with everyday matters. Yet the professors at the Paris Academy expected him to be familiar with grand ethical arguments and obscure cases that meant nothing on Île Feydeau.

But Verne studied, anxious to pass, though he had no desire to become an attorney. A far worse fate, he thought, would be to fail and return home to the wrath of his father. No, he would rather face rapacious pirates or typhoons.

Still, even when his head hurt, his eyes burned from lack of sleep, and his muscles ached from poor food and sheer weariness, Verne found time to spend in the company of stimulating intellectuals.

For hours, he sat with musician friends and aspiring poets in bistros and sipped his coffee oh-so-slowly so as not to have to purchase another cup. They spouted verse to each other, reminding Verne of the evenings his family had challenged each other to make rhymes. He also met other writers, one of whom had even had a two-act tragedy performed in a small puppet theater, which made him a celebrity in their circle.

His mind filled to overflowing, Verne's imagination caught fire. He remembered his literary ambitions, which had been quashed by the bemusement of his mother and utter lack of encouragement from his father. Yet now he became more infected than ever with the dream of becoming an acclaimed dramatist – and for that he needed to search out philosophical topics and devise grand commentaries on the human condition. Forsaking *Robinson Crusoe* and *Swiss Family Robinson*, Verne turned to Voltaire and Balzac, Byron and Shelley, reveling in their hot-blooded romanticism.

One day, waving a ticket that a sick friend had given him, Verne found a seat in the audience of the National Assembly, where a case was being argued. A publisher had been arrested and his newspaper, *La Presse*, forcibly suspended by the government. For Verne, the main attraction was when the great novelist Victor Hugo rose to speak with great passion for the cause of freedom of speech.

As a celebrity, Hugo had been elected as a deputy of the National Assembly. "He may as well serve his country," one of Verne's aspiring-writer friends had commented sarcastically. "It's been ten years since he published anything new." Then the students had begun to argue about whether Hugo could ever surpass his literary masterpiece, *The Hunchback of Notre-Dame*.

Verne hoped that with great minds such as Victor Hugo's in the Second Republic – and the election of the enlightened Louis Napoleon Bonaparte, nephew of the great Napoleon – Paris and France would finally embark upon a long period of stability and prosperity.

He paid little attention to either politics or rhetoric at the assembly, but instead nudged closer to the great Hugo. The man turned and met Verne's eyes for the briefest of instants, which would keep the young man in happy delirium for an entire week. . .

Mulling over these thoughts as he left the National Assembly, Verne found a few sous in his pocket, enough for one day's food. But he walked past the fruit carts and bakery baskets and stopped instead at a bookshop. There, he found the romances of Sir Walter Scott in thirteen volumes, a collection of the poetry of Racine – and, in a single magnificent tome, the complete works of William Shakespeare.

Verne counted the coins in the palm of his hand, studying the prices of the books. A person had to have priorities, after all. After dickering with the vendor, he settled on an amount. Verne walked home, penniless and still hungry . . . but carrying the book of Shakespeare.

He considered it a better investment of his money than mere food.

IV

Nemo was a stranger in a world where no human being had ever set foot.

Misty swamps spread out in the lost landscape, inhabited by strange and forgotten creatures. The ceiling of the incredible grotto became a sky of stone high above. Stalactites blurred in the distance, as far away as clouds, lit by a strange bright smear like a surrogate sun.

Nemo forged a path through the virgin wilderness. The primeval paradise simmered with subdued noises, shattered by occasional roars like that of the carnivorous dinosaur that had attacked his island. He pushed aside curled ferns similar to the tails of caged monkeys he had seen on the docks in Nantes.

In addition to his mushroom feast, he found brightly colored fruits and edible leaves in this uncharted Eden. Now that he was traveling again after so many years, Nemo felt even more restless. He moved one step at a time, pushing onward in hopes of discovering a passage that led upward. Home.

He trudged through swamps, sloshing in ankle-deep, peaty water. Huge flowers like sunbursts brightened the humid green-brown world. A dragonfly the size of a vulture skimmed by with wings like the glider he had built. Nemo ducked to one side as the mammoth insect swooped down to the sluggish water, scooped up a thrashing fish, and made off with its meal.

Nemo parted moss-covered branches to look out upon a dozen wading dinosaurs, immense beasts larger than any whale. Their long necks curled like a giraffe's. One plump creature gazed at him with placid eyes, its mouth full of uprooted swamp weeds. It showed no intelligence, only a dull interest. The plant-eating dinosaurs dismissed him and went back to their tireless eating.

Keeping track of time and direction as best he could, Nemo slept when he was tired, ate when he was hungry. In the smoky twilight, he used his best guess to keep a regular cycle of day and night. He fashioned a makeshift compass in a small pool of water, but could not verify its accuracy. He did not know his direction . . . only onward.

For weeks he continued through the deeper swamp into a cluster of conifers that sheltered a hoard of large, scaly bats. The startled bats took off with a thunderous flapping of wings toward the grotto ceiling, much as a flock of sparrows might have flown from a shooting party back in France.

At one point it rained for days on end. Salty-tasting water streamed from high above. Uneasy, Nemo wondered if he'd passed beneath a porous section of the ocean floor that allowed water to trickle through. According to his best estimates, Nemo had long since passed beyond the confines of the island.

The grotto seemed to go on forever, as if the earth had swallowed a bubble of the past and preserved it far from the surface. Nemo proceeded for what might have been months, clinging to a thin twine of hope that if he walked far enough, searched diligently enough, he would emerge again to civilization.

In the remaining, water-stained pages in his bound journal, he continued to document his travels, pressing a few strange leaves and flowers between sheets of dense description. Even with the daily entries and the specimens, though, he doubted anyone would believe his story – any more than he and Jules Verne had believed the tall tales told by sailors on the docks of Île Feydeau.

At last, the prehistoric forest thinned again, returning to low swamps that led out of the ferns to another grove of titanic mushrooms. For a gut-wrenching moment Nemo feared that the mushroom forest was the same one he had first encountered. What if he had circumnavigated the buried grotto and found no other passage to the surface?

As he studied more carefully, though, he realized that the forest, the water, even the far-off ceiling of stalactites, looked different. This was a new place, and the strangeness of it all gave him the energy to hurry forward.

Nemo parted the tall stems of mushrooms, disregarding the showers of spores, and came upon a sight that filled him with dismay. Where the spongy ground ended in an abrupt shore, the gray-blue waters of an incomprehensibly vast subterranean sea spread beyond the visible horizon, like spilled quicksilver. Currents stirred the water, as if from a bizarre tide in the center of the earth.

Nemo saw no way around the water. He looked left and right at the ocean that stretched as far as he could see. From here he had no place left to go.

V

Jules Verne had pressed hard to obtain an invitation to a "minor literary soirée." However, now that he stood in a large private house among the Paris literati, pretending to belong among them, he felt as if he were walking in the clouds. Simply being here, Verne felt as if he were making progress toward his own ambitions. . .

He wore his only good suit of clothes, which was a bit faded and tattered from continuous wear. Self-conscious, but affecting a haughty air to imitate those around him, Verne dipped into conversation with fiery-eyed young men who had political or dramatic ambitions. Still a hungry student, Verne also made frequent trips to the buffet table and ate four times as much as the other attendees, who only nibbled at the petits fours and hors d'oeuvres.

The months in Paris had already stretched to more than a year. During days in the Academy lecture halls, he dived into legal esoterica dating to Roman times. Although he remained uninterested, Verne knew he must do well enough to pass his exams and send appropriate reports to his parents. Otherwise Pierre Verne would bring him home, and he couldn't think of a drearier prospect.

He wrote regular letters, often mailing separate messages to his mother in which he complained of indigestion and various ailments, seeking sympathy. In missives to his father, he emphasized how hard he was studying and how difficult it was to survive in Paris on the meager allowance he received.

In the evenings, feeling out of his element, Verne met with acquaintances in coffee shops along the Left Bank and at the Sorbonne. In his correspondence, though, Verne took care not to express his literary ambitions. He did not describe times spent in salons or at social parties where he hoped to meet famous personages of the French art scene. His father had little patience for such dreams and would see no connection between meeting "idlers, buffoons, or subversives" and his son's future as a stable lawyer.

Verne paid for his double life through lack of sleep. He stayed up late and rose early, struggling to meet both his father's obligations and those imposed by his ambitions. Though he had no money and only a tiny attic apartment, Verne still managed to insinuate himself into the circles of those who held rich parties in the finer quarters of Paris.

Now, surrounded by a buzz of conversation, he listened with giddy interest to profound debates. With passion or feigned boredom, the literati discussed the plays offered along the boulevard du Temple, farces or romantic comedies, a few one-act tragedies told in lyrical verse. Many men chatted about the new play by Alexandre Dumas, who had adapted the first part of *The Three Musketeers*, to a stage production performed in his own playhouse, the Théâtre Historique.

Comparable only to Victor Hugo, Dumas was the literary light of French romanticism. For almost two decades, he had produced masterpieces of historical adventure. His most recent success, *The Man in the Iron Mask*, had appeared in 1847, the year before revolutions had forced him to close down his theatres. Now the Théâtre Historique had reopened, with the performance of a brand new play by the master.

Verne could never afford to see such a production, though he longed to. Still, it was a wonderful time to be in Paris, the pinnacle of human civilization.

When the topic inevitably turned from literature to politics, Verne found the conversation tedious. He wandered out of the drawing room in search of something else to hold his attention . . . and perhaps more food. He wondered how much he could hide in his pockets. Hearing a harpsichord and singing upstairs, he trotted up a long, curving marble staircase, so polished and smooth that it was like walking on wet ice.

Dozens of people milled about below, most of whom Verne didn't know. Their fashions dismayed him, their references to unrecognized names confused him, but he continued to wear a knowing smile and moved from one group to another before anyone could expose his ignorance.

As he hurried up the marble steps in his worn shoes, Verne slipped and grabbed for the stone banister to keep his balance. Missing it, he fell into a tumbling roll, just as an enormous man began to climb the stairs. Verne crashed into the mountainous, dark-skinned stranger, who caught him with a loud *oof*. They both tumbled backward like carts crashing in a crowded street, a flurry of legs and shoes.

While a few other partygoers tittered at the spectacle, Verne disentangled himself and mumbled his apologies, blushing as red as a sugar beet with embarrassment. He kept his gaze downcast, flustered. "Excuse me, monsieur! I stumbled. I couldn't help myself."

The big man laughed, and Verne raised his eyes, hoping he hadn't bumbled into a person in a surly mood. A haughty man just might challenge a gangly young student to a duel, and then Jules Verne would have to demonstrate just how fast he could run.

The stranger was one of the fattest men Verne had ever seen. He had kinky black hair that showed a strong Negro heritage and dusky skin, though light enough in color to indicate mixed blood. His fingers were studded with rings and he sported a cravat pin worth more than Verne's entire annual stipend. The man's cheeks were like balloons, and his dark eyes sparkled with amusement at the incident.

"Oh, ho! I'm delighted that I could rescue you by forming a barricade of my girth, young monsieur." He patted the sheer volume of stomach barely contained within his straining waistcoat. "My only disappointment is that you've unsettled the delicious Nantes omelet I have just consumed."

Verne brushed himself off, though the lint and tatters and faded spots in his clothes were not so easily whisked away. Trying not to appear such a buffoon, he remembered his mother's secret recipe. "A Nantes omelet?" He scratched at the stubbly beard he had begun to grow in imitation of Paris literary fashion. Perhaps he could extend an appropriate apology. "You have not tasted the best omelet, monsieur, because you have not yet eaten mine. I have a special recipe."

The fat man laughed. "Ho! Well then, since I have saved your life from such a terrible fall, I insist that you cook me a sample. I trust that it will be every bit as delicious as you've led me to believe. I am quite a gourmand . . . as you can see." He patted the barrel of his stomach, and it made a hollow, rumbling sound. "Would next Saturday do?"

Verne balked at what he had just suggested. He couldn't invite this well-dressed and obviously wealthy man up to his dingy room. He didn't have pans, ingredients, a dining table, china – not even napkins. He wanted to jump down the stairs again, and this time perhaps he would mercifully break his neck.

The dark-skinned man, observing Verne's distress, waved a pudgy hand to dismiss any concerns. "Young man, you need merely arrive at my chateau. I shall provide the cookware and supplies you require. I fancy myself something of a gourmet chef and would like to learn from such a master as yourself." His eyes twinkled.

"Certainly, monsieur," Verne said, trying to be formal as he recovered his pride. He searched for more lint to brush from his jacket. "Alas, I cannot give you the recipe. It is a family secret."

"But of course," the man said, then patted his stomach again. "You are fortunate that for me, the primary interest is in *consuming* the omelet."

The man continued up the marble stairs toward the harpsichord music, but Verne stopped him. "Wait, monsieur. You have not told me your name or your address."

The big man stopped in genuine surprise and turned to look down at Verne. "You mean you do not know?" He clapped his hands, then smiled even wider, flashing bright white teeth. "Oh, ho! So many fawning people cling to me at all times. Rarely does anyone bump into me truly by 'accident.'"

He extended a ring-studded grip; his palm could easily have folded around Verne's entire hand. "I am Alexandre Dumas. You must come to my chateau at Monte Cristo. I believe anyone here can tell you the way."

VI

After all he had been through, all he'd accomplished and suffered, Nemo refused to let a mere ocean stop him. So he decided to build a raft.

The monstrous mushrooms provided sturdy, woody stems that floated with ease. Squatting in the soft dirt, Nemo used a stick to sketch plans for building a simple, seaworthy craft. He took what he knew of engineering and added ideas he'd gleaned from Captain Grant's library – from the sketchbooks of Leonardo da Vinci to the designs of the steamboat inventor, Robert Fulton. It was a problem to be solved through time and ingenuity, and Nemo had both.

With his cutlass, he hacked down seven sturdy mushrooms. He removed the hemispherical caps, each one broader than his outstretched arms, and dragged the porous logs to a flat clearing at the shore of the sea.

Rather than using simple vines to lash the mushroom logs together, he took extra time to braid thin tendrils into a sturdy cord. He had no way of knowing how long he'd need this craft to last. He secured four of the large fungus caps together on the bottom of the raft to act as pontoons for extra flotation. Next he used his braided cord to tie the logs together on top.

After many hours of labor, Nemo stripped to swim in the leaden waters of the earth's central sea; then he went back to work again until, exhausted, he crawled under a mushroom canopy to sleep. . .

Once the completed structure was firm and stable, he looked across the cavern ocean. Seeing no end to the water, he gathered fresh supplies:

ripe fruit, hard roots, even the meat from a small plant-eating dinosaur he ambushed behind the thick ferns. He still had his two pistols taken from the pirates, but so far he'd found no need to use them.

Ready to undertake a long voyage, Nemo heaved his lightweight fungus boat into the water, using shaved mushroom logs for paddles and a tiller. The raft drifted along, carried by the strong subterranean current. Behind him, the underground shoreline faded into the distance, veiled by a mist that clung to the thick fungus forest.

Before long, Nemo found himself in the uncharted expanse of a featureless sea. The grotto ceiling above shone with pearly luminescence, far, far away, and Nemo had no stars or familiar land features to guide him. Only his dreams. . .

The hardest part was coping with the sheer boredom. For so long, Nemo had been forced to spend every waking hour on the simple business of survival, occupying himself with essential tasks all day long to feed himself, improve his life, or reinforce his defenses.

Drifting in the open sea, Nemo had nothing to do but lie back and think. He tried to determine his velocity by tossing bits of flotsam over the side, but had no fixed point of reference. Smiling, he let himself enjoy memories of his childhood days and the port of Île Feydeau, playing card games with his father, spending joyful times with Jules Verne, competing for the attentions of Caroline Aronnax, imagining all the adventures they would have in their lives. . .

Now he was at the mercy of the strong current, and his simple rudder could barely nudge him in one direction or another. He saw no reefs or shoals, still no sign of an opposite shore, or a passage leading to the surface. He began to think he might never see the real sun again.

He was lost at the center of the earth and defenseless in the face of whatever forces nature chose to inflict upon him.

VII

When a pounding came at the door of his small room, Jules Verne was not asleep, though the hour was late. He'd sat by the pale light from a salvaged candle, rereading scenes from the complete works of William Shakespeare. Tears were in his eyes from the tragic end of *Romeo and Juliet*, but the plotting and careful tapestry of characters made him weep as well. He wanted to publish great dramas, too – and perhaps Alexandre Dumas could help him. He wished he could afford to buy some of the esteemed author's novels and plays before visiting Dumas in his chateau. Verne was anxious to make a good impression.

The fist hammered insistently, and Verne assumed it must be one of his literary friends, possibly drunk, possibly wanting to borrow money that Verne didn't have. He got up, grumbling, and closed his book. "Coming, coming!"

But when he opened the door, he saw a broad-shouldered figure in the dimness of the hall. The stranger wore the striped pullover shirt of a sailor and tattered bell-bottomed pants, and he carried a smell of tar and sweat about him. Verne stopped, startled, as if seeing a ghost from the shipyards on Île Feydeau.

"I'm looking for Jules Verne," the man said with a gruff, Breton accent.

"I am he." Verne drew himself up, running a hand through his tousled reddish hair, though this sailor did not seem to put much stock in personal appearances. Rough and tumble, scarred, the sailor cut a fearsome figure, and Verne swallowed hard. He took an unsteady step backward, thinking of assassins and bullies. But who would want to rob him? "May . . . I help you?"

"You're from Nantes, then? I've been to your city and seen your father. He gave me your address here, but I've got to get back to my ship."

Now Verne was even more confused. His mind whirled – his father would never send such a man to check up on him, would he? He wished he'd been studying his law books rather than Shakespeare, just in case this ruffian reported on him. "What is this all about, sir?" He did not dare invite the man into his small room.

"I have a message for you. And a story." The sailor withdrew a thick, rolled-up sheaf of papers from his pocket. The pages were yellowed, curled, and water-stained, some torn. "I worked on a fishing trawler five months ago. We caught a shark, and when we slit his belly open we found a bottle inside. That bottle contained this journal – a long one, written by a friend of yours. Someone by the name of Nemo."

Verne's entire body went numb, and he reached out a trembling hand to take the roll of papers. As he unfolded them and looked down at the packed writing, he recognized his friend's penmanship. "Nemo . . . he's alive?"

The sailor shrugged his broad shoulders. "I expect so, otherwise he wasn't likely to write so much. Beyond that, I can't say. No telling how long the bottle drifted in the currents before the shark swallowed it. Says here at the top to deliver it to a Monsieur Jules Verne, from Île Feydeau. That's you, isn't it?"

Stunned, Verne stepped back into his room, holding the pages as if they were a rare treasure map. "Yes. Thank you. Thank you."

He had no money to tip the sailor, and he hoped his father had at least paid the man something for his trouble. The stranger didn't seem to expect money, though, and turned to depart without further formalities. Verne recalled that the brotherhood of the sea obliged sailors to perform such services for each other.

Nevertheless, he was relieved when the intimidating man creaked his way down the long staircase. Verne locked the door. He moved aside the volume of Shakespeare and sat down in a cold sweat. A strange amazement warmed his heart as he stared at the pages.

He read all through the night and well past dawn, astonished at the ordeals Nemo had undergone on the mysterious island. But the story came to an abrupt end after the pirate attack, without a resolution. Verne sat up, trembling, and wondered what had happened to his friend next.

VIII

As the weird, unchanging days passed, Nemo lost track of how many times he slept or ate. Estimating as best he could, he marked notches on the mushroom logs to make a crude calendar. The endless twilight passed in a haze of monotony as he continued to drift across the underground sea.

The character of the sky began to change so subtly that Nemo failed to notice at first. But then he saw that the air overhead had acquired a swirling, oily color, as if the cavernous ceiling had trapped strange thunderclouds. To him, it looked like a manifestation of the brooding vengeance he'd held for so many years against Captain Noseless and the pirates. Fluid arcs of electricity danced about, fading and vanishing . . . not exactly lightning, but pulses of electric current, discharges from some mammoth dynamo.

He sat up on the swaying raft, feeling a strong metallic-smelling wind in his face. The placid water around him had become restless. In the distance ahead, where the flow was carrying him, he could make out the frothy choppiness of a brewing storm that increased in intensity. Nemo's raft began to jostle and shake. Strange buzzing *cracks* stuttered through the air – not quite thunder, but something more exotic.

Deep in the strangely thick water, he noticed the movement of large, shadowy shapes. *Titanic silhouettes.* Not far away, a slick form like the back of a whale breached the surface and then plunged down again. Nemo withdrew to the center of his raft, though it offered little protection, exposed as he was. From his brief glimpse, Nemo knew that what he had seen was no whale or cachalot.

Another jolt of eerie *crackles* around him was broken by the sound of a huge beast emerging from the water. Its mottled back was studded with fins and armored with overlapping scales. Ice-pick fangs filled its long, narrow snout, like some hideous nightmare that had been the precursor to crocodiles. Black eyes like impenetrable volcanic glass stared at him.

Nemo remembered sketches of fossils from Verne's science magazines and noted that this creature was similar to an aquatic reptile called an ichthyosaur. The hungry-looking beast swirled in the stormy water and approached his raft. Gritting his teeth, Nemo withdrew his pistols and made sure both were loaded. He also propped the long cutlass in front of him.

Before the crocodile-beast could attack, however, a second prehistoric monster burst above the water, its head long and sinuous. Its forelimbs were wide flippers, like the rudders of a boat. Seeing its competitor, the new creature struck like an oceanic dragon. It was a sea monster reminiscent of maritime legends Nemo had heard on the docks in Nantes.

This ferocious sea serpent was by no means his rescuer, though. Nemo paddled frantically, doubting he had the strength to push his boat through choppy waters while these two titans battled. The sea serpent fell upon the first monster, striking with its snakelike neck and wide-open jaws. It bit deep into the dorsal flesh of the other, which snapped back until it tore a bloody shred from a flipper.

Both aquatic dinosaurs chomped and hissed. The crocodile monster thrashed again, tearing a gash in the neck of the sea serpent. But the other monster was larger and more powerful, and as the two battled, the grayish water turned crimson. The sea serpent bit hard, using its unwounded flipper to roll the other dinosaur over so it could avoid the sharp, spiny fins on its enemy's back. Then it bit deep into the soft, white underbelly.

The doomed creature squealed and splashed, but its long snout snapped on empty air. The sea serpent disemboweled it, ripping open the tough hide and spilling ichthyosaur entrails into the stormy subterranean sea.

Its teeth bloodied, the sea serpent struck again and again, taking a mouthful of meat each time, stripping the flesh off the cartilage and bones. As the carcass sank into the red water, the sea serpent circled.

Paddling with all his strength, Nemo had put some distance between his raft and the frothing combat. He had his cutlass and his pistols, but he doubted either would be sufficient to defeat the remaining monster. As the sea serpent turned its head, its obsidian eyes spotted the mushroom raft and the young man paddling. The sea serpent glided toward him.

Nemo got to his feet, cutlass in one hand and pistol in the other. He glared at the beast, as if his anger alone would be sufficient to drive it away. He shouted a blood-curdling scream. He had come too far and fought too hard to end up in a mindless animal's belly.

The wind increased, sweeping his shaggy hair around his face, but a defiant Nemo stood to meet the oncoming monster. The sea serpent circled the raft, more curious than hungry after its feast of the ichthyosaur. The sinuous neck rose up like a mammoth cobra's.

Unflinching, Nemo pointed the pistol at what he hoped was a vulnerable point for his single lead shot. The sea serpent opened its jaws and struck as if it expected no struggle from this morsel. Seizing the opportunity, Nemo screamed another challenge and fired the pistol into the pink flesh of its mouth. The sea serpent jerked back with a roar, startled as much from the loud *bang* as from the bullet sting.

Nemo dropped the now-useless pistol and yanked the second one from his belt, knowing he'd have no time to reload. Only one shot remained. After that, he would have to defend himself with the pirate's sword – and he vowed to hurt the monster as much as possible.

The sea serpent lunged again, faster this time. Nemo tried to remain steady on the rocking raft as he aimed for the beast's eye. When he fired, the puff of smoke obscured his vision at first, and then he saw that he had missed. Just barely. A bright splatter of red appeared below the sea serpent's left eyelid, perhaps enough to blind the beast from that side – certainly enough to cause it further pain. And rage.

Thrashing, the sea serpent submerged and doubled back for another attack. Nemo grasped the cutlass, turning in slow circles, feet spread on the uncertain deck of his raft. Around him, the thunderous *cracks* grew louder, and the wind howled as the magnetic storm grew in intensity.

With an explosive thrust, the sea serpent surfaced under the raft. Its armored head crashed through the tough mushroom structure, snapping Nemo's braided vine ropes. The raft broke into matchstick pieces in the water. The mushroom-cap pontoons broke free, and debris drifted in all directions. Nemo somehow held onto his sword as he plunged beneath the surface, taking an unexpected gulp of bitter water. He thrashed about, unable to hide in the ocean. He tried to reach the raft debris, where he could continue to fight.

At any moment he expected to find himself in the gullet of the sea monster, crushed in those jaws. He struggled to a floating toadstool cap and hung on with one hand. The enormous sea serpent rose beneath him, its head brushing against Nemo's legs. Out of instinct and fury, he swung with the cutlass and struck a deep gash across the beast's snout.

The sea serpent withdrew, and Nemo hauled himself into the bowl of the buoyant mushroom cap. The storm had turned into an electrical gale, and liquid lightning sparked through the air all around. The mushroom cap twirled and bobbed, nauseating him. He could see no way out of the crisis.

The serpent lurched up again, dripping blood from minor wounds. It looked straight down at Nemo – yet it came no closer, turning its head uneasily.

Gripping the puny cutlass, Nemo waited for the killing blow, tensing to make a final thrust. He planned to die fighting, never giving up. Instead, the dinosaur's serpentine head dipped beneath the water and vanished from sight.

Knowing it was sure to attack again, Nemo clung to the frilled sides of the mushroom lifeboat. But when he heard a change in the storm, he looked around to pinpoint the source of the growing din – and beheld a natural force awesome enough to frighten away even the sea serpent.

An enormous funnel bore down on him, howling and buzzing like a million souls in pain. The pillar of wind and water extended from the sea at the center of the earth, high up out of sight to the distant cavern ceiling: a waterspout with all the titanic strength of the greatest cyclone. It came churning across the sea – and drew Nemo inexorably toward it.

The mushroom cap spun around. Nemo clung to its sides as the waves churned, and whitecaps splashed over the rim. More fluid lightning skittered through the air. Nemo hung on for his life as he stared in awe.

The whirlpool hurled him around as if in an aquatic game of crack-the-whip. The waterspout drew him into its core like a grain of sand sucked into a hollow reed. He felt as if the wet skin was being torn off his bones. His eyelids were drawn open, his lips stretched back by centrifugal force.

The mushroom boat whirled and spun, and Nemo barely managed to hang on. Suffocation from the surrounding spray and the crushing weight of gravity filled him with black unconsciousness. He had no way to fight this.

He let out a long wordless cry of defiance, but even that sound was torn from him by the fury of the cyclone. . .

IX

Alexandre Dumas had designed his "Monte Cristo" chateau to resemble a fairy-tale castle, complete with turrets and Gothic towers. Across the expansive grounds, elm trees surrounded the main buildings and bordered artificial lakes that looked like sapphires. Swans drifted in the water, and raucous peacocks strutted across the manicured lawns. Topiary hedges and exquisite flowers added a filigree of colors to the landscape.

It all seemed like a fantasy to Jules Verne, which was no doubt the impression the great author wanted to cultivate.

Inside the main building, the writer's kitchen was immense (as was Dumas himself). The heavyset man waited for Verne, already wearing an apron; he held out another for his guest. Every imaginable cooking instrument lay strewn across an oak table, along with tomes of recipes that Dumas had compiled from all over the world.

Verne took deep breaths to calm himself in the face of such extravagance. He had never cooked in such a kitchen before; in fact, he'd made little more than cabbage soup for a long time. He had lost sleep for days – first out of amazement from reading Nemo's incredible journal, and now terrified that he might make a poor impression on the literary master. Too much was happening at once, and his studies were beginning to suffer.

If he ruined this family-recipe omelet he had bragged about, Verne might as well maroon himself on a deserted island.

But when he began cooking, he relaxed, cracking four eggs into the hot pan. With a smile on his face, he took out the secret packet of herbs he'd compiled in his room. He did not intend to show Dumas the exact ingredients, since he wanted to maintain a mysterious air. The enormous writer seemed amused by the pretense and brushed his thick, ring-heavy fingers on his apron strings, watching the preparations carefully.

Verne finished his fluffy creation and, beaming with pride, served it on a plain white plate. Despite his worries, the omelet neither stuck to the pan nor turned brown, nor did it break when his shaking hands used a spatula to remove it. He had added just the right amount of butter, sliced the mushrooms perfectly, added the precise dash of pungent herbs.

With minimal conversation, Dumas and Verne shared the omelet at a small servant's table inside the kitchen. Then the big man insisted Verne cook him a second one, which he devoured by himself. "Delicious!"

Later, Dumas showed the aspiring author around the chateau buildings and across the grounds. Verne grinned with delight, absorbing every detail, already promising himself that he, too, would live in a similar chateau someday (when he was a literary master as well). Servants worked in the various buildings, performing their never-ending tasks.

Dumas took him in a small boat out to an isolated island in the center of the estate's largest artificial pond. "Here, my friend, is where I do my writing, where no one can disturb me. I require complete silence to do my work."

Verne could see at a glance that the large gazebo was designed for creating literary masterpieces. Dumas stood at the doorway to his writing abode. "I must have concentration, you see. I've produced over four hundred short stories, plays, and novels in the last twenty years. I have a reputation to maintain – as well as my momentum!"

Dumas had been called a "fiction factory," and in order to maintain his prodigious output, he hired other writers to complete many scenes in his books. He concocted the stories and the characters himself, but sometimes he needed others to bother with the details.

"I admire you, Monsieur Dumas." Verne raised his chin. "I study law at my father's insistence, but I have literary ambitions of my own. Someday, I hope to be as successful as you are. I will work very hard at it."

Dumas laughed, dark chins jiggling. His chuckles echoed across the placid water. One of the swans stirred, then settled down as if it had heard the booming laughter many times before. "Oh, ho! I respect a young man with ambition and drive." Dumas raised eyebrows on a dusky forehead. "But do you have the necessary discipline and persistence, mmm?"

"I do," Verne said, then surprised himself with his own brazenness. "Would you help me, monsieur? Would you show me how to become a great writer like yourself?"

Dumas laughed again, but looked more seriously at his guest. "That remains to be seen, my friend. Many novices make the same request, but few are willing to do the necessary hard work."

"Oh, I *will* work. I've already completed two major historical plays and one comedy." He chastised himself for not having brought them along, for just such an opportunity.

"Oh, ho! Then I should like to read them."

Verne couldn't tell if the huge author truly meant it, or if he had simply expressed the sentiment out of a perceived obligation to his guest. He hoped for some advice – or better yet, connections. Dumas had it in his power to introduce him to the important publishers in Paris. Verne prayed the famous man might even hire him to help draft some of his scenes.

Verne looked around the isolated island study surrounded by beautiful trees, well-maintained gardens, and the fancifully decorated buildings of Monte Cristo. He longed for such fame and fortune. How could he ever hope for such luxury as a . . . as a country lawyer?

Many had aspired to similar success, but as he looked into the sepia eyes of the "fiction factory" himself, Verne also knew that he was different from all those others. He *would* work hard enough. He *would* be disciplined so that one day he could make a living by writing stories and plays.

The thought excited him vastly more than the prospect of an unending future as a small-town attorney, no matter what his father said. Verne vowed to stay close to Alexandre Dumas and learn everything he could from the master.

X

With the force of trapped pressure from below, the steam vent blasted Nemo into open air like a geyser. Stunned but protected inside the tough mushroom cap, Nemo was hurled high into the sky – a *blue sky* studded with real clouds – only to tumble down in a shower of sulfurous rain.

Around him, like a stark dream, he saw rough lava rocks and the curved wall of a volcanic crater. And snow . . . snow everywhere.

Then he slammed into the ground with an impact that knocked the wind out of him and drove all the senses from his brain.

Nemo awoke to find himself sprawled in a desolate caldera among the chunks of his shattered fungus lifeboat. At least the spongy mushroom flesh had cushioned his fall.

Groggy, he raised his head and looked at his surroundings, a rocky wasteland frosted with ice and snow. Brimstone-smelling fumaroles hissed from the inner walls of the volcanic crater.

When he sat up, shaking his head to clear the fuzziness of pain and unconsciousness, he was startled to see a man dressed in warm clothes standing behind him up the slope. The man, with spectacles and a neat white beard, furrowed his brow in perplexity as he appraised this strange and unexpected offering from the volcano.

He spoke in a nasal, looping language that Nemo did not understand. The young man shook his head, and the stranger spoke again in a different language, one he recognized as German. When finally the man attempted French, Nemo understood him. "I certainly hope you can explain your presence, monsieur," the stranger said. "I am most curious."

These were the first friendly words Nemo had heard in more than seven years – since the day he had climbed to the lookout post of the *Coralie* under Captain Grant's orders and saw a pirate ship approaching.

"I . . . can explain myself." His little-used voice sounded rusty and hoarse in his throat. "But I don't know if you'll believe me."

XI

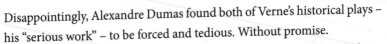

Disappointingly, Alexandre Dumas found both of Verne's historical plays – his "serious work" – to be forced and tedious. Without promise.

On his way back from his second trip to Monte Cristo two weeks later, Verne sulked in the carriage, staring at the piles of paper on which Dumas had scrawled his comments. The wheels crashed over a pothole, and Verne didn't even look up. He flipped from page to page, eyes burning, face hot, as he read insult after insult. Did the great man think he had no talent at all?

He picked up the next manuscript and tossed aside the romantic poetry – "pure drivel" – that he had also presented to Dumas. Verne wanted to just throw himself from the carriage and into the Seine. A man like Dumas couldn't possibly be wrong in his opinion.

Oddly, the enormous writer had actually found merit in a light romantic farce Verne had written, called *Broken Straws*. Still stinging from the criticism of his more ambitious works, Verne reread the encouragement as if he were swallowing medicine. In his own mind, this piece was but a slight comedy, nothing respectable, nothing like the important works of Balzac or Hugo. . . . But it buoyed up his confidence to read the words, in Dumas's own hand, that *Broken Straws* showed a bit of promise. "With appropriate fixing."

Then the most enthralling note of all: Dumas promised to stage the humorous production at his Théâtre Historique, after Verne (and Dumas) had made the necessary revisions.

* * *

Although *Broken Straws* was lost in the volume of plays and operas performed on the boulevard du Temple, it drew enough of an audience that it played for twelve nights running. This earned Jules Verne a few sous and, most important, paid back the production costs, so that it was not the utter failure he had feared it might be.

Heady with success and delighted at the expansive future before him, Verne did everything that Dumas suggested to him, though the great novelist still didn't ask him to join his stable of writing assistants. Verne would somehow have to make it on his own, work harder, try over and over again . . . and still maintain his legal studies, so that his father never knew.

Dumas urged Verne to write articles for popular science magazines and the children's publications of the day. Verne made only a little money at this, but even a few extra coins per month helped – and he was taking tentative steps down a glorious literary path that stretched in front of him. Seeing his name in print provided more excitement than the best passing grade in the most difficult of classes.

Jules Verne decided he just might become an author after all . . . if only he could find something interesting enough to write *about*.

XII

Nemo's bespectacled rescuer was named Arne Saknussemm, a cave explorer and amateur geologist, who enjoyed poking around in volcanic craters. He helped Nemo to his feet, steadying him on the steep slope of rubble.

"Which island is this?" Nemo shivered in his tattered clothes that had been pieced together for use in a tropical climate. "Where am I? It's so cold."

Saknussemm scratched his trim beard. "This is Iceland, monsieur. You are inside the crater of the volcano Scartaris."

Nemo reeled. *Iceland*? He had come from his mysterious island in the South China Sea. Yet he had descended close to the center of the hollow earth, drifted across a subterranean ocean, and emerged again at a different point on the earth's surface.

As Saknussemm led him up a toiling path to the crater rim, the old mountaineer explained that he had studied countless texts in many languages. "There's not much else to do on this island. The winters are long and hard, and I enjoy sitting by the fireplace."

Saknussemm had noticed a blast of steam venting from the volcano and had come to investigate. The mountaineer had witnessed any number of geological marvels – but never a bedraggled young man emerging from under the earth.

Nemo's limbs trembled with relief. He was unable to believe he had reached human company in a place which, while not exactly civilized, was at least a recognizable point on a map. From here, he could find passage back to Europe – back to France.

Back . . . home.

The two climbed to the rim of the tall volcano. Nemo looked across the sparkling glaciers and the white peaks of the great island that had been settled by Vikings so long before. Despite the breathtaking scenery, the wonder that captivated Nemo most was simply the sight of the bright yellow sun in a blue sky – where it belonged.

Saknussemm took Nemo back to his home, where the young man stayed for several months, recuperating and learning what had happened in the world during his absence (though Iceland was by no means privy to the most recent news, either).

It took Saknussemm until late spring to arrange passage for his guest aboard one of the infrequent sailing ships. Over many quiet nights, Nemo repaid his host by recounting his strange adventures on the island and in the fascinating subterranean world. The geologist queried him about the fine points of his story, hearing Nemo's tale with keen interest. The wise old mountaineer displayed far less skepticism than Nemo had expected.

When at last it came time for Nemo's ship to depart for Norway, the two made their way to the port of Reykjavik. Nemo embraced the mountaineer and said his farewells, then went aboard. He was a passenger this time, with a little spending money, fresh clothes – and a burning need to return to France. And Caroline. And Jules.

Nemo waited on deck, facing into the blustery high-latitude winds as the crew prepared the ship for departure. The vessel sailed away from Iceland.

Within a week after Nemo had gone, Arne Saknussemm gathered supplies and struck out for the mountains again, climbing the cone of Scartaris and intending to find a passage that would take him to the centre of the earth. . .

XIII

With its wooden siding and many narrow windows, the playhouse in Nantes seemed so much smaller and less impressive than even the minor theatres in Paris – but still, this was his *home town*. Jules Verne relished the thought of seeing *Broken Straws* performed for an audience he had known since childhood . . . and terrified as to what his parents would think. He attended every rehearsal, to ensure the best performance possible.

While in Nantes, he stayed at his parents' home, though Pierre Verne didn't know what to say about his son's unexpected literary ambitions. Surely, his parents would relish the fame as much as Verne did. "As long as you don't get too serious about it, Jules," Sophie had cautioned in the wake of her husband's stern admonitions for him to continue his efforts in the legal profession. It meant little to them that he had the unflagging support of the literary master Alexandre Dumas, but neither of his parents were readers of note.

In high spirits after the successful run at the Théâtre Lyrique in Paris, Verne had contacted Caroline Aronnax, back on Île Feydeau. (He still could not bring himself to think of her as Madame Hatteras.) The date had already been set for the performance in Nantes. Costumes had been made, and dress rehearsals had begun. Verne wanted Caroline to be there to share his moment of glory. It would be his finest hour, and he wanted her beside him, regardless of her marital status.

Urged on by his free-loving literary friends, and embarrassed by his continued bachelorhood, Verne had taken the train back to Nantes for the local theater production of *Broken Straws*. Using expensive paper and his best penmanship, he sent Caroline a special invitation to join him in his private box.

She had come to meet him at the train station, waving to welcome Verne back to Nantes. Cocking a parasol on her left shoulder, she allowed him to take her arm, which made Verne so giddy he could barely walk in a straight line. She strolled beside him along the street toward the blossoming lime trees in front of the Church of St Martin. "I look forward to your play, Jules, and I gladly accept your invitation to attend."

Behind them, the train let out a shrill whistle then began to chug away from the station. Loud bells clanged the hour at the distant dockyards.

Even through misty eyes, Verne could see that Caroline's smile looked friendly, but no more than that. "However, I believe it would be better if I sat a few rows away. Remember, I am a married woman, Jules."

In the two years Verne had been in Paris, Caroline's husband had sent no word about his search for the Northwest Passage. No one had heard from Captain Hatteras or his crew. Granted, the *Forward* had undertaken a long and hard journey, and it was still possible that everything had gone as planned . . . but she had been with her husband for only a short time in the first place, and now Caroline lived as a veritable widow – in reality, if not in fact. . .

Some time back, when Verne had informed her of receiving Nemo's letter and journal, Caroline had been overjoyed and vowed to do something about it. She had rallied support from her father's merchant fleet, and Monsieur Aronnax had sent letters to shipping companies and foreign ambassadors. The respected merchant had, after all, made the original arrangements to have Nemo ship out on Captain Grant's last voyage. Everyone agreed to search for the mysterious island, using the best descriptions in Nemo's handwritten journal – but there could be little hope of finding an uncharted speck of land in such a vast seascape.

Verne, however, knew never to underestimate his friend. Nemo had survived for years alone. He must still be alive. . .

On the opening night of *Broken Straws*, Nantes received Jules Verne as a minor celebrity, and he passed the hours in a daze. During the performance he looked across several rows of seats to catch Caroline's sparkling eyes. His heart warmed when he saw her laugh at the witticisms in his play, at the farcical plot. When the curtain dropped, she was the first to surge to her feet and clap her hands, beaming with obvious pride.

Blushing, Verne pretended to be humbled by the applause and adulation of his former townspeople. But it didn't last.

Though it was a gloomy autumn day in Paris, Verne felt confined and stifled inside his chill room. He decided to eat his lunch outside, despite the rain.

Though safely back among the literary salons and the intelligentsia, he continued to be troubled by unsettled digestion. As a student on a meager budget (much of which went to purchase books and library services), Verne ate far too much cabbage soup and far too little meat. After his success in the Nantes playhouse, he had hoped for a bit more extravagance and luxury in his life, but so far he had seen none of it.

After buttoning his thin coat, Verne gathered a broken half of stale baguette he'd bought at discount the day before and the dregs of a cheap bottle of wine. Not quite the same as when he'd dined at Monte Cristo with Alexandre Dumas. . .

He planned to carry his umbrella and sit out in the damp, just breathing and thinking, allowing his imagination to roam. He could soak up the details of life and people around him – as the great Dumas had suggested he do. It would be fodder for his writing.

Verne glanced out his narrow window and, looking down to the wet streets below, saw a huddled man facing the sidewalk. Paris had many vagrants and strangers, but they had never troubled him. As a student, Verne had few items worth stealing anyway.

Holding his bread, his bottle, and his umbrella, he stepped outside and drew a deep fresh breath. He strode out with his long legs, determined to reach a quiet spot on the Seine at the northern edge of the Latin Quarter, where he could ruminate while he ate his lunch.

Before he could move down the block, the bundled stranger turned and raised a hand. "Jules!" came an astonished voice. "Jules Verne, is it you?"

Verne stopped and looked around, but saw no one else on the street, no place he could hide. He became wary, afraid that this might be some beggar or cutpurse . . . though he had no money for either.

But as the stranger came forward, Verne stared at the dark hair and dark eyes, the changed shape of the face, now drawn and weathered . . . but still with a hint of boyhood familiarity. Verne opened and closed his mouth, yet could not force words to come out. He was unable to believe what he was seeing. The man came forward and embraced him.

Nemo had returned.

PART V
PARIS IN THE 20TH CENTURY

I

Nantes, 1852

Standing on the quay, Nemo looked across the Nantes shipyards, shading his dark eyes. It had been more than a decade since he'd departed on Captain Grant's ship, three years since he'd returned – and so much had changed, both in the world and in himself. He was a man now, though surrounded by boyhood memories that haunted this place – the best of times and the darkest of nightmares.

In the dry dock shells and launching ramps at Île Feydeau, he heard loud voices talking, mallets pounding. Someone with a squeeze box sang out a ribald tune to keep his mates moving as they strung rigging on a new ship. His heart grew heavy as he thought of his kind-hearted father working on the doomed *Cynthia*. How many ships and sailors had gone in and out of this port since Nemo had left as a cabin boy aboard the *Coralie*?

The tall ships were still here. A few clippers and brigs continued to sail up the Loire bringing in cargo from the Atlantic, though the main business of the city now centered on shipbuilding. The future of Nantes lay in that industry, and now – by the command of Napoleon III himself – it was

Nemo's job to modernize the old shipyards, to prepare them for the next century.

As a young man, André Nemo had left home penniless and fatherless, with no future. Now, with a commission from the Emperor of France, rebuilding the shipyards of Nantes would be but one of Nemo's complex projects.

Since his return from far-off Iceland three years ago, Nemo had attracted much attention because of his extraordinary adventures. But he hadn't wanted to become a celebrity. Instead, he had used his modest fame to arrange for a formal education – something he could not have achieved as a mere orphan who'd served on a lost sailing ship (and a British-commissioned one, at that).

During his time on the island he'd already learned how to put his imagination to practical use. Before, he'd had access to nothing more than the knowledge in poor Captain Grant's small library. Now, his engineering studies at the Paris Academy opened a new world of resources, and he excelled in public service by using his own skills combined with the raw materials and budget of the country.

The elected president of France, Louis Napoleon, had settled the unrest after the revolutions of 1848 and recently declared himself emperor. To shore up his public image and continue the illusion of working to benefit everyday lives, Emperor Napoleon III undertook numerous construction projects. The work had shaken the revolution-scarred populace toward a grudging optimism.

"The empire means peace," Napoleon III had said in one grand speech. "We have immense tracts of uncultivated lands to clear, roads to open, ports to create, canals to finish, our railway network to complete. These are the conquests I am contemplating, and all French people are my soldiers." Napoleon wanted Paris to make great strides ahead of the rest of Europe. France would lurch into the future, advancing toward the 20th century, years before its time.

So, André Nemo worked to design bridges and towers, and, because of his successes, he was also chosen to redesign the shipyards in his home town of Nantes. He would improve its capabilities as a port and industrial center, and increase its commercial value for foreign trade. The future looked very bright indeed.

Now, Nemo stood on the docks and made a mental list of proposed changes – dredging the estuary to accommodate larger vessels, widening and reinforcing the quays. He would suggest adding two more dry dock facilities on either side of the river, and he would recommend that the shipyards concentrate on building new clippers, which were in heavy demand for passengers as well as perishable cargo. The first merchant to bring a new harvest to market always commanded the highest price, and clippers could deliver tea from China or delicate spices from the Indies faster than any competitor.

Coming up the Loire with demonic snorting and clanking, a tall-funneled steamer approached the docks. Gouts of smoke poured from its stack, while paddles churned the river. Nemo had seen only a few of these so-called "pyroscaphes," named after the Greek for "fire ship." With continuing progress, he suspected the vessels would become more common, and noisier and smellier.

Nemo paced up and down the riverbank, lost in his own world. He had let his dark hair grow long, as was the fashion in Paris, and he sported a mustache and goatee. Every time he looked in the mirror, he still expected to see the imaginative boy who had left Île Feydeau; instead, he saw an adult stranger.

Out of practice for a decade, Nemo struggled to readjust to a modern life back among civilized men. After two years aboard an English exploration ship, after battling pirates, suffering hardships on his mysterious island, and exploring the catacombs beneath the earth, Nemo no longer knew how to exist as part of calm French society with its intricate politics and convoluted social graces.

Emperor Napoleon had entrusted him with a good many important projects. Yet, the more he worked on them, the more Nemo missed the challenge of constructing a simple counterweight elevator or excavating his cave dwelling. Despite its glamour and all the fineries, the availability of resources, this civilized life was dull and mundane. He had little patience for government bureaucracies and budgetary constraints, for deciding how best to widen roads in France's rural departments.

Now, he gazed back down the Loire, picturing in his mind where it drained into the sea at Paimbœuf. Far beyond, lay the Americas or Africa or the South Sea islands. Strange places to explore, mountains to climb, jungles to investigate. He sighed wistfully, then looked at the clock on a nearby church tower just as the bells began to ring the hour. It was time for the meeting he'd both longed for and dreaded.

Caroline would be waiting for him.

In new clothes and stiff boots, Nemo strode down the narrow streets of Île Feydeau to the row houses at the water's edge. He walked beyond the piers into the older, more expensive section of town until he reached the offices of "Aronnax, Merchant," which had been owned by Caroline's father.

The gray-painted wooden doors were open to let in a fresh spring breeze and the smell of flowers. Inside the business offices at rows of varnished tables and desks, diligent clerks jotted down manifests in thick ledgers. Others pored over the financial records of various shipments, while one rail-thin man placed pins on a chart of shipping routes, presumably marking the estimated positions of the Aronnax fleet.

Nemo paused in the tall doorway, a stranger, still uncertain of himself. Already, this seemed so strange. Because he had spent so many years without the need for speech, Nemo often found it difficult to begin a conversation. Two of the clerks looked up with questioning gazes, but before anyone could ask his business, Caroline emerged from a back room.

When she saw him, the sun rose on her face. "André!" Caroline had grown beyond the pretty young girl he had fallen in love with – she was still as beautiful, but more filled out, taller, more self-assured.

He'd seen her briefly several times since his return to France, but he hadn't yet grown accustomed to how much she had blossomed. Instead of the barely contained rebellion that had always shown in her blue eyes, Caroline now carried a hard business sense, a sharp intelligence, and a resolve that had not been there before. She had fought hard to reach her place here, and she would not let anything budge her from her position.

"I am so glad to see you." She came forward, stopping close to him.

"*Bonjour*, Madame Hatteras," he said, though it hurt him to remind her of her husband, who still hadn't returned from his polar voyage, even after four years. Nemo longed to kiss her, but instead forced himself to maintain his honor and his distance. After a brief, awkward pause, they shook hands like two business associates.

After taking over her father's shipping offices, Caroline had dispensed with the flowery colors and frills she'd worn as a young woman. Now she wore a gray woollen suit and a broad hoop skirt; she had more important things to do than bow to social niceties and expectations. Since her marriage to Captain Hatteras, Caroline had used her time and her intelligence well, carving her world into the shape *she* preferred, rather than the other way around. Nemo was proud of her.

"Shall we go, André?" She slid her arm through his and allowed him to escort her out of the merchant offices. He felt a cold sweat break out down his back. "I'm sure Jules is already at the cafe waiting for us." She turned a hard gaze to the clerks, who still seemed disconcerted at having a strong, independent woman as their boss. "The employees can do without me for a short while. They know who pays their salaries."

Caroline's father had died in 1849, mere weeks after a terrible altercation with his office manager. At the height of the argument, Monsieur Aronnax had fired the man on the spot; thereafter, indignant, he proceeded to work himself to the bone, refusing to hire a replacement.

Without revealing that she had secretly studied the workings of the shipping business for years, Caroline stepped in to assist her father as a surrogate office manager. Monsieur Aronnax brooded over how his supposed successor had betrayed him, while inadvertently continuing his daughter's training. When he'd died suddenly, the master merchant had appointed no official replacement, which left the business operations in turmoil.

Caroline, bearing the name and fortune of Captain Hatteras, stepped in to take over the business. The daughter of Monsieur Aronnax marched into the offices with a vengeance, sat at her father's big mahogany desk as if marking her territory, and began issuing orders. This had scandalized the conservative clerks, and she released two of them at once when they refused to follow her orders.

The former office manager, who had been discharged by her father, fought Caroline, insisting that a married daughter with an absent husband was not fit to run a great shipping company. He attempted to buy "Aronnax, Merchant" at a low price that would have devastated the family.

Caroline's bereaved mother understood nothing of the work, had never bothered even to know the names or trade routes of the Aronnax ships. After a long, tear-filled evening Caroline had convinced her mother not to sell, and suggested that she herself should acquire the rights to the company, ostensibly in the name of Captain Hatteras. But there would still be a legal fight.

Because of her long friendship with Jules Verne, Caroline had gone to his father as an attorney to challenge the contested ownership. Instead, the dour man with bushy gray sideburns had shaken his head. "I'm afraid there's nothing you can do, Madame Hatteras. A woman cannot run a business. You must sell."

Frustrated, she realized that Monsieur Verne had only enough legal knowledge for filling out ordinary wills and property deeds, and very little fire in his belly. She had long ago learned from Nemo never to give up, and so she continued to press the issue on her own. Caroline had taken a train to Paris, where she found an ambitious and vociferous attorney, who handily won her case. So, for three years, she'd been the owner and manager of "Aronnax, Merchant" – and she reveled in the challenge.

Now, Nemo and Caroline walked together under the sunshine toward their favorite bistro, and he looked at her, proud of what she'd accomplished.

Her other options had been to sit at home or become a society lady – neither of which fit Caroline at all. The gossips still talked about the scandal of the female merchant (but then, they always would), even though Caroline had been extraordinarily successful in rebuilding the family business according to her own instincts. She had uncanny luck in choosing paths and cargoes.

At home, alone, she wrote her own music as she had always dreamed of doing, maintaining the fiction of the non-existent composer "Passepartout," to whom she gave all the credit . . . though few people questioned her about it any more. Even her loyal maidservant Marie had married a tradesman and had left service.

Strolling along, he enjoyed Caroline's company. "I wish we could be alone," Nemo said. "It's so difficult, and I have so much I want to say."

Caroline shook her head. "We can't – and you should not." Then she smiled. "But I know what you must be thinking, even after all this time."

The two of them arrived at the open-air coffee shop next to the flower stalls and pastry vendors. Jules Verne, still tall and thin but sporting a new beard, waved at them. He had already ordered pots of dark coffee and *chocolat chaud* and munched on a gooseberry tart while he waited, wiping sticky jam from his lips. During his visits home from the Paris Academy, Verne made every effort to replenish himself in preparation for his fourth and final year at law school.

A disappointed frown crossed his face when he saw Caroline on Nemo's arm. She released her light touch as they both walked toward Verne's table. He stood halfway up to greet her, and she kissed the young man on his red-bearded cheek. "Thank you for waiting, Jules."

Blushing, Verne pushed one of the pastries toward the chair she had selected, then self-consciously wiped crumbs from his lips with a stained napkin. "I've ordered us some cheese, and I chose a currant pastry for you, Caroline. I know that's your favorite." It occurred to Nemo how much his friend looked like a wide-eyed puppy, eager to please.

Before Nemo could say anything, Verne turned to him, full of energy and news. "I've received a letter from one of the ships that went searching for your island, André. There's been a volcanic eruption in the vicinity of the coordinates you gave. Maybe your island has sunk."

"Like Atlantis," Caroline said, her blue eyes shining.

Nemo nodded sadly. "That could well be. The volcano was restless when I entered its caves."

"It's a good thing you left when you did." Verne scratched his curly hair, then took a bite of the nearest pastry, licking his fingers. Nemo poured a cup of *chocolat chaud* for Caroline and himself. Verne continued to watch them from across the table, as if keeping track of how often they looked at one another.

"And for you, Caroline, I've asked one of my lecturers at the Paris school." When Verne awkwardly cleared his throat, he looked very much like a lawyer. "I can draw up the papers if you like. In three more years, with no word from the *Forward*, it –" He hesitated, then forced himself to go on in a somber voice. "It is possible to begin proceedings to have Monsieur Hatteras declared lost at sea, if . . . if you should wish to get on with your life, that is." He added in a rush.

Startled, Caroline unconsciously glanced over at Nemo. "Seven years . . ."

"You are still a young woman, Caroline," Verne pressed, "with a great deal to offer –"

Nemo took her hand. "Your suggestion is premature, Jules. Let's wait the proper amount of time first, then let Caroline make her decision. Remember, I was gone for more years than that – and I am most certainly still alive." His voice was stern, alarmed at his friend's impropriety and at Caroline's obvious distress. "We've had enough on the subject for now."

"Running 'Aronnax, Merchant' requires all of my energy, Jules. I am quite content with my life and not anxious to take another husband just yet," Caroline said, but the troubled look on her face and the quick glance she sent Nemo suggested otherwise. "I never gave up hope on you, André."

Verne saw the look and tried to cover his frown, suddenly flustered. "There's no hurry."

Though he continued to dabble at writing plays and poetry, along with his stage manager's job at the theatre, Jules Verne still had too little success to justify any career other than to follow in his father's footsteps. It looked as if it would be an attorney's grave for him. "I'll be required to return home in another year or two after I finish at the Academy. And André, you'll be here at Nantes working on your engineering projects." Verne forced a bittersweet smile. "It could be like old times for the three of us. A world of adventure is waiting."

Nemo heard a ship's bell clanging on the distant quays, sailors shouting to each other as they cast off mooring ropes. His heart felt heavy again, and he looked across at Verne. "I'm not sure we can ever go back to those days."

II

The old stone bridge had been damaged by cannon fire during the revolutions of 1848, but moss, water, and time had weakened the supports long before.

Intent on his work, Nemo stood in knee-deep slimy mud beneath the pilings, searching for cracks, rapping with a steel hammer to listen for soft spots. Waving his hand in front of his face to scatter biting flies, he waded deeper to assess which repairs might be needed.

On the shady bank sat his designated work party, chewing on grass blades. Pieces of wooden scaffolding lay all around them, unassembled; a stonemason mixed a new batch of mortar, though it would probably dry before Nemo came back and told the laborers what to do. . .

While his plans to modernize the Nantes shipyards ground through the endless bureaucracy, he had been recalled to Paris. His sketches and ideas fought for notice among hundreds of worthy projects while the Prefect of the Seine, Baron Haussmann, juggled proposals to make Paris the most magnificent capital in Europe.

In the interim, Nemo dutifully designed reinforcements to weakening bridges or church steeples, and even outlined improvements to the expanding railway network. Though many of his innovative ideas were too strange to be accepted by formally trained engineers, Nemo did his best to find the most efficient way to accomplish each task. He recalled the inspirational words of Napoleon III: "March at the head of the ideas of your century, and those ideas will strengthen and sustain you; march behind them, and they will drag you after them; march against them, and they will overthrow you."

Nemo marched to the rhythm of his own imagination, though often his work crews didn't want to march at all. He slogged dripping out of the water and began to issue orders, already eager to face the challenge of the next job.

Nemo lived alone in a small room at the heart of Paris and often went to operas and the theatre, including several entertaining little farces that Jules Verne had written or staged. Sometimes, he made a point of meeting his red-headed friend, but their lives had diverged enough that the lost years became a gulf between them.

Verne himself had never yet managed to set foot outside of France. The struggling writer was enthralled by parties and literati, but Nemo preferred the silence of his own company to the posturing and naive "intelligentsia" who spouted opinions as if they were facts. The challenge of complex engineering projects was a better fuel to Nemo's imagination. Though the emperor's architectural repairs did not make use of his full abilities, the work kept him busy – and this left his mind free to absorb anything else that interested him.

Nemo wandered through the palatial halls of the Louvre, studying magnificent works of art – most particularly the *Mona Lisa*, an exquisite portrait by Leonardo da Vinci, whose drawings and notebooks had so captivated him aboard the *Coralie*. He also loved to travel to Versailles to admire the architecture of the "palace that was a city" built by Louis XIV.

A single man with no social aspirations, Nemo's tastes did not run to the extravagant. His greatest indulgence was to subscribe to the Parisian science magazines that young Jules Verne had shared with him so many years before. Nemo read voraciously to keep up with new scientific developments, reveling in the tales of explorers seeking wild paths across the globe. With only his memories of distant lands, he traveled in his mind, living vicariously through the other great men of the century.

He thought often of Caroline, though he didn't dare see her more than once every month or two, when business took him back to Nantes. He longed for her and mourned the circumstances that had built a barrier between them. The two of them did, however, exchange a regular correspondence, and he read and reread every note she sent. He would smell the faint scent of her stationery, look at her brisk but delicate handwriting, and imagine her slender fingers holding the pen as she gathered her thoughts.

By now, her husband Captain Hatteras was almost certainly lost at sea . . . but Nemo would not pressure her to file for a death certificate, as Verne had suggested. He would wait and think about her, and when his longing grew too intense, Nemo plunged with greater vigor into his daily work.

After the interminable seven years had passed, things might change for the two of them. He and Caroline had waited for each other so long. . .

One gloomy day in the Paris civil engineering offices, Baron Haussmann presented Nemo with a new assignment. The short-statured man had a cherubic face, and harried, bloodshot eyes. He spoke with a thick German accent. "I now require of you a supreme effort, Monsieur Nemo. It is my intention that you develop a plan for expanding the ancient, overburdened system of storm drains and sewers in Paris." He handed the young engineer a thick roll of oversized papers. "These are the blueprints. Please study them meticulously."

Nemo found it difficult to tap into his reservoir of enthusiasm for such a dreary job. But he took the blueprints, gave a formal nod to the powerful baron, and marched out of the government offices.

That evening, with the dizzying labyrinth of Parisian sewers hammering at his brain, Nemo sank into his reading chair with a cold meal of roast mutton at his side. He buried himself in his scientific magazines. A new issue of the proceedings from Britain's Royal Geographical Society had arrived. Since the articles were all written in English, Nemo kept up his proficiency in the language.

For more than a century, the exploration of darkest Africa had been an obsession of European explorers. Nemo had read with great interest the memoirs of James Bruce, a big-shouldered and tempestuous Scotsman who had traveled through Ethiopia and discovered the source of the Blue Nile in 1770. He also studied the 1799 journals of Mungo Park, who explored the interior of Africa and perished under a native attack on the Niger River.

Now, Nemo read a speech given at the Royal Geographical Society by an eccentric and vociferous – and possibly learned – doctor of biology named Samuel Ferguson. In an uproarious lecture to the Society, Dr Ferguson had proposed the preposterous yet intriguing scheme of taking a hydrogen balloon from the east coast of Africa across the unexplored continent all the way to its western shores. Other travelers tramped through clogged jungles and fever-ridden swamps, tried to navigate crocodile-infested rivers or negotiate foaming cataracts. Ferguson's idea, on the other hand, was to drift calmly *over* the African landscape, as if taking a quiet carriage ride.

The Royal Society had sponsored other expeditions, with the British government adding supplemental funding. Unfortunately, Ferguson's ideas seemed just a bit too unorthodox for the conservative members of the club, and they refused to finance the doctor's proposal. They allowed quite generous grants to numerous other expeditions, making certain that the world was explored and investigated to the fullest extent possible. The Society sent out veritable armies of scientists and collectors to the four corners of the globe.

But not Samuel Ferguson.

Not in the doctor's favor, was the evidence that two of his other "innovative" (or "crackpot") designs had failed to get off the ground, after the Society had funded them, and the members in control of the treasury did not want to waste further money on Ferguson's ideas. His remarkable double-balloon design would not likely progress beyond a scheme on paper.

While sitting in his room, ignoring the dull blueprints of the Paris sewers and storm drains, Nemo thought the explorer's idea had merit, despite his apparent arrogance and blustery personality. As he reread the article, excitement grew within him. But when he studied the diagram for Ferguson's balloon, he realized it would never work.

As planned, the balloon would not have enough carrying capacity for supplies, scientific instruments, and passengers. The vessel would never make it across the continent, but would instead sink into uncharted areas. Nemo had no doubt that if Ferguson persisted in this plan, he would never be heard of again.

Unless the balloon could be modified. . .

Nemo shrugged off all thoughts of Parisian sewers and set to work with pen and paper, making calculations, incorporating his own ideas. He did not sleep, but still felt more refreshed and alive than he had in many months.

III

Standing in front of an imposing door covered with peeling black paint, Nemo rang the English explorer's bell in the middle of the afternoon. He was still breathless but filled with ideas. He had never been to London before.

"I request an audience with Dr Samuel Ferguson, please." Nemo stood straight-backed and unwavering on the doorstep. He had spent his savings on a passage across the English Channel, then took a train into London, where he'd had no difficulty finding the doctor's address.

The gaunt manservant scowled, assessing the young man. He had a high forehead and drooping eyes as gray as winter clouds. His mouth drew together in a pinched frown like a flower bud shriveling in the sun. "And might I inquire as to your business, sir? You sound . . . French."

Nemo blurted out the sentence he had rehearsed, though his English was still a bit rough. "The doctor's proposed balloon design will not work. I have a better idea to share with him."

Skeptical, the manservant stepped back into the foyer and closed the door, leaving the young man to stand on the street. While he waited, Nemo checked his clothes and smoothed his dark hair, making certain he did not appear to be a wild-eyed madman. He tucked his rolled drawings neatly under one arm, as if they were weapons.

When the door was flung open again, Nemo looked up to see a long-legged man with hazel eyes, bushy dark eyebrows, and a ridiculously huge black mustache that balanced like a canoe upon his lip.

"Whatever is the meaning of this, eh?" Ferguson said, like a roaring lion. "How could you possibly know whether or not my balloon will work? Indeed, I have spent hours on the design, and I missed nothing."

Nemo held up his rolls of sketches and designs. "Allow me to show you why, monsieur." Without waiting for permission, he pushed past the doctor and marched down the corridor, following daylight to the large windows in a drawing room. There, he found a writing desk at which Ferguson had been compiling notes and a list. Nemo unrolled his blueprint on the flat surface.

"Why, I don't even know you, sir!" Ferguson hovered behind him. "This is highly irregular."

"Your idea to cross Africa in a balloon is also highly irregular," Nemo pointed out. "And it is brilliant."

"Brilliant, eh? Yes, yes it is. But because of my, er, unfortunate track record with similar balloon designs, the Society chooses to fund more conventional expeditions. I shall never get the chance."

"Your balloon designs are flawed, as I will demonstrate. You, of all people, Dr Ferguson, should listen to an unorthodox concept. I would hate to see your expedition fail because of several miscalculations that could have been avoided. I suspect that your earlier test flights failed for the same reasons."

"But what sort of . . . miscalculations can you mean?" He stroked his thick mustache like a man petting an unlucky cat. "Indeed, I cannot deny that my earlier balloons were disasters, eh?"

Nemo pointed to the columns of numbers, and the flustered doctor scanned them, pretending to redo the math in his head. "You'll need five weeks in a balloon to traverse Africa, monsieur. As is apparent here" – he jabbed a finger at his calculations – "even under favorable winds, you will not have enough flotation for three weeks. Your hydrogen gas will not last for the duration necessary to cross such a distance. Even if the Society had seen fit to fund your expedition, you would have crashed in the middle of the continent."

"Yes, yes, I see now. Perhaps they were wiser to fund traditional overland treks instead, considering. . ." Ferguson nodded, intent. His indignation forgotten, he stared at Nemo's drawing instead. "Indeed."

"My new balloon design *will*, on the other hand, succeed." Nemo squared his shoulders. "I am confident of it."

Ferguson tapped the sketch with his forefinger. "You appear to have two balloons?"

Nemo nodded. "One inside the other, with a valve so that gases communicate from the inner sphere to the outer sphere. I have also developed a mechanism that can heat and recondense the hydrogen gas to increase our buoyancy."

"And the purpose for that is?" Ferguson raised his bushy black eyebrows. He sounded testy now, but Nemo could tell it was only an act. The man was intrigued by the innovative design, and somewhat abashed at the clear mistakes he had made with his own proposal.

"For maneuverability," Nemo said. "In previous travel by balloon, one has been at the mercy of the winds. However, aeronautical studies have proven that the winds blow in different directions at different altitudes. Therefore, we must simply seek a height at which the winds will blow us on our westward course."

"*Our* course? *We*? What do you mean, *we*?"

"I intend to come along, doctor, since the design is mine." Nemo's gaze was calm and unshakeable. "Is that so much to ask?"

"An international expedition, you say? English *and* French? My, that would cause quite a scandal." Then Ferguson's excitement deflated. The long-legged man stepped away from the writing desk. He shook his head. "Alas, it is a moot point now, my friend."

"Why? The design is quite practicable," Nemo insisted. "I know it can take us across Africa."

Ferguson tugged on his enormous mustache, as if trying to remove it from his lip. "No, young man. The problem is with the Royal Geographical Society. They have sent out their quota of explorers already for the coming year. This afternoon they denied my second appeal for expedition funding, and therefore there will be no balloon trip. Unless you have a private fortune of your own, eh?" The doctor chuckled. "And that much I doubt, from your appearance."

Flushed with embarrassment and disappointment, Nemo realized the brashness of his scheme to come here. He should not have bothered the scientist. His new balloon design must have thrown salt on the would-be explorer's wounds.

"I apologize for taking your time, monsieur." Nemo gathered his drawings and backed out of the drawing room. "If circumstances should change, allow me to give you my name and address so that you can contact me."

Ferguson nodded, his thick brows knitting together. "Most certainly, my friend. I admire your verve – and audacity. Reminds me of your Napoleon Bonaparte, eh? Of course, he was defeated in the end, as well."

Nemo took his leave of the Ferguson residence and of London, and returned to his dreary job reconfiguring the sewers of Paris.

Two months later, when the post delivered an exuberant letter from Dr Samuel Ferguson, Nemo read it in his open doorway with great perplexity.

"Yes, my friend! Indeed, this is a most exciting time for us," the Englishman wrote. "I admit that your proposed terms took me by surprise. They are unorthodox, to say the least, and I needed to adjust my mental state to accept them. But why not, eh? The spirit of exploration requires us to open our minds to all things. Very well, young Nemo – as soon as arrangements can be made, we shall all be off to Africa."

Nemo read the note again with a pounding heart, but he could not fathom Ferguson's meaning. Had the Royal Geographical Society changed its mind, considering Nemo's modified balloon design? How had the explorer obtained the finances necessary for such an expedition? Nemo had assessed the costs of constructing his balloon-within-a-balloon, and he knew it would not come cheap.

His head was full of questions, yet it would take time for the post to carry a letter across the channel to London – and Nemo was mad with curiosity. However, before he could compose a note listing his questions, he heard a tentative rapping on his door. Nemo answered the knock to find Caroline standing there in sensible traveling clothes with a small valise at her side. "I hope you were sincere in your wish to travel across Africa, André."

Caroline removed her gloves as she smiled at him. "I have read your letters again and again – the ones in which you tell me of your ideas and your discussions with this Englishman Ferguson? I know this dream has attached itself to your heart."

"Yes, of course," Nemo said, "but –"

"So I wrote to your Dr Ferguson, and I guaranteed him funding for his supplies, his balloon, and his entire expedition. Both my husband Captain Hatteras and 'Aronnax, Merchant' have fortunes to invest. This expedition will honor my husband's lifelong ambitions of exploration. You will accompany the doctor, of course, because this must be your triumph as well as his."

Nemo could not contain his excitement. "Were those the terms Dr Ferguson refers to? That I must accompany him?"

Caroline gave him a mischievous smile, reminding him of the coy young woman he had fallen in love with back in Île Feydeau. But her bright blue eyes had an entirely different sparkle now. "I made my offer contingent upon several conditions. You are not the only one who longs to break free of a dull life here in France, André."

Nemo blinked at her, already sure of what she was going to say.

"The other condition is that *I* undertake this expedition with you and Dr Ferguson."

IV

The British and French press had a field day with Dr Ferguson's preposterous but wonderfully dramatic scheme to cross Africa in a balloon. Jules Verne read about Nemo's involvement in the daily Paris newspapers even before his friend came to see him.

Nemo sent a note asking Verne to meet him that Saturday on the steps of the Louvre. An unsettled Verne went to France's magnificent art museum to hear what Nemo had to say in person . . . and to try to talk him out of the madness, if at all possible.

A light rain and gray skies had deterred the usual crowds, but people still milled about on the sidewalks and grounds, seeking shelter inside. A mushroom forest of umbrellas sprouted on the street corners, like what Nemo had described finding at the center of the earth.

The dark-haired young man stood on the steps, smiling at Verne's approach. As Verne closed his umbrella and shook off the moisture, he saw that Nemo was wet, his long dark drenched, his clothes soaked. Verne raised his eyebrows. "I expected a man so accustomed to the hardships of survival to come prepared with an umbrella against the rain."

Nemo gave Verne a friendly embrace. "A man so accustomed to the hardships of survival does not mind a little moisture."

They passed under the white arches and entered the enormous museum. Verne had seen the exhibits many times before, often in the company of his artistic friends who spent more time criticizing than enjoying the artwork itself. Verne usually kept his opinions to himself, not understanding the complaints.

Together, the two men strolled past paintings of Napoleon Bonaparte, glorified portrayals of the French Revolution, bucolic landscapes, flowers, portraits of forgotten noblemen. In a casual voice that quickly heated with enthusiasm, Nemo laid out his case for the balloon trip, not surprised that his friend was already familiar with the details. Verne grew uncomfortable listening to every sentence, but he could see the fire in Nemo's eyes, the passion he had for this excursion, just like he'd shown when talking about his scheme to walk underwater. Nothing would ever sway Nemo once he'd made up his mind.

"I cannot argue with you that crossing darkest Africa is an amazing idea, André. I expected nothing less of your imagination . . . but still, I remain skeptical. Are you certain it's safe?"

He looked at Verne, his dark eyes flashing, an impish grin on his face. The expression reminded him of the times they had fashioned schemes down on the docks or pored through geography books, trying to outdo each other with tales of exotic lands. "My friend, can you truly be concerned for my safety, after all I have already survived?"

Verne gave a snort and turned away to scrutinize a rather dark and unimaginative still life of fruit and feathers. "Why should I be concerned about that? For a man who has walked underwater, sailed halfway round the world, fought off pirates, survived on a desert island, and explored the uncharted bowels of the earth – why, a simple trip in a balloon is bound to be downright tedious."

Then Verne drew a deep breath, trying to explain. "André, when I finish at the Academy, I am doomed to life as a small-town lawyer, forced to follow in my father's tedious footsteps. But you already have a useful, interesting job – an engineer who has captured the interest of Baron Haussmann and even the emperor himself. Why would you throw all that away?"

Nemo stared at the stoic expression of Bonaparte in an enormous painting that depicted the Battle of Borodino. "Haussmann has asked me to redesign the Paris sewers, Jules. Surely there will still be work remaining for me when I return from Africa."

They walked along in silence, then paused in front of a painting of an old fisherwoman holding a basket of herring. Nemo had a distant expression on his face, and he responded in a quiet voice that told how well he knew Verne. "Or are you more concerned about Caroline, Jules? Concerned because she'll be with *me*?"

He clutched his friend's forearm and stared at him. Always before the mutual attraction between Nemo and Caroline had sparked a bit of envy from Verne, but now Nemo was going away with her on a long and dangerous voyage across Africa. Verne's flushed cheeks and awkward silence told Nemo everything that his friend would not say aloud. "Jules, she is still a married woman. I won't forget that. Dr Ferguson will chaperone us at all times. On my honor, I will see to it that no harm befalls her."

The best Verne could manage was a faint smile. "She could ask for no better protector." The alabaster statues in the center of the wide hall seemed to look at him skeptically. He didn't dare say anything more.

He began to walk again, the tip of his umbrella clicking on the polished floor. In a side gallery a worker with a mop did his best to be unobtrusive as he wiped away wet footprints. "If you must know," Verne said, looking straight ahead in search of another work of art worthy of his attention, "I envy you for actually having the fabulous adventures we talked about as boys. You are seeing the world, experiencing the wonders that I can only imagine. I . . . I have never even set foot outside of France."

Nemo brightened. "Does this mean you'd like to accompany us, Jules?"

Verne jerked around in undisguised horror. "Of course not! I have my studies here in Paris, and my friends, and –" He sighed. "I'm afraid that would be impossible."

Nemo patted him on the back. "Never fear, Jules. I promise to tell you all about our excursion when we return."

After months of preparations, Ferguson's equipment was carefully loaded aboard a British naval vessel tied up in the London estuary. The ship was bound for a trip around Africa, around the Cape of Good Hope and back up to Zanzibar on the east coast of the mysterious continent.

Jules Verne did not manage to attend the launch of the ship, though. In his heart, he had wanted to be there to bid Nemo and Caroline farewell, but he could not summon the nerve to cross the choppy waters to England. He had heard that the Channel could be treacherous that time of year, and he was afraid of storms.

V

With full sails flapping in a brisk breeze, the British navy ship set off en route to India. Nemo stood in the open air, grasping one of the thick tie-ropes as he watched the African coastline roll by. He had a strange, empty feeling in his chest, remembering the fateful time he had made a similar voyage as a cabin boy with Captain Grant and Ned Land.

The British vessel journeyed southward, following the *Coralie*'s path around the Cape of Good Hope. This time, of course, Nemo was a passenger, not a crewman. And this voyage had one other tremendous advantage: he would spend a great deal of the time with Caroline.

In England, after the Royal Geographical Society had balked at funding the risky and unproven expedition – leaving Caroline Aronnax to finance the balloon, supplies, and equipment herself – Dr Ferguson missed no opportunity to point out to the press that a mere woman (and a *French* woman, at that!) had been willing to invest more in the furtherance of human knowledge than either the Royal Geographical Society, or indeed the entire British government.

Thus shamed, the president of the Society used his political influence to arrange for their passage aboard a British naval vessel around Africa and up the eastern coast to the British protectorate of Zanzibar. Still skeptical, the Society president said that they were willing to take this risk, even with Dr Ferguson's unproven designs, even despite his previous disastrous failures. The explorer himself dismissed any doubts.

The ship's hold contained the ingenious double-balloon, along with the weapons, foodstuffs, and clothing they would need for the journey across the continent. Nemo had spent a month supervising the construction of the lighter-than-air vessel. With staunch British pride, Ferguson had insisted on naming it the *Victoria* after the Queen of England, and Nemo did not argue. After all, he thought, the Emperor of France had assigned *him* to rebuild the Parisian sewers. . .

Nemo and Caroline walked the deck together in a fine afternoon breeze. Without speaking of their feelings, they had settled into a calm facade of friendship. "We must adjust to life's expectations," he said quietly to her, "regardless of our missed opportunities."

But just beneath the surface their thoughts burned hot, building an unrequited tension between them. Nemo refused to extend it beyond the bounds of propriety, and Caroline was comfortable with that, though he loved her even more now than during the hot-blooded days of his youth.

Aboard the ship, Caroline wore full skirts and appropriate "women's clothing" as a minor concession to social expectations. After the three of them boarded the balloon, though, she intended to wear trousers and serviceable clothes. Caroline expected to work just as hard as the two men, and Nemo knew better than to argue with her. After all, the scandal about her activities couldn't get much worse.

Since she had done so well running her father's shipping company, that gossip had no teeth. She had increased her family's wealth through a shrewd but unorthodox decision to refit merchant ships to carry more *passengers* instead of cargo. With the frenzied news of the California Gold Rush in 1849, hundreds of fortune-seekers were willing to exchange their life's savings for the fastest possible ship to San Francisco. Caroline had realized a higher profit in hauling people than she could ever have made by trading goods.

Before departing for Africa, she had left explicit instructions with the higher-level employees at "Aronnax, Merchant" – and paid a significant retainer to her feisty Parisian lawyer – to ensure that the business continued smoothly during her absence. She expected to be gone as long as a year, given the lengthy sea voyage around Africa and back.

Now, as they stood together in the open sunshine, Caroline withdrew a wooden flute from her small traveling bag. "The pianoforte was too large to bring aboard, but I could not bear to be away from my music for so long."

Nemo knew that her exuberant compositions had begun to draw attention back in Île Feydeau. During a dinner party, Caroline's mother had a pianist play one of the works found in her old room, and some local musicians had begun to suspect that the "mystery composer" might actually be living somewhere in Nantes. Caroline had considered the Africa trip an excellent excuse to remove herself from France for a while.

Now, with the wind thumping the sails above and the foaming waves applauding against the hull, Caroline toyed with melodies on her flute, letting her eyes fall closed as the music grew more complex, flowing out of her.

Nemo leaned against the railing, smiling with contentment. The sailors paused in their chores to listen. Dr Ferguson came up on deck, then clapped his hands when she was finished. Surprised, Caroline looked at her unexpected audience. Nemo complimented her with his warm expression instead of words. Ferguson nodded his vigorous appreciation. "That was lovely, madame."

"I call it –" she caught herself. "It's called 'Siren Song.'"

"Written by the French composer Passepartout, of course," Nemo added.

"Ah, yes. I've heard of the man," Ferguson said, wearing a serious expression.

Later that afternoon, Caroline looked out at the sea, listening to the hum of rigging ropes overhead. She drew a deep breath of salt air, then turned to Nemo. "I've always heard the call of the sea, André, but now I understand it better." She gripped the deck rail and faced the ocean-filled horizon. "There's so much more to the world than . . . Nantes."

"And I'll show some of it to you."

She strolled with him down the deck toward a patch of shade under the mizzen mast. "You must understand, André, that my options have been limited by the noose of social expectations. Even as a young man, *you* could do as you pleased and sign aboard a sailing ship. But I am a young woman. I had no such choices available. The only goal expected of me was to get married and stay at home. My parents even chose my husband for me. I have to pretend *not* to be the composer of the music I play in my own house."

Now her cornflower blue eyes flashed with anger. "But I want to do things, too! I want to accomplish whatever I can dream, just as you have. I want to be the first woman to cross Africa. That is an admirable goal, is it not?"

Nemo laughed. He looked at her beautiful face, saw the determination there. "Most certainly."

The ship put in at Zanzibar, a large island off the eastern shore of Africa south of the equator. The island was a staging point, a kingdom ruled by Sultan Seyyid Said, who had consolidated an empire spanning Oman and Zanzibar and Tanganyika. More than a decade ago, the old but powerful man had been forced to request English assistance to keep his kingdom.

Zanzibar was now a British protectorate, with a large fort and barracks in the middle of the island's main city. Britain's stated purpose was to put an end to the heinous practice of human slavery (of which Zanzibar was a willing participant), but years had passed, and the slave trade from Zanzibar to the West Indies and the Americas had not declined.

As the ship tied up at the dock in mid afternoon, Dr Ferguson came to greet Nemo and Caroline. He wore formal evening clothes, a stovepipe hat, and black coat, the very picture of a dapper Englishman. "Allow me to escort you into the town, my friends," he said, smoothing down his big mustache. "We are the representatives of science and exploration, eh? English and French in a spirit of cooperation to unlock the secrets of darkest Africa. Indeed, we must do our utmost to impress the natives."

In the port they passed swarms of people. Some wore British military uniforms and looked altogether too hot and sweaty in the equatorial climate; lighter-skinned Arabs wore voluminous pale clothes, and narrow eyes highlighted their lean appearance. Still others were dark-skinned African natives from the interior of the unexplored continent.

In the marketplace, Caroline stood beside Nemo, looking with anger and disgust at the groaning prisoners in chains. Zanzibar brought in great wealth through selling tons of cloves and clove oil, coffee, and coconuts – but slaves remained the most lucrative commodity. These captives had been taken from their villages during raids and shipped here to one of the world's largest slave markets, where they would be sold to Portuguese or Dutch traders.

Dr Ferguson and his companions were treated to a sumptuous but strained dinner with the British consul and plump old Sultan Said. The sultan seemed unable to comprehend why Caroline, a woman, would sit at table with the important men. But Caroline remained calm and self-assured without provoking the curious and skeptical locals.

Later, Ferguson supervised the unloading of his expedition supplies. He shouted at the porters carrying crates from the hold of the naval ship. "Those are delicate scientific instruments, eh!" He insisted on unloading his own firearms and ammunition. The doctor intended to shoot a great many specimens for study.

Nemo worked to set up the balloon with several of the ship's crewmen he had befriended during the voyage. With the basket tied down, he operated the recondensing apparatus that released stored hydrogen gas into the inner and outer balloons. As the enormous *Victoria* inflated, crowds came from all over the island to stare at the strange colorful sight.

The *Victoria* was an elongated oval fifty feet wide and seventy-five feet high, with seams sealed by gutta-percha, which enclosed a smaller balloon of the same shape. Blue, red, and green silk made the balloon look like a dragon floating in the skies. A mesh of hemp cords held the balloon in place, connected to the large open car, which would be their home for the next five weeks. The car was made of iron-reinforced wicker, with a network of springs to absorb the shock of any collision.

Caroline, under escort by two British officers, procured food and water supplies to supplement their dried provisions. In the Zanzibar market she purchased bags of coffee, fruit, and millet flour.

By the time the sun set across the misty line of the African continent to the west, their preparations had been completed. Nemo, Caroline, and Dr Ferguson ate a large meal and rested thoroughly.

At dawn the next morning, a British honor guard saluted the brave explorers. Resplendent in billowing clothes, Sultan Said arrived in a fine carriage. He waited while his personal slaves set up a pavilion near the balloon's anchorage point so he could sip his cardamom-and-coffee while watching the event.

Ignoring the growing crowd of spectators, Ferguson rechecked his stowed supplies and announced, "At last, we are ready to depart, my friends."

Nemo held out his hand to help Caroline into the balloon. They stood inside the swaying basket while Ferguson sprang aboard with a light step. He waved at the cheering crowd below.

At the military fort, three cannons were fired in a thunderous salute. The British governor stood outside the sultan's pavilion, formally at attention. He did not wave as all of the other people did.

At a signal from Dr Ferguson and another from Nemo, the workers pulled and strained at the ropes. Their muscles rippled beneath dark skin as they hauled the impatient balloon closer to the ground. Then they slipped off the anchoring ropes.

The *Victoria* leaped into the sky. Nemo's stomach lurched as the ground receded with dizzying speed, and Caroline peered over the side of the car at the receding crowd. Finally, as the British consul diminished against the landscape below, the stiff man deigned to wave them farewell. . .

The morning air was clear and still, but as they reached sufficient altitude, the breezes grasped them and nudged the balloon westward toward the mainland. For a long time, Nemo could hear the Zanzibaris celebrating below.

Soon they left the island behind, drifting across the straits that separated Zanzibar from the coast. The *Victoria* set off across the huge unexplored continent of Africa.

PART VI
FIVE WEEKS IN A BALLOON

I

African Continent, 1853

Upon reaching the mainland, the balloon drifted over low country covered with tall grasses and rich vegetation. They observed tall forests, trees studded with flowers or fruits, others covered with thorns. Dr Ferguson's hazel eyes drank in the scenery with boundless enthusiasm, taking copious notes for his expedition records.

Nemo shared the spyglass with Caroline as they looked down upon the unfolding landscape. She studied the maps and charts purchased from Zanzibar merchants, but it didn't take long to discover inconsistencies and gross errors. She diligently corrected each one, using the evidence of her own eyes.

Ferguson leaned over the balloon's basket, pursing his lips so that his mustache bunched up like a hissing black cat. "Far south of here, Dr David Livingstone took his wife and four children deep inland. Amazing that a man – and an Englishman, yet – would even attempt to bring his family, eh?"

"Some might call it foolhardy," Caroline said, appalled at Livingstone's callousness. "What about the safety of his wife, his children?"

"He was a *missionary*," Ferguson said, as if that explained everything.

"They took a wagon across the Kalahari Desert, without water and without food. I should say it's amazing they survived at all, eh?" The explorer patted the basket. "Indeed, my friends, this is the correct way to travel across hostile territory."

The *Victoria* continued at a gentle but respectable speed, and many miles passed beneath them. All that first day, the expedition seemed like a charming country outing. As they ate fresh supplies, Nemo imagined himself on a pleasurable picnic with Caroline, rather than venturing into unexplored and unfriendly wilderness.

At nightfall, Nemo operated the balloon's gaseous recondensing apparatus, cooling the enclosed hydrogen and decreasing their buoyancy so that the *Victoria* descended with effortless grace. They could have continued to float through the hours of darkness, but then Dr Ferguson would not have been able to see the landscape or take notes. Nemo tossed down one of their iron anchors, and the grappling hooks snagged in the tall trees. Thus, tethered to the ground yet still aloft in safety, they spent their first night with the evening breezes swaying the basket like an infant's cradle. . .

Over the next several days, the *Victoria* drifted inland, generally westward but with a tendency toward the north. The river they had followed from the coast took a sharp turn to the right and flowed out of sight. Before long the ground rose, and to the north they spotted the bulwarks of an enormous mountain far greater than anything Nemo had ever seen. Its crest was adorned with a glittering white that could not be explained by clouds.

Nemo stared and studied, then passed the spyglass to Caroline. "Snow," he said.

"Impossible," Ferguson answered, taking the spyglass from her. "We're on the equator. There cannot be snow at the equator." Then he let out a sharp cry of recognition. "Ah, indeed! I remember recent reports by a German missionary who also went inland from Zanzibar. He claimed to have seen a snow-covered peak in eastern Africa, and he became a laughing stock. He was German, after all."

Nemo thought for a moment. "Rebmann? Could that be Johannes

Rebmann's mountain?"

"Yes, the natives named it Kilimanjaro. Now it appears he was right." Ferguson began scribbling notes in his journal, while Nemo took out a sextant and other navigational devices. Using trigonometry, he estimated the height of Kilimanjaro at an impossible 20,000 feet above sea level.

The winds tugged them westward, where the ground flattened out into a sprawling veldt. Tall, dry grass rippled like golden waves on a stormy sea, and the sheer abundance of animal life took Nemo's breath away. According to the maps drawn by native slave traders and intrepid missionaries, this was called the Serengeti Plain.

Dr Ferguson removed his two shooting rifles, loaded them, and checked the sights. "Use the recondenser to take us down, eh? It's time to collect some specimens." He gave a formal nod to Caroline. "And madame, if you would be so kind as to sketch the specimens I shoot? Our friend Nemo insists that you are quite an accomplished artist."

Glad to be considered a part of the expedition, Caroline took out her sketchpad and used a small knife to sharpen the drawing points of her lead pencils.

The balloon descended toward the plain, where the vegetation was broken by strange baobab trees that looked like oaks uprooted and planted upside down. Tall termite mounds towered above the grass like abstract concrete pillars.

Nemo threw a grappling hook over the side and secured the balloon to one of the baobab trees. Using a winch, they lowered the balloon down to where Nemo could drop a chain ladder. Ferguson took his loaded rifles and scanned the congregation of animals. Some had already run from the odd apparition in the sky, but throngs of zebras and wildebeests remained, restless but not yet fleeing.

Long-necked giraffes stood at another cluster of baobabs, munching leaves from the upper branches. Caroline stared at them. "Those are the strangest animals I have ever seen. A spotted horse with a neck stretched like taffy."

A shot rang out, startling them, and Dr Ferguson lifted the barrel of his long rifle to watch a wildebeest tumble to the ground. "Good shot!"

The other herd animals ran about in confusion. Ferguson picked up the second rifle and aimed. It took him two shots to bring down a young zebra. Reloading, he fired four more times to secure a pair of antelope.

"That's quite sufficient for now." Ferguson gestured to the ladder. "Come along, my friends. We must take measurements and do our duty for science, eh?"

The three explorers climbed down the jingling chain ladder to the branches; Ferguson reloaded and took one rifle with him, slung over his shoulder. Nemo carried a satchel filled with scientific instruments, while Caroline followed, sketchpad tucked under her arm.

As they descended the baobab, startled birds took wing. On ground again, the explorers waded through a rustling sea of tall grasses that rose higher than their heads. Nemo kept a sharp watch for snakes in the underbrush, but Dr Ferguson strode with childlike determination toward his trophy.

The zebra lay sprawled on the ground. The black and white stripes on its hide formed a perfect camouflage among the rippling shadows of the Serengeti. "Magnificent specimen. Well fed and well muscled." Ferguson asked for the measuring tape, and he and Nemo noted the animal's statistics.

Caroline stood back, scratching her lead pencil across the paper to capture the major details. Later, she would spend the slow hours aboard the balloon to complete the fine points of the drawing.

With a sigh, the doctor gazed down. "A pity we can't take these specimens back with us, eh? Imagine what this one would look like stuffed in the Royal Museum in London."

Nemo looked back at the colorful balloon tethered to the tree. "We could never carry the extra weight."

"My sketches will have to do," Caroline said.

Next, they set off to where the wildebeest had fallen. They took similar measurements, and Ferguson used a bone saw to remove the beast's horns. Nemo put the souvenirs in his canvas satchel. By the time they reached the two dead antelopes, some animals had returned to the vicinity, wary and confused.

While Dr Ferguson again recorded the vital statistics and made meticulous notes regarding the differences among the three species, Nemo bent down with the hunting knife and began to carve steaming strips from the antelope's back. "This is the best meat we'll find in a long time, I suspect," he said. "We'll make camp on the ground so we can build a fire to roast it."

Caroline continued to sketch. She turned around, studying the particulars of the landscape to add to the picture. Ferguson puttered with his notebook, adding thoughts and details.

Then Nemo realized that the air around them had grown oppressively silent. His awareness raised to a high peak, as when he'd hunted wild boars on his mysterious island. Ears attuned, ready to protect Caroline, he heard a rustle in the grasses – then a muscular form like a tawny liquid shadow burst forward. He saw bright feline eyes and long teeth.

Nemo reacted without thinking. He snatched the rifle Ferguson had laid on the ground, swiveled, and fired. The booming sound startled the nearby herd of animals.

Caroline stumbled backward, dropping her pencil. Ferguson cried out, and Nemo stared in amazement as a lioness collapsed to the ground, a bullet hole blossoming scarlet at the center of her breast.

Dr Ferguson stepped away from the antelope, astonished. "Good Lord! I never expected a magnificent specimen like this." He went about making measurements of the lioness, wishing he could take the time to skin it. "This pelt would have made a marvelous display."

Nemo reloaded the gun and kept careful watch. "Just be quick about your work, doctor."

Taking their antelope steaks, the three adventurers returned to the balloon, scrambled up the baobab and the ladder and into the *Victoria*'s basket.

When he looked down onto the plain again, Nemo was alarmed to see that half a dozen lions had appeared from the deep grasses, as if by magic, and were feasting on the dead animals. Timid hyenas lurked around the fringes, waiting for their turn at the carcasses.

Shaken, but enthralled, Caroline began a new sketch, trying to draw the tawny lioness in mid leap.

II

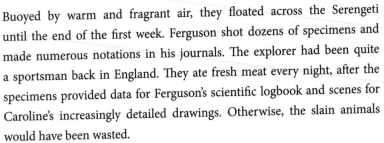

Buoyed by warm and fragrant air, they floated across the Serengeti until the end of the first week. Ferguson shot dozens of specimens and made numerous notations in his journals. The explorer had been quite a sportsman back in England. They ate fresh meat every night, after the specimens provided data for Ferguson's scientific logbook and scenes for Caroline's increasingly detailed drawings. Otherwise, the slain animals would have been wasted.

While drifting along, the crew of the *Victoria* had considerable idle time, and the doctor told them his life story. Samuel Ferguson's younger years had been rather checkered: he'd served aboard a ship from the age of eighteen and had sailed around the world before his twenty-second birthday. He had spent a year in Australia and Tasmania, and later trudged across India and into Nepal and Tibet, always bearing the British flag. He had a restless nature, a burning curiosity, and so much impatience to move on to the next conquest that he rarely enjoyed the fruits of his own discoveries.

Nemo got along well enough with the man, though Caroline grew weary of Ferguson's constant killing in the name of science. The doctor neither scorned her presence nor opposed her desire to do her share of the work, since Caroline's finances had made the entire adventure possible. The only things that inspired great enthusiasm in Ferguson were his hunt and the expedition.

* * *

As they floated over rock-studded plains, they came upon a ponderous herd of elephants. Beaming, Dr Ferguson insisted that they obtain a pachyderm specimen so that he could perform meticulous physiognomic measurements on the size and thickness of the ears, the biological hydraulics of the trunk, and the protective qualities of the hide. But the herd milled about in the open grasslands, far from any convenient tree for the balloon's anchorage.

"Drop the grappling hook anyway," Ferguson suggested, "all the way to the ground. Perhaps we'll snag it on a rock, eh?"

Nemo followed the command, but the colorful balloon continued to drift unhindered. The anchor plowed a furrow through the grasses, doing little to slow the *Victoria*'s progress. As if to spite them, the breezes increased, and the balloon drifted rapidly over the elephant herd.

Ferguson loaded both of his rifles then looked in dismay at the pachyderms. He didn't shoot because he had no way to retrieve his prize. But then, as the anchor dragged through the herd, its hooks snagged on something. With a lurch, the balloon jerked to a halt.

"Ah, we're caught," Ferguson said. "Now we can –"

The balloon began to move again, tugged along as if by a locomotive. Hearing a loud bellow, Nemo looked over the basket to find that the hook had caught on the curved tusk of a huge bull elephant. Tangled, the beast trumpeted with its long trunk and thrashed its head from side to side, which only set the sharp grappling hook tighter.

Furious, the elephant charged across the plain, dragging the *Victoria* along. Thinking of practical matters, Caroline secured the loose equipment to the wicker walls of the basket. Normally, the breezes gave them a gentle ride, but now the three were yanked about as the maddened creature stampeded, first in one direction, then the other.

Within moments, Dr Ferguson regained his senses enough to pick up his first rifle. He leaned over the basket, pointed the barrel at the elephant below, and let loose a shot. Against the thick hide, however, the bullet did little damage other than spurring the elephant to a greater frenzy. As the beast ran, the balloon bobbed along behind it like a fish on the end of a hook.

Ferguson shot his second rifle, and saw that the bullet struck the elephant squarely in the back of the head. He reloaded and fired again and again, until at last the animal slowed to a plod, bleeding from numerous wounds. With a great wheeze of pain and exhaustion, it dropped in its tracks.

Nemo and Caroline were both sad for the magnificent creature, but Ferguson saw it as no more than another set of descriptions to be entered into his logbook. They winched the balloon closer to the ground, and the doctor leaped over the side without even bothering to use the ladder. Enormous vultures and ravens circled around, waiting for the feast.

Nemo and Ferguson spent an hour poking and prodding the carcass, measuring, estimating weight, making notes. Then they stored both of the elephant's tusks, each worth a fortune in ivory, inside the balloon's basket.

From her lookout above, Caroline sketched the scene and added more poignancy to the dramatic flight of the elephant than pure scientific analysis required.

III

In misery, Jules Verne sat alone in a bistro by the river Seine. The waiter served him a bottle of cheap wine, strong cheese, bread, and poached fish with a mushroom cream sauce. At any other time, he would have savored every morsel; now, though, the future loomed like a yawning chasm, and made him lose his appetite.

The bistro owner presumed the red-bearded student was celebrating his graduation, though Verne's lack of enthusiasm suggested otherwise. "No, monsieur," he answered the grinning man's question. "This is most definitely *not* the happiest day of my life."

At the Paris Academy, Verne had reviewed every legal detail he'd learned in the past several years. The dry words crawled across the pages like listless insects, and he stared until his eyes burned and his head ached. He remained uninterested in the law – but he didn't dare face the consequences of letting his father down. . .

When he received his grade and discovered that his score was sufficient for a diploma (by a scant few points in his favor), Verne realized that he no longer had any escape. His dismal future had been set. Not as a literary genius, not a world explorer, not a brave adventurer . . . but a small-town lawyer.

As he watched a pleasure boat go by on the Seine, he took a forkful of fish and chewed. Now that he was certified as a practicing attorney, his father would expect him to settle down in Nantes and, over time, take over the family trade. Proud of his son's accomplishment, the older man had already mounted a new sign above the door to his offices: "Pierre Verne, et fils." *Verne & Son.*

The very thought horrified Jules. He felt as if he were on the deck of a sinking ship.

He forced himself to finish every scrap of his dinner and all the wine, regardless of whether his digestive system – queasy at the best of times – would appreciate it. Since he'd paid for the meal, he vowed to consume it . . . not that he ever let good food go to waste.

His theatre work had been both amusing and difficult, sapping his strength but teaching him many things (none of which, unfortunately, would benefit an attorney). He had earned little money in the theatre – just enough to repay his expenses and supplement the meager allowance his father sent him each month. If he defied his father and remained in Paris, the allowance would stop abruptly, no matter how much his sympathetic mother might argue. And Verne could not live on a theatre worker's salary.

By now he had hoped to become a renowned playwright. The poetry that had always delighted his family and friends did not seem brilliant enough to warrant publication. His historical novels, pale imitations of the works of Dumas and Hugo, were tedious, dry, melodramatic. The more he worked at them, the duller they became (at least according to his literary associates, who read them and gleefully offered their acid criticism).

But Verne wanted to find some way to be successful through his writing, no matter the cost. It was time to give up those aspirations and slink home in the night in the hope that no one had noticed his dreams . . . or he must swallow his pride and ask a tremendous favor from his strongest literary acquaintance.

By now, he vowed, it was no longer time to be polite or subtle.

Verne paid the waiter, then returned to his apartment where he changed into his best clothes, well-worn though they were. Alexandre Dumas hired writers to assist in the production of his novels and plays, and Verne had always hoped to join them. He had dropped hints during visits to the

Monte Cristo chateau, but the enormous man with his booming laugh and glittering jewelry had ignored each gentle reminder. Now, though, Verne would be direct, drop to his knees if necessary. If he could work for the great "fiction factory," perhaps he would earn enough to make a living. He had no other choice, besides being a lawyer.

As he rode in a carriage to the outskirts of Paris, Verne worked up his courage, remembering all he had learned in the theatre and in law school. He had to make a compelling case for himself. Nothing he'd ever done would matter as much as this.

When the carriage pulled up to the graveled courtyard of Monte Cristo, Verne handed the appropriate coins to the driver, along with a very small tip, then climbed out.

Into total chaos.

The carriage rattled away with a surly comment from the driver. Verne stood astonished as the front door was flung open and well-dressed men marched out of the entrance.

Inside the huge house, crews of workers bustled about, dragging furniture, taking down paintings, wrapping statuary for transport. The sound of hammers rang out from the magnificent marble-tiled ballroom as carpenters assembled storage crates. Grim-faced businessmen slapped labels on tapestries or alabaster busts of Dumas himself. Secretaries recorded the items in heavy ledger books.

"What is going on here?" Verne caught the elbow of a well-muscled workman who had extraordinarily hairy arms. He felt too intimidated to speak to any of the businessmen.

The worker brushed sweat from his forehead. "You another creditor? I only take orders from *him*." He nodded toward a small man with a wispy beard and a bright red cravat.

Gathering his courage, Verne hurried to the indicated man. "What is the meaning of this? Are you thieves? By what right are you taking these treasures from the great Dumas?"

"They're being marked for auction," the man said. "Monsieur Dumas is bankrupt. Even selling the chateau and its contents will not pay all his bills."

Verne was astonished. "Impossible! He is one of the most successful writers in France."

The small man gave a brief, maddening chuckle. "And he is also one of the greatest spendthrifts. Now be on your way."

Verne spluttered. "But . . . but have you no respect for books?"

"Aye – for ledger books. You'll have to find a new patron if you're another of those leeches who clung to Dumas and his wealth." The man sneered. "Or else find legitimate work of your own."

The haughty man marched off into another room, where a beautiful gilt-framed mirror was being hauled down with two ropes and a great deal of clumsiness. He bellowed an admonition to the workmen, and the startled brutes let loose the ropes. The mirror crashed into thousands of shards upon the polished floor.

Verne stopped another businessman on his way out to the reflecting pond. "Where is Monsieur Dumas? I must speak with him."

The pot-bellied man just snorted. "We *all* want to speak with Monsieur Dumas, but he has made himself conveniently scarce. If you find him, send him back to the main house."

With a sinking heart, Verne strode across the beautifully kept grounds, past hedges and flower boxes, fountains that now sat quiet instead of spraying torrents of diamond-like droplets. A handful of droopy-eyed writers stood in the manicured orange grove; two sat on stone benches. No one spoke, all their conversation smothered by a pall of despair.

Verne hurried up to them and repeated his questions, but got the same answers. They looked toward the tiny island where Dumas did his writing. Swans still drifted across the water, unconcerned about their future – although from the looks of Monte Cristo, there might not even be enough money left to feed the birds. No doubt they'd end up in someone's oven.

Even with his own dismal prospects, Verne found the moaning writers depressing. Dumas could pay none of them, not even for work they'd already done. Still, Verne found himself as much concerned for his enormous, good-natured mentor as he was filled with gloom about his precarious situation.

He wandered around the grounds, past the now-empty servants' quarters to the stables and the carriage house. There he heard people moving about with hushed whispers. Curious, Verne entered the carriage house and saw a footman lashing a harness to the single remaining horse.

The great Dumas stood outside a closed carriage, looking sullenly at a few baskets and sacks of possessions he had snatched from his estate. The man's generous lips were turned downward in an uncharacteristic frown. He had no room to store anything else inside the overloaded vehicle.

"Monsieur Dumas!" Verne called in delight and relief. The footman jumped, startled. The broad-shouldered writer whirled, almost losing his balance as his girth swung around. His broad face carried a look of dismay, as if he was ready to flee into the forests on the outskirts of Monte Cristo.

But when he saw Jules Verne, his face composed itself into a pale reminder of his former genial and welcoming expression. "Oh, ho, my friend Jules! Thank you for coming to see me, even in this dark hour."

Verne found himself at a loss for words. He had practiced the speech so many times, hoping to request work from Dumas. Now that the opportunity was gone, he had little hope left in his heart. "I . . . I am –"

"Well?" The dark man rubbed his thick fingers together. He had loaded them with more rings than Verne remembered having seen before. "Did you pass your law exam? You had a great deal riding on that test, if I recall."

"Yes, sir," Verne said with a groan. "I'm now licensed to be a practicing attorney."

"Delicious!" Dumas laughed at himself. "I myself could use a great deal of legal help. However, I'm unable to pay for it, at present."

"That's what . . . what I was given to understand. I'm sorry to hear about it, monsieur. I am afraid I have little experience and even fewer suggestions to offer you right now. Your situation is . . . beyond me."

"It is a good thing you have established your career. Unlike me, you have a solid future ahead of you, mmm?"

"A *dreary* future," Verne said bitterly. He bent to pick up a heavy box and helped to load it into the carriage, which already looked so stuffed the axles might bow to the gravel in the road. "I want to be a writer like you."

Dumas rumbled a great belly laugh. "Even now, when you see how my fortunes have fallen? Oh, ho!"

"But I've read your work, Monsieur Dumas. Surely your fiction has created a treasure for humanity far beyond" – Verne gestured around the carriage house, but indicated the whole estate – "beyond all this."

Dumas frowned at him. "At the moment, I'd gladly give up my novels if I could only retain possession of my home." The footman finished harnessing the horse and then climbed up to the buckboard. The great writer's single faithful employee would also drive the carriage.

Verne hung his head, astounded at the famous man's misfortune. His dreams for success had shattered into even smaller pieces. "I just wish my own fictions were more in demand. I haven't managed to capture the excitement as you have. My historical novels don't have the spark of life or the sense of wonder that you portrayed in *The Three Musketeers*."

Dumas beamed at hearing the praise, even at such a moment. "Ho! And I will continue to write books like that, mark my words – though I may have to rely solely on my own imagination from now on, as it seems I'll have considerable difficulty hiring other writers."

The big man opened the carriage door. "Every author is different, Jules. I have a flair for portraying historical charm, but if I were to devote my talents to the sort of stories that come from the pens of Voltaire or Balzac, I would fail miserably. Oh, ho! Jules, you have been working too hard to do what *I* have done. Perhaps historical adventure isn't where your special ability lies."

"Then what should I write about?" Verne said with an edge of desperation. He still hadn't heard any answers he could use.

"Write what you know, what you have learned, what you have lived. Write what is in your heart." Dumas looked at one of the laden sacks on the floor of the carriage house. With a grunt, he picked it up and tossed it onto the seat, the only clear spot wide enough for the writer's enormous buttocks.

Verne drew a heavy sigh. "But my life has been tedious and uninteresting. No one would want to read about my experiences. What am I to do?"

With great effort, Dumas heaved himself into the carriage, grabbed the heavy sack, and subsided into the seat with the sack on his lap. Eager to help, Verne trotted across the dirt floor and opened the doors of the carriage house. The footman flicked the reins, and the horse stamped, impatient to be off.

Dumas raised his eyebrows, looking out the carriage window. "What about your friend Nemo? When you told me about his adventures, there was excitement in your eyes – a fire. Delicious! You have the journal from when he was stranded on his island, correct? Certainly those are tales worth retelling?"

As if struck by a thunderbolt from the sky, Verne stepped back and his face lit up. Of course! He needed only to *tell* the adventures – not necessarily experience them himself.

Dumas swung the carriage door shut. "I hope to see you again someday, Jules Verne," he said through the window. "But now I must be off on . . . pressing business as far away from here as I can get."

"But how am I to find you?" Verne said. "I'd like to send you a new manuscript. I'm sure you'll like it."

Dumas leaned out the window of his carriage. "My dear man, at the moment my object is *not* to be found." The footman snapped a whip at the horse, and the vehicle rattled onto the cobbled path and out a side driveway. They fled toward a winding forest road that would eventually meet the main thoroughfare.

While his once-magnificent estate was ransacked, Dumas left Verne behind with his creditors . . . and his new ideas.

IV

Like a mythical air spirit robed in green, red, and blue, the immense balloon drifted across Africa for two more weeks.

Ferguson spent the daylight hours in scientific ecstasy, documenting swamps and forests, mountains and plains never before seen by an Englishman (or any other European, for that matter). He considered himself a "geographical missionary" for the Royal Society. On maps and charts, most of Africa's interior remained blank, but this expedition could fill in a swath of new territory. Caroline diligently sketched everything they observed.

Nemo tended the recondenser cylinder that controlled the exchange of hydrogen gas between the two balloons, which allowed him to raise or lower the *Victoria* through thick clouds and above storms. In relaxed moments, Caroline withdrew her wooden flute and played quiet melodies, adding her songs to the African veldt.

Comfortable against the wicker side of the car, she and Nemo talked about their lives, their hopes and disappointments, as well as simple matters of daily existence. "Did you ever think we'd end up here, in a place like this, André?" Caroline's fingers twitched, as if she wanted to take his hand, but didn't dare. Dr Ferguson puttered with his instruments and his notes, oblivious to the attraction between them.

"I always hoped I would be with you . . . but sometimes wishes don't come true the way you imagine. Our lives haven't gone the way we'd planned."

She drew a deep breath. "If only I had known you were still alive on the island, if only I could have –"

Nemo stopped her. "Caroline, even if you had known, you would still have married Captain Hatteras, and he would still have sailed off to find the Northwest Passage . . . and we would still be here now, in this same balloon." He smiled. "And there is nowhere I would rather be."

Leaving the Serengeti Plain behind, the *Victoria* crossed over a huge lake, but Caroline could not find the prominent inland sea on any of her charts. They gazed at the immense body of water, whose shore was dotted with small fishing villages like beads on a necklace. In the shallows, islands hosted numerous flocks of birds.

"It's large enough to be the source of the Nile," Ferguson said with a touch of awe. For a century, one expedition after another had searched in vain for the headwaters of the great river. The Royal Society had made the mystery its greatest priority, but so far none of the conventional expeditions had found any answers.

Unfortunately, Nemo could choose only the balloon's general direction of travel, and the body of water was so vast they would have needed to travel to the northern end to see if its waters drained in the proper direction. "Someone else will have to verify it."

"Mark it on the map with great care, madame," Ferguson said with a smile that made his huge mustache bristle. "Indeed, if I may be so bold, I shall even name this lake – for future cartographers, of course."

Nemo had never sought credit for himself. "That is your right, monsieur, as the leader of our expedition."

"Which name do you choose, doctor?" Caroline asked.

Ferguson looked up at the magnificent balloon over their heads. "Why not name it after the vessel that has carried us across such great distances and difficult terrain, eh? We shall call it Lake Victoria."

V

At noon on the nineteenth day, Nemo used a sextant to measure the altitude of the blazing yellow sun and, through trigonometry, determined their position. "We've drifted north of the equator," he said, pleased.

Caroline marked the spot on their charts. "As near as I can tell, we have traversed fourteen hundred miles – almost two thirds of the way across Africa."

"Indeed!" Ferguson perked up. "On foot it would have taken us a year to get this far, my friends . . . if we survived at all in such inhospitable terrain, eh?"

Caroline pointed out what the two men had not yet mentioned. "By drifting northward, we are heading across the widest part of the African continent. That will increase our time of travel."

"We can still make it in five weeks, my friends."

Nemo double-checked the *Victoria's* inflation gauges. "I hope so, since our hydrogen won't last much longer than that."

Caroline ran a finger across the blank, unexplored section of map just waiting for her notations and observations. The balloon passed over rolling hills and then river lowlands as Nemo worked the recondenser, raising or lowering them to find an optimal stream of wind. Finally they came upon a second huge lake surrounded by swampland and villages of huts built upon stilts.

Ferguson studied his map, comparing it with what he saw while Nemo took another set of positional measurements. The explorer's heavy eyebrows shot upward, and he grinned so broadly that his bushy mustache looked as if it might fall off. "That is Lake Chad! We've gone farther than I anticipated."

"We've also gone farther north than we should have," Caroline said.

But Ferguson would not be disappointed. He had already filled two journal volumes describing the landscape and recording the zoological specimens he shot. He'd also kept a careful log of how the wildlife varied with the terrain. Watching his diligence, Nemo recalled how Captain Grant had studied the various fishes and sea creatures they encountered on their ill-fated journey, also keeping detailed scientific records . . . now lost to the world.

Ferguson fiddled with the recondenser controls to drop the balloon far enough to study the marshes and shoreline of enormous Lake Chad. Nemo quickly intervened and operated the device himself. He knew they had to conserve their hydrogen gas to keep the balloon aloft for the remainder of the journey across the widest part of the continent.

They drifted low over swamps with reeds growing out of the water like porcupine quills. Natives in long canoes paddled about the shallows, casting fish nets. Crocodile silhouettes slithered along, while storks and flamingoes waded in the mud, probing for shellfish with their beaks.

Caroline pointed out a group of large dark forms perched on gnarled mangroves bent over the lake marshes. "Are those birds? They are larger than any vultures I have heard of."

Ferguson snatched the spyglass out of Nemo's hand. "Not just vultures, madame – condors. Rare and magnificent birds, perhaps the largest in the world. We simply must have a specimen, eh?"

He retrieved his sporting rifle and fired a shot at the clustered birds. One of the enormous condors dropped into the marsh with a splash of water and black feathers. The thunderous rifle blast startled the remaining birds, and they took wing with raucous, horrible cries. Each monstrous bird had a wingspan of fifteen feet, as big as the glider kite Nemo had built on his island.

Three crocodiles moved in to feast on the feathered carcass floating in the swamp. The other giant birds moved together like sharks of the air. Their naked heads were covered with skin that looked like sunburned flesh around black eyes, and a horny plate rose rudderlike from each horned beak. The condors headed toward the *Victoria*, as if they saw it as prey.

"Now they are coming for us, doctor," Caroline said, frowning at the explorer. "Why must you *shoot* everything?"

Ferguson blinked his hazel eyes at her, as if he'd never considered there might be another way to document scientific discoveries. "Don't worry, madame. Condors are carrion birds. They'll have no interest in us."

Then the gigantic creatures fell upon them.

"Give me the other rifle, Doctor!" Nemo said. "We'll both have to shoot now."

His first shot nicked the closest bird, severing a clump of feathers from its outstretched wing. Ferguson, with better aim and greater practice, felled another creature.

Caroline searched in the basket and came up with a boat hook they used to snag branches. She jabbed at one of the condors and struck its outstretched claws. The carrion bird flew away, only to circle around and come back.

The other condors rose higher to attack the *Victoria* from above. With razor talons they slashed at the balloon, ripping huge wounds in the colorful silk outer skin. The balloon began to leak gas, and dropped toward the swamp.

Nemo's second gunshot hit one of the condors. Then he turned desperately to the controls of the recondenser cylinder. He had to withdraw the hydrogen into the intact inner balloon before it all leaked out. "Caroline, help me! Get rid of all the ballast you can." He threw out the remaining sandbags, which briefly counteracted their descent.

Ferguson reloaded his rifle. "We'll be lost if they tear the inner balloon as well, eh?" He shot again, and another giant bird fell from the sky.

Caroline began tossing out everything she could find: spare clothing, cooking utensils, pots, empty containers . . . then full ones. With a satisfied expression, she jettisoned the heavy elephant tusks into the sky. Nemo decided they could do with only one of the two grappling hooks, so he sawed at the cable and threw the heavy anchor overboard.

The *Victoria* remained aloft, but now the colorful outer skin flapped like flesh sloughing from a leper's back. Ferguson shot again and again, with Caroline frantically helping to reload, until only two of the condors remained. Still, the sinking balloon careened toward Lake Chad. If the balloon crashed, they would all be trapped in the middle of unexplored Africa.

In desperation, Caroline picked up their largest water tank. She hesitated, knowing how much they needed the supplies, but judging by the rate at which they dropped, they would never make it across the vast lake . . . unless they could increase their buoyancy. Nemo looked at her, struck by how beautiful Caroline appeared even in extreme distress. He nodded sharply to her, and she threw out the water tank.

Nemo studied what remained of the wounded *Victoria*. He felt guilty that his ambitious dreams had tempted Caroline into this disastrous trip – though he would not have traded the past weeks with her for any treasure in the world.

Finally, with a grim sense of determination, Nemo knew what he must do: the only chance for the balloon to continue, the only way to keep Caroline safe. Down there, he could survive on his own resources, for as long as it took – he had done it before on the mysterious island. But he didn't dare tell her what he meant to do.

"Goodbye, Caroline." Unable to resist, he kissed her soft lips, startling her. The look in her eyes made his heart ache so that he almost lost his resolve . . . but if he did, he knew they would all die.

She moved forward to kiss him again, but Nemo slipped away to grasp the edge of the basket. Moving before his anguish and regret caught up with him, he stared at the approaching waters of Lake Chad and the swamps that extended to the horizon.

Now Caroline saw what he meant to do. "André!"

She reached for him, but he did not allow himself to be swayed. He took one last glimpse of her beautiful, heart-shaped face . . . and then decreased the weight of the balloon by one hundred and forty pounds – his own weight.

Nemo dropped through the air and into the water with a huge splash. Coughing but treading water in the murky shallows, he looked up in time to see Ferguson fire a final shot. The remaining two condors flew away, back toward their nesting trees.

He spat water and shook his head to clear his eyes. He could see Caroline's pale face leaning over the edge of the balloon's basket. She stretched out an arm as if to beseech him, but with its sudden increase in buoyancy, the *Victoria* rose again into a stiff breeze.

All alone and lost in the water, Nemo watched the balloon, out of control now, rise up and glide away into the distance.

VI

More than an hour later, the remaining anchor snagged on a twisted acacia tree. The damaged *Victoria* clung desperately, as if it needed a rest as much as its two remaining passengers did.

Drained and in shock, Caroline moved about like one of Mesmer's entranced subjects. Ever since they had departed from France months before, she had secretly begun counting the days until she could declare Captain Hatteras lost at sea. Caroline knew that Nemo would wait as long as necessary. But he had thrown himself overboard to save her.

Ferguson remained intent on the problem of the *Victoria* itself. His eyes were bright, and he tugged at his mustache as he pursed his lips and studied the gas-heating apparatus and the remaining inner balloon. "Our friend Nemo's design was brilliant, eh? Even after such a horrendous attack, we have survived. Remarkable."

"But *he* did not survive," Caroline whispered, her face pale and drawn. "André is gone."

Ferguson gave her shoulder a paternal pat. "There, there, madame – that remains to be seen. We mustn't underestimate our intrepid friend's resourcefulness, must we?"

She forced a smile at that, realizing that Ferguson had a point. Nemo had been lost before, and still he had made his way back to her. She hoped he would do the same now.

As they bobbed on the end of the snagged anchor rope, Ferguson pored over his notes and charts, searching for an answer. A scrubby forest covered the ground around them, broken by grassy areas and standing ponds. Caroline could see no paths, no signs of even primitive civilization. She didn't know where they were now, or how far they'd drifted from where Nemo had fallen into Lake Chad.

Caroline drew a deep breath. His quick, impulsive kiss still burned on her lips. She knew why he had sacrificed himself, but she would rather they had all crashed in the African wilderness; that way they could have worked together to make it to the coast.

But if Nemo had done such a brave thing for *her*, then she vowed not to waste his sacrifice. By all that she loved in the world, Caroline would find a way to get them out of this – and she *would* find him. Somehow.

Caroline looked up at the netting that enclosed the sagging silk envelope of the external balloon. "That outer fabric is doing us no good. If we strip away the cloth, we'll get rid of a lot of dead weight."

"Indeed!" Ferguson said with sudden eagerness. "The outer bag is over six hundred pounds of gutta-percha-covered silk. Removing it might give us enough buoyancy to continue our journey, eh?"

Grim and numb, Caroline took one of their long hunting knives. "I'll do it, doctor. *You* go and find Nemo." Her voice left no room for argument. Placing the knife between her teeth, she stood on the edge of the basket, then climbed the ropes to the outer webbing that held the balloon in place.

Ferguson took his rifle and a pack, then descended the ladder to the thorny acacia. Soon, whistling a tune to himself, he had disappeared into the tangled forest below. . .

Caroline planted her feet in the squares of netting. The monstrous condors had torn a four-foot gash in the scarlet fabric and another in the green section. The outer balloon was irreparable, even if they'd had more hydrogen gas to refill it.

Since they had already discarded most of their heavy objects into the lake, regaining six hundred pounds of lift required them to take on ballast again. That would also enable them to retrieve Nemo, if ever they managed to find him.

She replaced the despair in the pit of her stomach with iron-hard determination. Caroline pressed her lips together and lost herself in work. She had to slice the silk into strips and pull wads through the gaps in the webbing, taking special care not to puncture the inner balloon with the dagger point.

She thought of when she'd been younger, how she had enjoyed talking with Nemo from her window late at night, how she had flirted with him and strung him along . . . and Jules Verne as well. Because of her father's successful business and social standing, Caroline would never have been allowed to marry either of the young men, though she'd made her promises to a young Nemo, and had meant them with all her heart.

Yet now, with her father dead and her legal husband vanished somewhere in the Arctic . . . she knew she'd have been happier with Nemo after all. Angry, she tore strip after strip off the outer balloon, letting the tatters float away like colorful ribbons to adorn the top branches of the thorn trees.

She heard a gunshot and then a second, but even from her high vantage she could see nothing, could not tell what Ferguson was doing. Caroline imagined the English explorer fighting off ferocious beasts to rescue Nemo . . . though somehow she doubted that was true.

By the time she finished removing the outer balloon and climbed back into the *Victoria's* expansive basket, she heard a rustle in the branches and saw Ferguson returning. Tied to his belt were two ducks he had shot. "I've replenished our food supplies." He tossed them into the basket as he climbed aboard himself.

"But what about André?" she said.

He blinked at her as if in surprise, then shook his head. "Ah! No sign of him."

VII

Nemo managed to tread water long enough to catch his breath, and then he began to swim. The warm lake made him feel heavy and sluggish. He hoped to find an island in the huge shallow body, but low mists had risen from the surface of the water, and he could not see into the distance. He swam blindly, hoping he wasn't heading farther from the safety of shore. Creatures moved within Lake Chad – eels or snakes, even submerged crocodiles.

Twice he called out for help. His hoarse shout echoed in the air, reflected mockingly back at him. Finally, he heard soft sounds, a synchronous chant, and a splash of paddles in the water. He swam toward the noises. Before long, as the lake mists thickened, he spotted a long canoe filled with dark-skinned native fishermen gliding toward him. Nemo called out, hoping for rescue.

With a flurry of dipped oars, the canoes drew up beside the strange white man who had fallen from the sky. The boatmen seemed very excited. Their skin was remarkably smooth and ebony-colored, their attractive faces like statues with wide mouths and flat noses; gold ornamentation pierced their ears. They spoke in a musical-sounding language unfamiliar to Nemo. His French and his English would do him no good here in the heart of Africa.

Exhausted, drenched, and completely lost, he grasped the side of the canoe. The men said something to him, then consulted amongst themselves. Then, with such powerful muscles they seemed to be lifting a leaf, the fishermen hauled him out of the water and into their boat.

Nemo lay panting among the nets and fish. The fishermen began to sing again, dipping their paddles in the water with even, effective strokes. The canoe shot across the lake.

The boatmen made no threatening gestures with their fishing spears, though they could easily have clubbed him and thrown him back into Lake Chad for the crocodiles. Even so, Nemo saw a hardness in their onyx eyes, a predatory gleam that made him suspicious.

He knew there were many tribes, many nations in Africa, often at war with each other – some brave and honorable, some treacherous . . . just like all the other men he had known. He did not yet know to which category these fishermen belonged. Nemo drew a deep breath and coughed out water. At least his sacrifice had allowed the *Victoria* to fly on. No matter what happened, Caroline was safe.

The fishermen took the canoe into channels through the swamps. The ground became drier, and real grasses and shrubs replaced the marshy reeds, until the channel became a stream flowing out of Lake Chad. Ahead, Nemo saw a village of reed huts, thatched roofs, and stockades made of thorn branches.

Women chattered with great enthusiasm, welcoming the return of the fishermen. The man at the prow of the canoe loosed a musical cry. Then Nemo heard a startling gunshot, which seemed out of place in this wilderness. In the canoe, the boatmen took on harder expressions, and he felt even more uneasy. Nemo wished he could speak to the natives and ask their intentions, but for now, he waited stoically to see what fate had in store for him.

The canoe came to shore, and two boatmen leaped out to hold it steady while the others disembarked. Nemo climbed out after them, glad to stand on dry land again, though his knees quivered.

The men surrounded Nemo, then led him roughly along a worn footpath to the center of the village. Other villagers stared at the strange, pale-skinned captive. Two zebras pranced inside a thorny stockade; Nemo had no idea whether they had been captured as riding animals or beasts of burden . . . or just for food. Children sat in the dirt playing with twigs. Women wove fabric or pounded millet into flour.

Then with a chill he saw a group of narrow-faced men with pointed beards. They wore billowy garments with flowing burnouses, and swords thrust into sashes at their waists. By their lighter skin, Nemo recognized them as notorious slavers from northern Africa.

At the edge of the village, he saw dozens of people, obviously from a different tribe, chained together and tethered to the thick trees. Some of them huddled in the shade, others sat miserably in the hot, equatorial sun.

Before he could struggle, the fishermen grabbed Nemo's arms. He thrashed and kicked and yelled, to no avail. One of them cuffed him on the side of the head, making his vision spin. The slavers looked over at Nemo and raised their eyebrows in curiosity. They nodded with appreciation, then spoke in a guttural language which some of the natives seemed to understand.

One of the fishermen held out his hand for payment while the rest threw Nemo inside a small hut. He surged to his feet, fists clenched to attack, but the natives barricaded the door in his face.

Seeing red, Nemo growled through the thin walls, "I am not a slave." He didn't know if any of the others understood him, but he certainly comprehended their sharp, nasal laughter from outside.

VIII

When the stripped-down balloon was ready to fly again, Caroline and Dr Ferguson waited for a day, hoping Nemo would somehow make his way to them. The *Victoria* bobbed in the sky like a beacon; he should have been able to see them even from a great distance.

But still, he didn't arrive.

Caroline scanned the trees, the lake, the horizon, yet saw no sign of him. So, when the breezes changed and tugged them back in the opposite direction, she made up her mind. "If we take advantage of these winds, we shall drift back to Lake Chad. It's our only chance."

"We no longer have the means to control our direction, madame," Ferguson pointed out. "We cannot easily find new air currents. Indeed, we must go wherever the breezes take us."

Caroline's eyes were set with determination. "And now the breezes will blow us toward where we need to be. Nemo should spot us, and I know he can find a way to draw attention to himself . . . somehow."

Seeing her forceful expression, Dr Ferguson climbed down the ladder to disengage the grappling hook. The *Victoria*, as if anxious to be off, sprang into the sky as he climbed back up, mopping sweat from his brow.

Free again, the balloon wandered eastward across the sky like a drunkard, following the vagaries of breezes. Caroline refused to relinquish her grip on the spyglass, scanning for any sign of her lost Nemo. She knew that if they didn't find him soon, before the prevailing winds began pushing them in the opposite direction, she and the doctor would have no opportunity to return here.

At last, she made out the metal-blue haze of Lake Chad on the horizon. Now they merely had hundreds of uncharted miles to search for one lone man.

IX

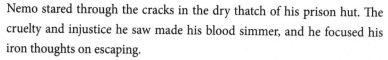

Nemo stared through the cracks in the dry thatch of his prison hut. The cruelty and injustice he saw made his blood simmer, and he focused his iron thoughts on escaping.

The other slaves, taken as spoils of battle in intertribal warfare, seemed crushed in spirit and unwilling to escape. Heartbroken, their villages destroyed, their relatives murdered in battle, they had nothing left to run to, no possibility for peace even if they escaped. The slavers had destroyed their very will to live.

But Nemo could still think, and he could still fight.

Ruthless slave merchants took captives to the coast, where they were sold in great markets such as the one at Zanzibar. The practice was so prevalent that the western edge of Africa bore the label "Ebony Coast," a euphemism for the slaves sold to Portuguese and Dutch ships.

Here, many of the hopeless women and children tied to the thorn trees were emaciated from a long trek across the wilderness. But Nemo was still healthy and strong. He would never be more fit. If he had to fight his way out, there could be no better time.

The hut enclosing him was not sturdy, with a floor of pounded earth – as if the slavers expected no outright resistance. Though Nemo had no knife, he knew he could break out. The main question was where he would go afterward. Where could he run? By now, if his sacrifice had meant anything, the *Victoria* would be long gone, far away . . . and Caroline would be safe.

The slavers gathered their horses and paid the villagers, making ready to depart at dawn the next day. Accompanying them, Nemo would be shackled and dragged along. Once the slavers put him in chains with the others and set off for the slave markets, he would never have a chance. It had to be tonight.

He sat motionless, studying everything around him, until he developed his plan. He didn't have the luxury of choosing among options.

At nightfall, the women built large cooking fires, and the visiting slavers feasted with their allies. Though the narrow-faced slavers restrained themselves, the fishermen drank millet beer from clay urns. Nemo ate the watery fish soup an old village woman gave him through the door of his prison hut.

During the loudest part of the revels, he found a sharp stone on the floor of his hut and sawed at the vine lashings holding the back wall together. Then Nemo waited until well past midnight, when silence hung thick around the village. Hoping he could move quietly enough to get away, he parted the back joinings of the hut. With a loud crackling noise, he pushed through and stood in the open again. *Free.*

Though his heart felt heavy at his inability to cut all the other captives loose, he knew they would be hunted down and killed, and would raise enough noise and alarm that none of them would get away. The vile slavers had horses, and the wilderness would be filled with predators. Nemo had no choice but to leave them here, resigned to their fates.

If he ran on foot into the jungle, though, he would not get far. Instead, Nemo made his way to the crude stockade, where he inspected the two captive zebras. The animals twitched their tails and snorted, moving back and forth.

Knowing he could be caught at any second, Nemo removed the thorny bars from the corral's closure. The striped animals backed away from him, but he approached slowly, trying to be calm. Not daring to risk even a soothing whisper, Nemo crept closer to one of them. In the starlight, the animal's black and white markings rippled like an apparition. Its mane was short and bristly.

The first animal trotted away, discovered the opening in the corral, and bolted out into the open. The second zebra, seeing its companion flee, decided to do the same. Nemo sprang toward it, throwing his arms around its muscular neck. He had no halter or saddle, but he had desperation. He grasped the stiff hair of its mane and hauled himself onto its back.

The zebra squealed as if a lion had clawed it, then bounded forward with the speed of terror. Nemo held on, low over the zebra's neck, squeezing its ribs with his thighs. He had no way to exert control – so the zebra just ran, galloping out of the village.

Behind him came the outcries of the wakened villagers. Gunshots barked into the night. Hunched low, Nemo kept riding, slapping the animal into greater speed, until the turmoil faded into the distance. The zebra plunged into the tree shadows and tall grasses, fleeing the marsh onto solid ground, toward the plains where it knew to roam. . .

Several hours later, while Nemo still clung to the zebra, the sun rose over the horizon, spilling golden light upon the grasslands. He cast a glance over his shoulder – and saw to his dismay a line of mounted dark-garbed raiders galloping after him. Though Nemo was only one slave, he had infuriated and shamed these men by escaping; he was an affront to these cruel people who expected all to tremble in fear of them.

The slavers' mounts were larger and stronger than his zebra, and they would catch up soon. Nemo swatted the animal's rump. Though its nose and mouth were flecked with foam, the zebra put on a burst of speed, charging across the plain.

Raising an angry fist at his pursuers, Nemo saw no place to hide in the great open space, no refuge. Then he looked up into the brightening sky and saw to the north a heavenly object, like a man-made moon drifting there.

The *Victoria*!

With a cry, he turned the zebra's head, changing its direction. The mount galloped blindly across the grasses. Behind him he could hear the thundering hooves of pursuing horses. One of the slavers fired a shot, though Nemo was still too far ahead to worry about any stray bullet.

When he heard a second shot from a different direction, he looked up and saw a tiny puff of smoke come from the balloon. Caroline had seen him. Ferguson had fired his rifle as a signal. Nemo raced forward on the zebra, but still the slavers came closer. Though frightened of the *Victoria*, still they would not let their escaped captive go free.

The zebra stumbled, nearly throwing its rider. The animal had very little strength left . . . but Nemo was so close now. He gasped a burning breath, raising one hand to wave at the balloon. The *Victoria* seemed to be descending. The anchor fell over the side and then the long ladder.

Nemo fought with the zebra, trying to influence its course, but the enormous balloon spooked it. He grasped its mane and squeezed with his thighs, trying to urge just a little more cooperation and speed from his mount. Then he hurled a curse back at the slavers.

The dark-garbed men closed the gap, still howling. As they shot their long rifles, bullets grazed the grasses near him. A lucky shot could kill him or the zebra. The slavers' shouts came across the still air, but Nemo paid them no attention. He drew closer and closer to the balloon.

The rope ladder dangled almost within reach. He would have only one chance, and he stretched out his hand to take it.

In that same cruel instant, a gust of wind jerked the balloon higher, and the bottom rung of the ladder rose out of reach. Above in the basket, Caroline leaned over the edge, her face filled with anxiety. She stretched out her arms, as if to grasp him. With a pang, he remembered how stricken she had looked when he'd jumped out of the balloon into Lake Chad – and he vowed not to disappoint her again.

As the zebra charged under the balloon, Nemo used the last of his strength and balance to rise up on the animal's back. He barely managed to plant his feet on the black-and-white striped hide. Snorting, the zebra wheeled and Nemo knew he was about to fall – but at the last instant, he grasped the lowest rung of the ladder. Relieved of its burden, the zebra galloped away into the veldt.

Caroline shouted and Nemo locked his other hand on the second rung, trying to haul himself up. His arms shook, yet somehow he had to find the strength.

The slavers rode beneath the dangling young man, furious, but he spat down at them. Dr Ferguson and Caroline began heaving out bags of ballast, and the balloon began to climb and climb.

A heavy sack struck a slaver's horse and it reared, throwing its rider. Ferguson fired his rifle, killing one of the pursuers, while the others milled about. The slavers finally began to shoot their inferior rifles up at the rising balloon, and Nemo knew the *Victoria* and her passengers were still in grave danger. If the evil men were to strike the hydrogen sack, the punctures would destroy their remaining balloon.

He scrambled up the swaying ladder, as Caroline threw out more ballast. The slavers circled and howled in outrage. A sack hit the tall, surly leader on the shoulders, driving him to the ground. The balloon climbed higher.

The slavers wheeled about and began shooting up at the *Victoria*, even though it had drifted high enough and far enough to be out of range.

Using every last ounce of energy, Nemo heaved himself upward one rung at a time, until Caroline and a grinning Dr Ferguson could grasp his arms and shoulders. They grabbed the back of his shirt and hauled him over the edge of the basket.

Nemo fell into Caroline's arms.

X

The balloon climbed until it reached a river of air that drove them north-west across a line of hills. While Caroline cleaned his minor injuries, Nemo devoured part of one of the ducks Ferguson had shot the day before.

Caroline used a few drops of their remaining water and a piece of cloth to wipe the sweat and grime from Nemo's forehead. The dampness felt cool; her touch was gentle, and lingered. Her bright blue eyes looked down at him with a depth of emotion that made him feel weak. Something had changed in her heart during his absence. Though unspoken, another pledge passed between Nemo and Caroline: soon, their time would come.

Listening to Nemo's tale, Ferguson leaned back against the wicker basket, scratching his extravagant mustache. With his logbook open on his lap, he used one of Caroline's lead sketching pencils to record the young man's story. "When we publish the record of our journey, this will make a fine addition, eh? Great excitement accompanied by numerous scientific observations. Perhaps even a biting commentary on the vile practice of slavery. Such a combination will greatly increase our book's readership, my friends."

Until this point, Nemo hadn't thought of publishing an account of their travels, except perhaps in the *Proceedings of the Royal Geographical Society*. Caroline had already suffered a scandal in France because of her independent ways and unorthodox ideas. The very thought of a woman participating in such an expedition across Africa – most especially in the company of a young man to whom she was not married (never mind Dr Ferguson's constant presence) – would set the high society tongues wagging again.

But perhaps the scientific merit of their work, especially Caroline's sketches, would stand in their defense.

For days they drifted north-westward, and the landscape became more desolate. The jungle vegetation gave way to scrub brush and leafless bushes. "We're approaching the edge of the Sahara," Caroline said, pointing to their charts with anything but enthusiasm. "Look."

Their water supplies were low, and they no longer had the recondenser apparatus to raise and lower themselves, leaving the *Victoria* at the mercy of the winds. They had to make the best possible speed, hoping their diminishing gas would keep them aloft for the thousand miles remaining to the coast.

Soon, the terrain changed from golden scrub to dark rocks and the taupe of unrelenting sand. Ahead, the dunes of the Sahara sprawled like an ocean whose sinuous hills and crests reflected the harsh sun.

Faint caravan paths led from Tangier or Fez across the Atlas Mountains, or from Tripoli across Sudan and the breadth of the desert. As they drifted over the dune sea, they saw no signs of life, no water, none of the wild herds they had observed on the Serengeti. Only the balloon itself gave them any shade in the cloudless sky. The shimmering sands created thermal updrafts that made the *Victoria* bounce and buck.

In the distance they could see a few rare, dark smudges that indicated oases. Nemo kept his eye on these patches for hours before he came to the grim conclusion that the balloon was no longer moving. Ferguson tested the stagnant wind with his scientific apparatus. His black mustache drooped as he scowled. "Indeed, it appears the wind has failed us. We seem to be at a standstill in the middle of the desert. Rotten luck."

Caroline saw the implications. "We must conserve our water and our food."

"The outlook does not appear good, my friends," Ferguson said at the end of a long afternoon. Caroline frowned at him for stating the obvious.

"The heat will expand our balloon," Nemo pointed out. "The extra buoyancy should keep us aloft longer."

But in the dead calm of the Sahara, they still made no progress whatsoever.

Then, after interminable hours of sunburn and sweat and parched throats, Caroline sniffed the air and held up her hand. "There is a breeze. We're moving again."

Ferguson grasped one of the support ropes and looked around. Nemo stared at the dunes below and saw that they had indeed begun to crawl along. "Now we are moving due northward."

Behind them, a hazy shimmer appeared in the air, moving across the desert. Caroline perked up. "If that is rain, can we refill our water tanks?"

Sickened, Nemo took out the spyglass. "Not rain, Caroline – that's a sandstorm."

The pillar of gusting winds picked up fine dust from the desert, leaving heavier sand grains at ground level. They had little enough time to fasten down loose objects. Thinking fast, Caroline gathered cloth for makeshift hoods to pull over their heads, mouths, and noses, leaving only a slit for their eyes.

The three huddled in the basket as the murky wind slammed the balloon off on a careening course. Choking grit coated them all with a layer of chalky, tan residue. The wind howled and shrieked, buffeting them back and forth. Caroline and Nemo clung to each other.

Ferguson said something unintelligible, then spat grit from his mouth and rubbed his dirty sleeve across his teeth, looking annoyed. The wind carried so many particles that it made a hissing sound. Static electricity created blue fingers of St Elmo's Fire that skittered up and down the netting.

The storm drove them along for many miles. When the whipping gale cleared and dust settled out of the air, the newly washed landscape of gentle sandy slopes appeared unchanged. Nemo scanned the dunes with the spyglass, while Ferguson and Caroline used rags to clear clinging dirt from the basket.

"Battered, but still intact, eh?" Ferguson said, optimistic. "If that storm cooperated, it could have taken us halfway to the coast by now."

They each took a ration of food and water, and drifted for another day on a brisk westward breeze. Like a miracle, the terrain changed again. The vagaries of weather had nudged them beyond the southern fringe of the Sahara, and even the scrub brush looked like a comparative paradise.

But Nemo realized to his dismay that their altitude was decreasing. He didn't voice his suspicions until he had stared at the balloon, watching the patterns of dust that clung to the silk. "The sandstorm weakened our seams. We're losing hydrogen faster than I had expected."

"We still have two hundred pounds of ballast to toss out, don't we?" Ferguson said. "Even though we have you aboard, my friend, we decreased our weight by six hundred pounds by removing the outer balloon."

Ferguson bent to pick up one of the heavy sacks at the bottom of the basket, but Nemo stopped him. "No. If we're going to descend anyway, let's take advantage of it. We can anchor for a while and replenish our supplies." By now, the near-empty water container held only a few cups of tepid liquid.

When they drifted close enough to the ground, they would tether the *Victoria* long enough to take on supplies; then they would get rid of ballast and hope to stay aloft all the way to the Senegal coast. From there, outposts of Portuguese, Dutch, British, or French would be within reach, even if the three explorers had to trudge overland and ask the locals for help. Coastal Africans were familiar enough with white traders and explorers that Ferguson expected to receive assistance without much risk.

After studying her charts, Caroline pointed out a river in the distance – the Niger perhaps – near which stood a city larger than the thatched villages they had seen before. Nemo looked through the spyglass, studying towers and walls. "It must be an important trading center." It reminded him of Zanzibar City.

"It cannot be . . . but it must be!" Ferguson's voice was filled with delight. "That, my friends, is the fabled city of Timbuctoo. You must have heard the legends? A magnificent metropolis filled with treasure, the caravan crossroads from desert and coastal dwellers."

Caroline looked at the settlement. "I've heard stories, but I don't believe them. Roofs made of pure gold, vast libraries to rival even those of Alexandria. Its citizens are said to be doctors, judges, priests, or scholars."

Though it was a large town by African standards, Timbuctoo proved disappointing in light of the legends surrounding it. The beige towers and mosques were fashioned from hardened clay mixed with sand, supported with timbers of dried wood. Window holes in the mud-cement gave the structures the appearance of wasps' nests. Men moved about the narrow streets wearing loose robes. Camels and desert asses hauled loads from what appeared to be a bazaar near a water well at the center of the city.

Ferguson leaned over the side of the balloon. "Only one white man has ever laid eyes upon Timbuctoo and returned to tell the tale."

"Yes – a Frenchman, René Caillié," Nemo said with a knowing smile. "He posed as an Arab, learned Arab ways, and joined a caravan. He started at the Senegal coast and journeyed inland until he reached Timbuctoo, where he spent a month recording his observations. Instead of returning the way he came, he headed north across the Sahara and finally reached Morocco two years later."

Dr Ferguson desperately wanted to descend, to be the first *Englishman* there, but Nemo didn't dare waste their precious buoyancy. As the balloon drifted beyond Timbuctoo toward a green line of hills, Caroline put a hand on Nemo's arm. They still had a long journey to the coast.

XI

Ahead, a black and brown buzzing cloud shifted with the winds, and then came straight for the balloon as if it were an intelligent, destructive storm. Ferguson stared perplexed at the oncoming apparition, trying to figure out what to write in his logbook.

But Nemo understood what it was. "It's a plague of locusts! They'll eat everything." In the distance, they could all see that the grasslands had been completely razed.

Helpless and adrift, the travelers had no way to defend themselves as the locusts attacked like a hurricane. A hail of winged grasshoppers pelted them, striking the basket, the ropes, and the balloon fabric itself. The insects chewed every scrap of vegetable matter. Nemo tried to keep Caroline covered at the bottom of the balloon car, but she insisted on fighting back and climbed up to swat the locusts off the basket and her clothing.

Coughing, Nemo slapped the insects away from his face and knocked them from the vital ropes. The voracious grasshoppers chewed at the cords and netting, clustering on anything they could devour. The sheer weight of the winged vermin made the balloon droop.

Ferguson hauled out his rifle, as if that might do anything, and then set to work crushing the insects himself with the wooden stock. Nemo, his hands smeared with ichor from hundreds of smashed locusts, crawled up the rope to reach the outer netting. He clambered around the cords, brushing grasshoppers off into the air, but they merely circled back.

The buzzing sound was deafening. Caroline shouted to Nemo, but he couldn't understand her words. He watched her climb the opposite side of the balloon, working desperately, and then he saw what she had realized. If they didn't keep the insects away from the surrounding mesh, the balloon and the ropes would all fall apart, and they would plummet to their deaths.

Ferguson stamped on the locusts chewing the *Victoria*'s basket. The humming made the air itself vibrate, as the swirling cloud of grasshoppers kept coming and coming. Nemo reached the top of the balloon and nearly lost his grip as a frayed strand of netting snapped.

"It's like one of the plagues of Moses." Caroline spat out a grasshopper that had flown into her mouth. Surprisingly agile, she climbed around the balloon, keeping the ropes clear, while Ferguson hurled curses at the grasshoppers.

Then, a few moments later the lush grasslands to the east proved a more tempting feast to the locusts. As the mindless swarm flew onward, some alighted, gnawed a mouthful of the basket frame or rope fibers, then moved on. They watched in awe as the buzzing cloud continued like a school of tiny piranhas to clear vegetation across the African countryside.

Nemo and Caroline at last lowered themselves into the *Victoria*'s basket, then spent several minutes picking grasshoppers from each other's hair and collars, pockets, and folds. At any other time, they might have found it amusing.

In the aftermath of the swarm, the balloon looked ragged and tattered, as if the whole vessel had been chewed by some giant beast and then spat out. The ropes were frayed, the colorful fabric of the inner balloon stained and spattered. Numerous tiny holes showed through the woven basket.

Luckily, according to Caroline's chart marks and Nemo's positional measurements, the *Victoria* had finally entered the environs of Senegal and Gambia, and they should be within a day of the west African coast.

This news cheered the travelers somewhat, but still the leaking balloon sank with discernible speed. After replenishing their supplies beyond Timbuctoo, they had discarded the last of their ballast. And now they needed to lighten their load more dramatically just to keep moving.

But the *Victoria* still had to pass over one more mountain range before they reached the coast. Unless Nemo could find some way to improve their buoyancy, the balloon would crash into the slopes.

XII

Covered with dense jungles, the line of low mountains loomed larger and more ominous by the hour. Beyond the hills, according to their maps, lay a river and lowlands that extended to the long-sought coast.

Then they would be across the continent, after five weeks in a balloon.

The sagging *Victoria* traveled in a weaving drunkard's course on the erratic winds. When they dropped to within a hundred feet of the treetops, they were close enough to see terrified animals even without their well-used spyglass.

Near the base of the rugged foothills, the balloon passed over a streamside village, where they observed a huge commotion. At first, Nemo thought the frenzied activity must have been caused by the natives' superstitious fear of their arrival, but then he noticed men tossing torches from one straw roof to another. The thatched huts went up in flames.

Tall villagers with glossy skin brandished spears defensively at men in billowing black robes riding muscular chestnut horses. The raiders carried swords and a few guns.

With a stricken expression, Caroline raised the spyglass and handed it to Nemo. Now he could make out the slaughtered forms of village defenders lying on the bloodied ground while the mounted raiders charged about rounding up women and children. Nemo's shoulders sagged, and he felt sick with disgust and rekindled anger at seeing the atrocity of the slavers.

One lean woman, her face a mask of despair, thrashed loose from her captors and dashed toward a burning hut. Her bare breasts were swollen, and Nemo suspected she was a new mother. Before she could reach the hut, which no doubt contained her child, one of the slavers galloped by and struck her down with his long sword. Wheeling his horse about, the black-robed raider charged through the cluster of captives, as if he wanted to kill even more of them. Intimidated and outnumbered, the villagers let themselves be rounded up.

Silent and slow, the balloon drifted over the massacre, low enough that they could hear screams of anguish from the captured and dying. Sour smoke snaked around them as the flames devoured the remains of the village.

"I will not just sit idly by and allow this to happen," Nemo said. "We must disrupt the slavers however we can."

Wearing a grim expression, Caroline grabbed one of Ferguson's rifles herself while the doctor picked up the other. She looked at the Englishman, studied his huge black mustache and bushy dark hair. "This time we are not taking specimens, doctor, and I am not just drawing sketches."

She fired the rifle at a raider and missed, but killed the horse beneath him. Ferguson aimed carefully and shot, knocking down a broad-shouldered man with a pointed beard. The other black-robed horsemen reined up and shook their fists at the balloon.

Several native women broke free of the circle and ran toward the tree-covered foothills. After Nemo reloaded Caroline's rifle, he killed another of the dark-clad slavers, but the surge of satisfaction did little to dampen his anger. Soon, however, the balloon had passed over the scene of the massacre and continued to drift westward toward the mountains.

Enraged, the mounted raiders left the burning village with only two men to guard the captives. They rode over the terrain in pursuit of the sinking balloon. The slavers had old-fashioned guns as well, and lead balls flew past the tattered *Victoria*; two struck the already leaking silk bag. The balloon kept ahead of the raiders, though with the fresh bullet holes they lost altitude even faster now.

"We must hope the wind keeps up," Nemo said, "and that the slavers follow until that village can rally its defenses."

Below, the horsemen howled in a language Nemo could not understand – but their intent was clear enough. In the lead, the tallest slave raider whipped his chestnut horse and thundered into the hills. Gradually, the travelers increased their lead, but as the wind carried the sinking balloon toward the mountains, Nemo realized the *Victoria* would never maintain sufficient altitude to cross the range. He hoped the raiders gave up before the balloon slammed into the mountainside. Yet the furious black-robed men showed no intention of slackening their chase.

"It appears we have gotten into trouble again," Caroline said, drawing a deep breath. "At least this time I have no regrets. We saved many people in that village."

"Indeed. Now we merely need to save *ourselves*, eh?" Ferguson reloaded both of his rifles. "I believe we're up to the task."

They sank lower and lower until the treetops were barely twenty feet beneath the basket. Nemo searched for any way to lighten their load. He threw out the last of their food and the remaining water container, as well as the heavy grappling hook. The bullet holes opened into wider gashes, and the *Victoria* began a more rapid descent as the mountains climbed beneath them.

His thick brows drawn together, Ferguson looked long and hard at his scientific logbooks, which he dared not sacrifice; neither would he give up his rifles. Finally, he opted to throw four pounds of bullets over the side: a symbolic gesture, gaining them only a few minutes of flight, at most.

The winds gusted against the foothills, slowing the balloon's progress. The *Victoria* drifted in a circular motion that would snag them in a tangle of trees.

As the slave raiders galloped after them, thrashing their mounts, the balloon's slackening pace allowed the horsemen to close the distance. From behind, two more gunshots rang out, and within moments the black-robed men would be upon the *Victoria*.

"We have no choice," Nemo said, looking up at the balloon, which sagged in its net. "We've got to get over these mountains." He picked up a rifle, loaded it and handed it to Caroline, then took the other for himself. "Doctor, please tie your journals securely inside your shirt. We'll be required to hang on tight."

"What are we doing? You've got an idea, eh? I can tell."

"I hope we're close to the river and the colony in Sierra Leone, doctor," Nemo said. "We are going to cut away the car and hang onto the ring and netting for the rest of this journey."

While Ferguson gaped at him, Caroline climbed onto the edge of the basket and up into the webbing. One of the locust-chewed strands snapped under her weight, but she grabbed with the other hand and climbed higher. Nemo hoped the tattered ropes would hold long enough for them to get over the mountains and away from the vicious riders.

Ferguson secured his logbooks and followed Caroline up into the netting. Nemo placed a long knife between his teeth, remembering how he had climbed ratlines on the *Coralie*, and crawled up from the basket.

Holding firmly, he sawed at one of the sturdy ropes until it came apart. The basket lurched and dropped. The *Victoria* continued to descend. Nemo worked his way around the balloon ring and cut the second of the four ropes, imagining that he was cutting the throat of one of those evil slavers.

Behind them, the raiders drew closer. The horses seemed to realize the closeness of their prey and put on an extra burst of speed. One of the black-robed men shot at the balloon, and Nemo saw another bullet hole open in the silken sack. As if to spite the travelers, the winds slowed again, bringing them to a near standstill in the air as their pursuers closed the distance.

Nemo viciously sliced the third rope. Stretched out beneath Caroline, the only remaining cable began to fray by itself where the locusts had chewed it. Caroline took the knife from him, bent down, and slashed the last rope. With a loud snap, the basket broke free and tumbled end over end.

Liberated from this dead weight, the balloon bounded up into the sky until it reached another current, which pushed them toward the mountain crests. Nemo lost his grip, clung to another rope, riding the balloon as if it were a wild animal.

Below, a chestnut horse reared as its rider tried to wrestle his mount to one side, but the basket crashed on top of them. Rather than accepting defeat, the black-robed horsemen rode even more furiously, as if hoping the balloon might snag on a rocky pinnacle.

Breezes carried the *Victoria* toward the boulder-strewn ridge summit, but Nemo still wasn't sure they would make it. He hooked his arms and legs through the ragged netting and held on, his feet dangling.

They scraped over the broad crest of the mountain. Still clutching the webbing, Nemo dropped and began to run, pulling the balloon forward. When they crossed the apex, he jumped back into the air. Like a gasping Greek marathon runner, the *Victoria* coasted over and down the western slope. Ahead, at the bottom of the foothills, they saw a broad fast-moving river that flowed toward a delta on the coast.

"That must be the Senegal, eh?" Ferguson said, reaching inside his shirt as if to consult his maps. "A British protectorate, if I remember correctly."

Nemo stayed the explorer's hand. "We'll have plenty of time to study the charts after we land, doctor," he said. "For now, we're at the mercy of wherever the winds take us."

"Will we stay afloat to cross the river, André?" Caroline asked.

He looked up at the deflating balloon, but doubted they would reach even the grasslands at the base of the foothills. "We can hope, Caroline."

On the far side of the Senegal River, they would find European settlements and a fort – and beyond that, the ocean. The Atlantic Ocean. The opposite side of the African continent, which they had traversed entirely, the first Europeans ever to do so.

But their triumph would be complete only if they *lived* to the end of the journey. Nemo looked at Caroline and promised himself that she would survive and return to France.

All too soon, however, like a horse that had been ridden until its heart burst, the *Victoria* simply gave up. The balloon sagged, and the explorers descended, clinging to the rope net, all the way down to the treetops.

Nemo had to hold his feet away from the tearing branches, but soon they scraped over the scrubby hills to the grasslands. The flatter terrain allowed them to keep moving with every gust of wind, though occasionally the dying *Victoria* struck the ground, before lurching into the air again like a bouncing ball. Each oscillation became smaller, the balloon no more than a wadded silk blanket around them. Dragged by ever-weakening gusts of wind, they struck the ground for the last time, half a mile from the wide Senegal River.

Nemo lashed the severed ends of the balloon ropes to low bushes, anchoring the empty sack. He suspected that inhabitants of the Sierra Leone fort might have seen their dramatic approach and would come to investigate.

Dr Ferguson steadied himself on his feet, then bowed his head, placing a hand over his heart. "Farewell, *Victoria*. You have served us admirably indeed. The remainder of our journey can be a mere epilogue." He patted the heavy scientific notebooks he had kept. "Despite our perils and misadventures, I must admit this has been quite a successful expedition. The Royal Geographical Society will be most chagrined that they refused to fund us, eh? Never again will they scoff at my innovative designs."

Caroline smiled at him.

"We should make camp here," Nemo suggested, looking around for food. The river would provide all the water they could want.

They built a large fire. As Nemo tried to doze, he gazed through the sparks and orange light to see Caroline lying on her back, staring up at the stars, also awake. Even disheveled from their long adventures, she still looked beautiful to him, just as when she had spent the night beside him under magnolia trees in the churchyard on Île Feydeau.

Their journey together was nearly at an end. Soon Nemo and Caroline would return to France and their former lives. Nemo had no doubt that she would continue to run her father's shipping business, while he would take up another of Napoleon III's engineering projects. He hoped that by now the emperor had found someone else to redesign the Paris sewer systems. . .

And they would try to pretend. But during these five weeks he and Caroline had experienced too much together, had come to know each other too well, had grown too close for their situation ever to be the same. . .

The next morning they awoke hungry, with no food left. Caroline brushed dry grass from her coppery hair. As she turned to watch the sun rise over the low mountains, her eyes flew wide open. While stealing a glance at her beautiful face, Nemo watched her expression change – then he too saw the dark horsemen bearing down upon them out of the foothills, still several miles away.

The slave raiders must have ridden over the mountains through the night, intent on striking back at the balloon travelers.

The Senegal was a mile wide, and the current too fast to swim. The treeless lowlands offered no place to hide. Ferguson had only one small box of ammunition remaining and the two rifles. At least a dozen armed and murderous slavers pursued them.

Ferguson looked with alarm at the distant horsemen, then sadly down at the *Victoria*. "Alas, my friends, our balloon can serve us no more. We're out of hydrogen gas."

Holding his knife and ready to fight, Nemo tried to think of some way they could use the empty balloon to float on the river, but he knew the fabric would grow waterlogged and drag them under. He looked down at their small campfire, the few supplies they had. "Wait! We don't need hydrogen."

"But how, my friend? We have no way to inflate the balloon."

"Yes, we do. Caroline, grab as much wood and dry grass as you can. Pile it on the campfire." He fixed his dark-eyed gaze on Ferguson. "We'll make another kind of balloon out of the *Victoria*, doctor. Remember the Montgolfier brothers."

"Ah yes, they were French." Ferguson barked out a loud laugh. "A hot air balloon, eh? The sack should still achieve enough buoyancy to carry us aloft."

Nemo grabbed one corner of the huge silk sack while Ferguson went to the other end. "We only need to cross the river. From there we'll go on foot to the fort. It's Portuguese, I think, or maybe Dutch."

"At least it won't be run by those fellows." Ferguson jerked a thumb at the oncoming horsemen.

Caroline came running back with an armload of twigs and dried grasses. Ferguson and Nemo arranged the balloon, tying more of its cords to the bushes. They built the campfire into a towering blaze that belched smoke, hot flames, and heated air into the sky. By the time the bonfire burned at its peak, the horsemen bore down upon them so close that the adventurers could hear the hoof-beats and the shouts.

"It's time," Nemo said. "We dare not wait any longer."

The three of them each took hold of a separate part of the balloon and stretched the opening over the flames. The hot air was like a heavy breath that blew into the sagging sack.

"It's not filling fast enough," Caroline said.

"Just be grateful the leftover hydrogen didn't burst into flames, eh?" Ferguson said, looking up into the wide mouth of the battered silk sack.

Nemo strained against the ropes to hold the opening over the rippling hot air. "The gas is much too diluted for that." He watched the torn holes in the balloon sack, wishing he had taken the time to seal them the night before, but now the hot air filled the dying *Victoria* faster than it could leak out again.

The black-robed raiders snarled, and the three companions could see teeth flashing in their cruel mouths. Several of the men had drawn long swords, ready to ride down and lop off the heads of those who had ruined their slave raid.

But now the *Victoria* bobbed upward, standing straight. Though its sides remained crinkled, it had become buoyant, straining at the ropes.

"Caroline, climb up," Nemo said, helping her. "Careful not to burn your hands." Without arguing, she scrambled onto the tattered netting that held the sack together. The fire continued to roar, and the revived *Victoria* strained upward like a restless spirit.

"Doctor, you're next," Nemo said as he took the dagger and slashed one of the ropes opposite Ferguson. The long-legged explorer did his best to climb onto the sack.

Released from one of its tethers, the hot air balloon bent sideways, and Nemo slashed the second cord. As he leaped onto the netting himself, he cut the remaining rope so that the *Victoria's* carcass rose into the air, no more than fifty feet above the ground – but buoyant enough.

The horsemen arrived, livid with rage at seeing the balloon escape again. They fired their guns, puncturing the *Victoria* twice more, but air currents carried the revived balloon over the broad river that flowed gently to the sea.

"Hang on," Nemo said, and they all clutched the ropes as their hot air balloon drifted low across the Senegal. It spun around like a top, letting Nemo see in all directions. He watched the black-clad raiders come to an abrupt halt at the muddy bank. Snarling and cursing, they shot impotently into the sky.

Although the cooling air leaked out of the sack, the desperate explorers approached the opposite shore swiftly enough. As Nemo looked toward the western bank, he saw that a cavalry troop of uniformed men – British, from the looks of them – had ridden out to intercept the balloon.

The *Victoria* kissed the water twice, dragging their feet in the turgid current, forcing the three to crawl higher onto the sagging sack. The balloon continued to bob across the water, buoyed by a slight breeze, then struck the mud on the far side and dragged them across the flatlands as the British troops advanced to meet them.

When the exhausted *Victoria* finally came to rest, the travelers sank into the folds of silk and panted with sheer relief. Within moments, the British troops galloped up in formation, smartly dressed, cleaner and healthier than anyone they had seen in five weeks.

Nemo didn't stand to greet them: his knees were too shaky and his muscles too weak from the exertions they had endured.

The British captain peered down at the mustachioed explorer in the mud, and tipped his hat. "Doctor Ferguson, I presume?"

Ferguson smiled so that his mustache curved upward like a black cat's tail. He glanced over at Nemo and Caroline. "Yes, sir – Ferguson, and friends."

PART VII
ROBUR THE CONQUEROR

I

Paris, 1854

Though he had been home for half a year now, still Nemo could not relax.

At dawn, with a cool mist slinking around the riverfront districts, Nemo gazed up at the painted building that overlooked the Seine. Three stories tall, the structure had gray and white shutters, and stone steps leading up to a tall, narrow door. Over the lintel hung a bright sign: "ARONNAX, MERCHANT, Paris Offices."

Only a month after she had returned from Africa, Caroline had purchased the expensive Left Bank property across from Notre Dame, where gulls flew around the spires, arches, and gargoyles. Boats passed along the river, ducking under bridge after bridge. Caroline's main office stood directly on the water, across from the Tuileries Gardens, not far from the impressive Palais Bourbon.

Nemo could not argue with her decision to move her shipping offices to Paris. Both in business acumen and in her creative arts, Caroline had made herself into a person to be reckoned with. But the thought of having her so close to him, and still so unavailable, tore his heart with conflicting emotions.

Six years had passed since the *Forward*'s departure, and she still had received no word from Captain Hatteras. The Arctic explorer had not sent her so much as a single letter.

But the law was the law. Nemo had to wait one more year for her. That was how it must be, though in his heart he felt that he and Caroline had made vows and commitments to each other that outweighed any mere certificate. . .

Perhaps it was a consequence of having encountered danger so many times, having faced death at each other's sides. Perhaps the exquisite agony of being so close for five long weeks had worked their secret emotions to a fever pitch. When he and Caroline boarded a northbound British naval ship at the mouth of the Congo and sailed for England, Nemo could pretend no longer.

Caroline's eyes flashed at him like star sapphires, and she flushed when their glances met. He could read her thoughts and desires as if she'd written them down and handed him a secret note. The British sailors treated Dr Ferguson as a hero, and the captain welcomed the explorer to his table, but Nemo and Caroline were often left to themselves.

On a still, moonless night filled with stars over a sea of glass, Nemo slipped into Caroline's cabin. She welcomed him without words, only kisses . . . and did not ask him why he had waited so long.

They had a full month together as the ship cruised toward the English Channel along the African coast, past the Strait of Gibraltar and along the edge of Portugal. The two of them remained discreet, though they fooled neither the sailors, nor the captain, who viewed Caroline as precious cargo. Only Dr Samuel Ferguson, who spent every waking moment editing and rewriting his journals for publication, was completely oblivious.

Nemo and Caroline cherished every moment.

But as they approached France again, they looked at each other with dread and indecision. While Nemo had nothing to lose – no reputation, no standing in society – Madame Caroline Hatteras owned a successful shipping company and was married to a man who had a proud and respected name.

"We will have to wait, Caroline," Nemo said as they stood together at the bow of the ship, looking at the approaching English coastline. "We'll have to pretend. Again."

Caroline's eyes shone with tears like crystal. "It doesn't matter to me anymore, André. We both know the captain won't be coming back from his voyage to find the Northwest Passage. Why should we delay, when we love each other? We have already wasted the best years of our lives apart."

"Because it would make all the difference in the world – and you know it. In a year, we can be together, and people will cheer. No one will blame you. I am an adventurer with my own mantle of fame, as well as Emperor Napoleon's blessing, and you are a successful businesswoman." He narrowed his eyes and clasped her hand earnestly. "But if we flaunt our love now, Caroline, I will be seen as a scoundrel, and you as an adulteress." She turned away, but Nemo gripped her hand more tightly. "You know it as well as I do."

She nodded, but refused to let her tears fall. "That is why we must make the most of every moment together now."

When they returned to Paris, with the public watching, time had dragged on. Nemo steeled himself to avoid the woman he loved as much as possible. He would not tempt her further . . . or himself. That would only make the wait more unbearable for both of them.

To Nemo, being near Caroline was like playing with fire, and he found it impossible to drive her from his thoughts. The sea passage to Zanzibar and the balloon journey across Africa held memories even more joyful than his carefree childhood on the Loire. And the voyage home had been heaven.

But now Caroline would be right here. In Paris. Close. *Too close.* It was going to be a very long year. . .

Once back in France, Nemo had grown restless. He often walked the streets before dawn, wide awake with memories and dreams, trying not to think of Caroline. At twenty-six, he should have been at the height of his ambitions. Yet he found his civilized life dreary, without adventure or goals.

In the early morning he enjoyed watching shopkeepers crank out their awnings, fish sellers set up their stalls with baskets of herring, mussels, and trout. He stopped in front of Caroline's new offices, just staring, thinking about her. So early in the day, he knew she couldn't see him. . .

The previous night, as on so many long nights, Nemo had joined Jules Verne for a light dinner, sitting at a cafe table not far from where literary students argued about symbolism and meter in the poetry of Racine.

Nemo found the intelligentsia dull and unimaginative. When they discussed current events, their focus remained on naive politics, with no mention whatsoever of scientific breakthroughs or new exploration. But, while Nemo talked to Verne about the loss of his boyhood contentment and sense of wonder, his friend's attention was obviously drawn toward the artistic debate.

Dr Samuel Ferguson had received a hero's welcome upon returning to England. Despite his protests, the Royal Geographical Society had granted the Englishman all the credit for the expedition, citing Nemo and Caroline only as "assistants" or "traveling companions."

When Nemo had told his story to Verne, drinking a pot of dark coffee while his red-headed friend toyed with a glass of cheap Bordeaux, Verne grew uncomfortable each time Caroline was mentioned. The writer had never got over his attachment to the merchant's daughter either. . .

Now, as Paris awoke in the early hours, Nemo turned away from Caroline's still-empty offices and strolled along the riverfront, across a stone bridge, and then down winding streets to his own apartment. He had a long workday ahead of him, and tomorrow, and the day after.

During his absence, another engineer had been assigned to rebuild the Nantes shipyards, and the refurbishing there was already under way. And then, hearing of Nemo's balloon exploits, Napoleon III had decided the adventurous young man's imagination and prowess were too substantial to be wasted on Parisian sewer systems. For that, at least, Nemo was thankful.

So, while he toiled at restoring bridges and fountains to increase the emperor's glory and keep the public happy, Nemo hoped for something more *interesting* to do. His long, long wait for Caroline seemed to drag on forever.

II

When war broke out in early 1854, it seemed like a godsend to him.

The Crimean War brought together the unlikely allies of France, Britain, Sardinia, and Turkey against Russian expansion. The weak and crumbling Ottoman Empire could not hope to stand against the "Iron Tsar" Nicholas I, whose armies were pushing to the Black Sea. Turkey had no choice but to ally herself with Britain, and France's Emperor Napoleon III entered the fray by citing a divine obligation to protect Catholic holy places in Turkish-controlled Palestine. If the Ottoman Empire fell to Russia, then all Christian shrines would be controlled by the Eastern Orthodox church, which simply could not be allowed.

France called for patriotic fighters to join the forces laying siege to Sevastopol on the Black Sea. All the armies fighting together under the "Concert of Europe" needed brilliant and imaginative battlefield engineers.

Men like Nemo.

Knowing he would never be used as a mere footsoldier, cavalryman, or cannon-loader, Nemo accepted a commission for military service in the Crimea. He had lived most of his life without fine things, and so he packed a small valise with only a few possessions. He was going off to war and did not want to be encumbered. He carried a recommendation from Emperor Napoleon himself, but volunteering was primarily an excuse to see exotic landscapes again – as well as to be distracted from Caroline for a year.

When he came back from service, they could finally be together. . .

Escorted by her carriage driver, Caroline Hatteras came to the bustling, smoky train station to see him off. She stood in full dark skirts, her waist cinched tight with whalebone stays, her high collar buttoned properly, just as a married woman's should be. To a casual observer, she seemed cool and aloof, unaffected by the crowds and excitement all around her. But when she saw Nemo standing there, her eyes lit with an inner fire.

He had gone to her again the night before, surprising her in the dark stillness so absolute it reminded him of when he and Jules Verne had slipped out to L'Homme aux Trois Malices for a celebratory drink before shipping out with Captain Grant. Nemo and Verne had stood below young Caroline's window and said their goodbyes.

This time, Nemo had given her another farewell but, oh, so much sweeter, so much more painful than that other one. He had tapped on her door, standing in the shadows in the silent streets. He'd seen her astonished expression and sudden welcome as she whisked him into her home, long after midnight.

Caroline begged him not to go off to war, promising him all her love if he stayed here in Paris. But Nemo knew he could never resist the temptation of her. Every secret meeting, every stolen kiss would grow easier, and they would grow careless. Someone would see, and disaster would follow.

And so they had made love one more time, bathed in the yellow-orange glow from a single oil lamp. They had room, and clean sheets rather than a crowded bunk on a British ship. Nemo wanted to stay in her arms forever.

But instead, he had departed before dawn, to prepare for the train.

Now, in this crowd where emotion hung as thick as a spring fog, Nemo just wanted to hold her, to smell her hair and feel her lips against his. But he could not. Not here . . . not for another year. Not until he returned from the Crimea.

Beside them, the locomotive hissed and snorted while its boilers built up steam for departure from the Paris rail yards. The sulfurous smell of coal smoke and thick grease lingered close to the tracks.

French volunteer soldiers kissed their sweethearts, accepted bouquets, took hair ribbons as mementos. Nemo felt pain at remembering how Caroline had given the same sort of gift to two young men anxious to set off to sea. Now, without any conception of the horrors of war, these eager soldiers crowded onto a train that would take them to eastern Europe, where they would board a ship to take them to the Black Sea. They cheered and teased each other about going off to fight for their country.

But Nemo had seen men slain by the violence of other men, and he was not so anxious to reach the battlefields.

Amidst cheering and clasped hands and tearful goodbyes, Caroline stood stiffly, keeping her promise to Nemo and not showing her feelings here, especially not in such a crowd. Instead, the two had to embrace with their eyes alone. But they communicated greater love with their soulful expressions than did any of the moonstruck couples in the train station, even without kisses or passionate words. Caroline's simple smile spoke more eloquently to Nemo than any love letter, any vows.

"Don't worry about me, Caroline," he said. "I am an engineer. I will make life more tolerable for our soldiers, and I will stay far from the fighting."

She gave him a wan smile. "Somehow, André, I cannot imagine you staying far from anything – but you must promise me that you will return."

"There is nothing I want more. Nothing . . . other than for time to pass more quickly. After a year, we can both be happy. I have waited all my life for you, but these last months will seem the longest."

"André, I will count the days." Her sigh turned into a smile. "Alas, I wore no colorful hair ribbons to give you this time."

"No need. I have more thoughts of you than I can possibly revisit in twelve months."

Nemo was the last man to board the car. Though her carriage driver waited impatiently, Caroline refused to move until the train was long gone. . .

Nemo rode with a motley crew of soldiers on the troop train across Europe, then aboard a fast ship through the Mediterranean and the Bosporus strait into the Black Sea, where battles raged on the Crimean peninsula.

The strategic deep channel in front of the Sevastopol naval base had been used for centuries, first by the Tatars and then the Ottoman Empire. The

Russian military had sought refuge in the walled city after sweeping through the Ukraine, taking over Moldavia and Bessarabia, before attempting to conquer the Crimean peninsula. Now, allied troops laid siege to the huge fortress city of tan and gray stones, and the Russians had been unable to break out for months.

After he disembarked on the dock, Nemo looked up at the prisonlike edifice, knowing the Tsar's soldiers must be starving inside. However, when he saw the deplorable condition of the European troops besieging the walled city, he doubted they were faring much better.

Cholera had raged through the allied camps as the French, British, and Sardinian soldiers outside Sevastopol coped with the changing weather. They'd already been through a damp spring and a hot summer and had no extra uniforms or supplies. As autumn chilled the air, the men could only dread the worse weather ahead. Napoleon Bonaparte's troops had been defeated by a Russian winter in 1812. Nemo hoped Crimea would not prove to be a similar debacle for France.

Nemo strode toward the tent headquarters, surveying the dry, hilly land. Using his written orders and a letter of introduction from Emperor Napoleon III, he met with the French troop commanders. Veterans of the Napoleonic Wars, they were doddering old men who spent more time bragging about the events of their youth than they did running the occupation forces on the Black Sea.

On his own initiative, Nemo studied the army encampments, sitting up late at night in his small white tent. He looked over terrain maps by the light of an oil lamp, determining how best to exploit the resources at hand, using only the few tools the army had given him.

Disregarding the war, the Crimean locals continued to take fishing boats out onto the Black Sea each morning and returned to port with full nets. The army purchased most of the fish (or commandeered it – Nemo didn't know which). Old women and their daughters worked on the rocky beaches, filling bottles and tubs with Black Sea water, which they left out in the sun to evaporate; later, they would use the sea salt for preserving fish.

Rolling hills covered with brown grasses and low trees encircled Sevastopol. The scenery reminded Nemo of parts of Africa he had seen from the balloon. Farther along the south-eastern coast, the rugged Crimean Mountains rose high, a bastion against any forces of the Tsar that might come to rescue the Russians.

In peaceful times, the land was used for growing wine grapes, herbs, and a variety of plants harvested for their essential oils. The countryside looked like a gentle place to live. Unfortunately, the Crimea's strategic importance had made it a battleground, again and again, for centuries.

Nemo's job was to embroider the hills with lines of trenches for the allied forces, so that the soldiers could take shelter while keeping the Russians bottled within the city. He oversaw the digging of ditches and the building of barricades using rocks scavenged from destroyed villages outside the fortress.

British cannons were hauled up and installed in place, surrounded by cushioning dirt berms, woven grass mats, and wicker supports. Wooden stools sat beside each gunnery emplacement so the cannoneers could tend their weapons for the daily bombardment of Sevastopol.

Month after month, the siege had continued, and still the Russians did not yield. Though the Tsar's invaders retained an enormous fighting force and many weapons, they were still trapped. Turkish and British armies blocked access from the north so that no Russian reinforcements could arrive. The siege went on.

Nemo devoted himself to designing sanitary facilities, draining standing pools, and improving latrines to check the spread of cholera – though the bureaucratic confusion and the lack of cooperation between allied military groups was maddening. He often had a difficult time obtaining supplies and men for his engineering projects, though everyone could see the efforts would benefit all soldiers.

The British and French forces were woefully underequipped, their uniforms not designed for the Crimean climate. Their boots did not fit, their weapons often did not fire, and medical supplies were inappropriate or non-existent.

Most of the budgetary resources had been diverted to developing unusual advancements. The British regiments used new breech-loading rifles, supposedly far superior to the traditional muzzle-loading guns that armies had used for centuries. British riflemen could fire more rapidly, though with more frequent muzzle explosions and misfires.

Explosive landmines – another innovation for the Crimean War – were planted beneath the ground and detonated with each Russian foray. The terror of these mines worsened when the allies could not remember precisely *where* they had been planted. Killing indiscriminately, the explosions took as great a toll on allied troops as they did against the enemy.

Correspondents from European newspapers made use of hastily laid telegraph lines, reporting daily events with unprecedented speed to readers of their periodicals. Never before had the public experienced a distant war *as it actually happened*. Armed with new camera equipment, intrepid photographers set up tripods and used bottles of chemicals, glass plates, and cumbersome light boxes to record visual images of the events. Photographs provided a starker realism than battlefield sketches, causing quite a sensation back in the civilized areas of Britain and France.

Nemo, though, was more concerned with setting up siege walls and defensive apparatus. He used pulleys and wooden cross-beams and adapted good old medieval technology to help in the war effort.

He already longed to go home to Caroline.

One morning, after the dawn fog had lifted over the battered siege ground, Nemo completed the intricate scaffolding for an observation tower atop a grassy hill. From this vantage, he saw a group of Turkish troops riding past for the regular exchange of soldiers. French troops moved into the front positions where Sardinians had camped, while British infantry moved to the fields that had held Turks. Though the number of fighters didn't change, the constant rotation of army encampments created a confusing hive of activity that accomplished no purpose. Was it part of a plot calculated to confuse the Russians inside the fortress, or just military incompetence caused by conflicting commands?

Unlike the battered and poorly supplied Europeans, these oncoming

Turkish warriors looked dashing in fine uniforms of bright silk. Though their weapons were more primitive than breech-loading rifles and long-range cannons, their eyes held a hard glint, and their stance was determined. Most of the Turkish soldiers Nemo had seen were dedicated fighters, vigorous to protect the Crimea.

But these men were harder, both pompous and dangerous. The horsemen paused to stare at Nemo's crude construction. Wearing loose outfits, sashes, and turbans, they sat astride sleek brown horses, surveying the quiet battlefield . . . and at the same time somehow assessing *him*. Nemo stared back.

The broad-shouldered man at their lead had a long face, a neatly trimmed beard that etched out a silhouette of his pointed chin, and long eyebrows that curled like insect antennae. A green silk turban covered his head, adorned with an emerald the size of a walnut. He rode proudly on the largest stallion, which pranced about as if charged with energy.

Nemo could tell from the man's embroidered clothing and stiff bearing that he was an important man, a *caliph* or military leader in charge of Turkish troops. When the caliph rode up to the scaffolding, Nemo stopped what he was doing, set aside his blueprint sketches, and waited.

The caliph's stallion snorted and shifted on its hooves. The man's eyes flashed with black fire, as if his head could not contain the ambitious thoughts in his mind. A long scar shaped like a lightning bolt marred the tan skin of his left cheek. He stared at Nemo in silence for a long moment, and the engineer wondered if the caliph could speak English. In his time on the Crimea, Nemo had spent enough time in Turkish camps to pick up a few words of the language.

The caliph nodded at the jury-rigged siege tower and said in accented but clear French, and then again in English: "Good work. Very good work indeed, engineer. I have been watching you."

Then the caliph yanked his horse's head around and dug in his heels. He and his troops rode off down the hill toward the army encampments around the walls of Sevastopol.

III

By late October, 1854, the siege showed few signs of letting up. The Russians trapped inside the Sevastopol fortress had lit fires and burned down buildings. At night, occasional deserters slipped out and fled alone across the countryside.

Supplies began running out for the British and French forces as well. When a Sardinian cargo ship arrived, the food and clothing were rapidly distributed – and came up far short. Spotters stood on the beaches, looking across the Black Sea in vain for other sails.

In hill camps, the Turkish warriors kept to themselves, separated by culture and language . . . as well as the knowledge that, though this war was supposedly being fought on their behalf, theirs was the weakest army here.

After centuries of greatness, the Ottoman Empire had recently been led by several generations of self-absorbed sultans whose vision rarely strayed beyond the palace boundaries. Regardless of the religious or patriotic overtones imparted by other European leaders, the Turkish lands were seen as lush prizes in an imperial game. Though claiming altruistic motives, the leaders of Europe had their eyes on the riches of the Black Sea region.

Nemo's quiet engineering work had improved the lives and strategic positions of the allied armies. His ingenuity became so well known among the troops that he was recognized in any camp. Many soldiers wanted to hear about his balloon trip across Africa, or about being marooned on a desert island, or about fighting against pirates in the South China Sea.

Others just wanted Nemo's best guess as to when they would all be going home.

For two days he bedded down on the plain with the British Light Brigade: six hundred mounted troops that could move quickly, unencumbered by heavy artillery. They could be ready at a moment's notice to charge against an enemy. As the siege dragged on, the proud brigadiers had grown restless for action.

Though the Earl of Cardigan was ostensibly their commander, friction among the British officers had thrown leadership of the Light Brigade into question. Often, conflicting orders were issued, either by or against Cardigan, just to spite him or to plunge the troops into confusion. Morale had reached its lowest point, and nothing in Nemo's engineering repertoire could fix that.

After crawling out of his tent, he ate a meager breakfast, refreshed himself, and went to check his horse. For now, Nemo had spent enough time studying the Light Brigade's encampment to the north of Sevastopol, and he intended to move on that morning.

Before he could leave, however, an alarm sounded, and the brigadiers sprang out of their white tents. They blinked in surprise and confusion – then excitement. "The Russians are moving! They're trying to break free from the north."

Bugles shrilled, and members of the Light Brigade rushed to saddle their horses and gather their weapons. "They're heading toward Balaclava," one of the commanders yelled.

Remembering his terrain maps, Nemo realized the military significance of Balaclava, a small fortified village not far from Sevastopol. The Russian troops had lost Balaclava early in the siege – but, if they could retake it, they would expand their foothold on the Crimea and gain desperately needed supplies.

The Earl of Cardigan stepped out of the officer's tent in full commander's uniform and raised his ponderous voice. "Upon our honor, men, the Brigade shall be the first to meet them." Cardigan lifted his ceremonial sword in the air and sawed the reins of his horse. The heavy mare reared up, making the earl look every inch the commanding military figure. "Light Brigade, prepare to charge!"

Nemo climbed into the saddle of his horse and looked across to where the fortress gates had been thrown down. The frantic Russian army poured forth with all their forces, cannon, rifles, and infantrymen.

Observing the enemy troop strength, though, he saw the folly of Cardigan's maneuver – as did some of the British soldiers. A second commander rode up to Cardigan, and the two exchanged quick, harsh words. The earl shook his head, his face clouded with anger, and he rode his mare around in circles as his men formed up on their mounts.

The second commander said, "Stand down, men! We must wait for our other divisions. The Russians are closing in a pincer formation."

"Belay that order!" Cardigan said with a huff. "We shall strike first and hard."

A third commander approached from the side. He hadn't heard the Earl of Cardigan's orders or the confrontation with the other officer. As if it were his perfect right to give orders, he shouted, "Light Brigade, follow me! We must head south and meet up with the British divisions. We'll lead the vanguard, and all attack at once."

Cardigan wheeled his horse and turned to his men. "All of you, follow me. *I* am your commander. We shall charge now – and be victorious this day."

Before the soldiers could think, the earl launched off on his confused but energetic mare. For a moment it looked as if he would be all alone in his charge, then those behind him urged their horses into a gallop. All the men drew their swords.

Nemo shook his head, appalled. The Brigade was a mere six hundred men against ten thousand heavily armed and desperate Russian troops. The brigadiers would be slaughtered.

One of the second lieutenants rode up to Nemo and thrashed him on the shoulder with a quirt. "What are you waiting for, man? We're charging! Back with the group."

Nemo flinched and looked at the Second Lieutenant in angry surprise. "I am not part of the Light Brigade, sir," he said in careful English.

The flushed man lashed him again with the whip, then tore a pistol from his belt. "You're a bloody deserter and a coward. If you don't ride right now, by God, I'll shoot you where you sit on your horse."

Nemo wanted to fling himself upon this blustering idiot and pull him from his horse. He cursed himself for his error. He should have spoken in French, pretended not to understand the lieutenant's commands. But the glowering man leveled the barrel of his pistol, and Nemo had to decide in an instant.

"You are making a mistake," he said in a low growl. But he could not argue with the lieutenant, not while the Light Brigade advanced into battle, however misguided they might be. So he turned his horse, grabbed his sword – a dull ceremonial one, since his primary weapons had been pen and blueprint – and rode with the Light Brigade to meet the ever-swelling horde of Russians trying to escape Sevastopol.

Enemy troops flowed out, pulling cannons and mounting rifle squadrons. On the hills surrounding the fortress, British infantry and French reinforcements moved in at a fast march, hauling heavy weaponry to arrive at the town of Balaclava before the enemy did. Unfortunately, the Light Brigade, a pathetically small David against the well-armed Russian Goliath, would reach the enemy much sooner.

Nemo galloped beside a fresh-faced young cavalryman who had asked him about his African balloon adventure just the night before. The man's blue eyes were wide and sparkling, and if he felt any fear, he did not let it show. His innocent optimism exasperated Nemo, who said, "Can't you see this is madness?"

"We're following orders, mate," the cavalryman said. "We've been instructed to charge. We are the Light Brigade, and we'll bloody well strike a mortal blow against our foes."

Nemo looked at the size of the enemy army and choked back his fury. "But this brigade doesn't even know what it's doing."

"Aww, you're only an engineer from France," the man snapped back, pride adding derision to his voice. "In England, a bloke doesn't question orders. Our duty is to do as we are told, and die if we must."

Nemo checked his weapons, knew that if he continued to argue against this insane charge, he would be executed by his supposed allies. So, fuming at the foolishness, he determined to survive.

The Light Brigade crashed into the Russian army like a sledgehammer into an anvil.

The enemy troops were taken by surprise, unable to believe that this gnat of an opposing force would attack them. Russian gunfire rang out. Cannons blasted, and invading infantry troops marched toward the British horsemen.

The acrid smell of black powder and raw blood filled the air, mingled with dust from explosions. The scattered troops stumbled onto leftover landmines, which exploded, harming both sides. A sleet storm of lead bullets rained down. British brigadiers began falling like stalks of wheat under a scythe.

Nemo saw the brash young officer beside him thrown from his horse, a red wound in his throat. Nemo could barely hold on to his own charging horse, which had been a mere riding animal, not a trained war mount. The clash and thunder of war deafened him, crushing his terror, crushing thought itself.

British and French reinforcements were approaching. From a distance, their cannons fired – but they were too far away and traveling too slowly. *Much too slowly.*

The Russians continued to fire upon the Light Brigade as if for sport. Few of their own number died, but the Light Brigade riders, blindly following the Earl of Cardigan to the slaughter, fell one after another after another.

Something slammed into Nemo's lower left rib cage with the force of a club, and he clung to the reins of his horse. He couldn't breathe. His vision turned dark for a moment, filled with clouds.

He touched his side to find a heavy flow of blood seeping from a burned hole in his jacket. His horse ran in blind panic.

A cannon blast erupted at ground level beside him. Nemo tried to hold onto the saddle and reins, but his fingers had turned to water. The world spun around him. More blood stained his hands and his chest. Soon all of his vision turned the same color of red, then black.

By the time he dropped onto the churned and war-torn battlefield, he couldn't even feel his body strike the ground.

IV

When Nemo awoke from a crimson haze of pain, he smelled blood and chemicals and sharp tobacco smoke. He instantly tried to assess his surroundings, to snatch at recent recollection that fled like the tattered remnants of dreams. He heard the moans of injured men, the snores of the blissfully unconscious, the deep silence of the comatose. The uncertain light around him seemed grimy, tainted with shadows.

Nemo gradually understood that he was no longer on the battlefield, but inside a building that must be an army hospital. He lay without sheets on a pallet made of hard wood. Only a little starlight seeped through the narrow windows that lined the walls.

He reached out with stiff fingers, following the nerve lines to sketch the extent of his pain. His left side was bandaged with ragged swaths of red-stained cloth. After touching the soaked and crusted dressing, he determined that he must have been here for at least a full day. The smells of vomit, urine, and blood made the close air as fetid as the oppressive marshes around Lake Chad.

The large room held only a few actual beds occupied by wounded soldiers, some so bandaged that they looked mummified. Other injured men lay on the bare floor without even a pallet like his own. A few groaned and stirred in the restless night; others huddled in a pain-fogged sleep. Some did not move at all, unconscious . . . or perhaps dead and not yet taken away.

Lying motionless, Nemo reached out with his precise memories of the landscape and soon determined where he must be. He recalled a huge old Turkish barracks outside of Sevastopol, unfurnished and dirty. Considering the crowded conditions, the hospital must be full of casualties. He wondered how many of those brave but foolish British cavalrymen had survived Cardigan's ill-advised attack. The ineptitude of the commanders and the blind compliance of the Light Brigade made him distraught.

The war, the suffering, the sheer waste disgusted him. How could he ever have wanted to come here? How could a battleground ever seem preferable to Paris, even with the sweet torture of Caroline's presence always nearby?

He propped himself on one arm and winced as the gunshot wound caught fire and singed the already ragged nerves. When he tried to take a deep breath, his lungs hitched. Fresh blood soaked through his untended bandage. He used the pain as a crutch to keep himself conscious through a wave of clammy nausea.

When he remembered the horrific battlefield, he was amazed to have survived at all. He caught his breath and then sat forward a little more. No matter how long it took, he had to see more of where he was. He thought of all the things he had already survived, and promised himself he would survive this, too. Now, he had Caroline to live for.

None of the other soldiers responded to Nemo's gradual, pain-wracked movement. The crowded and smelly room held too many wounded soldiers, each wrapped in agony and despair. He heard two men talking to each other, lying side by side on the cold floor. By starlight, Nemo made out that one man's leg had been amputated; both of the other man's arms were wrapped in wide splints held together by meager strips of bandages.

"We drove the Russians back, aye," the man with broken arms said in a cocky British accent. "At least we done that much. Our forces kept the buggers from getting to Balaclava."

The man with the amputated leg coughed, then hissed as it sent a burst of pain through his system. "Gor! But at what bloody cost? Goddamn that arse Earl of Cardigan! Not one of the bloody officers knew what he was doing. They just chose opposite paths to spite each other." He propped himself on one elbow, while the man with splinted arms watched with a twinge of envy. "Damn! Half an hour was all it took. Half a bloody hour, an' two-thirds of the Light Brigade were killed or wounded. What's the goddamned sense in that?"

"History will remember us as heroes, aye," said the man with the splinted arms, though he didn't sound as if he believed it himself.

"They'll remember us as bloody *fools*," said the other soldier.

From down the corridor a pale yellow light appeared, like a will-o'-the-wisp. As the wounded men noticed it, they stirred and came awake. "It's the lady with the lamp." They seemed to hold their breath.

When the woman finally arrived, Nemo was surprised to see a thin, stern-looking nurse in an ugly gray uniform. She was in her early thirties, with a weak chin and a rounded nose. Arched eyebrows graced her smooth forehead over deep-brown, intelligent eyes.

Her dark hair, parted in the middle, was tied back severely under a bonnet. Though intensely weary, she walked with fluid movements, like a ghost carrying an eerie spectral light. Her expression softened with compassion as she looked at all the miserable soldiers. In a low voice she soothed those men who were conscious and could look at her. She promised to write a letter home for one, gave a cup of water to another.

When she came to Nemo, she looked at him in surprise. "You're not one of the British troops. Do you speak English? Can you understand me?"

Nemo nodded. "I am French, but I speak English."

She brightened, then spoke to him in his own language. "What are you doing here, monsieur? You were wounded on the battlefield. This hospital is full of the survivors of the British Light Brigade."

"I was . . . with them, at the wrong time, mademoiselle," Nemo said. "I didn't have any choice. A lieutenant said he would shoot me if I didn't ride in as part of their foolish charge."

A look of disgust crossed the woman's face, making her appear much older. "All officers should be forced to spend a day here in the hospital. They would see what destruction their stupidity causes. I have written repeated requests for additional supplies." She gestured helplessly. "There aren't enough medicines, or beds – not even rags for bandages. How can I tend the sick under these conditions?" She took a deep breath, as if forcing back her despair. "Who is your commanding officer? We must report you to the French forces."

Nemo let out a bitter sigh. "Every contingent here is so confused with bureaucracy, I'm surprised they can find the latrines by themselves."

He explained what he had been doing to improve the conditions, and the woman raised her eyebrows appraisingly. "So you're not just one of the killers, then? Very good, monsieur. What is your name?" He told her, and then asked the nurse to introduce herself. The other men watched, envying his conversation with her.

"I was born in Florence, so my father gave me that name – Florence Nightingale. I was shipped to the Crimea by the British Secretary of War to help, and not long after I arrived, that idiotic attack at Balaclava happened. Now there are more wounded than I know what to do with. I have thirty-eight nurses and, just in one day, close to five hundred wounded in a hospital that was never meant to be used as such a facility."

Florence Nightingale frowned again, stealing beauty from her beatific face, then she smiled in such a generous way that it struck to Nemo's heart. "We shall tend you as best we can. Many others will die here, and I can't help that, but I will give comfort wherever I can. I promise not to let anyone travel that long, dark road due to neglect on my part or on the part of my nurses."

Nemo touched his injured side. She looked at the old dressing, her face awash with despair, but she drove back the emotion. "You'll survive, Monsieur Nemo. Your wound is serious, but not life-threatening unless it becomes infected. Of all the casualties I've seen in this endless war, three-quarters have died from disease or ill-treatment, rather than the wounds themselves."

Florence Nightingale stood straight, her face hard again. "But that will change." She touched the bandages and shook her head. "This needs a fresh dressing, but I have no more cloth. In fact, we are boiling uniforms cut from dead soldiers just so we can tear them into strips for bandages. I will do what I can." She gave him a wan smile, indicating the conversation was over. "Thank you for allowing me to practice my French."

Stern again, she pointed a finger at him. "My main command for you, André Nemo, is to get better – but not completely well, because they will send you back to the battlefield. Since your own commanding officers cannot keep track of you, I need you to heal so you can help me clean this place and tend the other soldiers."

He smiled back, then winced as another bolt of pain shot through his ribs. Her orders made more sense than anything he'd heard from true military commanders. "I will do my best to obey you, Mademoiselle Nightingale."

V

Sitting with other wounded men in the crowded hospital, Nemo ate a thin gruel, drank copious amounts of tea, and tended his own injury. The smelly air was heavy with the sounds of coughing, groaning men. The nurses couldn't possibly do enough to help their patients – and given few resources, supplies, materials, or even personal vigor, Nemo could think of little he could do to help.

After his days aboard the *Coralie*, then living alone on the rugged island, and even during the balloon trip across Africa, Nemo had learned some first aid. As a healthy twenty-six-year-old, his stamina worked to his advantage. Most of the other injured men had lived in trenches for months during the siege of Sevastopol, and were much worse off.

Soldiers in the infirmary rooms smoked cigarettes, a paper-wrapped form of tobacco that had recently come into fashion during the war. But the acrid smoke did little to mask the hospital's sour stench of sickness, chemicals, and death.

One night, the man with two splinted arms unexpectedly died from a blood clot. His one-legged companion wallowed in such deep depression that Nemo was convinced the man wanted his stump to fester with gangrene. The peripheral horrors of war continued to dismay him, and he did not understand why people had to do such things to each other.

When Nemo attempted to walk, he could feel the bones and skin knitting in his side. Since he was more mobile than most, he gave up his hard pallet to a more seriously injured soldier. Still, he limped around like Victor Hugo's famous hunchback. Every evening Florence Nightingale took her lamp and walked the halls of the huge barracks hospital, one floor after another, speaking softly to the wounded soldiers. She did it without complaining.

Nightingale's nurses were as devoted as she, and worked just as hard. The driven women took shifts sleeping for a few hours apiece, then continued their duties. The soldiers called them "angels." Indeed, the dark-dressed women were the only spots of brightness in the gloomy hospital.

Nemo and other half-healed victims rinsed and boiled rags for bandages, swept the floors, and removed bodies. Piles of corpses were stacked downwind from the hospital windows, and daily funeral pyres blazed high. Nightingale insisted that rapid disposal of cadavers and amputated limbs was crucial to prevent the spread of disease.

Sitting at her wobbly, splintered desk, she wrote dozens of letters and pleas for supplies. She even sent notes via the new telegraph lines used by war correspondents and army commanders. When she insisted that her demands be transmitted back home, no telegraph operator dared to stand in her way.

The nurses had sent the required documentation to the French commanders regarding Nemo's injury – unfortunately, the old Napoleonic veterans had not even noticed the loss of a lone engineer. If he'd been killed on the battlefield at Balaclava, no letter of condolence would have been written, no death certificate signed. Caroline would never have known his fate.

Forgotten, Nemo was content to remain here helping the nurses. . .

On November fourth, the Russians again attempted to break the siege, this time striking toward the village of Inkerman. The British, French, and Turks once again drove them back, but it was an expensive victory for a relatively minor battle.

After the horrific fighting at Inkerman, wagons hauled bleeding men to the giant hospital barracks where there were no more beds. Nightingale appealed to the army commanders for supplies and assistance, but they refused to lend any of their troops. Nemo and a few volunteers worked harder, but he didn't mind. The toil drove back boredom and made him forget the twinges of pain.

In the midst of this chaos, a tall, lean man came in search of Nemo: the green-turbaned Turkish commander who had noticed him building siege towers. With a retinue of burly personal warriors, the haughty caliph marched through the hospital, asking questions until he tracked down the engineer.

Florence Nightingale and her nurses were too occupied with emergency duties and triage to waste time with these Turks who, unlike their fellow countrymen, did not lift a finger to help in the frenzied emergency. The caliph discovered Nemo himself, however. Five armed guards stood behind him, dressed in white garments, with ceremonial sabers in their sashed belts and rifles over their shoulders. None of them seemed interested in the war or the politics.

"You are the engineer?" the caliph said in passable French. He studied Nemo's features. "I have come to take you away."

"I am busy." Nemo continued tearing strips of cloth for bandages. "You have no right to command here, sir. I don't even know who you are."

The Turk's skin flushed darker, making the lightning bolt scar on his cheek stand out. "This is a British hospital. You are a French soldier. I have obtained papers to take you to your appropriate assignment." The caliph held out a sheet of paper that was written in unintelligible Turkish.

"I have work to do." Nemo gestured around him. "Can't you see all the wounded?"

"They should have died on the battlefield." The green-turbaned man jabbed a finger against Nemo's bandaged ribs. "You have been deemed sufficiently healed and should no longer take up space in this hospital. You will come with me."

Florence Nightingale bustled in, her sweat-soaked hair in disarray, her gray dress spotted with blood. She hurried over, wearing a stern expression. "What do you want with this man, sir? I need him here."

"The engineer is to come away with me. The British hospital

administrator has given orders that no French soldier may be tended here. British supplies are to be used only for British victims. No French, or Sardinians, or apparently Turks."

"We're supposed to be allies," Nemo said, digging in his heels.

"We're supposed to be a *hospital*," Nightingale snapped. "We tend the wounded without regard to which flag they salute. This man is too badly wounded to go back to the battlefield."

"Nevertheless," the caliph said, squaring his shoulders. His bald guards put their hands on the hilts of their scimitars. "He does not belong here. It is simply a bureaucratic matter."

Florence Nightingale sagged. Like Nemo, she was all too familiar with the paperwork and ineptitude that characterized this entire war.

"You have my guarantee he will receive the proper care and treatment," the caliph said, his voice more pleasant. "But this man must come with me. I am a caliph – Caliph Robur."

At the far side of the room, a soldier shrieked in pain. Two nurses held him down while a battlefield surgeon did his best to saw off the man's left leg, but the surgeon had trouble getting the serrated blade through the thick femur.

The caliph looked at Nightingale. His black eyes were impenetrable, and he stroked the pointed beard on his narrow chin while the amputee continued screaming. "You *do* have wounded to tend to, nurse. Why are you questioning my legitimate orders?"

In disgust, Nemo held up his hand to stop further argument. "I will go with him. It makes as much sense as the rest of this war." Though troubled, Florence Nightingale seemed more concerned about the new arrivals. Nemo followed the Turk, limping slowly. He looked back at the busy nurses; already Nightingale had gone to work with the flood of new victims. . .

Caliph Robur had a cart and driver waiting outside, and the bald guards helped Nemo climb in. He saw no other legitimate Turkish soldiers, none of the brave but ragged fighters from the battlefield. These men seemed to follow their own law, with no regard for the overall battles. Without speaking to Nemo again, they mounted their prancing horses and set off from the hospital as another funeral pyre poured a column of greasy smoke into the sky.

The cart jostled away from the Sevastopol fortress. Every bump in the road sent jarring pains through Nemo's side. Weak as he was, he endured the rough ride. He did not know how he could be effective on the battlefield, even to perform the less physically challenging tasks of engineering.

Instead, the caliph took him far from the battlefield, into an even worse situation. . .

VI

Under cloudy skies, Robur's escort led the wobbly cart far from French and British military trenches. They proceeded in silence across the rocky terrain on narrow, rugged roads. In pain, Nemo propped himself up to watch as they approached the battle lines held by Turkish forces, then went beyond the main camp to their own settlement. Many of the Ottoman soldiers slept on the ground beside smoky campfires built out of scrub brush.

When he called out questions, demanding an explanation, the cart driver ignored him, as did the scimitar-carrying guards. Robur himself rode ahead out of earshot. He seemed aloof from the rest of the Turkish military.

In the center of the sprawling camp, the caliph and his generals had erected large multicolored pavilions that bore clan markings. Deep in the heart of the broad encampment, the driver halted the cart in an open area surrounded by the caliph's private tents, which blocked the view from outside. Nemo saw with sudden dread a line of well-armed guards – none of them wearing the uniform of the Turkish troops – standing around a fenced enclosure.

The thirty men gathered inside the fence wore the uniforms of French, British, and Sardinian troops. "I am to be a prisoner of war, then?" Outraged, Nemo tried to stand up in the cart, but the pain in his ribs struck him like a bolt of lightning. "I am a French citizen. You have no right to hold me, or any of these men."

Caliph Robur rode over and gestured for his guards to "assist" Nemo in dismounting from the cart. The bald guards, though strong and well-armed, did not treat him with undue viciousness. Nemo considered struggling, but feared that he would rip open his wound again.

Upon seeing his arrival, the other prisoners stirred. Most scowled in frustration, though a few of the French captives looked at him with barely restrained excitement.

Robur stroked his pointed beard and turned his angular face from the camp prisoners toward Nemo. "You will remain here and recover, engineer. I promise we shall treat you well. We have important work for you, far beyond this mere squabble among nations."

"But why did you bring me here?"

"Everything will be explained to you in time – when you need to know." Dismissing him, Robur rode off as the guards hauled Nemo through an opening in the fence.

Bound by their common predicament, the other prisoners welcomed him and introduced themselves, explaining their backgrounds and how they had come to be in Robur's camp. Like Nemo, none of the prisoners understood why they were here. Each man had been taken under bureaucratic pretense, then abducted for some unknown purpose.

An Englishman named Cyrus Harding was a professional boatbuilder by trade. Harding had square-cut brown hair and a large chin that sported a crater-sized dimple in the center. Though his flinty eyes watched his surroundings, Harding kept his mouth shut in a grim line unless he was forced to speak.

Conseil, a mousy man from Marseilles, had been brought to the Crimea as a *meteorologist*, of all things. Months earlier, after storms in the Black Sea had severely damaged the French fleet, Conseil had been assigned to collect regular weather reports from the war zone, which he then telegraphed to a central station. The meteorologist had an amusing habit of withdrawing his simian head in a cringe. His eyes were wide and round, as if on the verge of popping out of his head; he kept his gray-brown hair scraped close to his skull, but when it grew longer, the short strands stood out like bristles on an old brush.

Liedenbrock, an odd member of the group, claimed to be Sardinian but spoke with a strong German accent. Trained as a metallurgist in Salzburg, he had found work with industrial investors in Sardinia. Unfortunately, he had gambled away all his money, lost his home and his mistress, and would have gone to prison – unless he volunteered to join the Sardinian forces in the Crimea. Liedenbrock was rail thin with a curly fuzz of gray hair like a cloud that had settled on his cranium. His heavy brow extended like a shelf over brown eyes, casting his face into shadow.

Some of the other prisoners had worked as craftsmen or mechanics, others as lathe-turners and glassmakers. What could Robur possibly want with an outcast metallurgist, a timid weather scientist, a stoic boatbuilder – and himself? None of the men were officers or important political prisoners . . . few even had families or obligations back in their home countries. The caliph seemed to have chosen the *least* significant men as hostages from the battlefield. Nemo thought no one would even notice their disappearance. . .

After his initial anger, he studied the camp objectively. Knowing the hospital conditions he had just endured, and having experienced daily life in military camps, he noted with surprise that Robur's war prisoners were treated better than most troops in the Crimea. The men had grass bedding and awnings to protect them from the sun. They received regular meals, usually lamb or goat stew; at other times they ate fresh vegetables, olives, bread, and wine. In fact, they ate better than the loyal Ottoman troops fighting on the siege lines.

For days as he pondered the problem, he circulated among the captives, learning their names and their situations. As a point of survival, Nemo had long ago learned to assess available resources – and these men and their diverse skills comprised his only resources in this strange situation.

The quietude was marred only by the constant presence of mounted guards who rode the camp perimeter. Glowering bald guards stood with scimitars drawn and spoke not a word, not even in their own language.

Over the next two weeks, Nemo ate, and rested, and recovered, regaining strength to fight, if necessary. He tended the other prisoners as best he could, using first aid he'd learned from Florence Nightingale. Even under such good conditions, though, three of the injured conscripts died.

Liedenbrock clung to the fence and raged at the guards. "Ach! You are inhuman. Why are you not taking these men to doctors?" But Nemo realized the wounded prisoners would have died in any case. In fact, he suspected the men had lived longer *here* than they might have in the overcrowded hospital.

"No, no," Conseil mumbled in misery. "None of us will leave this place alive."

Caliph Robur rode in, not deigning to get down from his horse. He stared them all to silence with his black eyes. "We will now begin a rigorous regimen of exercise. Your rations will be increased, and you will also be required to develop greater endurance."

"Why?" Nemo said, stepping forward. "Explain why we are here."

"Aye, we deserve some manner of explanation," Cyrus Harding said, startling them with his words, which he usually kept to himself. The boatbuilder's nostrils flared as he spoke.

One of the guards snatched out a long whip, but Robur raised his hand to forestall any brutality. "These men are free to ask questions. We chose them because of their inquisitive minds." He gazed down at Nemo and gave him a thin smile. "However, engineer, I am not yet at liberty to provide answers."

"Ach! We would rather be back on the battlefield," Liedenbrock snapped.

"No, no," Conseil said with a vigorous shake of his head. "No we wouldn't."

Raising his green-turbaned head high, Robur rode out of the fenced circle. After he departed, the guards forced the prisoners into a routine of calisthenics to tone up their muscles. Aching and sore, they repeated the activities the next day, and the next. Their increased rations barely compensated for the extra work. Even though Conseil seemed ready to drop from exhaustion, he somehow managed to keep up.

Nemo helped the mousy man whenever possible. "We must bide our time, Conseil. Do this for *you*, not for him. We still don't know what Robur wants." He moved from prisoner to prisoner, passing the same angry message in an attempt to maintain morale.

Over the course of a week, the exercises became more strenuous, and Nemo felt himself returning to full vigor. Given the monotony of prison camp life, he even began to look forward to the daily workout.

When the weather grew colder with the onset of hard winter, the caliph ordered all prisoners to stand in ranks inside the encampment as he rode in to inspect them. The stallion tossed his head, but Robur clamped his legs and squeezed the mount into submission, guiding it past his carefully selected captives. He found nothing to disappoint him and returned to his starting point without saying a word.

Then he spoke to the captain of his private guards in Turkish. By now, Nemo had picked up enough of the words to understand, though he did not let the enemy realize this. "They are ready. Tomorrow we leave."

The next morning the prisoners heard distant gunshots, bugles of command, and military charges. The standard Turkish troops had all left their camp and rushed off to the main battle, leaving Robur's camp to themselves.

"Ach! They are fighting another battle at Sevastopol," Liedenbrock said, furrowing his broad brow. Nemo nodded. Stony-faced, Cyrus Harding just stared into the distance, imagining the unseen battlefield.

With the major armies occupied with the fighting, Caliph Robur and his guards surrounded their prisoners. They marched the men past the colorful pavilions, beyond the now-empty camp of Turkish soldiers and smoldering cook fires. Next, the men began trudging across country toward the Crimean Mountains and the coast.

Nemo's feet grew sore, but he drove back any thought of complaint with a dour resistance. Encouraged by his comrades, Conseil staggered along, muttering unintelligible complaints. When the little man stumbled, Cyrus

Harding draped the French meteorologist's arm over his shoulders and helped him to keep going. . .

In two days the ragtag group reached the gravelly shoreline, where the Black Sea spread out in front of them, calm and dark. White clouds rode in the sky, distant storms that would pass far to the south.

Far from the busy anchorage of Sevastopol – and prying eyes – a large and low-slung Turkish dhow had anchored off the rugged shore. There, no one but a few fishermen and farmers would see its triangular lateen sails or the armed men waiting on-board like corsairs.

At dusk, longboats came ashore and took the twenty-seven prisoners out to the dhow. The guards and sailors helped them aboard, seating the captives on benches under flapping shades and striped awnings. Liedenbrock said in disgust, "Ach! We are being converted into miserable galley slaves. We will be forced to row across the sea."

"No, no, no," Conseil said, his eyes round. "We can't do that!"

Nemo shook his head and spoke with harsh assurance. "Caliph Robur would not have spent so much effort on us if he meant to use us for such a menial job." He drew his dark eyebrows together as stormy thoughts continued to kindle his temper. "He's got something else in mind for us."

"Wish I knew what the crazy bloke wanted," Harding said gruffly. He found a spot to sit, hunched down against the low-slung boat's poop deck, and scowled in silence.

Instead of being asked to row, they were all given water and extra rations after the long march. The dhow raised anchor and sailed into the night across the rippling Black Sea. . .

Next morning the triangle-sailed ship was far from land as it crossed the water. Nemo looked at the sun and tried to determine their course, drawing on the knowledge of maps in his mind. Conseil commented on the weather, relieved that the storms had passed far to the north of them; Cyrus Harding remarked on the construction of the dhow, rapping the deck boards with his knuckles and studying the way the prow of the Arabian boat cut the water.

Within days they had crossed the Black Sea and reached the narrow Bosporus strait. Without stopping, they glided past Constantinople, where huge mosques with gilded domes and pointed minarets towered over the waterway. The dhow crossed the shallow Sea of Marmara to the Dardanelles, where the Trojan War had been fought more than three thousand years earlier.

Under favorable winds, they sailed into the deep blue waters of the Mediterranean Sea while hugging the shore of the Aegean. They cruised among a rocky kaleidoscope of Greek islands – Khios, Samos, and Rhodes – then turned south-east again, along the mountainous coast of Turkey.

Robur's sailors followed a hilly coast covered with olive groves, brown grasses, and vineyards. But as they proceeded, all signs of population faded. Nemo and his companions found themselves in a wasteland, far from any port or city. The craggy shoreline folded, creating a deep cove surrounded by tall cliffs between which the dhow navigated. The curious prisoners watched, certain that they were close to their destination, where perhaps they would receive their answers.

Farther into the cove, out of sight from passing ships, stood an entire industrial city. Rock quarries and ore smelters marked the mountains. Docks extended into the deep channel, and lines of barracks rose up the slopes. Nemo blinked at the astonishing site. Everything looked so modern – austere but efficient. Newly built.

Like a performer playing his audience to increase suspense, Caliph Robur stepped to the bow of the ship. He turned, placing his hands on his hips. Ocean breezes whipped his shimmering pantaloons.

"This is my city of Rurapente," Robur said. "With the guidance of the sultan, I have spared no expense to make resources available. You men will receive every allowance to complete the work I give you. In the sultan's name, I expect great things from you. You will be made comfortable and therefore productive, for you will spend years here – perhaps the rest of your lives."

In a babel of languages, the captives cried out in indignation. "We are not slaves!" "We do not belong to the Turks." "We are citizens of our own countries."

The caliph's face remained stony as he stared at them, unaffected by their complaints. Nemo held his tongue and studied the man, keeping the dark wings of anger at bay. Robur was without question his enemy.

When their clamor had died down, the caliph spoke again. "You men are all officially *dead*. The proper paperwork has been completed. Your governments believe you were killed in battle. For those few of you who had families, they have already received letters of notification and posthumous medals." His voice was harsh and utterly confident. "No one will look for you. No one will find you. *You are mine.*"

The prisoners gasped in disbelief, but Nemo knew the caliph could easily have done as he said. The tangled bureaucracy and confused ineptitude of the Crimean commanders would have made such a trick pathetically simple to achieve.

Robur smiled at them. "The Ottoman Empire is falling apart. Your own European press calls us the 'sick man of Europe.' We were one of the greatest empires in the world, and now Britain and France see us only as the spoils of war. They dicker over how to divide the fallen corpse when Turkey falls." Beneath his jeweled turban, the caliph's eyes blazed. He scratched at the jagged scar on his cheek.

"But I am an enlightened military ruler. I look ahead, and I act for myself. I know that the old Ottoman ways are doomed to failure – but I must have experts. I need engineers, metallurgists, meteorologists, boatbuilders, chemists, opticians. You men are my technological advantage. You shall work together to create invincible machinery of war, ingenious new defenses that will help the Ottoman Empire draw a fresh breath and return to life."

The caliph strode down the deck, looking at them all. He saw anger among the prisoners, and defiance, but his gaze did not waver. "I have selected *you*, the best and brightest minds that were senselessly wasted on the battlefield. You should thank me. I will allow you to be creative and use your talents." His next words hung like a heavy weight over them. "You will cooperate – or you will be executed."

He stopped in front of Nemo, who glowered at him, but kept his angry words in check by clenching and unclenching his fists. During his time among the prisoners, Nemo had already bound the men together. Though he had no aspirations of grandeur or power, the prisoners looked to him with respect, as their nominal leader. Robur had noticed him and singled him out.

Someday, Nemo vowed to lead his companions out of here.

"I consider myself a learned man," the caliph said. "I will allow you certain freedoms and certain rewards – but I expect much in return." He looked down at Nemo. "In your Latin language, my name Robur translates as '*powerful*.' I intend to live up to my name."

Nemo looked back with a bland expression that masked his anger. "And I am called Nemo. In Latin that name means '*no one*.'" Now he allowed himself a smile. "But I don't put too much stock in a name."

VII

Writing by candlelight in Paris, Jules Verne sent letter after letter to his parents, explaining his daily work and his dreams. Even with nothing more than a cold attic room and little to eat, he badly wanted to remain here. Knowing the quaint country life of Nantes, he felt he could not survive anywhere but in the vibrant bustle of the City of Light.

After all this time, Verne had achieved only the most modest success with his writing, and no fame whatsoever. In the letters he downplayed his poetry, plays, and theatre work, knowing what stern Pierre Verne would think. The older man would be baffled, incapable of understanding why his son would brush aside predictable security.

But even after graduating with his law degree, he had dawdled and made excuses to stay in Paris. Despite his father's plans, Verne did not want to settle into the dull attorney's office on Île Feydeau.

Now, though, as he finally returned home to Nantes, fresh plans brewed in his mind. He needed to put forward his own case in a way that would make even the greatest lawyer proud.

Pierre Verne and his son sat in silence together in the withdrawing room after an exquisite dinner his mother had prepared. They each drank a glass of tawny port, each puffed on a cigar. Nothing would ever change, and the elder Verne seemed to prefer it that way.

Scratching his sideburns, the elder Verne sat shrouded in a contented, peaceful silence of routine as he read the Nantes newspaper. With his son beside him, the gruff older man enjoyed the luxury of making pointed and opinionated comments about the news of the day. He read the headlines aloud – "Treaty of Paris signed" – and grumbled his appreciation. "It's about time this whole Crimean debacle ended." He jabbed the paper with a fingertip. "I knew that once Tsar Nicholas died, his son Alexander II would prove more reasonable."

Verne perked up. "Is it true then? The war is at an end?"

"What an awful mess for three years." The older man shook his head. He continued to read as if he hadn't even heard his son's questions. "Ah! Here's another triumph for France." While Verne waited, his father took a long puff on his cigar and exhaled a heady sweet cloud. "Ferdinand de Lesseps, a French diplomat and engineer, has been selected to undertake the largest excavation project in the history of mankind."

"Greater than the pyramids of Egypt?" Verne asked, as he was expected to. He knew all the rules of conversation with his father.

"Pasha Mohammed Said has granted permission to excavate a channel across the Isthmus of Suez. It'll take years, but someday ships will be able to sail directly from the Mediterranean to the Red Sea and down into the Indian Ocean. That cuts six thousand miles off the journey from Europe to China." He took a drink of the tawny port. "Good thing a French engineer is in charge."

"A Suez Canal? There'll be enormous repercussions for world trade," Verne said, trying to keep up his end of the conversation. "I wonder if Caroline Hatteras has heard the news, since it will have a dramatic effect on her shipping company." His father muttered an acknowledgment.

Now that the Crimean War was over, Nemo would be returning home. It was entirely possible that his friend's experience as an accomplished engineer might land him a prestigious assignment on de Lesseps' crew. It would be wonderful if Nemo could help accomplish such a magnificent undertaking . . . and it would also keep him in Egypt, far from France and Caroline.

Though nine years had passed without word from Captain Hatteras, Caroline still refused to go through the formality of declaring herself a widow – at least not so long as Nemo remained away. . .

"Father, we must consider my future," he said abruptly. The elder Verne looked up at his son, bushy eyebrows knit in puzzlement, though Jules knew he was aware of the situation. He had written home often enough about his dreams for a palatable livelihood. "I have studied all the information, sir, spoken with all the appropriate people. I'm certain that I have discovered a way for us to become rich." His words came out like pattering hailstones. "A true career that will be engrossing to me, and successful, too."

"The stock market?" his father said. "Yes, yes, you mentioned something about that in a letter." His voice was unwelcoming, but the younger Verne did not allow himself to be dismayed. To him, anything – even working in a stock exchange – seemed preferable to becoming a country lawyer.

"If you have enough faith in me to put up the money, I can invest in a brokerage house," Verne continued. "I will handle my own securities, as well as my family's and friends.'"

"And how can I be sure you know what you're doing? You have spent years training to be an attorney," Pierre Verne said, still devoting most of his attention to the newspaper. "What is wrong with being a lawyer? Will you not change your mind again in a month?"

Verne took a sip of the syrupy port. It burned at the back of his throat. "Father, I need to change my way of living, because the present insecure situation simply can't continue. This is the best way for me – and our family – to become wealthy."

Without looking up from another news story, his father said, "Dallying with your poetry, and your stories, and your theatre work when you should have been concerned with the law – you have always been a reckless young man who gets excited about any new scheme. The stock market is nothing different."

"But this isn't entirely new, sir. Many in Paris have been successful at it." He lowered his voice to quash the whining tone. "I know I can do this, Father."

Then he raised the point he knew would be most convincing to his mother, who would, of course, be one of his primary defenders. "If I get such a position on the stock exchange, I will be seen as a man with a stable career and ambitions. I must have that if I am ever to be . . . married. I am twenty-nine already. You do wish me to get married soon, don't you, sir?"

Now Pierre Verne folded the paper and sighed. "Your mother certainly does." He puffed on his cigar in silence and stubbed out the butt in an ashtray.

Verne waited until he could contain himself no longer. "I need to be happy – nothing less than that, sir."

His younger brother Paul had gone away to sea and was successful in the French navy. His sisters had both married, and now Jules Verne was the last of his parents' children still unattached and unfocused.

"Very well," Pierre Verne said gruffly. "At least it has better prospects than writing those silly plays of yours."

Overjoyed at his victory, Verne pumped his father's hand in gratitude. As he thought of the Paris stock exchange and the bustle of well-dressed men buying and selling securities and commodities, Verne knew that he had a very exciting life in store for him.

VIII

☼

Even though hostilities had ended in the Crimea, for Nemo and his fellow prisoners the war was never over. Not while Caliph Robur held them captive.

It had taken them only a few days to explore their facilities and take stock of their situation. In their temporary barracks of canvas and piled stone, the boatbuilder Cyrus Harding had spoken in a hushed voice with the metallurgist Liedenbrock as they concocted a possible plan of escape. "We could steal a boat, and I could sail her," Harding said. "We'd cross the Aegean to Greece."

"Ach! Why do we not just find another city on the Turkish coast?" Liedenbrock smacked a fist into his palm. "Any place will be better than to remain here in slavery."

"No, no, no! The guards will stop us," Conseil said, eavesdropping. "We are in a strange land. None of us could ever pass as Turks."

Nemo joined the conversation. "Consider how isolated this compound is, men. Far from prying eyes. Robur chose Rurapente well – the mountains, the deep water, the lack of roads. He is an evil man, I sense, but he is not a fool. Besides, there are almost thirty of us. One or two might slip away, but never the whole group." He looked at the prisoners, who listened to him intently. "I say we should all help each other. We have no chance if we try to act alone."

Harding nodded, thrusting out his square, dimpled chin. "Got to agree with you there, captain." Surprised, Nemo realized the boatbuilder had used the title as an honorific. It felt . . . right to him.

The German-born metallurgist heaved a heavy sigh. "Ach, even if I am making it back to Sardinia, I will be thrown into the prison again – unless Caliph Robur intends to give us each a purse of gold when we go." He gave a bitter laugh.

From what the prisoners had seen thus far, the caliph was not a man to pay for anything he could simply take. The industrial laborers at Rurapente had been recruited from Turkish villages in the Anatolian highlands, probably without the sultan's knowledge. Some were slaves, others hostages; a few seemed content with their tasks, which were no more difficult or onerous than any other service for their masters.

By now, Nemo had learned that the industrial complex was capable of producing the finest materials, and the Europeans were allowed free access to books and experimental apparatus. But as yet, Robur had given them no specific instructions, only the speech about his grand vision. Then the caliph had ridden away up a steep mountain path on important business, which had kept him away for several days.

His mind sharp, Nemo refused to waste any time. He spent every daylight hour memorizing the details of Rurapente and the surrounding landscape, hoping to find some way to use it against the caliph. At the same time, he struggled to pick up as much of the Turkish language as his mind could hold. It would be useful. . .

By himself at night, he spent many restless hours trying in vain to engineer an escape that would leave none of his comrades behind. When he grew too weary to think and threw himself onto one of the narrow sleeping pallets, images of his beloved Caroline – just out of reach – haunted his dreams. Far more than a year had passed. By now, Captain Hatteras would have been legally declared lost at sea, and he and Caroline could have been together, married . . . happy.

But instead, he was trapped here, a prisoner.

Caliph Robur returned after a week, riding on his magnificent stallion. The guards sounded a blaring note from a strange musical instrument to summon the group of captive scientists, engineers, and technical experts.

"Men, we are taking a journey into the mountains," Robur said. His jaw clenched, and the jagged scar on his cheek wrinkled up. "I have a demonstration to show you."

The men mumbled in consternation, but displayed no overt disobedience. Robur turned his horse and called over his shoulder. "Once you observe what I have done, you will share my enthusiasm about our future. Mine is the ultimate vision for progress. " Thrusting his pointed beard forward, he smiled . . . but no mirth reached his glittering eyes. "Then you will all agree that I am an enlightened leader, who will rule through technological advancement, rather than fanaticism. If I succeed, the world will indeed be a better place."

Though wary, the prisoners were in good shape and well nourished. Robur set off up a zigzagging mountain path that took them along sheer cliff sides. Guards followed their every move. Even mousy Conseil did not lag behind as they trudged past trickling waterfalls and rockslides, until they reached the Anatolian Plateau, a wilderness peopled only by a few nomads.

They camped at night on the grasslands, wrapped in blankets as the warm wind picked up. In the distance they could hear the bleating and copper bells of a shepherd's flock, but the melodic tinkling was soon overwhelmed by the sound of Liedenbrock's loud snores.

The next morning the twenty-seven men and their armed escorts marched along the edge of the plateau until the trampled dirt road ended. There, they saw a secret installation Robur had built into the stark cliffs. Gazing at the out-of-place facility, Nemo found himself intrigued. The other engineers and scientists gasped in amazement. Conseil squawked in disbelief.

Robur had built an enormous weapon mounted into a notch in the stony cliffs: a cannon barrel longer than an entire ship. The black tapering cylinder thrust into the sky, supported by iron girders. The muzzle was aimed high, pointing upward out into the Mediterranean distance.

Robur reigned up his horse. He said nothing at first, just letting his captives stare down at the incredible cannon barrel. The German-born metallurgist placed a hand on his jutting brow to shade his eyes. "Ach! How is this possible? To cast such an object will have been too difficult even for a master craftsman."

Robur's Turkish pride got the better of him. "The *Columbiad* is the largest cannon in the world – the longest gun barrel ever constructed in human history. It is named after the great Western explorer, who discovered new continents, though many told him it was impossible. We do not listen to the impossible." His thin smile had no mirth. "Its length from breech to muzzle is nine hundred feet. The diameter is ten feet. And I, Robur the Conqueror, have created it." He looked straight at Nemo. "Imagine the projectile that can fit inside, engineer."

The captives mumbled to each other, but Nemo stepped forward and squinted along the angle of the barrel. "It's an artillery piece that lets you fire cannonballs across the Mediterranean?" In his mind, he calculated the range of such a cannon, but had trouble believing his own answer. Robur must be as mad as he was ambitious.

The Caliph brushed the comment aside. "Your assumption is false, engineer. Not every creation is driven by war – as you will see, once I rule the world. An enlightened leader can foster many wonders for the human race."

He gestured toward the gigantic *Columbiad*. "No, this cannon is not a weapon of war, but a device for scientific pursuits." He smiled again. "With it, I will fire not an explosive artillery shell. . . . I intend to launch men to the moon."

"I'd not want to ride in such a ship," Cyrus Harding observed. Nemo refrained from comment, his brow furrowed as he considered the parabolic trajectory. Offhand, he did not know the velocity required for such a shot to escape the earth's gravity and reach outer space.

"Everything is prepared," Robur said, "and today we test the *Columbiad*. That is what you must see." He swiveled to take in the group of captives.

His flushed face held a passion that infused his words with a plea for understanding. "You, my technical experts, must understand what I can accomplish, what *you* can be a part of . . . even if the sultan himself does not yet grasp the concept."

Busy people moved in the outbuildings around the facility, making preparations for the exhibition. Nemo felt a sudden dread that the caliph would ask for a volunteer from among the prisoners, a test subject to ride in this fanciful projectile to the moon . . . and if so, he planned to fight.

Robur led them to the cliff side, his movements electric with enthusiasm. He remained on his horse and gestured for the others to enter a doorway and descend carved stone steps into chambers excavated from solid rock. After Nemo and the others had entered the complex, Robur dismounted, giving the stallion to one of his white-clad guards, then he followed.

The stone-walled chambers held workers, supplies, and materials to fulfill the technical requirements of the purported moonshot. The base of the immense cannon nestled in an iron cradle mounted into the living rock.

Dominating the echoing room stood a conical projectile that resembled an armored pavilion. Climbing ladders to reach the capsule's hatch, slaves loaded crates of supplies, cages of chickens, cushioned chairs, and even a goat through the opening. Pudgy, well-dressed men in flowing robes inspected the operations from ground level, looking very important. The men turned toward the newcomers, then bowed deeply when Robur entered.

"We are completing the final preparations, Caliph," one of the men said, tapping his knuckles together with a clink of jeweled rings.

"We are most gratified that you have given us this opportunity to prove the correctness of our calculations," another said in a watery voice, more terrified than eager.

"I would have it no other way." Robur's voice had a warning edge.

By now, Nemo understood enough Turkish to deduce that these men must be court astronomers and perhaps an ambassador of the great sultan who ruled the Ottoman Empire. Caliph Robur had chosen them as his representatives to the Moon. Nemo considered them all fools.

Robur stroked his pointed beard and straightened his turban. He continued to watch the preparations, explaining nothing to the captives. Judging by the glint in his eyes, he wanted the prisoners to figure everything out for themselves.

Cyrus Harding spoke up. "Do you intend to send these men on a journey into space? They're going to be launched in that capsule?"

"I have chosen them as emissaries – in the sultan's name, of course. They will take everything they need, including fresh food and water, supplies, even baubles for any Moon men they encounter. I intend to open the lunar world for trade with the Ottoman Empire. When he learns of our success, the sultan will be most pleased."

Nemo narrowed his eyes. So, the sultan did not know everything Robur intended. Several of the astronomers trembled with poorly disguised fear at the prospect. Though he resented the warlord, Nemo had to admire the grandeur of the man's dreams and the lengths to which he would go to achieve them.

"How long do you expect the flight to take, Caliph?" Nemo asked. "And how will the men return to Earth after they succeed in reaching the Moon?"

His expression stony, Robur clenched his jaw. "Those questions remain to be answered."

As he watched the slaves loading the supplies, Nemo remembered the bustle of preparation before the *Coralie* had sailed from Nantes. This journey would be far different from a simple sea voyage.

Conseil's round, blinking eyes displayed his astonishment. "No one has ever been to space. No one knows if the Earth's atmosphere extends to the Moon . . . or what strange air the Moon men might breathe."

"Nevertheless, our astronomers have no choice but to risk the journey," Robur said. "I have ordered them to do this for the glory of their omnipotent sultan."

When the slaves finished loading the crates and animals and jugs of water, the astronomers climbed up and poked their heads into the capsule opening, one by one. Whispering among themselves, they finally agreed, then stepped back down, gesturing with ringed fingers and flowing robes. Robur climbed the ladder and peered inside the crowded shell. Satisfied, he climbed back down and bowed to his astronomers and ambassador.

Servants bustled in and laid out colorful rugs for the astronomers. Each man knelt and prayed vigorously. Then they stepped off their rugs, rolled them, and tucked them under their arms before climbing into the capsule. Robur saluted them, and the men waved back before another slave sealed the hatch from the outside.

Using a system of gears and pulleys, massively muscled slaves loaded the heavy artillery shell into the enormous breech of the *Columbiad*. With a clang, the end cap slammed shut and locked.

At a signal from the caliph, the guards commanded everyone to evacuate the complex. Though the workers had little understanding of the experiment, they did not need to be told twice, having seen the huge amounts of black powder poured into the explosive chamber.

Robur took one last look at his magnificent cannon, then gestured to the stone stairs that led out of the caves. His eyes glistened with a fire of anticipation. The prisoners followed him to the plateau, from which they could watch the *Columbiad* fire its shot.

Nemo had seen much smaller cannons fired aboard ship, and from his engineering studies he knew all about dynamics and inertia. He did not envy the volunteer astronomers who sat inside the capsule. In fact, he wanted to be far from the mountain when the mammoth gun blasted its projectile to the skies.

"Don't know about you, but I'd watch out for the recoil," Cyrus Harding said.

After the prisoners emerged into the bright sun, they hurried along the cliff side paths. One of the slaves was commanded at swordpoint to return to the cave and light the cannon's long fuse.

Back on his stallion again, Robur galloped to a clear area on an elbow of land that had been designated as an observation point. The guards herded their European captives over to stand beside the caliph. "My best engineers made their calculations, and my best metallurgists completed this construction," the caliph said, staring at the gun that protruded from the cliff. "I have every confidence that they did their jobs correctly."

The giant gun remained silent in the sunshine, its muzzle pointed upward. Seconds passed, and the waiting became an agony.

The hapless slave came running out of the cave complex, his face filled with terror after lighting the fuse. His legs pumped as he dashed along the path; he tripped and sprawled on his face, but managed to gain his feet within an instant.

With a thunderous roar and a belch of smoke like an iron dragon vomiting fire, the *Columbiad* spoke.

An explosive clap hammered the observers like a physical force. Poor Conseil fell backward, and Nemo reeled on his feet. Caliph Robur's horse reared in panic, but the turbaned warlord gripped the reins and viciously brought his stallion back under control without once taking his eyes from the spectacle.

The projectile leaped from the muzzle of the 900-foot-long cannon, soaring into the sky with the speed of a bullet. Nemo couldn't even imagine the horrendous forces that must be slamming the passengers against the rear of the capsule. Within seconds, the artillery shell dwindled to a dot, arcing high into the Mediterranean sky, far beyond the stretch of the Aegean Sea and out of sight. . .

Then, an unexpected avalanche occurred at the breech end of the cannon. The *Columbiad*'s recoil proved so terrific that the gigantic artillery weapon hammered back into the mountainside and broke free a chunk of the cliff. Huge slabs of rock sloughed off in a spray of powder and stone dust, then fell down the sheer precipice into the deep blue waters below.

Fire burned from the rear of the cannon and slowly, slowly the muzzle broke from its iron strut supports, groaning and drooping.

Caliph Robur stared, his expression grim. The other captives, who had been amazed at the triumphant shot, now groaned as the *Columbiad* broke free of its mounts. With inexorable grace, the huge gun dropped away from the cliff with an excruciating shriek of torn metal and falling boulders.

Nemo watched with hidden satisfaction as the rest of the tumbling cliff side accompanied the cannon in its plunge. Once it struck the water, the enormous black gun barrel took several seconds to become completely submerged. It sank without a trace into the churning froth.

After a long moment, Caliph Robur turned to his European experts, who stared in disbelief at the disaster. His voice was cold. "As you can see, I needed better engineers."

IX

When the group returned to Rurapente the following day, Caliph Robur summoned them to the center of the compound. The sun crackled through the air, making them all restless and uncomfortable. The independent warlord had brooded throughout the tedious journey across the plains and back down to his secret industrial city.

During their absence, the miners and smelters had continued to produce raw materials and metals. Slaves and indentured workers awaited the orders of their master. Everything was prepared . . . but the engineers still didn't know why they had been brought here.

Robur stood on a platform, ready to give instructions to his engineers. "You have seen a demonstration of my ambitions. The sultan rules the Ottoman Empire, and the caliphs are his military advisors. Others whisper conservatism and cowardice in his ear, but only I have the vision, and so I must act on my own, to prove I am right. I intend to provide the sultan with everything he needs – including weapons and my own wisdom as his primary advisor."

He drew a deep breath. "You men were brought here for one purpose. In Egypt, Pasha Mohammad Said has given his permission for the construction of a massive canal across the Isthmus of Suez. When completed, this waterway will bring a flood of European trade through the Mediterranean to the Red Sea. If unchecked, this Suez Canal will mean the destruction not only of the Ottoman Empire, but of Egypt as well.

"I, however, intend for my Turkish people to use this to our advantage," Robur said, his voice rising. "Just as we control the bottleneck of the Bosporus and the Dardanelles, we must also maintain an iron grip on the Suez. For that, I require an unprecedented *weapon*. A vessel that can raid and hold for ransom any ship that passes through this canal."

The emerald in his turban gleamed in the sunlight like an evil green eye. He looked at the Europeans, then squarely met Nemo's eyes. "You men will invent, construct, and test a powerful warship – but not just any warship. I must have one that can travel unseen under the water, like an armored fish, so that I can strike at all who defy our tolls."

"Ach! An underwater boat?" Liedenbrock said. "This is impossible."

"Your word *impossible* does not translate into my language," Robur said.

Cyrus Harding maintained his silence, but his brow furrowed as if his mind were already imagining solutions to the problem the Caliph had posed.

Nemo remembered the drawings Captain Grant had shown him of the prototype submarine boat that Robert Fulton had designed and built for Napoleon Bonaparte. That idea had always intrigued him. "We can do it," he said in a low voice, already calculating how he could turn this task against the caliph.

Robur made an instant decision. "You, engineer – I place you in charge of the project." Nemo couldn't tell if the caliph had planned this assignment all along, or simply rewarded the young man for his quiet confidence.

"You shall have all the resources you need. Any calculations you desire, any raw material, any assistant. We expect you to work and to cooperate. Once my underwater boat is functional, you will all be given the greatest riches you desire. Perhaps you will even be allowed to go home."

The captives grumbled, still uncomfortable to be assisting a man who – though ostensibly an ally to their European countries – had already proven his complete disregard for the rights and freedom of so many people. The caliph could well become a tyrant . . . especially given such a weapon.

But this was not the moment to challenge him. Nemo would bide his time.

"The Suez Canal will take many years to complete," Robur continued. "You must succeed in your task before that time." He turned to descend the raised platform, but stopped and spoke again as if in an afterthought, stroking his beard. "If you fail me, or if I sense your work is progressing too slowly, I will execute you – *all of you* – and find myself another group of engineers."

Then, leaving them stunned, he mounted his stallion and rode off down the streets of Rurapente to his ornate pavilion.

PART VIII
MASTER OF THE WORLD

I

Amiens, France, 1857

By the age of twenty-nine, Jules Verne had resigned himself, and so he finally married. Someone other than Caroline Aronnax.

While spending two weeks in Amiens for a friend's wedding, he met a sturdy woman named Honorine Morel, a widow whose husband had died of consumption a year earlier. She was pretty enough in a plain sort of way, though encumbered with two young daughters, Valentine and Suzanne.

Drowning in the celebratory atmosphere of the friend's wedding, swept along with the joy and love and well-wishes, Verne convinced himself that he could make a life with the widow Morel. While she wasn't Caroline, he had decided to be pragmatic. Thanks to the inheritance from her first husband, Honorine had a solid dowry, and Verne was weary of being a bachelor. Having few other prospects, he decided to give as much of his heart to her as he could spare. So long as she allowed him to continue writing his stories, even if in secret. . .

Years earlier, Verne had joined a bachelors' club, Les Onze Sans Femmes, sanguine young men who had declared their total independence from female company. Together, they shored up each others' beliefs, convinced each other of their continued bliss without the encumbrances of a spouse and children. But recently many of his "bachelor society" friends had finished university, settled down in marriage despite their earlier smug protestations of disinterest in feminine company, and started their own lives. Some seemed quite happy with their new situation – and Verne felt restless again.

Gloomy and impatient, he convinced himself that Caroline would never accept the obvious. Although Captain Hatteras could have been legally declared lost at sea years before, she vowed not to make any such decision until Nemo returned from the Crimean War. But their friend's last letter had been dated a year before the peace treaty, and they had heard nothing from him since. . .

Verne had a decent job at the Bourse, the Paris stock exchange. Once married, he would settle into a normal existence, without adventures and without anxiety. Over the years, much to Pierre Verne's satisfaction, his red-headed son had grown more serious toward life. Though he continued to write plays that were never produced and scientific articles that never got published, Jules Verne no longer talked about becoming a famous writer like Dumas or Hugo. He kept those dreams to himself, but they did not vanish entirely.

For his wedding, Verne managed little more than a simple ceremony and a sparse dinner for the dozen attendees, including his parents. Honorine's lacy wedding gown emphasized her broad shoulders, wide hips, and dark brown hair that curled against her skull. Stoic and placid, she had pale eyes and a wide mouth that rarely showed any expression: not a scowl or pout or smile of joy. Still, she had a steady keel, and Verne welcomed the stability she would bring to his life. Though passionless, at least Honorine was quiet. And he could still work on his stories to his heart's content.

Verne lived in a small flat a few minutes' walk from the Bourse. He'd found the place comfortable enough as a bachelor, but it was unsuitable for a man, a wife, and two young girls. Valentine and Suzanne were shipped off to spend several months with the parents of Honorine's first husband, while Verne and his new bride settled in.

Though she was a devoted wife who did everything society required of her, Honorine spent little time in conversation with her husband. She showed no interest in Verne's stories and did not share his creative needs. She felt no particular obligation to understand: after all, what wife *did* know about her husband's interests and activities?

Instead, Honorine supported him in her gentle, sturdy way. Verne rose at five o'clock every morning and retreated to a small room where he closed the door and spent hours reading newspapers and magazines, scribbling notes, and writing drafts of manuscripts.

Honorine brought him freshly brewed coffee or tea and a small breakfast. Most importantly, she left him in peace. When her two daughters stayed with them, making the place oppressive and crowded, Honorine did her best to keep them silent until ten o'clock came around and Verne emerged from his writing study to dress. He would then leave for an early lunch and spend the remainder of the day in the stock exchange.

Although Verne was not *happy*, he could not ask for more. His wife did not intrude on the time he spent in his writing room. He read scientific journals voraciously, clipping articles for his folders – though he spent far more time in research than in actually putting words on paper.

Each day he scanned the news for events of the world, new discoveries and reports of far-flung lands – places he and Nemo had dreamed about in their youth. Most of all, he tried to be satisfied with the life he had accepted and never to think of Caroline Aronnax again. . .

One morning, a bizarre article in a Paris weekly caught Verne's attention. German explorers in a caravan marching south into the Sudan from Tripoli had discovered a strange wrecked vessel in the sand dunes of the Sahara. The iron-walled capsule, shaped like a gigantic artillery shell, had been embedded in a crater in the rolling ocean of desert. The projectile seemed to have fallen out of the sky and crashed.

While the uneasy nomads hung back on their camels, the German explorers had pried open the wreckage. Inside, they found the remains of several men squashed to jelly, bones pulverized by an explosive acceleration of inconceivable magnitude. Desiccated supplies, dead chickens and goats lay in a mashed clutter. But the explorers could find no explanation of how these poor wretches had got here, what they had been up to, or why they had undertaken such a terrible risk.

Puzzled, Verne used his heavy scissors to snip out the article. Such mysteries tantalized him. Even without additional information, Verne could perhaps invent a tale to explain such a fantastic occurrence, but he could think of no circumstance outrageous enough to fit the facts.

He added the clipping to his growing pile of notes and ideas, wondering when he would ever have the freedom or enthusiasm to pursue all the stories that floated in his head. Perhaps he needed a "fiction factory" of his own, like Dumas . . . but for that, he would have to begin making money at it, and that seemed a long way off.

Honorine knocked on the door and quietly reminded him of the time. With a heavy sigh, Verne finished his cold tea and stood to get dressed. Once again, he had written nothing all morning, had made no progress toward creating a famous work of literature.

Instead, he spent the rest of his day at the dreary stock exchange, making and losing other people's money.

II

Over time, Nemo came to love Auda, his assigned wife in Rurapente.

She was a beautiful Turkish maiden with silky black hair and creamy tan skin, her sepia eyes large and catlike, her mouth full, her body lean and supple. Auda would have become part of the sultan's harem in Ankara, if Caliph Robur had not given her to Engineer Nemo as a reward...

For more than two years now, Nemo had managed the caliph's ambitious project to create an armored submarine boat. He had been given comfortable accommodations, good food, and various amenities, all of which were intended to make him forget his situation – and he had demanded the same for every one of the captive men.

But even his beautiful wife and luxurious dwelling could not disguise the fact that he remained the caliph's prisoner, forced to work against his will on a terrible weapon of war. Every time he saw the dusky, exotic features of Auda, he could think only of Caroline, their stolen moments of love aboard the ship home from Africa, and in her own bedchambers on his last night before departing Paris by train to the Crimean front.

Every day, he saw Auda's caring in her deep-brown eyes, and he felt sorry for her situation as well as his. His own guilt and longing for Caroline had made him avoid this unwanted young woman for many weeks, but Auda was patient, and loving. The only bright flower in this miserable place.

Caliph Robur would never let them leave Rurapente.

With his European comrades, Nemo had developed a plan for the

CAPTAIN NEMO

submarine boat. In a written list to Robur, he proposed a long series of tests to determine the best method for building an underwater war vessel. Together, the men set to work, clinging to their only hope of freedom.

The boatbuilder Cyrus Harding assisted with the overall concepts of a watertight submerged boat based on what Nemo remembered of Robert Fulton's design. The metallurgist Liedenbrock experimented with alloys to create a strong but light material for plating the hull of the vessel. Conseil strove to develop ways to contain atmospheres inside the craft, compressing air and mixing blends of oxygen and nitrogen to produce the best breathing gas for underwater explorers.

Other engineers expanded upon Nemo's childhood idea of enclosing one's head in a breathing sphere so as to allow a man to walk beneath the sea. Glassmakers, hydraulic engineers, and mechanics all pitched in, resigned to their fates as the years passed.

The facilities and resources of Rurapente gave them everything they requested, any necessary supplies or materials. Throughout the work, Caliph Robur scrutinized their progress, riding about on his dark stallion and keeping a watch on the smoke belching from the smelters and glass-blowers' huts. He demanded regular reports, and Nemo had long ago given up any pretense of concocting exaggerations. He let the intense man see for himself how much progress his captive experts were making.

After six months of satisfactory work, Robur had brought in a group of women and assigned them as wives to the European engineers. He seemed intent on making his pet scientists settle down and forget their former lives. Under the caliph's watchful eye, Nemo knew they might remain trapped here in this hidden city for years. Though he pretended to cooperate, at night Nemo seethed over his stolen life, and his lost Caroline. . .

The lovely Auda was one of twenty daughters sired by another caliph, Barbicane, a conservative rival of Robur's. The jewel of the group of assigned wives, Auda was quiet and intelligent, a prisoner of fate as much as Nemo was. Though he still thought of Caroline, despairing that he had broken his promise to return to her, he also knew that Auda would be punished and ridiculed if he refused her. And she did not deserve that.

He treated his wife well, and she proved to be a warm companion for him. When Nemo came in after a day's hard work, Auda would rub his shoulders, bathe his feet, and wipe cool perfumed cloths over his forehead and neck. She spoke a little English, much to Nemo's surprise, and over the following year and a half she taught him to be fluent in Turkish, while he reciprocated by teaching her French.

Late at night, while he stared at his blueprints and calculations by lamplight, Auda often sat by his side and studied the drawings herself. Not until she began to make insightful and relevant suggestions did he realize that she understood the intricacies of his diagrams. Though he had accepted her as his wife, he'd never imagined Auda might be as educated or clever as his beloved Caroline.

"I studied in Ankara, my husband," Auda answered. "I learned mathematics, astronomy, alchemy, and even some surgery. The eunuch in my father's house was fond of me and shared his books. But my father, Caliph Barbicane, abhors science – especially if it is taught to women. When he discovered what the eunuch had done, he executed the man and banished me here to Rurapente. He considered it a great punishment to place me in the clutches of Caliph Robur."

When she smiled at Nemo, her sepia eyes glittered like mysteries in the yellow lamplight. "But it is no punishment after all. I find each day with you to be a reward, my husband. You treat me as a friend and teach me even more. How could I have hoped for so much?"

After that evening, Nemo made a point of discussing the submarine development with her, though she warned him not to mention their conversations to the other engineers – and most particularly not to Robur.

Auda explained how, in the politics of the Ottoman Empire, the great sultan was pulled in various directions by his military advisors, the caliphs, who often held secret and enormous power. Some caliphs, like Robur, wanted Turkey to become a modern nation, comparable to the European states, while others – conservatives such as her father – wanted to return to rigid Islamic principles and blindfold their people to changing times.

Now Nemo understood why Robur so often disappeared from the isolated industrial compound to ride inland for days. He was running back to Ankara to sit in the sultan's palace and advocate his new weapons and technology. When Robur returned from his sojourns in a foul mood, he roared at Nemo for not making sufficient progress. "Your men *must* complete the submarine boat in time to show the sultan its wondrous power. My own fate depends upon it – and yours as well."

Nemo and his men developed a metal-walled chamber to be submerged in the deep cove of Rurapente. It was not meant to move, simply to test the hull metals and the watertightness of the seals. The first unmanned test chamber broke apart in the deepest water, its window panes shattered.

The caliph wanted to behead the glassmaker whose work had failed, but Nemo stood up for the man, placing himself in mortal danger. Robur grudgingly backed down in his rage, and all the captives looked relieved.

After the second experimental tank retained its integrity, Caliph Robur insisted that a "volunteer" slave be placed inside for the third test, as a demonstration of human endurance. The chamber sank to the greatest depths of the channel and remained intact. Unfortunately, it took Nemo and his engineers several hours to raise the vessel again . . . by which time the poor man inside had suffocated. Conseil, who had designed the air-storage systems, shuddered with guilt over the man's death.

Though Nemo and his team learned a great deal from each experiment, Robur considered the failures to be dire setbacks. The stern caliph punished the men by reducing their rations, and Nemo had to argue furiously with the stubborn warlord to have their full privileges reinstated. For days afterward he fumed, once again trying to determine how they could all escape from Rurapente – and once again he came up with no answers. Auda comforted him, and told him to be patient. . .

Two years after they were married – five years after he had left France for the Crimea – beautiful Auda bore him an infant boy who became the bright light in Nemo's life. After the birth, her face drawn with the effort and her silky hair streaked with sweat, Nemo found his wife more beautiful than ever. In that moment he realized that he had indeed come to love Auda.

Looking back over everything he had lost, Nemo took comfort in this one thing: at least he had gained *her*. As he remembered his childhood and the happy days in Nantes, he held the baby son in his arms and smiled.

"We will name him Jules," he said.

III

Long after the Treaty of Paris ended the Crimean War, soldiers continued to trickle home from the Black Sea battlefields. They were a sorry sight, wounded in mind and body, completely without the songs or hurrahs they had carried in their hearts when they'd gone off to war.

But André Nemo was not among them. Month after month, he did not come home, nor did he send any word. He had vanished somewhere in the war.

Preoccupied with his new family, his struggles as a writer, and his daily work in the stock market, Jules Verne spared only an occasional thought for his old friend. He and Honorine, with her two daughters, traveled to Nantes for a spring holiday, where Verne ate well of his mother's cooking. In Paris, their personal finances had been tight, as always.

During the visit home, he held the usual brief conversations with his father while reading the newspapers and reviewing the events of the day. The "Iron Tsar" Nicholas I had died the year before, leaving the country in the hands of his more open-minded son Alexander. Autocratic Russia had grudgingly resigned her protectorate over the Orthodox Church in Turkey, and the great sultan of the Ottoman Empire promised privileges for his Christian subjects. The Black Sea became a neutral body of water, and the world began to settle down.

France's parliament engaged in heated discussions about the outrageous ineptitude of the military bureaucracy during the conflict. Others challenged Emperor Napoleon III's clumsy foreign policy that had unnecessarily drawn France into the war in the first place. In Britain, the outspoken reformer Florence Nightingale used official records and damning statistics to show that of the 100,000 fatalities in the Crimea, fully a quarter of them had died of disease, exposure, and lack of supplies rather than from battlefield injuries. *Inexcusable.*

Tennyson's scathing but heroic poem immortalized the Light Brigade's senseless and futile charge against murderous odds. The victims – "Theirs not to reason why, theirs but to do and die" – became symbols for the confusion and tragedy of the Crimean War. . .

Thus, by virtue of his brief vacation in Nantes, Verne was at his old house when the terrible message came from the French war department.

When enlisting years earlier, Nemo had written down the names of Jules Verne and Caroline Hatteras as "next of kin." The war department letter, identical to so many others, gave few details aside from the stark announcement that André Nemo had been killed at the battle of Balaclava. According to military records, he had been buried with other brave soldiers outside Sevastopol. He had left no personal effects.

Standing in the doorway, Verne held the official communiqué with trembling hands. While arranging flowers in a vase in the back room, Honorine watched him blocking the sunlight, observed her husband's reaction as he opened the note and read the words. She came forward, grasping the flowers in her hand, as she instinctively tried to comfort him. Instead, Verne walked in a daze away from his father's old house to wander the streets of Île Feydeau.

Not surprisingly, he found himself on Caroline's doorstep. Despite her new offices in Paris, she still lived much of the year in Nantes. Now he heard music inside, her delicate fingers on the keys of the pianoforte, no doubt playing one of her own secret compositions, a mournful and ethereal melody that sounded like a dirge. When she answered his insistent ringing of the bell, Verne saw from her drawn face, reddened eyes, and tear-streaked cheeks, that she too had received a letter.

"He went to the Crimea because of me," Caroline said. "He wanted to get away for a year. We should not have waited! I cared nothing for any public scandal." She looked at him with her glittering blue eyes. "Ah, Jules, I pushed André from Paris, and he went off to the fighting so that he could forget about me until I was free."

Verne didn't know what to say – but then, he had always been tongue-tied around her. Just seeing the beautiful woman who had consumed his youthful, imaginative passions reminded Verne of all the things he had not achieved in his life. "No one could ever forget you, Caroline," he said.

Without a further word, she leaned forward to let Verne awkwardly gather her in his arms. He embraced her, thinking of all the times he had longed to do just this. But now grief made her touch cold and desperate.

"I will survive somehow, Jules," she said. "I cannot believe André is gone, when his memory lives so strongly in my heart. Could it be a mistake? We thought him dead before, and yet he returned. He promised me he would return."

"I . . ." Verne found himself at a complete loss for words, again. "I would not want to give you an unreasonable hope, Caroline. This letter leaves no doubt." He held up the paper note he had wrinkled in his grasp.

"We must remember André as the wonderful man he was, you and I. No one knew him better." She brushed her fingers across Verne's unruly reddish-brown hair, sending a shiver down his spine.

His heart pounded, and his blood grew hot from reawakened longing. But now that she might finally give up waiting for her lost captain, and waiting for Nemo . . . Verne himself was married. They stood together for a long moment, until Caroline pulled away.

"Yes, I'll certainly remember him. He was closer to me than my own brother," Verne said and understood that he had to go. His wife was waiting for him back at home.

IV

Rurapente's cove had become a massive construction site. Ramps and scaffolding extended into the deep water. The sounds of Robur's slave workers hammering rivets echoed like gunfire off the close mountain walls. The slaves pounded hull plates, bent framework pipes, and twisted steel support ribs into proper shapes. Gritty smoke and chemical fumes from the refineries filled the air faster than ocean breezes could sweep the stench across the Mediterranean.

Nemo stood on a platform deck, directing construction and supervising the captive engineers and indentured workers. Rather than just watching, though, he spent most of his time up to his knees in water that sloshed into the dry docks. He tried to maintain the morale of the men, while searching for subtle ways to resist their despised captor.

The skeleton of his submarine craft was taking shape. Despite being forced to this labor against his will, Nemo admired what he had accomplished and felt pride in his design. If only the innovative vessel had been for a different purpose, other than hated war . . .

The bottom hull had been reinforced according to Cyrus Harding's instructions. The British boatbuilder teamed up with the German-born metallurgist to inspect the progress. Riveted plates crawled up the walls, sealing the underwater vessel so that it floated like a dragon inside the construction dock. Muscular Turkish slaves used handpumps to drain water from the bilges.

Nemo's son Jules was a year old now, a bright joy in an oppressive life. The boy had his mother's black hair and full mouth, and his father's determined, optimistic spirit. The child had no idea that his loving home was a prison camp. At times, the toddler's laughing eyes even made Nemo forget for a while.

The captive engineers had been away from their homelands for so long that they hardly remembered what a normal existence could be like. Few had left families behind, and after so many years their longing for Europe had deadened to a dull ache. Their lives were here, and now, and they had little hope for improvement. They worked on the undersea vessel and devoted their hearts to its completion – for their own pride, not for their captor's.

When Caliph Robur returned to Rurapente after a three-week sojourn with the great sultan, he rode his stallion down to the construction site. As he haughtily studied the incomplete vessel, his expression was not pleased. The warlord's narrow face twisted, and his skin darkened with rage, highlighting the scar along his cheek. Nemo looked at him and guessed that Robur was losing his continuing political battles against the conservative caliphs in Ankara.

Conseil, the French meteorologist, peeped out from his instrument shack at the end of the docks, noted Robur's stormy expression, and hid himself again. His bristly hair had grown into a haphazard shock of gray; his hangdog face continued to sunburn regularly despite years in the Turkish heat.

Nemo watched the angry caliph, then climbed away from the skeleton of the undersea boat to face him. For the sake of his men, he had to fend off Robur's capricious moods. He stood straight-backed in front of the turbaned man on the horse. "As you can see, Caliph," Nemo said, masking his sarcasm with pride, "we have made substantial progress during your absence."

The warlord scowled in disgust at the frame of the vessel. He spoke in a loud, sharp voice. "I bear news from Egypt that actual excavation has begun on the Suez Canal. Your French engineer de Lesseps is already digging the channel that will bring the downfall of the Ottoman Empire." His stallion pranced and snorted, sensing his rider's rage.

Robur's mouth twisted, as if he wanted to spit on the ground. "Unfortunately, my sultan is blind to the implications, and so I must act alone, for his own good. He dismisses my concerns and listens instead to Barbicane and other fools who have no understanding of the new world we live in." Robur narrowed his dark eyes and stared for a moment at his captive engineers and scientists. "The sultan thinks we are still fighting against primitive Tatars or Mongols. He does not see the need for my underwater warship."

Nemo wondered if the caliph would cancel the project now, but knew the arrogant man would never surrender so easily. Perhaps the sultan had commanded him to free all of his European prisoners – but Nemo could not hope for that either. He suspected instead that he and his companions would be quietly disposed of, their bodies hidden. His fists clenched at his sides. He would fight with his bare hands, if necessary.

"Therefore, I must prove my vision is superior," the caliph continued, stroking his sharp black beard. "The Suez Canal must not be completed before we are ready. Your men must work faster and harder."

Skeptical, Nemo looked back at the construction site. He knew how frantic his men had been laboring in the hope of freedom once their task was completed. Nemo was certain by now that this hope was false. Caliph Robur would never allow the men to return to Europe, where they could reveal what this megalomaniac had done to them. He also knew that a project as massive as the Suez Canal would require years of labor from thousands of people.

But Caliph Robur seemed to think it would be completed overnight. Instead, the warlord thrust a long finger toward Nemo and his men. "You have one year from today to complete this work. If at that time my submarine warship is not ready, I will execute one of your men, and then another for every additional month you fail me."

The men voiced their objections. Nemo stepped forward, angry and defiant. "Sir, that cannot be done. We are already –"

Robur cut him off. "Everything can be done, given sufficient incentive." He placed a menacing hand on the hilt of his scimitar, wheeled his stallion, and rode back toward his lavish pavilion.

V

The first full-scale prototype of the underwater vessel was completed and launched ten months later, a gleaming metal predator able to submerge beneath the cove.

Instead of experiencing triumph as he watched the vessel sway against its moorings, Nemo felt deeply uneasy. Under Robur's threat of reprisals, the rushed engineers had worked haphazardly, cutting corners. The slave workers did not understand their work, and Nemo's engineers had no time to perform sufficient safety checks.

All around the construction site, Robur had increased the presence of his private guards. The bald men now stood with prominent scimitars tucked into waist sashes around their billowy white uniforms. Some of the burly guards made a point of carrying whetstones with which they sharpened their blades in the afternoon sun.

During an actual underwater voyage, Robur would need all of Nemo's trained men to sail the vessel – but for the initial test, they would simply submerge and maneuver the submarine boat to the end of the cove to prove the vessel's integrity. The caliph sent seven of his trusted guards along, but refused to climb aboard the vessel himself. *With good reason, too*, Nemo thought with an unspoken sneer. The undersea boat was not safe.

Under the caliph's watchful eye, the hatches were sealed. Nemo took the helm, and the electrical engines thrummed, turning gears and motivators. The submarine boat pushed away from the docks into deeper water, its screws turning. Underwater propellers and mechanical fins swung back and forth.

Through the thick glass windows, Nemo watched the receding dock and saw Robur, still on his horse, his face expressionless. Nemo knew that Auda and their young son would be in the crowd, watching as well, and that thought tempered the constant ache of anger in his heart.

When the metal-walled vessel reached the end of the cove, Nemo tried not to think of the caliph's unreasonable demands. He scowled at the brutish guards aboard with him, then pushed them from his mind. Staring out to the blue panorama of the Mediterranean, he smiled at Cyrus Harding and the other two engineers he had brought along.

"Prepare to submerge, Mr Harding."

"Yes, captain." When Harding formally relayed the order, his gruff voice sounded tinny within the plated walls. The crewmen worked controls to open the ballast tanks, forcing air out and filling the chambers.

Holding tight to the helm rail, Nemo watched the waterline creep up on the thick glass portholes. He heard pumps and turbines, water gushing into the tanks, saw air bubbles foaming around the body of the vessel. Though the hatches were sealed, Nemo glanced at the visible hull seams, watchful for leaks. Though this vessel had been created under duress, for an evil purpose to spread warfare across the seas, he still felt a pride in its design and construction.

Frothing water covered the dome of the ship. Perspiration glistened on the shaved scalps of the uneasy guards. They looked at each other and fidgeted, hands on the golden hilts of their scimitars, as if swords could do anything to conquer their fear.

Nemo made sure each one of the caliph's men saw his confident smile. Here, far from Robur, *he* was their master. Then he commanded more ballast tanks to be opened, and the vessel sank deeper.

In the rear of the main deck, one of his men shouted in alarm. Too late, Nemo heard the agonized groaning of stressed metal. Plates bent, and rivets popped like small bullets. Two of the lower ballast tanks burst, spraying gouts of seawater into the bottom decks. It all happened so fast.

The caliph's guards lumbered about in confusion, barking toothless threats at the crew. Nemo shoved them aside, ignoring them as he ordered the inner hatches sealed. Harding yelled for the crewmen to crank armored covers into place over the glass ports, but it was no use. The submarine boat began to fill with water from the ruptures. The stern tilted downward.

"We have no choice but to evacuate," Nemo said. The deck was at such an angle he had to climb to the upper hatch. Below, more of the main hull plates bent inward as the vessel sank deeper. "This ship can't be saved."

One of the guards drew his scimitar and snarled, but Nemo stopped him with a commanding look. He replied in clear Turkish, "Remain here if you like."

Robur's forced construction schedule had been too hectic. Additional support girders and hull reinforcements he had suggested on his original design had not been added. Forced by their tight deadline, Nemo had chosen to omit backup systems. Now they would pay for the oversight.

If they did not abandon the vessel now, they would plunge too deep into the channel for anyone to escape. His crew would never manage to swim to the surface before they drowned.

Nemo reached up to open the primary hatch, and a thunderous waterfall of brine poured down upon his head. Oddly, he now remembered the bladder helmet he had used as a teenager on the river Loire – even that crude invention would have given him a few more breaths of air on his way up. But they had left Conseil's undersea helmets and diving suits in Rurapente. Robur had insisted they'd have no need for undersea exploration on this test voyage.

Nemo grabbed Cyrus Harding and his two engineers and forced them to climb through the water pounding from the hatch. The ship continued to plunge deeper and deeper. He looked at Robur's panicked guards, pitied them for a moment – and chose to let hell take the allies of the man who had stolen their lives from them. His heart felt utterly cold as he left them to die.

With powerful strokes, he swam into the deep water, surging toward the bright surface that seemed miles above. The pressure squeezed his skull and chest, but he stroked and kicked. In a dizzy, sickening instant he recalled when he had tried to rescue his father trapped beneath the Loire in the sinking hulk of the *Cynthia*. He saw the shadowy forms of his crewmen overhead, rising with the flow of bubbles toward daylight. His need to get away grew more urgent.

Below, a cyclone of escaping air accompanied the plunge of the submarine.

Nemo swam until his arms ached and his lungs wanted to explode. He burst to the surface, heaving huge lungfuls of air. His men were beside him, panting, bedraggled, and exhausted. They looked at each other in dismay. Five of the caliph's guards also surfaced, while the sinking craft claimed the other two lives.

Sick at the disaster, seeing all their work wasted – and dreading the consequences Caliph Robur was sure to impose – Nemo and his weary men swam toward the distant shore.

VI

Caliph Robur began his bloody punishments before the full year was up.

Strident horns blew across the compound, summoning the dejected engineers from where they had begun work on a second vessel based on Nemo's modified design. The caliph's guards marched out, their shaved heads glistening in the Turkish sun, their loose white garments looking too clean.

The captive engineers knew something terrible lay in store for them, though they had done their best under impossible circumstances. Robur's own foolish impatience had been the root cause of the disaster.

Standing at the docks with industrial smoke hanging like a pall over the cove, Nemo stepped to the front of his team in an attempt to reassure them. During the Crimean War, Robur had coolly selected each man because of his individual expertise. Each one was valuable to this project, vital to the completion of the undersea vessel. But Nemo feared the warlord's rage would provoke him to unwise actions. . .

The night after the first submarine craft had sunk, two-year-old Jules had played innocently on the carpets in their home, laughing. He was a good-natured boy, whose vivid imagination made a toy out of any scrap of material. Auda played a stringed musical instrument and sang to Nemo, trying to soothe his despair.

"I have word from the sultan's court at Ankara, my husband," she said in a low voice. "Caliph Robur finds himself in a terrible situation. My father has grown stronger, and Robur has lost the sultan's support."

"Why?" Nemo said. "Because of what happened today?"

Auda shook her head. "For years, Robur has secretly diverted much of the sultan's treasury to Rurapente, yet he still has nothing to show for it. My father, on the other hand, knows the power of sweet words, compliments, and promises . . . and he uses them daily on the sultan's weak will. Caliph Barbicane gives the sultan little gifts to show his loyalty, while Robur does not." She stroked his dark hair. "It is a game of politics, my beloved – and Robur does not play it well."

Nemo looked at her, distracted by her beauty. Young Jules chuckled in a corner, playing with a small twig studded with dry leaves. He waved it about like a flag.

"Much as I despise him, Robur does have the truer vision," Nemo told her. "He sees the future, while Barbicane does not. The Ottoman Empire *will* fall if the Turks persist in old ways and ignore how the world will change once the Suez Canal is completed."

Auda leaned forward to give him a gentle kiss, then played her musical instrument again. "Husband, this matter has nothing to do with who is correct and who is wrong . . . only which of the caliphs can persuade the great sultan."

When she had begun to sing once more, Nemo closed his eyes and listened to her voice, but she hadn't been able to lull him out of his misery. . .

Now, months later, Robur's voice boomed out with the grim threat of a cannon strike. "You have failed me. All of you." He looked from one captive engineer to another, his gaze like a stiletto dragged across their throats. "But I shall be merciful – and only one of you will pay the ultimate price. This time."

He made a brisk gesture with a ringed hand. Nemo could see that the whole spectacle had been rehearsed beforehand. The muscular guards marched forward and grabbed fidgety Conseil, the meteorologist. "No, no, no!" The small man from Marseilles flailed and cried out, but they pinned his arms. His sunburned face turned beet red, and his eyes looked as if they might spring from their sockets. The guards dragged Conseil to the end of the docks.

"Caliph Robur, you must not do this!" Nemo stepped forward, but guards shoved him back.

The Turkish leader gave him a withering glare. "You do not command me, engineer. You are my *slave*."

Nemo did not blink. "I am the one building your submarine boat – and if you want it finished, you cannot deprive me of my men."

Robur fixed Nemo with a stony gaze. "Nevertheless, you will learn to work without this man."

Conseil's arms and legs had turned to jelly. Desperation turned Nemo's voice deeper, gave it a ragged edge. "You must not do this!"

At the caliph's quick nod, the guards shoved Conseil down onto his knees. His face was now pasty white, and his arms fluttered. He tried feebly to get away, but the strong men held him down.

"I said stop, or I swear to you that we will all sabotage our work and you will never have your submarine boat!" Defiant and angry, Nemo pushed against the crossed scimitars of the guards. He struck out with his fists, trying to make his way to the doomed man, but one of them hammered the hilt of his weapon against Nemo's forehead, making him crumple to the ground.

"Then you will all die, in the most horrible manner I can imagine. I suggest that you do not challenge my ingenuity in concocting tortures." Robur looked at him as a man might inspect a bug. "I do as I wish, engineer – just as *you* must also do as I wish. All of you."

Nemo struggled to his knees, wiping a scarlet splash of blood from his eyes, and snarled in desperation, "No! If you insist on doing this, then you are a *fool*." The threat in his voice made the guards glare at him. Nemo had dealt with thugs and pirates and warlords before, and he hated them all. "Robur, you have my word that if you spare him, we –"

Caliph Robur gave a barely perceptible flick of his right hand.

The curved scimitar struck downward, and Conseil had time for only a brief squawking cry that was abruptly cut short as his head rolled onto the dock boards. The guards released his decapitated body, which slumped forward like a dropped sack.

The engineers staggered in shock, as if they, too, had felt the blow. Some stared with a thunderstorm of rage across their faces. Liedenbrock swore under his breath, then began to weep.

Nemo clenched his jaw, trying to contain his absolute loathing for the man who had forced them here. He vowed again that he would never cooperate for the caliph's aims. They had been here for seven years already and had grown too complacent. It would take cleverness and determination, but he *would* find a way to use Robur's own technology against him.

The warlord's men used their booted feet to shove Conseil's body off the dock and into the cove. Then, three workers ran forward with buckets of water to wash away the blood.

His green turban in place, its emerald staring like a third eye from his forehead, Robur scowled at the gathered prisoners. "Now, get back to work."

VII

As daylight seeped through the red silk curtains that hung over his windows, Nemo stood motionless, hypnotized by the fish swimming inside their tank. A glass-walled enclosure contained ten fish of various sizes and species, gliding back and forth. He had spent hours observing how their bodies and fins moved for propulsion, how their gills pumped water, how the fish *existed* beneath the surface.

His mechanical, armored war vessel would have to do the same.

Auda, who knew not to interrupt him during these contemplative times, had taken their son Jules, now four years old, to play in the back room of their home. Nemo's many years of enforced work and research at Rurapente would culminate today with the launching of the new vessel. Despite the caliph's self-imposed urgency, the Suez Canal had not yet been completed.

But the submarine warship was truly ready after many long years of labor, of sweat and blood. Either Nemo would succeed today . . . or fail utterly. With so many lives dependent on him, failure was not an option. Conseil had already paid for their work with his life.

A muscular guard marched through the door covering without announcing himself. "Caliph Robur wishes to depart. Now." The bald man stood, intimidating, and waited for Nemo to turn away from the fish tank. His shaved scalp wrinkled with consternation at the delay.

Still, Nemo refused to hurry, resisting in every small manner he could find. With a deep feeling of dread, he went to Auda and Jules. While the guard glowered and made impatient noises, Nemo embraced his wife and son, promising them that nothing was wrong . . . but he wondered if this might be the last time he ever saw them. What did Robur have in mind for his engineers if the submarine vessel did perform as expected?

Hanging his head in resignation, Nemo followed the guard. He took one last look at the gracefully swimming – though still trapped – fish, then at the modest possessions he and Auda had gathered during their life in Rurapente. He marched behind the white-robed guard out to the crowded docks.

The new armored vessel lay like a half-submerged predatory fish tied up against the pilings. Eyelike portholes made of thick glass stared from the control bridge within the bow. Overlapping armor plates reminded him of the scales of the shark he had fought while adrift on a raft of flotsam from the *Coralie*. Jagged fins like saw-teeth lined the dorsal hull, the better for causing severe damage to wooden-keeled ships traversing the Suez.

In secret, Nemo had named the boat the *Nautilus*, after Fulton's turn-of-the-century design. In nature, the real nautilus was a cephalopod cased in a beautiful corkscrew shell, but the ethereal name could not disguise the fact that this was a powerfully armed ship of war, designed for causing death and destruction, nothing else.

Workers and slaves had gathered from the barracks, and Nemo hoped Auda would also come out to join them. The ever-present guards stood watching as the *Nautilus* was prepared for her maiden voyage. Nemo had taken the craft up and down the cove several times, testing her movement and stability while submerged in the deepest water. His men had worked hard, and with care, proud of their accomplishment even as they hated Robur. They had learned their lesson from the first ruined prototype. Allowing themselves to be rushed had led to the death of poor Conseil.

Nemo meant to avenge the hapless meteorologist . . . somehow. Robur had much to atone for.

Torn by even greater political strife back in Ankara, Caliph Robur had threatened further executions. He insisted that Nemo's team work to complete the construction as fast as humanly possible. Nemo held the stubborn man's bloodlust at bay only by emphasizing how the loss of more good workers would cause further delays.

Nemo had grown cold inside, feeling the guilt on his conscience, no matter how much Auda tried to soothe him. He had lost an innocent comrade because of this warlord's mad ambitions. Any enthusiasm he'd had for the project had been killed with the same scimitar that had murdered Conseil. Even after such a long time at Rurapente, Nemo had never accepted his fate, had never believed in the caliph's barbarous ambitions. But he would have to do something soon.

The *Nautilus* functioned perfectly. Once Nemo had demonstrated the vessel's capabilities, Robur could easily convince his sultan of its necessity. All political power would shift. With such a clear triumph over conservative Caliph Barbicane, Robur would once again become a favorite in the sultan's court.

Nemo knew the warlord would never keep his promises of rewarding his captive experts with freedom, though. He could see it in Robur's dark, calculating eyes.

His twenty-five remaining engineers were already aboard the *Nautilus*, a full crew. Food and supplies had been stored in the submarine's chambers. The men had said farewell to their families, because Robur had announced his intention to explore the Mediterranean on this trial voyage. Accompanied by his most trusted guards, the caliph meant to be gone for a full week.

At the edge of the docks, Caliph Robur sat on his stallion as if he intended to bring his big horse aboard the vessel. When the warlord saw Nemo walking toward the launch site under escort, he dismounted and handed the reins to a servant. He motioned to a troop of white-robed guards who climbed through the hatch down into the armored submarine. Smiling above his pointed beard, Robur stood proudly beside Nemo, congratulating his chief engineer. Nemo wanted to spit at him.

"We will now depart and explore the realm beneath the seas," Robur shouted for all the gathered workers to hear. "We will journey into unknown territories, and when I return, all of the Ottoman Empire – in fact, the entire world – will know the power and terror of this invincible warship. The Turks shall once again be masters of the Mediterranean."

Nemo scanned the slaves and workers. Though they cheered on cue, many seemed agitated in a strange way. The warlord remained oblivious to the changed mood – Robur had never heeded the feelings or motivations of the people who were forced to serve him.

Then, even in his red haze of resentment, a relieved grin broke across Nemo's face as he recognized beautiful, long-haired Auda pushing through the crowd. He'd known she would come. His wife clutched little Jules's hand in her own and made her way to the dock. In her other hand, she grasped a bouquet of flowers.

"Wait!" she called in Turkish. "I must give these to my husband. It is a tradition from his home country."

The guards let her pass, and she hurried forward. After years of knowing Auda so well, Nemo could read the concern in her sepia eyes. "Take these flowers, my husband," she said, using French this time. While Robur could still understand her, the guards could not. "Put them in your stateroom and think of me on your journey."

Then she bowed formally to the caliph himself, though her eyes remained as hard as flint. "It is my way of offering prayers to Allah," she said. "A gift of beauty for my husband."

Robur gruffly nodded to her. "Take the flowers from your woman, engineer, and get aboard. I am anxious to be off."

Concerned, Nemo took the bouquet from her trembling hand – perhaps she was afraid for him on this trial journey? But Auda had not shown such fear on his other test voyages. Why now?

Impatient, Robur gestured for him to climb through the hatch into the vessel, then rapidly followed, scrambling down the metal rungs. The hatch clanged shut with a sound like a coffin lid closing.

The *Nautilus*'s front chamber consisted of a raised bridge deck made of anodized metal plates. Corrugated steel steps dropped down to the main control deck where workers manned the apparatus. Wide plate-glass portholes showed a forward view, as if through the eyes of a fish; side windows also looked out upon the undersea world.

Within the main body of the submarine boat, private cabins for Nemo and the crew members lined the hull. A large sitting room and salon – which Robur intended to use as his throne room – filled the central section of the *Nautilus*. On the lower deck were supply closets and a dressing room complete with undersea suits and brass helmets, as well as a double-lock door to allow egress beneath the water. The engine room, with propulsion screws and pounding pistons, was crowded into the narrow aft chambers.

Nemo deposited Auda's flowers on the table in his cabin and hurried back to complete preparations for submerging. By now, his European crew was well practiced, and he merely gave the orders to reassure them. He took his formal place at the bridge controls. Robur stood next to him, domineering, as if he meant to take the helm as soon as he had observed Nemo's piloting skills.

The submarine's engines started. Electricity pulsed through the motors; the crew tested the rudders. Finally, the ballast tanks were opened as the *Nautilus* drifted free of the dock.

The metal deck hummed beneath them. Solid and sturdy, the undersea vessel showed no distress as water filled the tanks, and the ocean rose above the porthole windows until it swallowed the ridged upper hull. The *Nautilus* sank, and then moved forward.

Away from direct sunlight, the bridge deck darkened. "Lights," Nemo said. Brilliant cones of white illumination stabbed into the water as they proceeded through the mouth of the cove into the Mediterranean.

Robur gasped with childlike glee at the new world beyond the thick portholes. He saw confused fish swimming about, rocky outcroppings far below on the ocean bed, waving tendrils of seaweed.

"Marvelous, engineer." Robur startled him by clapping a firm hand on Nemo's shoulder. "My ambitious dream has come true."

Nemo considered guiding them down the Turkish coast to where they would find the rusted wreckage of the gigantic cannon *Columbiad* – just to show the caliph evidence of his hubris and his technological folly.

"You need never have doubted us," he answered, trying hard to keep the vindictive tone out of his voice. The round, terrified face of slain Conseil swam in front of him.

The caliph and two guards observed Nemo closely, studying the man's every movement to learn how to pilot the *Nautilus*. Nemo wondered how soon the caliph would consider his crew obsolete – and what Robur would do to them then.

They traveled all day, covering many leagues under the sea faster than any sailing ship. Propelled by the *Nautilus*'s powerful engines and ignoring the vagaries of wind or water currents, they could choose their own direction.

The muscular guards eventually relaxed. After all, where could Nemo and his men go? They could never escape. Robur soon insisted that he take the helm on his own, giving Nemo no choice but to relinquish command. He pretended to do so willingly, feigning weariness. "I'll retire for a while and rest, caliph."

In his cabin Nemo sat down, his thoughts in a turmoil. He stared at the bouquet Auda had insisted on giving him. He smiled at the thought of his wife and their boy Jules, fastening on the one shred of pleasure remaining to him. Although he had never surrendered the place in his heart he would always hold for Caroline, his first love, he adored Auda and their son. They had made him happy during what would otherwise have been an impossible time.

He sniffed the flowers – and discovered something strange around a thick stem at the center. She had folded and wrapped a thin scrap of brown paper which matched the color of the twigs. Curious, Nemo unraveled the scrap and found that she had written him a note in tiny letters, painstakingly translated into French. He held his breath as he read, feeling cold horror grow within him.

"Nemo, my love, Robur intends to kill you and your men on this voyage.

He no longer has any use for you. He does not realize, though, that it is already too late for him. While he is gone during these seven days, my father's troops will sweep down from the mountains and overthrow Rurapente. The sultan has issued an order for Robur's execution.

"Protect yourself. Stay on your guard and be prepared to fight when the caliph makes his move. My father has promised me safety – yes, all along I have been his spy at Rurapente, and I have sent regular reports via the shepherds on the plateau, who are my allies.

"I will take Jules into isolation and protect the families of your men – but you *must not return* for at least a year. There is sure to be terrible bloodshed and political confusion. Because you have built this war vessel for an enemy of the sultan, your life may also be forfeit.

"Do not worry about me, my husband. Just find me when the time is up. I shall wait for you, counting the days. I will make sure your son never forgets you, and when you return, you will receive the honor and glory you deserve."

Nemo reread the letter through a hot haze of betrayal. He had expected treachery from Caliph Robur, and he vowed again that the evil warlord would not succeed in his mad goals. Robur represented the worst of mankind.

Grim and determined, Nemo knew he would have to rally his crew. They must find a way to outwit the caliph's murderous guards.

When he felt ready to return to the bridge, he looked down and discovered that in his cold fury, he had crushed the delicate flowers in his hands.

VIII

Like a metal shark, the *Nautilus* glided through the Mediterranean. The vessel cruised over ribbony masses of coral and underwater forests of seaweed. Schools of silvery fish flitted through the glare of the dazzling front lights. The captive crew watched for legendary mer-people, marvelous sunken cities, or frightening sea monsters.

Knowing the death sentence Robur had secretly pronounced for them, however, Nemo could see no beauty there.

Seeing that the burly guards were occupied and complacent, Nemo took aside Cyrus Harding, whom he had named as his second-in-command, and quietly told the English boatbuilder of Auda's warning. Then, speaking a polyglottal combination of French, English, and Italian, passed the word among the captive crew. Now vigilant, they began making plans for their defense against Robur's betrayal. Since the senseless execution of poor Conseil, the men had been eager to strike back against the bloodthirsty warlord. . .

As they journeyed for days, Nemo stood at the helm, silently aware of Caliph Robur and his murderous guards. He watched the caliph's narrow face for any sign of impending treachery. Robur seemed to grow more eager, his motions impatient, as he demanded that Nemo show him every control of the undersea boat. He overheard two guards whispering in Turkish, confident their language could not be understood, as they caressed their scimitar hilts and chuckled about "the true uses of steel."

By the caliph's command, Nemo guided the *Nautilus* south, following the coast of Lebanon toward Egypt. Robur grew agitated and then smugly satisfied, when they reached the northern Egyptian coast. Though de Lesseps's massive excavation of the Suez Canal had already been under way for two years, the French engineer had fallen behind schedule.

Now, the *Nautilus* cruised up and down the coast, watching the trawlers and dredging ships. Silt from the gargantuan project had turned the water murky. Everyone aboard could see that this supposed threat to the Ottoman Empire would not be completed for many years. Caliph Robur had imagined the speed at which this entire "emergency" would develop.

One by one Nemo's crew stared out the window at the embarrassingly incomplete trench. Then, with barely concealed bitterness, they returned to their duties tending the submarine. Conseil had been slain for no purpose.

Nemo knew what he had to do. He made signals to his men and held brief whispered conversations with a few, who then spread word to the others. He had stalled long enough. It was time for revenge.

Nemo prepared to fight Caliph Robur and his men to the death.

Turning northward, they headed across deep water toward the Aegean Sea. Beneath the surface, gigantic underwater mountains rose from the sea floor to form numerous sun-washed islands. Crevasses split their steep sides, filled with colorful fishes that flitted away from the submarine's brilliant light. High above, fishing boats and oyster divers went about their daily routines.

After four days, the tension of wondering when Robur would make his move had reached a peak for Nemo and his men. When the crew finished morning operations, the caliph, resplendent in green turban and brilliant cape, turned to Nemo. "Engineer, I have seen everything this sub-marine boat can do, and it has performed flawlessly. Your work is at last complete." He glanced meaningfully at his nearest guards; their fingers shifted toward the hilts of their scimitars. "Now it is time –"

Nemo was ready for him, though. "Oh, not entirely, Caliph." He held up his hand and feigned a smile. "I have kept one important and marvelous thing until the end. A special surprise for you." Robur scowled, but Nemo offered his most disarming smile, hiding an automatic expression of hatred for the man. "Come, you must see for yourself."

Forcing himself to appear calm, he led the warlord to a closet, which he opened to reveal five diving suits. The bronze helmets were reinforced to hold air pressure and fitted with thick glass viewplates. The garment itself was leather and canvas, coated with gutta-percha to make it watertight; all the seams were shellacked.

"You have not yet walked on the bottom of the ocean, caliph. This is the final honor reserved for you: to set foot where no other man, not even your sultan, has gone." By appealing to Robur's pride, Nemo knew the decision was foreordained. "Surely you cannot pass up this miracle? We have enough time."

Robur studied the brass helmets, air tubes, and metal tanks. After a moment's hesitation he stroked his black beard. "Yes, we shall do that." Then he glared at Nemo. "And *you* will accompany me, engineer, to ensure that there is no danger."

"Why should I wish to harm you, caliph? Will you not soon reward us for the excellent job we have done?" He studiously looked away from the burly guards. "However, it would be best if I bring one of my men along – to assist in case of any technical emergency."

Robur's brows knitted in concern beneath his turban. "Then I will take one of my guards, as well." Nemo shrugged, suppressing a smile. These bald, muscular guards had never fought with anything but a scimitar: they would be completely helpless under the sea.

He trusted Cyrus Harding most among his men, but he would need his second-in-command on-board to handle the other part of the plan. Instead, he chose as his companion the German/Sardinian Liedenbrock. "Ach! This should be a fine expedition. And eventful, I hope." He and Liedenbrock looked at each other, and understanding flashed between them. Both knew how much was at stake here. They could not hesitate.

"When we return, engineer, I will finally set you and all your men free," the caliph said, removing his green turban so that he could wear the reinforced bronze helmet. "Now help me into this suit."

Not believing him for an instant, Nemo lowered the sturdy metal covering on Robur's head, sealing the brass collar into its padded gasket. Robur's anxious guard watched. Nemo made no threatening moves as he secured the chest and leg fastenings on the warlord's diving suit, then attached an air hose to the tank of compressed air developed by Conseil before his execution.

Nemo and Liedenbrock donned their own suits, while others assisted the cumbersome guard, forcing him to leave his curved sword behind. The muscular man did not understand why he couldn't carry the blade inside his heavy, waterproof suit. The impatient caliph commanded him to cooperate so they could go outside and walk on the ocean floor.

Leaving the rest of the *Nautilus* crew with the remainder of the white-clad guards, the four suited men stood inside the small, double-walled exit chamber. Nemo grasped a long, barbed spear from a rack on the wall. In his heavy suit the caliph's guard moved clumsily to grab the weapon away from him. Robur's helmet plate opened. "What is the meaning of taking this weapon, engineer?"

"We must defend ourselves, caliph," Nemo said in an innocent voice. "We are entering unexplored territory. We do not know what dangers may wait for us beneath the sea. Is it not better to be prepared, than to be slaughtered by a man-eating fish?" He looked intent, making certain he increased the uneasy guard's fear. "Or perhaps a sea monster?"

The caliph grumbled, "Very well, but my guard will carry the weapon himself. Now, let us be off so I can experience the last of the *Nautilus*'s wonders."

Nemo forced a tight smile again and looked at Cyrus Harding waiting just outside the airlock hatch. His anger had turned to ice, and he was completely prepared for what he must do. "Yes, caliph, we will have much to celebrate." The second-in-command gave a curt nod to show that he understood.

The four suited men sealed the airlock chamber. Nemo turned a rotating wheel to open a valve that allowed sea water to pour in. Both the guard and the caliph became frantic at the gushing flow, but Nemo raised his gloved hand, gesturing for them not to fear. When the water filled the chamber, they stood together for a moment, testing their breathing apparatus and looking through their helmets.

Nemo tasted metallic air in his lungs and again saw a bright vision of the meteorologist lying beheaded on the docks. Conseil had developed these systems, much improved over the crude bladder helmet young Nemo had used to walk under the Loire, when he'd been unable to save his drowning father. . . . With renewed determination, he opened the outer door, and the party stepped out of the submarine boat and onto the bottom of the sea.

Nemo's boot sank deep, sending up a cloud of silty mud. For a second he wondered if he had stumbled upon a murky trough of quicksand . . . but then he struck hard rock. With slow, fluid steps, he left footprints that the ocean erased.

Caliph Robur walked beside him like a child, struggling to keep his balance, but soon he was filled with delight and wonder. Liedenbrock followed them, letting himself become accustomed to the suit. The reluctant guard used his harpoon like a walking stick. Nemo watched them every second, ready to strike the moment either man made a mistake or showed any weaknesses.

They passed through a garden of olive-green seaweed that waved like ferns around their knees and provided shelter for darting, exotic fish. The ground rose in rippled mounds of volcanic rock mixed with colorful coral like the antlers of a stag.

When Nemo saw the twined coral, he felt another sharp pang. He recalled that long-ago morning when he and Jules Verne had each promised to obtain a coral necklace for the beautiful young Caroline Aronnax. Now he stood looking at a fortune of the substance . . . and he was farther from Caroline than he had ever been – and far from his wife Auda, as well, who had risked a great deal to warn him of the dangers he faced.

Robur intends to kill us all.

Hidden among boulders, they saw a cluster of giant clams, each one like a wide set of gray lips rimming a hard shell. Nemo wondered if they might find enormous black pearls inside the crushing bivalve jaws of the clams.

The explorers were so intent on the mollusks that only Nemo noticed the shadow like a sharp canoe over their heads. He tilted his armored helmet to see the sleek form of a hammerhead shark swimming in search of prey.

The air bubbles escaping from their tanks had attracted the predator. Nemo froze, hoping the shark would swim away, but the hammerhead circled back. Nemo grabbed Liedenbrock's arm to get his attention. Seeing the movement, the caliph looked up and recoiled in astonishment. The guard holding the spear flailed in terror as the shark swam closer.

Nemo bounded forward, the water's embrace forcing him into a slow-motion dance. He wrested the spear out of the befuddled guard's gloved hand, then made certain he had a strong foothold on the rough coral surface.

The hammerhead stroked its angular tail back and forth, propelling itself toward Liedenbrock. As the shark passed overhead, Nemo thrust the spear upward with all his might. The barbed tip plunged into the shark's belly. The hammerhead shuddered, but Nemo refused to let go of the spear. He pushed and tugged, using the jagged blade to rip open the fish's abdomen and spill its entrails along with a cloud of red blood.

The shark wheeled away, thrashing as it died. Trembling from the effort, Nemo ripped the spear loose. The air tasted hot and metallic inside his helmet. Liedenbrock stood beside him, poised for further action. The caliph's guard lumbered forward to retrieve the spear. His dark eyes glowered with anger and shame at his own inaction.

Both Nemo and Caliph Robur looked with contempt at the burly man, but Nemo surrendered the weapon without argument. He wouldn't need it for what he had in mind anyway. He gestured for the men to begin the return trek to the *Nautilus*, whose lights gleamed in the distance like a lighthouse beacon. The dissipating blood from the shark would attract other aquatic predators . . . and Nemo had enough human enemies right beside him.

* * *

Aboard the *Nautilus*, after he'd waited long enough for the underwater party to be far away, Cyrus Harding sounded the alarm. The other crew members had been primed, and they reacted to the emergency, pointing toward one of the ballast chambers. Harding raised his voice in false panic. "Sabotage! Sabotage, mates! Someone's in the ballast rooms!"

The confused guards sensed the urgency, but they understood little. Harding could have spoken in perfect Turkish after so many years at Rurapente, but he stumbled over the foreign words with feigned confusion, explaining little. A loud siren and a flashing beacon flustered the well-muscled guards even more.

The Englishman ran toward the rear ballast chambers, and three of the five remaining guards stormed after him, drawing their scimitars. While the other crew members scrambled about, faces filled with mock terror, Harding flung open the metal bulkhead door. He pointed in alarm.

The three guards plunged inside, swords raised, ready for battle with saboteurs – and Harding slammed the metal door, sealing them into the ballast chambers. Then, coldly and without remorse, the British boatbuilder opened the valves and filled the sealed room with cold sea water.

The trapped guards shouted and hammered their sword hilts on the other side of the door. Harding stood stony-faced. These men had executed Conseil without mercy and would have happily dispatched every member of the *Nautilus* crew. The followers of Caliph Robur deserved to drown.

The other Europeans turned on the remaining guards, overwhelming them. One of the engineers had retrieved the scimitar left behind by Robur's bodyguard; now the men threw themselves at the white-clad guards, using metal bars and equipment to fight for their lives. They knocked the curved swords away from Robur's men and retrieved the blades for themselves. Their enthusiasm and anger ran unchecked.

By the time Cyrus Harding went to meet them, turning deaf ears to the final cries of the drowning men inside the ballast chamber, the caliph's murderous guards had already been slain with their own swords. They lay in pools of blood on the *Nautilus* deck plates.

After the successful revolt, the captive crew members stood in shock, drenched in sweat. Blood spattered the uniforms Caliph Robur had forced them to wear, identifying them as prisoners of Rurapente. The long silence extended for more than a minute.

Finally, without a word or sign from Cyrus Harding, the men let out a loud cheer that signified their victory and their freedom at last after so many long years held hostage. Now the *Nautilus* belonged to them.

Harding went back to the helm and stared out the thick windows, watching for his captain to return.

Nemo waited until they approached the *Nautilus*. The running lights from the submarine boat shone out, overpowering the shimmering illumination from the sun far above.

He moved his gloved hand in a secret signal to Liedenbrock. Nemo fumbled inside a wide pocket in his underwater suit and withdrew the long knife he had secreted there. He stepped in front of their captor and turned so that his eyes, dark with hatred, could stare through the viewing plate at Robur's scarred face. He had waited long years for this moment.

When Robur saw the knife, a burst of bubbles evacuated from his air tank as the caliph flailed backwards, clumsily trying to get away. Nemo gracefully slid forward and slashed the air hose behind Robur's brass helmet. Helpless, the warlord struggled, but to no avail.

Air poured from the severed hose the way blood had sprayed from Conseil's neck. Nemo watched impassively as the once-powerful caliph fought to breathe . . . but all of his air bled away. Gratified, thinking of the years of oppression he and the other captives had suffered, Nemo watched every moment and felt no sympathy whatsoever. . .

Liedenbrock struck at the same moment, cutting the guard's air hose with another knife. As the burly man lumbered about in confusion, the pressurized air propelled him like a jet, knocking him forward and off balance. In desperation, the guard swung his spear, but the metallurgist sidestepped the jagged blade, then plucked the weapon from the guard's gloved hand as if it were a welcome gift.

Liedenbrock lowered the spear and thrust it into his enemy's chest, killing him instantly. Nemo regretted that extra bit of violence, because now it would take longer to repair the valuable watertight suit.

When Robur finally ceased his struggles, Nemo looked down to see that the warlord's helmet had filled with water, and his eyes and mouth were open. The fearsome caliph looked like nothing more than a dead fish. With a heart of stone, Nemo had no regrets for what they had been forced to do. He grasped Robur's body by the thick sleeve and dragged him to the *Nautilus* airlock.

Liedenbrock did the same with the guard. The crew would have plenty of time now to repair the underwater suits. When Nemo emerged from the airlock into the submarine, dripping and exhausted, he saw that Cyrus Harding had done his part. They had succeeded in capturing the *Nautilus*.

Nemo lifted the brass helmet from his shoulders as the ecstatic crewmen set up a loud cheer. He was their captain, and these men would follow him around the earth, if he asked it. They had lived and worked and suffered together for years. They had built an unparalleled submarine vessel, they had slain a brutal warlord who wanted to be master of the world – and now they were free again.

The *Nautilus* remained submerged while the crew washed the blood off the deck and disposed of the bodies, feeding the caliph and his hated guards to the fishes.

Nemo stood at the helm of his great submarine boat and studied his loyal and devoted men. They were now in command of their own destinies. According to Auda's note, it would not be safe to go back to the Ottoman Empire for some time. Instead, he would take the *Nautilus* and head out of the Mediterranean.

"Captain . . ." Cyrus Harding said, looking at the other men as if they had elected him to speak for them. "We've all been away for six or seven years. The things we've done, and the things we've seen since then – well, sir, our homelands are just memories now. They ain't nobody's *home* anymore."

Liedenbrock stomped his foot on the metal deck plate of the *Nautilus*. "Ach! If we were having anything to return to, why would we join the war in the first place? I want to stay aboard this ship that we built, with these men who are closer comrades than anyone I knew back in Europe."

A Sardinian glassmaker with long hair said, "If it's all the same to you, captain, I'd rather wait out the year and go back for my family in Rurapente. I want to take them away from there. When it's time."

Hearing his men, Nemo nodded. He longed to go back to France and see Caroline again, and Jules Verne – but he had traveled so far along life's path since he'd last spoken to them. He was married to Auda now, and he loved her. Thanks to the vile deception Caliph Robur had perpetrated, Nemo knew that Caroline had believed him dead for years . . . lost to her. By now, she would have gone on with her life, perhaps even married again. He could not bear to torment Caroline – or himself – with things that now could never be. Better to let her keep thinking him lost than to suffer more regrets. . .

The *Nautilus* headed out into the depths of the Mediterranean Sea, setting a course eastward. Nemo would not forget what lay behind him. He vowed someday to return to his wife and son.

"For now," Nemo said, "perhaps we will simply enjoy our freedom."

PART IX
20,000 LEAGUES

I

Paris, 1862

At the age of thirty-four and bored, Jules Verne considered his life a failure.

When a brown-wrapped package arrived with the afternoon post, Verne took it from the delivery man himself, trying not to let Honorine see – knowing, dreading, what it was.

The sky outside was a robin's-egg blue, the air sharp and autumn cool, pleasant enough to make pedestrians smile as they walked the streets. The delivery man tipped his hat to the bearded writer and strode away, whistling. Verne envied the man's optimism.

With a growing sense of resignation, he shuffled over to the low writing desk and used a pocketknife to snap the twine on the packet. Honorine watched from the other side of the room as she gathered her hoops and threads to begin a new needlework pattern for a pillowcase. She smiled encouragement to him, but Verne turned his back on her. He already feared what the parcel contained.

Year after year, he had continued to strive at his writing career, and achieved just enough success to keep him doggedly trying. No one would sing his praises in the halls of literary fame because of the few minor plays he'd had produced. No one would remember his clever verse or his magazine articles. Still, he tried . . . and tried.

He had spent a full year on an ambitious new manuscript, burying himself in clippings and books and journals. He had devoted his research attentions to a massive scientific study based on the uses of balloons in travel and exploration. He himself had never been up in a balloon or explored distant lands . . . but he had talked with Nemo and Caroline, and had read Dr Ferguson's published account of the voyage across Africa. That should have been sufficient.

Now, if only someone would publish Verne's tome. It had begun to seem hopeless. . .

After five uneventful years, his marriage to Honorine had settled into a quiet numbness. He paid scant attention to his wife, spending but a few minutes with her at meals, during which he spoke little before dashing back to his writing study. This wasn't how he had fancied his life as an author. Perhaps Alexandre Dumas had been kind in trying to discourage him, or at least make him face the realities of the career.

His tedious job at the stock market provided enough money for them to live in reasonable comfort, though without extravagances. Verne had managed to represent every member of his extended family who had any money at all to invest. Sometimes his advice was good, sometimes it failed, but he did nothing so rash as to make his relatives consider his performance disastrous. Jules Verne made no waves, no ripples in life whatsoever.

He and Honorine became the parents of a baby son, Michel, more through a fortuitous accident rather than any ambitious effort on Verne's part. A colicky baby, Michel spent most of his time fussing and causing disturbances. Dreading the future, Verne assumed the baby would grow up to be a difficult youngster as well. In stories, life never seemed to happen this way.

In the household, with her daughters visiting their grandparents again, Honorine's task was to keep the infant as quiet as possible so her husband could concentrate on his writing. Later, after he had trudged off to the dreary stock exchange, Michel could wail to his lungs' content.

As his creative frustration built, Verne became a more impatient person, sharper tempered. The stamina he needed to continue his unflagging (and unrewarded) writing efforts began to wane. The noise and disruptions at home made concentration even more difficult. Even the plots of his own adventures gave him diminished enjoyment.

Still, Verne had been proud to complete his exhaustive balloon manuscript, convinced that he had found his path to success. Honorine could sense her husband's excitement about the project, and she smiled at him whenever he bothered to give her a glance.

Full of optimism, he had selected the best Parisian publisher and submitted the completed manuscript. Surely, the hungry minds in France would want to read everything there was to know about lighter-than-air travel. And the book came back – rejected.

Undaunted, silently dubbing the editor a blind fool who could not recognize talent, Verne sent the balloon treatise to his second choice, an equally reputable and impressive publisher. Again the book was returned to him.

Angry, but still determined, he submitted the manuscript over and over . . . and waited for the return post. Each morning, like a sleepwalker, he went to the Bourse, uninterested in the endless routine of selling and buying shares. Days, sometimes weeks, passed – but always his manuscript came back with similar verdicts. "Too long." "Too dull." "Too unfocused."

Verne's co-workers knew of his ambitions and joked about him being a lightheaded dreamer. While they thought he wasted his time at writing, they themselves spent extra hours in the stock exchange, making (and losing) fortunes.

As the balloon book repeatedly failed to find a home, Verne's mood soured, and co-workers stopped teasing him. In fact, they stopped conversing much with him at all. . .

Now, with his palms sweating, he unwrapped the parcel and closed his eyes. He drew a deep breath and removed the handwritten note on top of his fastidiously produced manuscript. *Deemed unpublishable.*

Again.

Verne had lost a substantial sum in the stock market that day, and the baby's loud crying exacerbated his headache. The letter from yet another ignorant publisher only reinforced his doubts and his foul mood. Rejected seventeen times. How could an 800-page manuscript about the history and engineering of ballooning possibly be *boring*? It went beyond all reason.

Giving in to frustration, Verne strode across the room with the heavy manuscript in hand, his only copy of the work that had taken him a year to complete. He threw open the iron door of the stove where a fire burned, warming the house against the autumn chill. With a wordless gesture of disgust and a dramatic flair, he tossed the thick manuscript into the fire and slammed the door with a nod of petulant satisfaction.

Honorine froze in place, and her dark brows furrowed with concern. "Jules?" She looked from him to the torn brown postal wrapping, to the letter from the returned manuscript. Then she noticed his smug expression directed at the stove. "Jules, don't you dare!"

Stern and uncompromising, she shouldered her husband aside and flung open the stove door. Without a moment's hesitation, she reached into the fire, burning her own fingertips, and yanked out the stack of manuscript pages. She dropped it onto the floor and stamped on the edges to extinguish the flames.

"You are even more a child than Michel," she said. When he reached for the manuscript, confused and guilty but still full of rage, Honorine snatched it up and turned away from him. "No. I see that I must keep this safe until you come to your senses."

Marching over to the desk, she opened a wooden file drawer and dropped the stack of papers inside. She locked the drawer and then placed the only key in a pocket of her dark skirts. "You worked far too hard on that book, Jules. It took you away from me for a year. You have been obsessed by it. *I will not let you throw it all away.*"

"But I have tried every publisher," he said, cowed. "It will never see print."

"It will never see print if you give up and burn the manuscript, foolish man," she said, wagging a finger at him. "You have friends who are writers.

I hear that Dumas has returned to Paris. Ask *him* for advice . . . but don't you dare give up now."

Though Honorine had never shown an interest in his writing, she did have a concern for her husband and knew how the passion drove him. He looked at the locked desk drawer and fumed.

Verne didn't speak to Honorine for the rest of that evening – didn't thank her, did not apologize – but the wheels began turning in his head, and he considered other options he might pursue. He went to a brasserie and read his newspapers, keeping an eye out for old writer acquaintances. He found none. He did, however, spot an article about a bloody civil war sweeping across the Turkish peninsula – rumors that had been denied by Ottoman officials. He considered clipping out the article for possible use in a fiction piece, but decided he had no interest in a struggle among the barbarous Turks.

The next day he went to see the great Dumas. The enormous writer had returned to Paris, pretending that his financial troubles had never occurred. Once again the big man indulged in the extravagant lifestyle that had caused him so much misery before. Verne just wanted to hear some of the famous author's advice before Dumas went bankrupt again.

He welcomed Verne, patted his young friend on the back, and insisted that the younger man join him for a glass of wine. He seemed unsurprised that Verne had achieved minimal success in an entire decade of struggles as a writer.

"Oh, ho! Don't worry about it, Jules," Dumas said. "Most of those who come to me for help never succeed. Most never really try – they just want it *given* to them." His generous lips curved into a smile, then Dumas burst out laughing, his cheeks and jowls vibrating like a bullfrog's. "You, however, have an actual manuscript, a completed book. You don't understand that this already puts you far closer to success than most of your peers."

"But no one will publish my manuscript. I've tried everyone."

Dumas raised a pudgy, ringed finger. "We shall see what we can do about that, mmm?" Already the big man looked distracted, as if he needed to be about some other business.

He gave Verne the name of another new author who had succeeded in getting a few pamphlets printed. That author then forwarded Verne to his own publisher, Pierre-Jules Hetzel. Hetzel had launched a children's science magazine, the *Magasin d'Education et de Récréation*, and claimed to be in search of new writers for his fledgling publishing house.

Assuring Honorine that he would not harm the book, Verne coaxed her to unlock the desk drawer and remove the singed manuscript. Before giving it to him, she brushed away the burnt edges, restacked the pages, and carefully wrapped them. Verne took the precious package and, without much hope, hand-delivered it to the offices of Hetzel & Cie.

A consumptive clerk took the package. Although Verne made certain to drop the name of Alexandre Dumas – several times, in fact – the clerk seemed unimpressed. He merely assured Verne that Monsieur Hetzel would respond as soon as possible.

Within a week, in mid October of 1862, Verne received a card inviting him to meet with Monsieur Hetzel at his earliest convenience. Excited, Verne gave up his morning's routine of writing, dressed in his finest clothes, and nervously ate a croissant for breakfast. He waited and waited for an appropriate hour.

When at last he strode up to the rue Jacob offices at mid morning, he learned that Hetzel – a night owl – entertained morning visitors only in his bedchambers in an apartment to the rear of the publishing offices. Though he was not ill, Hetzel liked to remain in bed for most of the morning. Horribly embarrassed, Verne turned to go, but the coughing clerk ushered him around the back through a small garden courtyard and up a flight of creaking stairs to meet the publisher in person.

Years ago, Pierre-Jules Hetzel had made his mark in the publishing world, though he was a Protestant and had thus suffered many difficulties during the turmoil in France. An outspoken supporter of the Second Republic after the revolutions of 1848, he had managed to escape arrest when Napoleon III proclaimed himself emperor. While hiding in Brussels for eight years, Hetzel published the work of fellow exile Victor Hugo until an amnesty in

1859 allowed him to return to Paris. Back again, Hetzel had rapidly become very successful, and now was ready to expand his publishing endeavors.

The man remained in bed, sitting up in his blankets and pillows to greet his visitor. Despite the fact that he was about fifteen years older than Verne, Hetzel had an energetic intensity that shaved years from his age. His pale hair was not entirely gray, and he appeared healthy as an ox.

Both men had full, stylish beards, but the publisher's face had sharper angles, a hawkish nose, and close-set eyes that brightened when he saw the young writer enter his bedchamber. Without a word, the consumptive clerk disappeared. Verne remained standing, looking down at the important man sitting in his nightshirt on the canopied bed.

Beside him, on the blankets, lay the manuscript of Verne's balloon book.

Jules Verne's heart pounded. He smelled the beeswax candles in the enclosed room, noted the publisher's picked-over dinner tray lying on the floor on the opposite side of the bed. The heavy velvet curtains were drawn, and only dim morning light intruded. He felt like an intruder here, but he didn't dare leave – not until he had heard what Hetzel had to say.

The publisher looked at him for a few moments. Verne wondered desperately what to say. None of the other publishers had bothered to call him in person; they'd merely sent declining letters. His hopes ran high. The other man picked up the thick stack of papers, and Verne held his breath.

"I am sorry, monsieur, but I cannot publish this manuscript," Hetzel said.

Verne felt as if the building had crashed down upon him. Already lacking confidence, he felt that this man had made a fool of him. His face reddened, and cold sweat trickled beneath his collar. "I apologize for wasting your time, monsieur," Verne choked out the words. He reached for the manuscript to snatch it away. This time he would burn it far from where Honorine could see and stop him.

"On the contrary," Hetzel added, raising a scolding finger. His thin, businesslike voice held no anger. "I cannot publish this book *as it is*. I do believe, however, it can be *made* publishable . . . if you are willing to do the work. I want authors who are hard workers. Are you a hard worker and persistent – or will I never see you again?"

Verne didn't comprehend what the publisher was saying and wondered if the man were taunting him. Hetzel tapped the thick manuscript. "What you have written, Monsieur Verne, is nothing but a dry lecture about balloons and their potential. I am convinced that you have apprehended the facts, but you have not presented them in an interesting manner."

Verne drew a deep, cold breath. "My book is about science, sir. It is not meant to be a comedy or a farce."

"But why not an adventure?" Hetzel locked his gaze with the young writer's. "It must be a *story* with a scientific basis, not a treatise about scientific fact. To captivate your readers, you must wrap your research within a tale so exciting that the people will cry out for more." His eyes sparkled. "You will become a teacher, introducing the public to new concepts without their realizing it." He chuckled.

Verne stopped, allowing the words to penetrate. What was this man saying? What did he truly mean?

Now Hetzel lifted the manuscript and extended it toward Verne. "I believe you can salvage much of this, my friend, but you must give me an entirely different work with the balloon information in a novel form. Write a new kind of book, a fiction that depends upon scientific knowledge and exploration – but you must engage us with *characters* who learn these things in the course of a story, rather than simply recounting bald facts as a lecturer."

When Verne took the manuscript, his hands were trembling. Hetzel sat up straighter in bed and yawned, plumping the pillows behind his back. "Buried in your paragraphs, you mentioned offhandedly some travels your friend made in a balloon across unexplored Africa. I suggest you use *that* as your framework, create an epic quest with brave explorers traveling in the fabulous balloon you have postulated. Certainly that would make for more interesting reading?" He raised his eyebrows.

Shaken, Verne nodded and backed away. "Yes, Monsieur Hetzel. I understand. I . . . I will work without pause, and present you with a new manuscript within two weeks' time."

Hetzel smiled. "If you can perform that miracle, Jules Verne, we can publish your book in time for the Christmas holiday season."

Verne emerged from the back apartment, his mind spinning as he stumbled across the garden. He did not yet allow himself to accept the joy of what had just occurred. He still had a great deal of work ahead of him, so he wasted no energy in dancing with excitement. He thought of his long-dead friend, André Nemo, and his escapades with Ferguson across Africa.

He would change the names of Nemo and Caroline, of course, and create new, fictional characters to accompany the good doctor. Even so, Verne had a wonderful story to tell. . .

II

The following spring, Jules Verne found a mysterious message slipped under his door during the dark of night. Standing in his robe the following morning, he picked up the scrap of paper; his brows furrowed in curiosity.

"Jules, old friend, come to Paimboeuf on April 2nd and prepare to be gone for a week. One mile up the coast, you will find a sheltered cove. Meet me there at midnight. I promise you an extraordinary voyage you shall never forget – a journey you have always wanted to take."

The note was unsigned, and extremely intriguing.

Scratching his full beard, Verne stepped back into his flat and closed the door with a click. Honorine had already spent an hour in the everyday battle of washing, dressing, and feeding young Michel, but Verne decided not to show her the note . . . not yet. His pulse raced as he thought of the mystery.

Who might have sent such a message? Was it a hoax, or some sort of treachery? Should he be concerned for his safety? Despite his longings and his dreams, Verne rarely had cause to seek out "adventures." Not real ones, anyway. He actually preferred to travel in his imagination, as his father had made him promise to do.

But few people knew that. They expected a different sort of person after reading his novel. . .

In early 1863, Verne's *Five Weeks in a Balloon* had been published to wide acclaim. Readers all across France had snapped up the adventures of

Dr Samuel Ferguson and his intrepid companions (vastly different from Nemo and Caroline) crossing Africa in his remarkable balloon. Foreign publishers had translated the book into diverse languages.

Seeing the success, Pierre-Jules Hetzel had offered his young author a lucrative publishing contract to write additional novels in the same vein – books grounded in science, combined with extraordinary journeys to fascinate the reading public. Verne was to write three novels a year, for which he would be paid 3,000 francs – not a fortune, but more than he made in the stock market. And certainly more than he had ever made from his theater work. He was an unqualified success as a writer after so many long years.

After breathlessly signing the contract that bound him to Hetzel, Verne had rushed home elated. In the foyer of their flat, he danced with a stiff and surprised Honorine and kissed her on the cheek before trotting off to the Bourse.

Crowing like a proud rooster, he had stood in the middle of the trading floor surrounded by paper-laden work tables to attract his co-workers' attention. "Well, boys, I am off to another career. I will now make my living as a writer while you stay here among your dreary numbers and stocks."

Although the others congratulated him, it was clear from their expressions that they thought him a fool for giving up a stable career. Verne didn't care. . .

Now, as a successful writer, Jules Verne had the freedom to do as he wished – and this strange note promised him an "extraordinary voyage" of his own. How could he pass up such an opportunity? It might even turn into the basis for a new novel, whatever this adventure might be. He tried to place the tantalizing yet familiar handwriting, the tone of the sentences.

Chewing his lip, Verne paced in the foyer, scuffing the rug. He knew he should travel more, experience more. He had always longed for such things, theoretically. But somehow he never got around to doing so. He had a secure income – so, why should he not take advantage of his success?

Impulsively jamming the note into the pocket of his robe, Verne decided to take a chance – for once. He raised his chin in the air in a show of bravery. He would tell Honorine he needed time alone to concentrate on a new book. While he adored the bustling civilization of Paris, he longed to see the ocean again. He liked the cool, damp weather, and the lullaby of the Atlantic.

Even if this message were merely a practical joke, Verne could still relax by the ocean, all alone. It would be a holiday, and he didn't have to tell anyone. Either way, he had nothing to lose.

He gave Honorine a cursory goodbye, glad to leave her behind with their fussy toddler. Verne boarded a train carrying a small valise that contained a few toiletry items and three changes of clothing, as well as a bound journal in which he could write down notes for stories. If he should not encounter the promised "adventure," at least he would get writing done.

On the appointed night, nervous and anxious, Verne took his valise, and walked along the shingled beach north from Paimboeuf. As the time grew near, he began to feel like a fool for believing what was most likely a prank – but he had to see for himself.

A mile up the coast from Paimboeuf, just as the letter-writer had described, he found a deep, calm cove far from the nearest village. Faint white breakers stippled the dark water.

Verne waited, listening to the brisk wind and calm whisper of the ocean. He smelled the brine, the iodine tang of seaweed, the odor of dead fish. There were no campfires, no fishermens' huts, no one at all. Clouds scudded across the sky, obscuring the silvery circle of the moon. He saw no roads nearby, heard no wagons or horses.

Drawing a deep breath, Verne reached into his vest and pulled out the pocketwatch he had purchased with money Hetzel had paid him for the balloon book. He remembered how his father had always kept a telescope trained on the distant monastery clock: now Verne could tell time whenever he wished.

He snapped the lid shut. It was midnight.

He sighed, convinced that no one would appear after all. Some rival or dissatisfied reader must be back at a Paimboeuf inn right now, snickering at Verne's gullibility. His cheeks burned; maybe someone was watching him from the rocks even now.

Then a stirring caught his eye in the water out in the cove. Air bubbles rushed to the surface like a pot coming to boil. Verne whirled and faced out toward the ocean. To his astonishment, a great metal sea beast rose from the waves.

Its round portholes gleamed like the infernal eyes of a demon. Jagged fins looked like the ridge on a dragon's back. As it surfaced, Verne backed away, stumbling on the loose rock of the beach, but he could not stop staring.

The armored beast floated in silence and then, with a scraping sound and a heavy clang, a hatch opened on its top. The lean, shadowy figure of a man in a dark uniform rose up from the thing's gullet. He raised his right arm to wave toward the lone figure on the beach.

"Jules Verne, is that you?" the man called in an oddly familiar voice. It was deeper and rougher . . . yet it reminded him of someone he'd known as a young boy. "Come aboard and see my *Nautilus*."

At a loss for words, Verne opened and closed his mouth. The terror had trickled away, leaving him numb with awe . . . and, yes, even a little curiosity. A small boat detached itself from the armored craft, and the lone man rowed toward him. "Jules, don't you recognize your old friend? It's me – Nemo."

Verne stared at the man as he brought the boat to shore and stepped into the shallow water. His friend's face had changed: now in his mid-thirties, Nemo had grown leaner, his muscles tougher. A neatly trimmed beard covered his chin, and his dark eyes had a hard look, as if he had seen much more than he could ever explain.

"Nemo . . . but I – we – thought you were dead. Caroline and I both received a notice from the Department of the Military. It said you were killed in the Crimean War." His legs felt as if they were about to give out, and he would faint backward onto the beach.

"Not exactly killed, as you can see." His smile was grim, without a trace of humor. "You and I will have plenty of time to share the entire tale, Jules. I think you'll want to hear about my adventures." He reached out to haul Verne's valise into the metal-hulled boat. "Follow me – you will be amazed. It's about time you came along on one of my voyages."

Taking Nemo's hand, Verne climbed into the small boat and sat unsteadily. "I . . . I've always meant to go on an adventure." As Nemo rowed back out to the armored vessel, Verne thought of the tiny rented skiff he had taken down the Loire, which had broken apart and stranded him on the isolated sandbar. "I would have gone on the *Coralie* with you. Honestly."

"And now you can go on my *Nautilus.*"

After Nemo docked against the iron-plated vessel, the two men stepped onto the wet outer hull. Verne felt wobbly on his feet. Awkward, he leaned forward and embraced his old friend, still numb with shock. Nemo patted him on the back, then laughed with genuine warmth. "Come below into the vessel. You have a grand adventure ahead of you, just like we always talked about."

They descended a metal-runged ladder into the submarine boat. Verne stared in wonder. A square-jawed British man with a prominent dimple stood at the bridge, calling orders to the crewmen, all of whom wore the same strange uniform. When Verne asked about it, Nemo tugged at the dark fabric on his shoulder. "We kept these outfits as a badge of honor, after we escaped from Rurapente." Seeing Verne's confusion, he said, "I hope you brought along a journal to take notes. Do you still want to be a writer?"

Verne nodded, patting his valise.

One of the crewmen sounded bells, just as on a sailing ship, but the crew had no ropes to tie, no sails to set, no anchors to cast off. The propeller of the *Nautilus* began to turn with the vessel's powerful engines. One sailor climbed up to seal the upper hatch, and then the craft headed away from the coast of France.

Verne stared out the portholes, but could see little in the ocean shadows. A cold shiver crept down his spine as the angle of the deck tilted and water covered the thick windows. His heart constricted with the realization that they were now beneath the ocean. Sweat popped out on his forehead. The *Nautilus* struck out into the wide Atlantic, and Verne hung on for dear life.

For hours he observed landscapes he had never imagined. Fishes darted to and fro, glittering in the illumination from the forward lamps. Rocks never touched by human hands made strange formations and undersea mountains.

Nemo stood beside him with a satisfied smile on his face. When Verne's astonishment had faded to a manageable level, Nemo clapped him on the shoulder. "Come into the salon. Let me tell you everything that's happened to me in the past ten years."

In the large, opulent room they sat at a narrow table and drank a strange-tasting tea. Verne continued to gaze out the broad, thick-paned portholes as his friend began the tale.

"The Crimean War was terrible, but I suspect no worse than any others. I watched pirates slaughter Captain Grant on the *Coralie*. I saw slavers in Africa killing innocent women and children. In the Crimea, I was with the Light Brigade when they made their foolish charge on Balaclava. And then I spent time in a hospital, surrounded by all the pain and suffering caused by foolish orders and petty squabbles between officers."

Nemo's face darkened, and he looked down at the table. Several beautiful shells were strewn about, specimens taken during his underwater explorations. Verne glanced away from the porthole, noting the tremble in his friend's voice.

"And then the things Caliph Robur did to some of my men." He drew a deep breath. "It never ceases to amaze me how human beings enjoy inflicting violence upon their own species."

As he drank more tea, Nemo's voice took on a firm resolve. "Here on the *Nautilus*, we are isolated from the political turmoils of the world. We can be safe. My crew is devoted to me – they are at home on this vessel, more so than in any place in Europe."

He scowled. "Their countries sent these men to fight in the Crimea. They saw and did things their families could never accept. Due to bureaucratic error, every one of them was declared dead when Caliph Robur captured them. These men endured fear, and threats, and long imprisonment. They started new lives with new families in Turkey – only to learn that Robur intended to execute us all when we'd done what he wanted." Nemo's fists clenched and unclenched. "And now we have escaped, and found peace here . . . until such time as we return to Rurapente to retrieve everyone and everything we left behind."

Verne had lived in Paris during the revolutionary years, had been there for the formation of the Second Republic and then the new empire. "Peace is a hard thing to come by in this world," he said. "Even the United States of America is now embroiled in a terrible civil war. I'm glad I've managed to remain safely away from it all."

Disturbed, Nemo changed the subject by inquiring into Verne's life. He told Nemo about his law certificate and his years at the stock market, but how he had continued to write his plays and poems. With some embarrassment, Verne explained about *Five Weeks in a Balloon*, for which he admitted borrowing heavily from his friend's exploits.

"Forgive me, my friend. I believed you were dead, and I saw no harm in it." Nemo gave him a quixotic smile, and Verne continued in a rush. "The novel has been such a success that my publisher has contracted me for three books a year. I am developing a new kind of fiction. Each volume will be a strange and exotic adventure based on technology and the best advances in geographical exploration. We are calling the series 'Les Voyages Extraordinaire.'"

"I should like to read this *Five Weeks in a Balloon*." Nemo looked at his friend with some amusement. "Not bad for a man who has never set foot outside of France – in fact, never traveled farther than from Nantes to Paris." He chuckled. "Until now."

Verne huffed. "I did take a journey to England and Scotland two years ago. An entire week on a boat. And I've been to Amiens, too – several times. I think I may even like to live there someday." At the time, those trips had seemed breathtaking and exotic, but now they seemed . . . embarrassingly inadequate.

Nemo raised his eyebrows and said nothing for a moment, though his smile spoke volumes. "Perhaps I can give you ideas and background for more stories, Jules. I've done quite a lot in the past few years."

For the next several days, as the *Nautilus* cruised the Atlantic, Nemo talked to his friend about being held captive by Caliph Robur. He described the debacle of the gigantic moon cannon and how it had tumbled into the deep sea. Then he explained how he and his men had designed and built the submarine boat, which Verne could now see with his own eyes.

Standing on the bridge of the *Nautilus*, Nemo gazed ahead as their journey continued. "There are two types of men in this world, Jules: those who *do* things, and those who wish they did." Hearing the words, Verne felt stung. He sensed some implied criticism, but did not challenge his friend.

One evening as they sat together at a dinner of poached fish and steamed mollusks, Nemo asked in a quiet voice, "Have you heard from Caroline, Jules? How is she? What is she doing these days? Even after I escaped I . . . I thought it might be better if I let her continue to believe I am dead."

Reluctant to talk about the woman they had both loved since childhood, Verne professed to have little knowledge about what had happened to her. "She's quite successful, I believe, since she moved her merchant offices to Paris. She invested well and keeps busy, probably still writes her own music that she lets few people hear."

"And . . . her husband?" Nemo said. "Captain Hatteras. Has he ever returned? Is there any word?"

Verne snorted. "No, and I doubt there ever will be. It's been sixteen years. She'll never remarry now, though she could have done so legally long ago. I think she rather likes being on her own. She's so independent."

"I . . . I am married," Nemo said, taking Verne by surprise. "Her name is Auda, a Turkish woman. Caliph Robur presented her to me and I had no choice . . . but we've come to love each other. The two of us have a son." He smiled. "I named him after you, Jules."

Verne flushed, and admitted his own situation. "I have a wife, myself," he said, unable to believe that in all the time they'd talked, all the stories they had told, the two men had neglected to mention their families. "We've had a son, too. I named him . . . uh, Michel."

Nemo wistfully scratched his dark beard. "My men and I will return to pick up Auda and my son, and their families as well. I'm afraid I have let Caroline down again." He hesitated a moment, then looked back toward the bridge and his crew. "We intend to live together aboard the *Nautilus* and never come back to France. I've had enough of so-called civilized lands, and leaders with their constant struggles and murderous intents." A storm crossed Nemo's face. He picked at his food, then pushed the plate away.

"Excuse me, Jules. I must go to the helm. I plan to take us deeper into the Atlantic – where even I have not yet explored. Three-quarters of the earth is covered with the oceans, you know. I could travel" – he waved a hand, making up a number – ". . . twenty-thousand leagues without ever touching land. And I think I just may do that."

He left Verne to finish his meal alone.

III

The *Nautilus* descended to incredible depths. No daylight penetrated the vast underwater canyons. No ray of sunshine passed through the inky black water.

The submarine's layered hull groaned from the pressure. Verne paced the bridge deck, glancing sidelong at the thick porthole glass, as if expecting to see cracks appear at any moment. Nemo seemed calm and confident, with complete faith in his vessel. From time to time the crewmen looked at their captain, then returned to their duties. Liedenbrock, the metallurgist, examined the hull plates, then placed his ear against them. He nodded to Nemo, who gave the order to go deeper still.

Strange, phosphorescent sea creatures swam about in the blackness like glowing candle processions. Tiny cold lamps sparkled from bizarre beasts that no fisherman had ever caught.

"We will compile charts of this landscape, for the sake of science," Nemo said. "But I will not provide this knowledge to the world's governments. Their leaders would find some means to turn it to a violent end."

Verne opened his mouth to disagree, then clamped his lips tight. After everything his friend had endured, a mere author had no right to argue with him. After the oppression of Rurapente, Nemo seemed to have lost some part of his heart; his old spark of enthusiasm had turned into a gray ember.

Nemo said in a distant voice, his face expressionless, "Here, embraced in the womb of the oceans, my men and I can be at . . . peace with the world."

Moments after that pronouncement, the sea monster attacked.

Emerging from the depths, a giant squid darted in front of the *Nautilus*. The hostile environment had transformed it into a leviathan of incredible proportions. The beast swam backward, pumping its tentacles, attracted by the dazzling lights of the submarine boat.

Liedenbrock gasped in alarm. "Ach! Such a brute."

Verne's eyes widened as he saw the enormous suckered tentacles thrashing toward them.

Nemo barked an order. "Reverse the propeller screws, Mr Harding. We must avoid this creature."

But the *Nautilus* could not move as fast as the enormous mollusk. Its numerous appendages surrounded the vessel like a net. The *Nautilus* rocked as the tentacles encircled the plated hull in an unbreakable embrace.

"Forward – now!" With a groan, the submarine's powerful engines pushed them in the opposite direction. But with an abrasive straining sound, the propellers ground to a halt.

Cyrus Harding said, "Tentacles are caught in the screws, captain. We cannot move."

The sea beast rocked them like a crocodile trying to shake its prey to pieces. The giant squid's conical head pressed against the thick portholes, displaying only a cold predatory intent. Its hideous round eyes, larger than serving plates, stared without recognition or intelligence. Verne scrambled away from the thick window with a cry of terror.

Nemo's brows furrowed with desperate concentration, and he scratched his close-cropped beard. "We must surface, Mr Harding. We will bring this thing to the light of day. Out in the open air, perhaps it will release us."

With a clang, the squid raked its sharp, parrotlike beak against the iron-scaled bow, chewing on the metal hull.

"Brace yourselves!" Harding called. Verne grasped the bridge rail with all his strength and squeezed his eyes shut. The ballast tanks were blown, and the vessel began to rise. Nemo watched the external pressure gauges and the depth indicator. "We are rising rapidly." The creaks and groans of the hull emphasized his words.

Verne hoped that a monster from such depths could not survive at the surface, but he had read old sailors' tales, accounts of titanic battles between giant squids and sperm whales. He had never desired to see one with his own eyes.

The submarine continued to rise for many minutes, and the uncertain light grew brighter as they climbed toward sunlit levels. But the squid refused to relinquish its suckered hold.

As if with a sigh of relief, the *Nautilus* breached the surface – yet still the giant squid did not relinquish its hold. The writhing tentacles flexed and tightened, like a python's grip. One untangled itself and slammed the top of the hull. The battering sounds echoed like explosions within the vessel's metal walls.

"We must put a stop to this." Nemo's jaw clenched until Verne could see his muscles move beneath his dark beard. He looked at his crew. "Take your weapons, men. We will go out and face this monster here and now."

While Verne hung back, sure he could be no help whatsoever, the *Nautilus* crew members grimly followed their captain's orders. They secured spears, axes, and long throwing knives; four even carried curved scimitars taken from Robur's overthrown guards.

Telling Verne to stay clear, Nemo led the way up the metal ladder to the hatch. "Beware of the tentacles. Each one of those suckers has a central hook that can rip your guts out."

Nemo drew a deep breath – and threw open the hatch. The men scrambled out, carrying their weapons. Outside, the Atlantic was choppy, and a low, cold mist covered the sky. The giant squid quested with its tentacles like deadly bullwhips.

Nemo jumped onto the outer deck, carrying the jagged spear with which he had killed the hammerhead shark. Cyrus Harding, his dimpled chin thrust forward in determination, set to work with a heavy ax, chopping one of the tentacles. The other crewmen yelled as they attacked – but the deep-sea creature did not seem to hear.

Two of the squid's tentacles probed toward Harding, but a crewman sliced off the ends with a scimitar. The oozing stumps continued to flop about. Harding used his ax to sever another tentacle.

One man, a long-haired Sardinian, plunged a long throwing knife into the round expressionless eye, ducking away from a spurt of jelly. The creature stank of sour slime and half-digested fish. Slippery, oozing gel from the smooth skin covered the riveted hull plates.

The squid lifted more tentacles, releasing the *Nautilus*'s propeller to turn its efforts against new opponents. One of the serpentlike arms wrapped around the Sardinian who had stabbed its eye. The long-haired man screamed in pain, poking his dagger into the rubbery flesh, with no effect. The squid raised him high. The others rallied to save their comrade, but a storm of tentacles rose – and the crewmen had to defend themselves.

The squid dragged the poor crewman toward the clacking jaws of its parrotlike beak. Inside, a horny, tooth-filled tongue slashed from side to side.

His face a mask of fury, Captain Nemo strode into the midst of the tentacles and thrust his spear into the squid's mouth, jamming the jagged tip past the open beak and thrusting it deep into the soft tissues. With another scimitar, a crewman lopped off a fourth tentacle.

Terrified at the mayhem above, Verne tentatively climbed the ladder, trying to see.

One man stabbed his splintered spear into the soft conical head, but struck no nerves or brain. Verne had read somewhere that a squid had three separate hearts, and he doubted a single weapon thrust could kill the beast.

Snarling like an animal himself, Nemo pushed his spear deeper into the monster's mouth, until the squid finally let go of its captive. The long-haired Sardinian dropped to the deck, bloody and mangled. The hooks within the squid's suckers had left long lacerations in the victim's flesh. One of the other men grabbed the hapless Sardinian by the shoulders and dragged him toward the hatch. Verne tried to get out of the way, but the crewman snapped, "Take him, man! Can't you see he needs help?"

Squirming and stuttering, Verne helped carry the injured Sardinian down into the submarine. The long-haired man bled profusely from dozens of deep wounds, and Verne's clothes were soon soaked with scarlet. He felt ashamed that he could do nothing more to assist the man. He wasn't a doctor, and knew little about first aid – had never even seen such terrible wounds before in his life.

Up above, the giant squid grew more agitated. The stumps of its severed tentacles thumped against the *Nautilus*, while the other appendages thrashed like angry cobras. When Nemo tried to tear his spear free from the mangled mouth, the parrot-like beak snapped its shaft, leaving the captain without a weapon.

One brash crewman, a broad-shouldered Englishman, ran forward and slashed with his scimitar between the squid's eyes. The monster reached out a huge tentacle as if to swat a fly and grabbed him. Before Nemo or the other men could react, the giant squid released a burst of black dye, spraying clouds of acrid-smelling ink. The terrible fumes stung their eyes and blinded them.

Then the squid plunged back into the ocean, still grasping the hapless Englishman as if demanding some small victory in payment for its pain. . .

Nemo and the other survivors trembled with exhaustion. Covered with slime and blood, they stared at the black murk dissipating in the waters. Though the cold Atlantic mist made the vessel's hull slippery and treacherous, at least the moisture rinsed away the oozing ichor.

Nemo shuddered as he looked around himself, grieving for the loss of the crewman. He looked as if he wanted to collapse and weep. After a long, uncertain moment, they staggered back down the ladder into the submarine.

On the deck below, a helpless Verne sat holding the bloodied man. He had fashioned makeshift bandages, but it was no use. Before Nemo could reach his man, the Sardinian also died.

* * *

The *Nautilus* crew wrapped the victim's body in a pale shroud. During a somber ceremony, the crewmen said their farewells, each in his own language, both to the dead Sardinian and to the lost Englishman. They had all been together for years, laboring in Rurapente under the worst of circumstances. . .

Maintaining a wounded silence, the *Nautilus* cruised aimlessly until Nemo found a private reef studded with waving seaweeds and beautiful shells. He and several of his men suited up in underwater garments and cycled through the airlock. Verne declined to accompany them, feeling that it wasn't his place. Instead, he went to the salon and watched through the broad windows.

The funeral procession plodded in slow motion through the waters, carrying their wrapped burden. Verne's heart grew heavy watching the poignant march as the *Nautilus* crew – men without a country – laid their slain comrade to rest.

Moving like a machine, Nemo helped pile undersea rocks in a cairn over the body, leaving a watery grave that no other man could ever visit. They built a second mound in honor of the lost Englishman. . .

When they returned to the vessel, Cyrus Harding piloted the *Nautilus*, while Nemo isolated himself in his private cabin to mourn. He didn't emerge for an entire day. Finally he came out to speak with Verne.

"I must take you back now, Jules," he said, his expression dark and his voice grim. "It was a mistake to bring you here. This is no picaresque journey, no amusing adventure for a starry-eyed dreamer. I have no time for sightseers."

The *Nautilus* dropped Verne off late at night on the coast of France, north of Paimboeuf. Afire with enthusiasm, his journal full of ideas from Nemo's stories, he watched the armored submarine sink beneath the water, cutting a wake out into the ocean.

Verne waved farewell, and headed back toward home, thoroughly inspired to write further books.

IV

For most of his life, whenever Jules Verne had an opportunity to see Caroline Hatteras, he leaped at the chance . . . and dreaded it at the same time. She still made him tongue-tied and light-headed, and he still imagined a life with her, though that fantasy was even more unrealistic than his strangest extraordinary voyages.

Caroline and he always had much to discuss, old-time reminiscences and shared experiences. Though Verne had already been married for eleven years now (and Caroline, ostensibly, for twenty-one) the thought of being alone in a room with her, face to face, still gave him chills.

Before leaving his flat on a blustery day, Verne told Honorine that he had a "business luncheon," such as he often scheduled with his publisher Hetzel. In spite of the many years that had passed, he'd never talked about Caroline with his wife, had never confessed how the fiery-blond woman still haunted his dreams with lost opportunities.

A similar reticence kept Verne from telling Caroline about Nemo and his submarine vessel. Nemo had strongly hinted that he preferred for her to continue believing him dead, now that he could never come back to her. He wanted Caroline to make her own life, without him – but Verne knew she never would.

Now, the prospect of explaining that her long-lost love was still alive, against all odds (as usual), raised a morass of unresolved emotions in him. Five years had passed since his voyage aboard the *Nautilus*. Caroline divided her time between Paris and Nantes, yet Verne had not gone out of his way to see her. He had stewed over the secret long and hard, and had decided that she must know.

Though Verne had kept his distance from her over the years, not trusting himself, he had also kept track of Caroline's successes. Madame Hatteras's rivals resented the fact that a powerful, outspoken woman managed such an important business concern, but customers who admired her verve and ingenuity trusted her to take risks that more conservative merchants would not consider.

The sleek ships of "Aronnax, Merchant" often brought commodities to port weeks sooner than those of her competitors. Caroline was willing to consider new designs for faster clippers, and she investigated alternate sea routes. Her childhood fascination with geography had served her well, though long ago her mother had scolded her for 'unseemly pursuits.' The captains of her fleet – many of whom had worked for her father, or had been loyal to the famous Captain Hatteras – were now devoted to Caroline.

To gain further business, she had also capitalized on her notoriety from the balloon journey across Africa. With delight she had read Verne's fictionalized and melodramatic account in *Five Weeks*, and had written him a congratulatory letter. He still kept the handwritten note in a locked drawer in his study, treasuring it. . .

In the end, it had been Caroline who'd invited *him* to her offices and, despite his better judgment, Verne didn't have the heart to refuse.

Now, striding brightly down the river walkway, past Left Bank brasseries and bookshops, Verne smelled the fresh air. A brief rainstorm had passed during the previous evening, infusing the morning with a brisk dampness that made his nostrils tingle. Gulls flew above like kites. Whistling with the anticipation of seeing Caroline again, Verne could think of no more admirable place to live than Paris. The City of Light had become so beautiful since Emperor Napoleon III had rebuilt it after so much civil unrest.

When he arrived on the tulip-surrounded doorstep of "Aronnax, Merchant," he gave his name to the clerk. "Monsieur Jules Verne?" The clerk squinted at him through gold-framed spectacles. "The author? Esteemed storyteller of the Extraordinary Voyages?"

Both pleased and embarrassed, Verne nodded. His full beard, long nose, and penetrating eyes had become a trademark in Hetzel's magazine. People often recognized him on the streets, and he still didn't know how to respond.

In the years since *Five Weeks in a Balloon*, readers had come to anticipate each new Jules Verne novel. He had followed his balloon adventure with a massive epic called *Captain Hatteras* – named for Caroline's husband – about a man's quest to find the North Pole.

Of course, Verne had no special knowledge of what had happened to the real Hatteras, who had disappeared two decades earlier. Using an author's license, he had made up a story about bleak and unexplored lands. In the novel, the obsessed but admirable hero had succeeded in his magnificent quest, though his incredible ordeals had driven him mad in the end.

Even believing Nemo dead, Caroline clung to her own reasons for not remarrying, preferring a life alone to a dreary marriage. By day, she ran an important business and made her decisions, while she kept evenings free for painting or sketching or composing music.

How would she react to the news he brought today? He cursed himself for having waited so long, but he had always made excuses, both intimidated by Caroline and longing to see her. Every month, he kept expecting Nemo to change his mind and come back to civilization, but now he knew that would never happen.

The enthusiastic clerk startled him by reaching out to shake his hand. "Monsieur, I have read *A Journey to the Centre of the Earth*. Simply amazing. My congratulations on your remarkable imagination."

Pierre-Jules Hetzel couldn't have been more pleased at the public reaction to these stories. Each holiday season, Verne's novels were bound in illustrated gift editions, after being serialized in Hetzel's *Magasin d'Education et de Récréation*. The number of readers grew with every volume.

Verne and Honorine now lived in a larger flat with a separate vacation residence on the damp sea coast he loved so well, though his wife and her daughters found it dreary and cold. Feisty Michel just seemed fussy. Even at seven years old, the boy had to complain about everything. . .

Verne's imagination went farther afield for his fourth novel, *From the Earth to the Moon*, in which he accepted Caliph Robur's idea of a gigantic cannon that could fire a projectile with sufficient force to escape earth's gravity. Intrepid explorers – super-confident Americans, in this case – rode inside the capsule to reach the moon. Because he'd been in a good mood, delighted to have secured a writing career at last, Verne added much humor to the moon book, poking gentle fun at overly ambitious Americans.

In his most complex novel to date, *The Children of Captain Grant*, he took details from the *Coralie* and added Nemo's reminiscences of the great and honorable Captain Grant, the pirate attacks, and being marooned on an island. *Nemo* again . . . always inspired by Nemo. *What is it about the man?*

"I . . . I have come to see Madame Hatteras," Verne told the clerk. "I believe she is expecting me for lunch?" Bright and eager, the bespectacled man bustled off to fetch Caroline. . .

With such a string of novelistic successes, Jules Verne could now stand next to the great Alexandre Dumas as a colleague, rather than a mere sycophant. However, as he continued writing furiously and researching adventure after adventure, Verne grew uneasy because he owed practically everything to the experiences of Nemo.

There are two types of men in this world, Jules: those who do things, and those who wish they did.

His friend's words kept haunting him. Verne had never been one to experience things first-hand. At least he had sailed with Nemo on his *Nautilus* and shared a terrifying undersea adventure. Someday, he hoped to travel and see a far-off land or two, but with a wife and young son and a contract for three books every year, he had no time. He could make do, as he always had, with research alone.

He knew, though, that Nemo was out there, still having adventures . . .

and Jules Verne would tell the world about them. Readers would remember his name as a visionary, because Nemo shied away from public attention.

After the battle with the giant squid and traveling so many leagues beneath the sea, Verne had not seen Nemo again. France had changed greatly in the fourteen years since his companion had gone off to the Crimean War. Verne wondered if, after living so long apart from civilization, his boyhood friend could ever again become a man of society. Not that Nemo wanted to. . .

Caroline came down from her upstairs offices, her face flushed with delight. Verne wrung his hat in his hands as she handed a stack of papers to the clerk. "Jules, it is lovely to see you." She embraced him, brushing her lips across his cheek.

He clasped her hand. She wore no gloves, no distinctive perfume. Her nails were trimmed short, and he noticed ink spots on her fingertips, like the stains on his own fingers when writing at a furious pace. Her hair, which he'd once described as "honey caught on fire," still retained its vibrant color, but now it was pulled back in a no-nonsense twist, tucked out of her way at the nape of her neck. She wore comfortable clothes unhindered by lace or frills, and had not cinched her corset. The outfit was formal yet serviceable, without drawing overt attention to her beauty. Caroline's natural prettiness shone through, though, in a way that no roses or Chantilly lace could adequately emphasize. Her blue eyes remained bright, like a ray of dawn crossing his face when she looked at him.

"Jules, I do not understand why we fail to see each other, since we both live in Paris. It has been . . . five years?"

"Too many obligations, I believe," he said. "I have my writing, and you have your" – he waved his hands around the offices – "your business."

She laughed. "I can always find time for old friends. You are my only reminder that I was a child once. Come, I've had *chocolat chaud* sent in, for old time's sake, along with those gooseberry pastries you enjoyed so much." Verne's eyes brightened, and he followed her up the stairs and into the back room from which she ran her business.

A tray on her broad mahogany desk held one silver pot of *chocolat chaud*, and the other contained coffee. Both smelled delicious. Verne selected one of the tarts arranged on fine doilies. "You remembered my favorites!"

Despite his rehearsed words, the conversation began to go wrong as soon as Caroline spoke up. "Tell me about your mysterious wife, Jules. You've never brought her to meet me. And what about your son, Michel? You must be so proud of him."

Verne covered his surprise by taking a bite of the pastry. "Honorine is well. She . . . she's rather quiet and withdrawn, not much for meeting people. I apologize that you haven't made her acquaintance yet. On the other hand, Michel is . . ." He heaved a sigh. "Well, they tell me he's just like any boy, but still I find much of his behavior . . . distressing."

Caroline chuckled and leaned back in her chair. "Or at the very least, distracting, no doubt."

Verne countered before he could take his words back. "And what about your husband, Caroline? Is the good Captain Hatteras still lost?"

Her face turned stony. "I still have not heard from him."

Verne shook his head. "I don't understand why you so steadfastly refuse to remarry. You're a . . ." – he swallowed – "a beautiful woman, still young. You have no children, no man to run your personal affairs." He knew the words were wrong even as he spoke them, but years of longing for a woman out of his reach had built up behind a dam of bitterness that now began to break. "It can't be that you loved Hatteras – you barely knew him. What are you waiting for?"

He pretended that he didn't already know the answer. Caroline faced him as she poured a cup of chocolat chaud for herself. "No. It is not that, Jules." She lifted her cup to take a sip.

Verne leaned his elbows on the mahogany surface. "It's because you miss Nemo so much, isn't it?" When she didn't answer, he nodded in triumph. "I thought as much. Well, I have something to tell you, Caroline. I've kept it secret for years, because I wasn't entirely sure anyone would believe me."

Caroline gave him a wry smile, suspecting nothing. "What could be so preposterous that even I would not believe you, Jules?"

Verne took two bites of the pastry, finishing it. He had opened his mouth and let the truth spill out; now he had no choice but to tell her all of it. "Everyone thinks I simply concoct my novels – but I've used *experiences*. You, more than anyone, saw how much I took from your balloon trip across Africa, how much I extrapolated about your Captain Hatteras at the North Pole, and . . . Nemo's experiences underground for *A Journey to the Centre of the Earth*."

"I have read every one of your books, and of course I recognized the inspiration." She gestured to the wall, and he was surprised to see the bound illustrated editions on her shelf. "I am very proud of your success and whatever small hand I may have had in encouraging you when we were younger."

"I have something to tell you," he repeated. And her cornflower-blue eyes widened, as if she already guessed. "Nemo isn't dead, after all, Caroline. His death was falsified in the Crimea."

Caroline clutched his hand, then sat back to listen. While consuming two more pastries and two more cups of *chocolat chaud*, Verne explained how Nemo had been taken captive by a Turkish caliph and forced to build a submarine vessel. Her eyes widened to hear of his journey for days beneath the sea. Stunned and thrilled, she was rapt with a sense of wonder. "You are right, Jules. But I know you, and I know André. If anyone could do such things, *he* could."

Verne looked at her, his face grim as he told her the most important part. "Nemo also has a young son – and a wife. He married her in Turkey, and he told me he loves her very much." He watched as Caroline struggled to compose her expression; his heart went out to her, but she needed to know this.

"In fact, when Nemo dropped me off on the French coast, he said he was going back to get them." He brushed crumbs from his beard, avoiding her gaze, not wanting to see if tears sparkled in her eyes. "I haven't heard from him again, not in five years. He knows you've thought him dead all this time, and he was sure that by now you would have made your own life, married someone else. He said he doesn't want to torment you by coming back to visit you, when he is already bound to another woman."

Caroline managed to cover the flicker of dismay that crossed her beautiful face with a stoic expression. "Thank you for telling me, Jules. I hope they are very happy together. After all he's been through, André deserves to be happy."

"We all deserve to be happy, Caroline." Verne regretted hurting her, snuffing her dreams. But his own dreams of a life with her had long ago been vanquished. "It just doesn't always work out that way."

V

The *Nautilus* traveled secretly beneath the waters, circling the oceans of the earth. All aboard remained isolated from the world . . . and at peace. Following their years-long ordeal, Nemo and his crew reveled in freedom.

Finally, after staying away for as long as Auda had asked, the submarine boat passed again through the Strait of Gibraltar. With growing anticipation, Nemo headed east toward the Turkish coast. He felt cold and uneasy about returning to Rurapente, which bore so many violent memories for him. Isolated on the *Nautilus*, they had learned little about world news, but he'd had enough of war and bloodshed. He hoped the political turmoils had settled down in the Ottoman Empire, as Auda had promised.

He longed to see his wife and son again, and the rest of his crew missed their families as well. On the *Nautilus* they would take their wives and children and be free to make their lives wherever they wished. They clung to that hope.

In his gruff British accent, Cyrus Harding proposed that they search for Nemo's mysterious island, which presumably remained uninhabited. There, they could establish a wonderful new colony, a utopia based on principles of cooperation and support. With the extensive engineering and technical knowledge the sophisticated crew possessed, they could build anything they wished. The Swiss Family Robinson would be mere amateurs by comparison.

Nemo set a course through the sparkling blue waters, threading a maze of scattered Greek islands until they reached the isolated cove where they had been imprisoned for so many years.

As they traversed the deep channel to the rocky shore of Rurapente, Nemo kept the *Nautilus* submerged. Through the round windows they could see dock pilings and other wreckage covered with silt. When he blew ballast to raise the craft and the sea washed clear of the portholes, Nemo and his crew pushed forward, hoping to see cheering, victorious rebels.

Instead, Rurapente had been devastated. The entire industrial compound, its factories and dry docks, its ore smelters and kilns, its village of dwellings – all had been burned and destroyed. Reduced to charred rubble, nothing more.

The *Nautilus* rested against the empty docks, and a moan of despair rose from the crew. Nemo said nothing, jaws locked in a grim expression only partially hidden by his dark beard. His intense eyes stared at the devastation. Somewhere in the dead emptiness of his shock, the fires of anger sparked and blazed.

He opened the upper hatch and emerged blinking into the sunlight. The air smelled of greasy smoke. "Come with me," he said to no one in particular. Every member of his crew felt as desperate and shocked as he did. He didn't try to provide false assurances or unrealistic hopes. "We must learn what we can."

After tying up the submarine boat, the men stepped carefully across rotting dock planks. When they reached the compound itself, they hesitated, afraid to proceed.

The foundations of buildings stood like blackened stumps of teeth. The smelting refineries had caved in, windows smashed, bricks crumbled. The living quarters had been burned to ash and slag. Everything . . . destroyed.

The oppressive silence was broken only by a faint whistle of wind that trespassed in the cove. Nemo thought he could hear the shouts of raiders, the crackle of flames, the clang of scimitars against makeshift weapons . . . or against soft flesh, hard bone. Screams of pain and pleas for mercy from the desperate slaves, the women, the children – everyone who had endured life at Rurapente.

Auda had allied herself with her father, Caliph Barbicane; she had known about the impending attack and arranged for her own rescue and the safety of the others. . . . But now it appeared that no one had listened to her. Nemo could only pray that she had escaped. Or had she and young Jules been victims of the terrible revolution? Where were they?

The *Nautilus* crew picked their way among the rubble, not speaking, searching for some sign to give them hope. Instead, they found skeletons picked clean by carrion eaters and time.

This massacre had occurred many months ago, perhaps at the same time they'd killed Robur and escaped in the submarine vessel. While the captive engineers had fled, masters of their fate and oh-so-pleased with their victory over the bloodthirsty caliph, their families were being slaughtered at Rurapente.

The men could identify none of the remains, but the faces of wives and friends and children shone in every man's imagination. Nemo held back the tears in his eyes as he surveyed the charred wasteland. He turned to his second-in-command, and his voice struck fear in even the gruff Englishman's heart. "Mr Harding, take teams and recover anything you can find – keepsakes or memories, and then give a respectful burial to these poor people."

"Aye, captain," Harding said. He had never argued with Nemo's orders before, but now he hesitated and said, "And what will you be doing, sir?"

With his chin, Nemo gestured toward the steep cliff paths that led up to the plateau. In her note, Auda said she'd used the shepherds as couriers. Many of them were involved in the plot. "I need to find someone," Nemo said.

He took a pack and food from the *Nautilus*, then began his long uphill trek. He plodded throughout the hot day until finally, at sunset, he reached the top of the plateau. Finding a small windbreak of low bushes, he built a smoky campfire, but remained awake most of the night, staring at the stars . . . and remembering.

For two days he wandered the Anatolian Plateau, searching for the nomadic shepherds who had acted as secret watchers for the sultan and his advisors in Ankara. At last he came upon a small group sitting cross-legged in front of their patched tents, while women tended a cookfire, roasting cubes of mutton.

Seeing a lone man in inhospitable territory, the shepherds brandished their ancient rifles at him, making signs to ward off evil. Indeed, the stricken expression on his face made him look like a vengeful spirit – but Nemo made appropriate placating gestures, then a religious sign of Allah he'd learned during his time in Rurapente. He called out in their own language, claiming to be a friend. He wished merely to share their fire and ask them some questions over cardamom-spiced coffee.

The shepherds were dirty and scarred, and looked far older than their actual years. They grudgingly accepted his presence, following the rule of hospitality to wayfarers on the Turkish highlands. Nemo told them that he had spent much time in Rurapente, but that he'd been gone for a year.

"Can you tell me what happened?" His voice cracked with need.

The shepherds discussed the matter among themselves, wondering if he might be a spy testing their allegiance, or a deserter from the sultan's armies. Though Nemo had dark eyes and dark hair, he did not look at all Turkish. But Auda did . . . and so did his son Jules.

He took a chance, and the grief in his voice softened the men. "My wife lived in Rurapente – and my son. She was Caliph Barbicane's daughter. I'm trying to find her. I have companions who also wish to find their families. Can you help us? Please?"

One of the shepherds stood up, stepped away from the smoky fire, and stared appraisingly at him for a long moment. "You were Auda's husband?"

Nemo cringed at hearing the past tense. "Yes. She warned me and my men of the uprising, and we managed to survive. Caliph Robur is dead." Not knowing the loyalty of these men, he did not admit that he himself had killed the warlord.

"Auda was an infiltrator," the shepherd said. "She was sold to Robur to become your wife, but she continued to watch Rurapente. Through us, she reported to Caliph Barbicane, for the sultan in Ankara. We were part of the army that came to free them." He patted his chest, then shook his head. "But there was great bloodshed, much fighting. Another caliph sent forces that swore no allegiance either to Robur or Barbicane – and a slaughter ensued."

"Senseless and terrible," one of the other shepherds said. "The men enjoyed the killing very much."

Nemo listened with a heavy heart. Smoke from the cookfire stung his eyes and nose.

"When it was discovered that Auda was a spy, she and several others loyal to Barbicane took a boat and tried to escape across to the Aegean Islands. But on the way they were attacked. Their boat sank. All aboard were killed."

After that, Nemo heard little else as anger and despair clamored in his head. He didn't care about the changing politics in the Ottoman Empire, or the sultan's current advisors, or plans for the site of the industrial compound. In a daze, he finished his coffee with the shepherds and thanked them, but refused their offer of a full meal.

At dusk, he wandered across the plateau into the deepening night. He felt as destroyed inside as the entire city of Rurapente.

VI

Aboard the *Nautilus*, the crew sank into a heartsick silence. The men from a hodgepodge of countries and cultures drew closer together than ever, unified by their circumstances and their losses. They performed their duties like the walking dead, all hope of happiness lost in one cruel stroke of fate.

Feeling hollow, Nemo stood at the bridge, gripping the metal rail. Finally, out of desperation, he gave the order to depart from the Turkish coast, taking painful memories with him and leaving nothing else behind. With engines at half power, the *Nautilus* cruised away from the ugly scar of Rurapente.

He vowed never to return. Never. He'd had enough of warfare, suffering, and death. He wanted nothing to do with humanity's bloodshed and cruelty.

As the ocean folded over the underwater boat, he stared into the blue-green wilderness. Every time he encountered people, every time he tried to make peace with society and live with his fellow man, the results were disastrous.

He thought of the pirates attacking the *Coralie*. . . They had killed Captain Grant and stranded him for years on the desert island. Then he'd traveled across Africa and been captured by slavers. Next, he'd experienced the horrors of the Crimean War, and then lived as the prisoner of a murderous caliph . . . which caused him to lose Caroline in the bargain. And he'd just seen what had happened to Rurapente, to Auda and Jules.

Fate hadn't claimed their wives and children: people had. *Warmongers.*

For years Robur had extolled dreams of benign technological superiority for the benefit of his people. But the *Nautilus* had been designed for no purpose other than war. The caliph had meant to terrorize peaceful sailing vessels and extort a ransom for all trade entering the Red Sea.

After so much time, Nemo remained appalled at the ability of men to cause pain and suffering. Certain men were bred to be bloodthirsty killers, and they brought crimson shadows to the entire world. Violent conflict had always been abhorrent to him, and now his hatred of it grew even worse.

He had lost so much already.

The submarine boat cruised through the Mediterranean, as if in a daze itself. The crew remained withdrawn for days, eating just enough food to keep themselves alive. They had no goal now, no destination. Their dreams of utopia with their families had died along with Rurapente. . .

Nemo considered abandoning the submarine boat, returning to Paris, and trying to recapture peace in the arms of Caroline. Surely she would welcome him again, though it had been so long, so many years. Jules Verne had said she still refused to remarry.

But in his moments of solitude he could imagine only the death cries of Auda and his young son. He could not bear to rush back to Caroline as if nothing had happened, as if he intended to forget his wife and boy. The thought of trying to fit in with French society terrified him.

Nemo tried to salve his grief by staring for hours upon end at the bliss beneath the seas. He never wanted to leave here, never wanted to face any aspect of war again. But even as he hid under the sea, warmongers continued their painful march across the canvas of history. No one would ever stop them.

None of the men even suggested heading for their respective countries. Nemo did not want to return to the world at all. He was through with mankind. He would let the so-called "civilized" people continue their vicious fighting until they learned their own lessons. . .

Days later, at the height of his anguish, it occurred to Nemo that he *could* strike back, that he need not spend his days in passive misery. The *Nautilus* itself was a tremendous weapon. It had been designed to inflict terror upon other ships sailing the seas. But while Caliph Robur had intended to prey upon merchant ships or peaceful travelers, Nemo realized he could use the submarine boat against another kind of vessel.

Warships.

He could sink navy craft filled with weaponry – battleships whose only aim was to wage war. In so doing, he could prevent the slaughter of innocents, stop warships in their tracks, and sink their deadly cargoes to the bottom of the sea.

He could make a difference, and only the guilty need pay the ultimate price.

Nemo felt no loyalty to any particular nation. He had seen patriotism used as an excuse for further bloodshed, and he wanted none of it. No more innocents must die – even if that meant *he* had to strike against the murderous ones, the invaders, the soldiers. The warmongers.

With the *Nautilus*, Nemo could declare war *on war itself*.

VII

As chance would have it, the first battleship they encountered flew the Union Jack of the British Empire. With running lights extinguished, the *Nautilus* passed five fathoms beneath the broad wooden hull. Nemo's crew peered upward through the portholes, assessing the size of the war vessel.

Standing off at some distance, the *Nautilus* surfaced like a dozing whale. Her front lights glowed a brilliant yellow. Nemo climbed the ladder and opened the upper hatch. With a spyglass to his eye, he peered toward the warship as the sun set, coloring the distant horizon with yellows and orange.

"Mr Harding, prepare for our first . . . statement." Nemo studied the ship and counted the cannons protruding from hatches above the waterline. Wearing a grim expression, he descended back to the submarine's bridge. As if wearing blinkers, he fixed his thoughts on a single point in the future, not allowing himself to think too much on what he was doing. He had made up his mind and would not be swayed.

"She is a vessel of war, gentlemen," Nemo said. "Perhaps even a privateer, government-sponsored pirates who are free to attack other ships . . . so long as those ships fly the flags of an enemy nation."

Aboard the British warship, men in Royal Navy uniforms marched the decks and gathered to look at the distant metal-hulled sea creature. Lying partially submerged, the *Nautilus* must have appeared to be a strange monster with a razor back, armored skin, and glowing yellow eyes.

Nemo's crew fidgeted, though they had discussed their plans at great length. Scratching stubble on his dimpled chin, Cyrus Harding voiced his reservations, which echoed those of the other men. "Britain was my home, captain, a long time ago – and that warship carries a good many English sons. Where –"

Nemo raised a hand to interrupt him, not in a display of temper, but of firm resolve. His anger was directed outward, not at his crew. "The *Nautilus* is our only country now, men. We have no allegiance and no territories. If that were a war vessel from France, I would be just as willing to strike our blow. We have separated ourselves from the rest of our race. And, ironically, we must become crusaders for the rights of humanity."

"But, captain, what about the humanity aboard that ship?" Harding persisted. "Do they all deserve to die?"

Nemo glowered, agonized, but intent on his decision. Like ravens' wings, he heard the dying screams of innocents around his ears. "Gentlemen, that vessel was built to serve one purpose alone – *to commit acts of war*. Her crew is trained to fight and kill. Should we follow her until she fires her cannon, until she spills more innocent blood, and then take our revenge?" He could not drive away the image of burned Rurapente, the thoughts of Auda and young Jules drowning after their fleeing boat was sunk by enemy cannons.

"We must attack any target we find, any bully of the seas. By doing so, we save every person that battleship would have killed and prevent the destruction those cannons would have caused. The only victims are the warmongers themselves, not the innocents . . . like our families were." The other men looked away, cowed and ashamed. "Today – now – we remove one more weapon from the hands of the world's navies."

Seeing the blaze in their captain's eyes, the men went back to their stations. The air stank of nervous sweat. Nemo stood motionless at the bridge and waited, gathering his nerve. Finally, speaking for himself as well as the crew, he said, "Men who make a living by waging war do not deserve our mercy. Remember Rurapente. Remember what happened to your wives and children."

He pushed away images of Caroline and his happy times with her, the five weeks in a balloon over Africa, their precious intimate moments aboard the ship on the way back to France. No, those memories would not keep him strong. "Remember."

In his mind, Nemo saw it all again: the flames, the screams, the scars . . . the warlords fighting each other. The Light Brigade led into slaughter in the Crimea. The villains like Caliph Robur and the ruthless slavers in Africa. The pirates who had sunk the *Coralie* and slain Captain Grant. . .

Nemo gave the order for the *Nautilus* to submerge. He had never tested his beloved vessel in such a terrible manner, but he knew the integrity of his design. He knew what the *Nautilus* had been created to do.

He closed his dark eyes for just a moment and summoned an image of beautiful Auda and little Jules. He tried to find peace, tried to find a purpose. But he could no longer think of them without envisioning the charred bones in the ruins of Rurapente. He thought of Auda murdered, of young Jules pulled beneath the dark water, trying to suck in a breath of air as their ship sank.

"Full ahead," he said. "Ramming speed."

The engines growled, and the propellers turned. The *Nautilus* leaped forward like a hungry shark, spewing a wake just below the surface. Yellow eyes from the forward lamps burned the seas ahead of them.

"Brace yourselves, mates," Cyrus Harding said, cool and collected, an engineer to the last.

The dark shadow of the British warship's hull loomed closer and closer. The *Nautilus* streaked toward it, picking up speed. The armored metal saw-ridge on its bow was sharp, ready to eviscerate.

With a hideous, resounding crunch, the submarine boat crashed into the underbelly of the battleship. The impact sent a deafening *clang* through the hull of the *Nautilus*, and the shock hurled the crew to their knees.

The relentless engines continued to roar. The submarine boat sawed like a battlefield surgeon's blade amputating a diseased limb. The hull of the British warship tore open, a mortal wound that shattered its keel and burst the bulkheads.

"Full stop!" Nemo called and turned to watch, sickened at what he had done and yet refusing to regret his actions.

The gutted warship seemed unable to grasp what had just happened. An explosion sent a muffled boom through the water, probably from a ruptured powder storehouse ignited by stray sparks.

At a safe distance, Nemo gave the order to surface again. Several silent, awestruck crewmen climbed up through the hatch to stand on the outer hull of the undersea vessel, where they observed the death throes of the warship. At least they were far enough away that they could not hear the cries of pain and pleas for rescue from the doomed British crew. . .

Then, with a morbid fascination, Nemo submerged the submarine boat and cruised beneath the wrecked hull. The shattered warship continued its slow and ironically graceful plunge toward the bottom.

Outside the windows of the salon, he could see burned and broken hull timbers, tangled rigging, and bodies . . . many bodies of dead navy men who'd had the misfortune to go to sea on the wrong battleship. His breathing became quick and shallow.

Many of the *Nautilus* crewmen turned away, but Nemo stared with glassy eyes. He had a mission in his hardened heart now, and he owed it to himself and his crew to face his conscience, to see the frightening reality of what he had done.

When he left the salon and addressed the crew, his voice carried no guilt. "Henceforth, if a warship bears arms and carries cannon to sink other ships – then I declare that vessel fair game." He drew a deep breath and stared at the destruction for another long moment, trying not to let questions rise like spectres in his memory, trying not to think of the people who had been on-board that vessel.

"We will show no mercy."

VIII

Back in Paris, Jules Verne continued to write and read, using his imagination for extraordinary voyages, which the readers devoured. He studied the newspapers every day. World events gave him ideas to add to the adventures Nemo had shared with him aboard the *Nautilus*. Sitting alone in his study, he could hardly bear the excitement of the stories he intended to tell. He was glad he didn't have to waste time actually experiencing the adventures. . .

For months now, the international press had carried remarkable stories about warships sunk, vessels attacked and destroyed by a terrible "sea monster." Oddly, the creature attacked only ships of war, but did not discriminate as to nationality. The naturalists of the world held a conference in London and argued about the origin of this creature, imagining a gigantic narwhal or some prehistoric beast arisen to attack ocean-going craft.

Day after day Verne read the reports with interest and horror, unable to deny the obvious answer. He told no one, of course, but he understood immediately what must be going on.

The *Nautilus*, an armored submarine boat designed for purposes of warfare, had to be the culprit. And Nemo himself was behind the attacks.

IX

French readers loved Jules Verne's *Twenty Thousand Leagues Under the Sea*, published in two volumes beginning in 1869. Verne accepted his success in a daze, believing the wonderful comments he heard, and finally he allowed himself to revel in it. He felt his heart swell with the long-sought literary fame.

At lunchtime, as Honorine prepared a plate of cold meats, cheese, and fresh berries, Verne received his copies of the newly released gift edition from Hetzel. The book had been released several days before, but Verne often didn't see copies of his own novels until some time later. Engrossed in new stories, he often didn't notice.

Opening the package, he held up the volumes, delighted with the illustrations and pleased to see his name on the cover. A good wife, Honorine dutifully admired the books, as if they were her husband's trophies. She never read his stories, but she placed them lovingly on shelves and displayed them for all visitors.

He grinned at her. "As soon as I completed this massive novel, Honorine, I knew in my heart that I'd written my masterpiece," Verne crowed. "This one . . . this one would make even *Dumas* proud."

He tapped on the cover with a satisfying thump, then bustled to his writing study where he could pore over every page. Once again, Verne owed this epic to Nemo, his dark-haired and daring friend who had succeeded in so many areas where the author himself had failed. . .

Over the many months of writing the book, locked away in his study and scribbling in bound journals, Verne had shamelessly borrowed from what Nemo had shown and told him. He'd described the metal-hulled submarine boat and even added how it preyed upon warships. He wrote about the exotic landscapes of the sea bottom and even included the terrifying adventure with the giant squid. The novel was his masterpiece.

By couching facts in fiction, Verne made sure no one would scoff at him, though he alone knew that the events were indeed true. He had even gone so far as to name his main character, the diligent and curious Professor "Aronnax," after Caroline, of course. It was his way of honoring her in a manner that she could perhaps understand.

The readers of the magazine serialization, though, were most captivated by the brooding and mysterious Captain Nemo, an angry and impassioned man who had isolated himself from the world, divorced his very existence from human society. Verne's intent had been to make him a dour, driven fellow, consumed with the fires of vengeance, scarred by some terrible (and unspecified) event in his past – yet the public loved him for his dark passion. They saw Nemo as a romantic hero, an enigma that captured their imaginations.

Verne accepted the accolades with good grace, though at home with Honorine he remained perplexed. Even after years of total absence, Nemo still managed to steal Jules Verne's thunder. *What is it about the man?*

In the novel, Captain Nemo took Professor Aronnax prisoner, along with the blustery Canadian harpooner, Ned Land, and the professor's faithful manservant, Conseil. The three accompanied Nemo on a remarkable voyage to underwater volcanoes, sunken cities, seaweed gardens, and polar ice caps. At the end, the three captives managed to flee just before the *Nautilus* was lost in a terrible maelstrom off the coast of Norway.

In writing the novel, Verne had exorcised his own demons, his jealousy for the man who had done so many of the things Verne had denied himself. The magnificent submarine and Captain Nemo himself were both gone, sucked down into a water vortex, never to return. Verne had felt satisfied, and it was a grand ending.

Caroline, though, was outraged.

She pounded on the door of the flat while Verne was still locked in his private office. When Honorine let her in, Caroline looked appraisingly at Verne's wife, and then marched toward the closed door of the writer's study.

Honorine tried to stop her, but Caroline flung the door open and stood like a valkyrie in the doorway, her russet-gold hair in disarray. Verne turned around, astonished to see her, his face lighting with a surprised smile until her enraged expression registered on him. He faltered. "Caroline! Uh . . . Madame Hatteras, to what do I owe –"

"Jules, how could you do this?" Caroline's bright blue eyes flashed with anger. By the sweat on her brow and the rumpled appearance of her clothes, he guessed that she had marched all the way from her shipping offices on the left bank of the Seine.

Honorine hovered in the background, wearing an expression of stern reproof. "Jules, what is it? Who is this woman?"

In all the years he'd been in Paris, Verne had never introduced Honorine and Caroline. At the moment, however, it did not seem to be an appropriate time. He blushed and sweated, brushing his wife away. "Honorine, would you give us a moment of privacy, please?"

Confused but willing to obey her husband, Honorine retreated to the other rooms and busied herself with housework that Verne would never understand.

"So . . . you must have read my new novel?" he asked Caroline disingenuously, then flashed a nervous grin. "Did you see how I –"

Caroline slammed down her own copy of *Twenty Thousand Leagues Under the Sea*. It made a crack like thunder on his desk. "You used my name! You used André's. You made up this preposterous adventure . . . and then you killed him. *Why?* To get even with him for some imagined insult – or to get even with me? How could you do that? Nemo was your friend."

"But –" Verne said, flustered. He leaned back in his chair, swallowed hard, and scratched his beard, at a loss. He searched over the newspaper clippings and scientific journals in front of him, as if he might find an answer among the summaries in his collection. "I have often used names and experiences from my real life." He sat up, gaining conviction. "As you well know, I used your own lost husband as a hero in *Captain Hatteras*. You didn't complain then."

She stood, fuming. "Because I did not care about him, Jules. What did it matter? But André . . . André –"

Verne's heart fell like a stone, and he stared at his notes on the desktop. In a brisk gesture, she swept away the piles of clippings from the wooden surface, and they scattered like a flock of geese fluttering to the floor.

"How can you do so much research, Jules, how can you know so many things about the world – and yet understand so little about people?"

Caroline shook her head, and Verne saw that reading about Nemo's death had pierced her to the core. She'd always held out hope, since Nemo had survived one ordeal after another . . . yet he had never come back for her, not in all these years, even though she knew he was alive. That had stung her to the core. Reading his book, she must have felt her spirits rise at first, delighted with the story, her sole connection to the only man she had ever loved . . . and then been crestfallen when Verne blithely sank his character in the deep whirlpool.

But that was just fiction. He also knew, from Nemo himself, that his friend's crusade had driven him to kill many men who happened to sail aboard vessels of war, regardless of the country's flag they flew, and that included many French military men. And Nemo truly killed them, not just as an imaginary tussle in an adventure story.

But he could never share that with Caroline. Instead, he received her displeasure and disappointment in silence.

"I have always encouraged you in your writing, and I have hoped for the best success and happiness for you," she said. "But must your friends pay such a high price for your dreams? You are not the only one who has dreams, Monsieur Jules Verne."

Then Caroline stood straight and composed herself. She smoothed back her loose strands of hair, ran a hand across her damp forehead, and took a deep breath. "He has always been your friend, Jules, and you know he is still out there somewhere." She gave a sad shake of her head. "Many men envy you – do you know that? You have fame, money, a kind and devoted wife. Why did you need to do this? What more could you want out of life?"

As if slapped, Verne slumped back in his chair. *What more could I want?* He envied Nemo for the life he had *lived*, rather than just imagined. But Verne had missed the opportunities – some had been taken from him, like the voyage on the *Coralie*, like Caroline's love for Nemo . . . and some Verne had been too reluctant to reach out and take.

But he could say none of these things to Caroline. She watched him intently, as if she could read his thoughts, then she left his writing office and made her own way out the door of the apartment. Before Caroline turned away, he thought he saw a single tear in her cornflower-blue eyes.

Honorine went about her routine, her face worried and curious, but Verne knew it would be a long time before he could explain everything to his wife.

He feared that he had lost Caroline forever.

PART X
AROUND THE WORLD

I

Nautilus, 1870

For two years, Captain Nemo's armored submarine boat was the nightmare of the seas.

While standing like a grim statue at the helm of his *Nautilus*, he wrecked dozens of heavily armed war vessels, and the navies of the world sent out hunting craft in search of the "sea monster." Though a few of these ships blundered across Nemo's path and opened fire with their cannons, the *Nautilus* never faced any real danger.

He continued without remorse and without any sign of stopping – but after two years Nemo began to question whether his crusade was of any use. His anger had become a habit, his revenge a routine – and he felt that his heart and soul had died. Even Auda and young Jules became mere haunted shadows in his past. He was afraid to think of Caroline, how he could return to her at any moment and ask for her forgiveness and her love. He dared not.

To the dedicated crew, this had never been a game, but a deadly statement that the political leaders of the world must hear. Sending that message had become their job, repeated often. With the blood of countless hundreds on his hands, with the tortured screams of drowning seamen unheard in the depths of the oceans, Nemo's shoulders grew heavy. His conscience trembled on the brink of despair. What had it all been for?

He convinced himself that the victims he'd killed had all been willing participants in war, and thus guilty. But . . . had *he* not himself been a soldier in the Crimea? In fact, every crewman aboard the *Nautilus* had been recruited from that terrible war. And had *he* not charged into battle because of confused orders or misguided loyalties, like some of these men?

Did Nemo have the right to mete out his personal justice on such people as he and his men had also been? Had he become just as bad as the butchers of Rurapente, preying upon innocents who knew no better?

What would Caroline say about what he'd done? And hadn't he and Caroline been passengers aboard a British navy ship to and from their African balloon journey?

He took his vessel through the calm waters of the Red Sea to the southern end of the Isthmus of Suez where the great canal had at long last been finished. Though well behind schedule, the French engineer de Lesseps had accomplished his tremendous feat. The narrow thread of land that separated the Mediterranean from the Indian subcontinent had been severed. Sailing vessels no longer needed to make the long trek around the bottom of Africa's Cape of Good Hope and back up again.

At the mouth of the canal, the *Nautilus* lurked underwater. The crew watched the first triumphant French ships cruise through the waterway, firing celebratory cannons and waving colorful banners.

In his dream to become master of the world, Caliph Robur had intended to use the *Nautilus* to sink those ships, to trap them in the bottleneck of the Suez Canal. Now Nemo simply watched the procession from inside his technological dream. . .

That night, Nemo took his submarine boat northward through the shallow channel out of the Red Sea, reentered the Mediterranean, then headed west toward the Strait of Gibraltar.

In the following weeks, Cyrus Harding took over the less pleasant chores whenever they encountered prospective victims, vulnerable warships.

Nemo found himself spending more and more time in the great salon, admiring the wonders of the oceans, the cradle of life on earth.

He rested, reading his treasured books, even some of Jules Verne's amusing "Extraordinary Voyages," obtained through secretive forays into dockside cities where they could purchase newspapers and learn what was going on in the world.

He had read *Five Weeks in a Balloon*, and though the adventure was certainly entertaining, Jules Verne's inexperience had shown, depicting many of the African people in a distorted and highly unflattering manner, painting sinister pictures of Arabs and calling them all slavers. Nemo himself had encountered many groups and tribes engaging in the heinous practice, and many Arabs who did not. It was a matter of evil *men*, not a matter of their race. But Verne's civilized readers knew no better, and accepted the broad-strokes account as well-researched fact.

Nemo felt empty and dejected, aimless and lost, but could not articulate exactly why. How much would have been different if he'd just stayed with Caroline, so long ago? Or if he'd gone back to her, like a sensible man?

He was forty-two years old now and had seen many things and many places in his life. For amusement, he'd even taken the *Nautilus* up to the coast of Norway and seen the fabled maelstrom from Verne's story, in which the fictional *Nautilus* had sunk. The real submarine vessel swam through the whirlpool with ease, though, looking down on a graveyard of less-fortunate ships. . .

As Nemo relaxed in the salon, looking into the depths of the Atlantic, Cyrus Harding came to him. "Captain, sir, we've encountered another warship. A vessel from the United States. She carries forty cannon and rides low in the water. Full of armaments, I believe."

Searching for the passion that had driven him to such a crusade in the first place, Nemo left his books and his moment of peace, and walked to the porthole, yet said nothing. Harding, a man of calm demeanor and intent, waited for his captain's response. "Should we attack, captain? She fits the criteria we've established."

Nemo detected no eagerness in Harding's voice. The British second-in-command was never eager for the kill, but he did know his duty. "At your discretion, Mr Harding," Nemo said, taking the other man aback.

Finally, Harding gave a brief nod. "She does meet the criteria, Captain. I recommend we engage."

"Very well." Nemo ran a hand along his dark, trimmed beard. "I will meet you on the bridge momentarily."

He should have returned to Paris, asked Caroline to accept him again, even with the dark blots on his past. At any time he could go back to her, if he could gather the courage. What would he say to her? Why had he taken so long?

The submarine boat crested the calm surface while Harding and two crewmen emerged from the hatch. It was late afternoon; the sun would set within an hour. They used spyglasses to assess the American warship.

As soon as the armored vessel was visible, the United States ship began blasting with its cannon. Orange tongues of flame shrank in the distance to the size of firecrackers. After several seconds' delay, the booms of gunpowder reached their ears across the still sea. A scattered pattern of cannonballs splashed in the water. None of the projectiles came close to the *Nautilus*, but Harding and the other crew members went below.

Nemo was standing at the helm controls. "She's begun firing at us, captain," Harding said.

Nemo nodded, waited for them to secure the upper hatch, then gave the order to submerge. "Mr Harding, this is your hunt." He stepped aside to let his second-in-command take the controls, but the captain of the *Nautilus* displayed a greater degree of uncertainty than ever before. He felt no passion, only numbness, a blind momentum that led them nowhere.

"Power up engines," Harding called.

The grim men had been through the routine numerous times before and responded with military efficiency. The growl of the electric engines built to a loud roar, and the *Nautilus* leaped forward, cutting a wake across the surface. Its brilliant spotlights shone like the eyes of a dragon in the sea.

Distant vibrations followed them as the American ship continued its cannonade. The *Nautilus* picked up speed – a bullet streaking toward its doomed target.

Nemo gripped the railing, breathing heavily and trying to focus his thoughts. His obsession, his war against war, had given him a purpose during the bleakest time in his life. But the men aboard the naval vessels he destroyed also had wives and families. Perhaps some of those sailors had been conscripted against their wills. By what right did he rob them all of their futures?

He squeezed his eyes shut.

I could have been with Caroline all this time.

The saw-blade spine of the *Nautilus* struck the hull of the American battleship. The impact ripped the vessel's keel open, breaching the lower decks. Within moments, the wooden-hulled ship exploded, spewing debris into the unexplored waters of the Atlantic.

Nemo didn't even know the name of the ship. Nor did he care. . .

Within an hour, the American war vessel had fallen over on its side and began to go down, dragging victims to the bottom. Nemo remembered the wrecked *Cynthia* at the docks in Nantes, his father trapped in a sealed stateroom as the boat sank. He thought of Auda and the boy Jules, trying to flee Rurapente, drowning after their ship was attacked. . .

But somehow the fury was gone now. He saw only more misery caused by others, caused by *him*. He had not helped at all, merely made the situation worse.

After dark, Nemo ordered the *Nautilus* to surface. With engines humming at low speed, the vessel crept toward the floating debris. A few fires glowed in the ocean's night, and he wondered if the sharks would come. He stood in silence outside the hatch, inhaling the tang of smoke, gunpowder . . . and death in the sea air.

He felt no exhilaration at what he had done, no triumph at striking another blow against the warmongers. Evil men would always find evil things to do, and innocent men would always become cannon fodder. By destroying so many warships, he had only added to the number of victims sent to their deaths by incompetent commanders or politicians.

Nemo wondered if he should isolate himself, take the *Nautilus* and go somewhere away from the world. Surely, he deserved a respite from his dark quest by now? What more must he do?

And then there was Caroline.

As his eyes adjusted to the distant firelight and the pale moon, Nemo saw a lone human figure clinging to the wreckage. The man waved a long, angular arm, trying to draw attention to himself. Nemo froze, considering options before finally calling down to the bridge deck and ordering Cyrus Harding to pick up the castaway.

In all their attacks, never before had Nemo chosen to take prisoners or pick up survivors. But now, with his heart heavy, the silhouette of the single refugee made him think of how he himself had clung to flotsam after pirates had captured the *Coralie*. This man would die out here if the *Nautilus* didn't pick him up . . . and somehow turning his back on that one soul seemed even more cold-blooded than destroying the ship itself.

When the *Nautilus* drew up to the wreckage, Nemo remained outside, looking down at the bedraggled survivor. He and two crewmen reached over to help the spluttering man onto the metal-plated hull.

The stranger had dark hair, a trim mustache, and gangly legs that seemed even more awkward in his wet, though dapper, clothes. His face was gaunt, his eyes close-set. The survivor's expression and his huffy demeanor puzzled Nemo. He expected the refugee to express either terror or outrage – or even pathetic appreciation for being rescued. Instead, the man stamped his feet on the hull plates of the *Nautilus* to shake the water from his drenched clothes.

With long-fingered hands he wrung out cupfuls of water, and then neatly arranged his hair. He met Nemo's gaze with a stern look and didn't seem the least bit curious about the *Nautilus* or its wonders. He looked more ruffled and indignant than frightened.

"My name is Phileas Fogg, sir." He sniffed with great displeasure, then looked over his shoulder at the remains of the sunken warship. "You and this abomination of a vessel have just cost me a very large wager."

II

Though space was at a premium in the submarine, the ornate salon was large enough for Nemo and the odd-tempered refugee to stretch their limbs and make themselves comfortable. Fogg looked as if he had settled into a dark and smoky gentleman's club, perfectly at home.

As the *Nautilus* departed from the wreckage of the American warship (a vessel ironically named the *Invincible*), Nemo saw to it that his lanky passenger recovered, was well fed, and received new clothes. This done, he found himself in a dilemma as to what to do with Mr Phileas Fogg. Nemo did not want to keep this tall and fastidious man a prisoner aboard his underwater craft forever.

He intended to keep the *Nautilus* a secret, mainly to make sure that no other warlord like Robur decided to build such a vessel for his own ambitions. Though the submarine had been observed numerous times, most people still considered it a sea monster. Even after his friend's novelistic account in *20,000 Leagues Under the Sea*, no one suspected that Verne's "Extraordinary Voyages" had any basis in reality.

Fogg accepted his situation with grace and lounged in one of the chairs in the salon. He folded his long right leg over his left and sat at an angle, ignoring the undersea wonders that passed by the salon's circular viewing window. He seemed entirely uninterested in the armored underwater vessel.

Anxious to learn more about his new guest, Nemo stayed close to the man. Fogg asked no questions concerning the *Nautilus*, paid little heed to the engineering innovations designed into the craft. When the prim man finally asked a question, he looked Nemo in the eye and said, "My good man, might you happen to have a cigar? My own were irreparably soaked, and after all these inconveniences, I have a powerful craving for tobacco."

Taken aback, Nemo went to a cupboard in the salon, opened a sealed case, and removed a box of brownish cylindrical objects – a new delicacy invented by Cyrus Harding. "Try these. I believe you'll be satisfied."

Phileas Fogg lit one of the unusual cigars and sat back, puffing and concentrating as he tasted the smoke. "Most unusual." His brows furrowed as if his brain were working over the convolutions of an extraordinary mathematical problem. "Is it your own label?"

Nemo wondered if he could surprise the unflappable man. "They're made of a dried seaweed that is high in the substance nicotine. We prefer not to put ashore and buy land-based supplies except when absolutely necessary. Thus, you have our substitute."

"Seaweed, my good fellow? Most ingenious, I'd say," Fogg said, showing not the slightest desire to pursue the matter any further. "Well, we do what we must for good tobacco."

Nemo sat forward in his chair. "Tell me about this mysterious wager of yours, Monsieur Fogg. What have we cost you?"

"You and your infernal machine have caused me to lose a very ambitious race, sir." Fogg pointed with his seaweed cigar, deftly tapping ash into a receptacle beside his chair. "At one time I belonged to a rather prestigious, formal, and – yes, let us admit it – *stuffy* gentleman's club in London. A group of bored, wealthy men, who sat and read the newspapers, had afternoon tea, played whist, and . . . and did little else. Pompous asses, if you ask me – and I fit right in with them.

"One day, after pondering the worldwide commercial implications of the new Suez Canal, I calculated that it would be possible for a man with sufficient resources and careful attention to scheduling to travel around the world in eighty days." Fogg smiled, as if expecting Nemo to disbelieve him, but the captain of the *Nautilus* maintained an expression of polite interest.

"My colleagues in the club treated such a suggestion as preposterous. So, with my honor at stake, I made them a wager – a very large wager – that I myself could actually perform such a feat. I would attempt the impossible. We do what we must in the name of honor, do we not?"

Nemo brooded. "You might say that."

Fogg took a long drag from his cigar, as if he were attempting to siphon thick oil from a container. "Well, naturally, I had the schedules and timetables before me and the utmost confidence in my own abilities. I departed that very evening, and I have made nearly a complete circuit of the globe. That is, until you sank the ship on which I was traveling. Most inconvenient."

He drew on the seaweed cigar again and savored the smoke. Nemo lit a cigar of his own, though he usually did not indulge. He motioned with the glowing tip for the man to continue.

"I began by crossing the English Channel and took a railway to the south of France, where I caught a ship that carried me across the Mediterranean, through the Suez Canal, and into the Red Sea. From there, we sailed to India, which subcontinent I crossed using a train and an elephant. No time for tedious sightseeing – just rapid motion westward. From Singapore I traveled to Hong Kong, then Japan, across the Pacific to San Francisco, and finally by rail across North America.

"Alas, due to an unforeseen scheduling mishap in New York Harbor, I was forced to book passage upon the only vessel that could take me to England in time – a warship with orders to cruise the oceans in search of the notorious sea monster demonized in all the papers." Fogg raised his eyebrows and turned his gaunt face to study Nemo. "I presume that monster is your own ship? Rotten luck."

Nemo nodded. Fogg pursed his lips in acceptance.

"I had to use the last of my monetary resources to bribe the navy captain. If the *Invincible* had indeed kept to schedule, I would have been a very wealthy man . . . and, more importantly, I would have been proved correct in my convictions." Fogg stubbed out his cigar, as if he hadn't a care in the world. "Now, however, I am ruined. I believe Hell must be a place where no schedules are ever kept."

With growing disappointment in himself, Nemo listened to the fastidious Englishman's account. Phileas Fogg had survived the *Nautilus*'s attack on the American naval vessel, but all others aboard had died. How many civilians had drowned, mere innocents who'd had the misfortune of booking passage aboard a ship marked for war, as Phileas Fogg had? As he and Caroline had done, with Dr Ferguson, in order to return from Africa? How many people had been attempting to go from one place to another, and never had violence or bloodshed in their hearts?

Nemo had killed them all. That, he was forced to acknowledge, made him as bad as Caliph Robur.

Outside the circular salon window swam a great white shark, its soulless eyes peering into the illuminated interior of the submarine boat. If Phileas Fogg noticed the predatory fish, he gave no sign.

"Monsieur Fogg," Nemo said, arriving at a decision, "my *Nautilus* can travel faster than even a warship such as the *Invincible*. By journeying beneath the waves, we are not at the mercy of winds or weather. We can increase the power of our engines and cross the Atlantic within days." He stood. "I know I have inconvenienced you terribly, sir . . . and I have committed a great many other crimes, for which I must atone in my own way." He held out his hand. "I can offer restitution in your case, however, provided you grant me assurance that you keep the existence of my submarine boat a secret and not reveal how you returned to England." He squared his shoulders. "If you agree to these things, I will provide you passage to London in time to win your wager."

Fogg's narrow face brightened for just a moment, then he nodded at Captain Nemo. "You leave me no choice, sir. I agree to your terms. Anything, in order to get back on schedule."

III

In misty weather and calm seas, the *Nautilus* cruised along the surface of the Atlantic. As the vessel cut a bright wake across the waves, Nemo stood outside, taking in the fresh air and cool dampness. He listened to the quiet ripples of the armored boat's passage and stared into the distance . . . just thinking.

Entering the English Channel, they passed the northern coast of France. Being so close to continental Europe and his homeland reminded Nemo of his days in Nantes and Paris. Inevitably, his thoughts drifted to Caroline, how very close they had grown, and how he had given it all up.

If only he'd returned to her immediately after discovering the destruction of Rurapente. He had been consumed with anger and vengeance, cruising the seas on his quest to stop war, like Sisyphus rolling his stone endlessly uphill. What had it gained him, when he could have returned to a beautiful woman instead? He had been scarred and changed after the Crimean War, and he had turned his back on happiness, forsaking love for revenge.

For a man who'd been brave enough to fight the greatest battles and confront the deadliest adversaries, why was he afraid to face Caroline and ask her to accept him as he was?

Even before the war, if only he'd had the courage to remain in Paris for a year – a mere twelve months – he and Caroline could have been married long ago. A smile of bitter irony twisted his lips. He had truly believed that waiting for one year in Paris until he could hold her again would have been unbearable torture. Instead, he'd gone to the Crimea, been captured by an evil caliph, and been forced to work for ten years. Oh, if only he had stayed in France!

But if he had remained, Nemo would never have known Auda, or played with his son Jules. Despite the tragedy, Nemo would not have been willing to surrender those memories for any sum. . .

Phileas Fogg joined him outside in the fog. In silence, they watched the approaching white cliffs of Dover, ready to round the point to the Thames estuary. The lanky Englishman had spent most of the journey in his enclosed cabin, attending to his journal, displaying no interest in the *Nautilus*. Nemo was glad to have his privacy, yet could not understand this man's apathy toward new things. Fogg had traveled around the world, but had shown little curiosity about the wonders of the earth even as he'd passed through them.

Now, though, Phileas Fogg wore a pained expression and looked at the captain, as if he had distractedly eaten too many prunes at breakfast. He brushed down an offending loose whisker in his narrow mustache. Something troubled the traveler, but Nemo waited for the gangly man to speak. Finally, Fogg cleared his throat. "Captain Nemo, I am concerned as to how I may cope with your demands."

"Have I been unreasonable in any way?" Nemo raised his dark eyebrows.

Fogg reached into his salvaged coat and withdrew a bound volume wrapped in oilskin, with the words *Fogg's Log* embossed on the cover. "This is the precise and detailed record of my journey. I keep it with me at all times – otherwise it would have sunk to the bottom of the ocean, along with the wreckage of the *Invincible*. I would have had a terrible time retrieving it."

He opened the battered book and showed Nemo the colorful stamps from customs officers, inscriptions by local officials, postmarks and clippings from newspapers. "This is how I intend to prove that I did indeed complete my journey, that I traveled around the world in eighty days."

Fogg turned to blank pages. The date ended with the sinking of the

American warship. "If I must keep the existence of your *Nautilus* a secret, how am I to document my travel across the Atlantic? The sinking of the *Invincible* will be a matter of public record. How shall I explain my travels?" He scratched his head. "I doubt I can convince the members of the club that I managed to swim the remainder of the distance. . ."

Nemo pondered for a moment, continuing to look off into the mist. The shadows of chalk cliffs pressed closer. "You will have to concoct a story, Mr Fogg. You must think of some way to explain your travels – and I suggest you find an alternative other than swimming. I *will* hold you to your promise, monsieur."

Phileas Fogg's long fingers clutched the logbook in a tight grip. "But everything in here is true and documented, sir." His voice now took on a tone of indignation. "How can I falsify such an important part of my trip? That would be . . . most dishonest."

Nemo refused to back down. "Monsieur Fogg, one thing I have learned in my life is that what is written down and published is not necessarily the *truth* – even if it is purported to be so." He brought to mind how his adventures had been recounted in the novels of Jules Verne, how the events had been altered for the sake of the story.

"At its core, you will not be lying. You will have done as you proposed, according to the terms of your wager. You traveled around the world in eighty days. No one can argue that fact. The rest of the story is just . . . details."

"But details are like schedules. Too many people ignore them." Staring into the cold, moist air, Fogg remained stoic for a long moment until he broke into a broad grin, the first overt emotion Nemo had seen from the scarecrowish man. "Well . . . it will, after all, be only one more falsehood." Fogg turned to the dark-haired captain. "I've just realized that of all people in the world, you are the one person in whom I can confide. I can tell you my secret, Captain Nemo, because you have no means and no motivation to reveal it to the authorities."

"I have no respect for authorities," Nemo agreed bitterly.

Fogg continued. "As you might guess, sir, arranging such a trip around the globe involved more than careful scheduling. It required substantial monetary resources as well. While I had a comfortable enough life in London, I was by no means a rich man, not the sort of person who had the funds to engage in such a lengthy and expensive trip. So I was forced to acquire the financing by . . . unorthodox means."

Phileas Fogg fell silent for a moment, and Nemo looked at him as the *Nautilus* cruised onward. "You stole it?"

Fogg met his dark gaze. "I robbed a bank."

Nemo stared at the tall Englishman in astonishment.

"Oh, not with a gun or any sort of violence, I assure you." Fogg waved a long-fingered hand. "I simply found the means to walk off with a large stack of pound notes that were left unattended by a careless clerk."

Fogg sniffed, twitching his large nostrils. "And while the Bank of England and Scotland Yard were in a frenzy searching all over London to track down the thief, I was traveling around the world to great fanfare and popular reception. No one has ever suspected that the stolen money is in my possession – or *was*, that is. It's all been spent on my trip.

"However, if I do return home in time, the amount I shall win in my wager is several times greater than the sum I . . . withdrew. Before I left England, I devised a plan for returning the money discreetly – call it an impromptu loan. Then the books will balance, the details will add up properly, and all will be right with the world. Never fear, Captain Nemo, thanks to your assistance, everything will turn out as it should, according to schedule."

Nemo thought about the man's situation, but did not accept or condemn Fogg's actions. "We all have our secrets, monsieur. And since I trust you to keep mine, the *Nautilus* will bring you to London on time."

IV

Late at night, in the dark of a new moon, the *Nautilus* churned the murky waters of the Thames and delivered Phileas Fogg to a deserted wharf in London. The fastidious man packed a few meager possessions and his logbook, then prepared to disembark. The emotionless man didn't look at all triumphant, but accepted his arrival as a matter of course.

After climbing out of the hatch, Fogg stood beside the captain of the *Nautilus*. He glanced at his pocketwatch, released a contented sigh. "After you depart, Captain Nemo, have a care to avoid the French coast. I doubt you would wish to become involved in that terrible war and its repercussions."

Nemo studied the tall Englishman. "What do you mean, monsieur?" He felt uneasy, even a bit ill. "What war?"

Fogg returned the glance, surprised. He raised his eyebrows and sniffed. "Why, France is at war with Prussia, of course. Didn't I mention it? A dreadful, bloody conflict – and France is losing badly. A terrible situation, I do believe even the trains are no longer running on time.

"Your Napoleon III was captured at Sedan and capitulated to von Bismarck . . . but Paris itself refused to surrender. Some months ago Prussian troops laid siege to the city. The situation is dire, sir. Some of the trapped Parisians have sent out letters by hot-air balloon or carrier pigeon. Rather ingenious, eh? It seems one of your ministers of state even escaped the city by balloon." Fogg smoothed down his dapper mustache. "By all accounts, though, the people are starving. They've even resorted to eating animals from the Paris Zoo, just for the meat. Parts of the city have been burnt."

The Englishman stepped onto the vacant dock. To the curious press on the following day, Fogg would have miraculously appeared out of nowhere. "A terrible situation, simply terrible. I hear there are also Prussian warships patrolling the Atlantic coast of France." Then he raised his eyebrows. "Ah, if I might inquire? Should your *Nautilus* be sunk, might I then be allowed to revise my log to include passage aboard your vessel? It seems only proper –"

In shock, Nemo thought immediately of Caroline, knowing she would have been trapped in Paris. He imagined her starving to death, unable to get out of the city. . . "Mr Harding, prepare to depart," he called down to the control bridge. With a brisk farewell wave to Phileas Fogg, he descended the ladder and slammed the metal hatch over his head.

Nemo knew exactly what he must do. He directed his men to turn the submarine vessel about. They headed back toward the English Channel.

He would return to Paris and save Caroline.

V

Cruising along the coast of Brittany, the *Nautilus* found the mouth of the Seine, then traveled at top speed against the river current. Taking the helm again, Nemo guided the submarine boat through the maritime channel. All commerce to the interior of France had stopped due to the devastating Franco-Prussian War, and the *Nautilus* proceeded unhindered.

With winter setting in, the fields had already been harvested, the grasses and trees turned brown in anticipation of snow. At times, shallow water and sandbars forced the vessel to surface. Nemo's urgency allowed him no time for caution. Peasants who picked through crop stubble on the fertile bluffs looked down to see a scaled monster pass by. Nemo was oblivious to their superstitions; he thought only of reaching Caroline.

By this time, he had learned enough about the Franco-Prussian conflict to know that it was as foolish a set of circumstances and as poor an excuse for bloodshed as any other conflict. *Again, the folly of war.* Earlier that year, the Prussians had attempted to put their own candidate on the vacant throne of Spain. The shrewd Prussian chancellor, Otto von Bismarck, had maneuvered the now-bumbling Napoleon III into declaring war against Prussia to stand up for Spanish interests. What pointless folly!

It was a war that everyone knew France couldn't win. The Prussians had superior numbers, superior artillery, superior leadership. In an inept debacle, Napoleon III had countermanded the orders of his generals and personally led the French army into battle at Sedan, with disastrous consequences. The emperor and his troops were captured, and the Prussian army marched unopposed across the French countryside. In seventeen days, they had placed Paris under a siege that had not been broken for months. And now the people were starving, and the city was burning.

And Nemo was sure that Caroline would be there.

Riding low in the water like a giant crocodile, the *Nautilus* continued up the Seine, past Rouen, past St Germain. When they finally drifted beneath the numerous stone bridges spanning the river in Paris, Nemo watched the encamped Prussian army continue to bombard the city with artillery.

Confident of victory, the massed enemy troops did not even risk their lives by marching on Paris. They remained camped in position, untouchable and unbeatable. Their cannons launched incendiaries into the city, starting conflagrations that the beaten people could barely fight.

Still half submerged, as the *Nautilus* passed under the thick bridge pilings, Nemo's crewmen pressed close to the portholes to look out at the besieged city. The ruined buildings and smoke were a grim reminder of the devastation at Rurapente. Dusk had fallen, and night was on its way, but fires splashed the sky with unrelenting orange.

"The City of Light," Nemo remarked grimly, thinking of Emperor Napoleon III's grand rebuilding program. He shook his head to see the waste, the destruction, the mayhem.

"Looks bad, captain," Harding said, jutting his dimpled jaw forward.

"No matter, Mr Harding. These Prussians cannot stop us from doing what we must."

As the cannonades and artillery thundered into the deepening night, Nemo ordered the *Nautilus* to surface, blowing all ballast. He opened the upper hatch and listened to the water as it trickled off the hull plates. The air of Paris smelled acrid with smoke, piled refuse, and raw sewage. *And death.* In the distance he could hear crackling flames, pounding guns, and the moans of a defeated people too tired and hungry to continue the fight.

Long ago, he had worked here as an engineer for the emperor. He had helped build these bridges, designed some of the palatial buildings with the civil engineer Haussmann. Now, in a matter of months, the Prussians were destroying all the restoration Napoleon III had accomplished.

But Nemo could not find it in his heart to mourn the loss of *things* – not buildings or boulevards, not sculptures or fountains. With his rediscovered conscience, after causing so much mayhem of his own, he cared more about the lives at stake. He now knew he couldn't single-handedly stop the wars. How had he ever been foolish enough to believe that more killing was the answer? There were some things men would have to learn for themselves. . .

Right now, Caroline's very life might be at stake. Nothing mattered more than that. He had failed her so many times before.

Perhaps as the Prussian armies approached, she had been wise enough to gather her possessions, close down the offices of "Aronnax, Merchant" and flee the city . . . but Nemo knew she wasn't that sort of person. Caroline Hatteras would never have given up. She would have stayed at the offices even under artillery bombardment.

Cyrus Harding guided the submarine toward the crowded docks and row houses. When the armored vessel had tied up to the high brick bank, Nemo took a pistol and a scimitar – odd and archaic choices in the face of the modern Prussian army, but the *Nautilus* carried few other weapons.

"I will go alone," he called to the anxious crew. "Mr Harding, you are in command of this vessel. There is . . . someone I must see." The second-in-command nodded knowingly and took over the bridge controls.

Nemo leaped across the intervening gap to the cobblestone walkway alongside the river. Dirtying his old uniform from Rurapente, he hauled himself up to the street level. The handful of scurrying citizens looked as if they had been stunned, like kittens being chased with a broom. Rail-thin refugees ran back and forth, searching for something . . . safety, perhaps. Few of the downtrodden people even noticed the submarine boat lying like a dark fish in the oily Seine.

The shelling continued. Explosions rocked the night. Ducking low, Nemo ran along the quai Anatole France, beside the smoking buildings. Spreading flames spilled out of broken windows. New fires encircled this section of the Left Bank, and these venerable structures were doomed.

As he approached Caroline's place of business, Nemo was dismayed to see the row house already threatened by fresh flames. Earlier, before he had set out for the Crimean War, he had stood in front of this place in the dark of early morning. Now, fire flowed up the brick sides, gnawing at the half-timbered reinforcements. The plank floors and wooden furniture inside only served to fuel the blaze. Nemo hoped Caroline hadn't remained here – but he had to check. He would not let her down again.

With his shoulder, he broke through the tall door; it had been closed tightly against the jamb, but not locked. Several of the windows had already smashed in the rising heat. Over the growl of spreading fire, he could hear someone moving about in the back upstairs room.

"Caroline!" He ran up the stairs. The thickening smoke made his voice hoarse. The flames grew louder as they ate their way through the walls and timbers. His time was running out.

In the back room he found her, and his knees went weak. All of the clerks and workers had gone, probably weeks ago at the beginning of the siege, judging from the cluttered condition of the desks. But Caroline had remained, long after the others had fled.

He barged into the well-appointed office and saw her – face streaked with grime, hair loose and in disarray. She scurried about, gathering documents from drawers in her heavy desk. He couldn't imagine what business records could be so important that she would take such a risk to protect them.

When Caroline saw him standing in her doorway, framed by firelight, she froze. "André?" Her voice was the barest whisper.

Words caught in his throat. Caroline looked so familiar and yet so changed. After many painful years, she was even more beautiful than he remembered. His heart ached as he drank in the sight of her.

"I knew you'd come," she said, her voice thick with relief. "Somehow, I knew that if I waited long enough . . ."

Nemo stepped into the room, shoulders squared, refusing. "I've come to take you away from here, Caroline. You must leave Paris."

She shook her head, haunted. "No one can break the siege, not even you, André. The Prussians control all exits. We have had no food, no peace." Then she blinked. "But – how did you get into the city?"

Nemo extended his hand. "I have a way. Let me take you to safety. Leave your papers behind. They won't mean anything where we're going." Then he noticed the circles, dots, and slashes of musical notes, long compositions in her own hand. *Her music.* Of course she would have come back for it.

"No, I have to take this. I kept the papers hidden here, locked away, so no one would find them in my house. A full symphony, some concertos, sonatas –" As the fire grew brighter, she grabbed more sheets of music that had been stored in her desk drawer.

Nemo snatched up the compositions she had already piled on her desk. "If you come with me, you won't need to hide your music anymore." Their eyes met in a long, deep silence. "I have something to show you, and then everything will change. We have both lost so much." His voice became quiet, aching. "It is time we both gain something at last."

Windows shattered as the heat increased, and Nemo grasped her arm. "That's all we can take. Hurry!" They ran down the stairs and out of the row house, leaving the inferno behind. . .

Prussian cannons thundered without respite, and gunfire rattled from outside the city – either an enemy attack, or just bored soldiers letting off volleys to intimidate the Parisians. Together, the two ran down the streets, pushing past scattered people who ran in circles, terrified but with no place to go.

Nemo took Caroline along the river's edge, dodging broken stones and bricks from the buildings pounded by Prussian artillery. Finally, they reached the shadows beside a bridge embankment.

Caroline looked down at the river and saw the armored hull of the floating vessel. "That . . . that is the *Nautilus*? The real *Nautilus*? Jules's descriptions did not do it justice."

Nemo helped her step across to the hull. "This is how I will get you out of Paris. We'll dive beneath the river and slip out with the current. The

Prussians won't see us. I'll keep you safe."

She touched his arm. "Since we were little more than children, when you and I stayed out all night under the magnolia trees at the Church of St Martin, I have always felt safe at your side."

VI

In normal days, Jules Verne loved to be aboard his private yacht, out on the sea just like a bold sailor. But during the dangers of wartime, he would have preferred to be safe at his vacation home in Amiens. Unfortunately, too many people in the French government expected him to be like one of the heroes of his novels.

The conflict with the Prussians grew desperate enough that Verne found himself conscripted into the military, even at the age of forty-two. Because of his fame, he was not asked to fight on the battle lines; instead, he was assigned to the coastguard, due to his love for and proficiency in sailing.

Jules Verne, defender of France!

Several years earlier, the bearded author had purchased his own yacht, which he'd christened the *Saint Michel* in a moment of parental guilt. Before the war, Verne frequently sailed the *Saint Michel* up and down the Loire; he also cruised the Atlantic coast from Paimboeuf all the way up to Brittany. Every trip had been a fine outing.

Now the French military, in its bureaucratic wisdom, had decided that Verne should command his own boat – like his fictional captains Grant and Hatteras – crewed by a group of old veterans from the Crimean War. The legendary author would patrol the coast around Le Crotoy and protect France from invaders. Surely von Bismarck would tremble to learn of such a foe. . .

Just before hostilities had begun, Hetzel called in numerous favors to get recognition for his extraordinarily successful author. In one of his last actions before the outbreak of war, Emperor Napoleon III had summoned Jules Verne to the palace to present him with the Legion of Honor – and Verne had been as pleased as he could be.

To celebrate, Verne took Honorine and Michel away from Paris to visit his parents in Nantes. Gray-haired Pierre Verne's health was declining, and the elderly attorney had grown even more sour-tempered over the years. Yet given Verne's celebrity as a writer, he grudgingly admitted that his idealistic son had made a good career choice after all. Sophie Verne took pleasure in her rambunctious grandson, tolerating even Michel's worst behavior.

Then the war had erupted, the emperor suffered a shameful defeat at Sedan, and Prussian troops converged on the capital city. Verne's younger brother Paul was off in the navy, fighting against the enemy warships said to be prowling the Atlantic shores. While in Nantes on holiday, Verne had received his call to service. With the escalating hostilities, all citizens were obliged to contribute to the defense of their nation. . .

Thus, he spent the winter months off the north-western corner of France, patrolling the shores and remaining as far from the actual fighting as possible. Since Verne was completely unschooled in how to command the twelve grizzled veterans, they ran a rather chaotic ship. These aging, battle-scarred men were not healthy enough to fight on the front, so they rode with the author in the choppy waters near the coast. They were driving Verne insane with their incessant chatter, bragging, and scatterbrained ideas.

Though his crew had been designated a military unit, they possessed only three flintlock rifles among them, and Verne was forced to supply all of their food out of his own pocket. A single tiny cannon had been mounted on the bow of the yacht; whenever it was fired, the gun barked like a poodle.

For week upon dreary week, the *Saint Michel* sailed in a tight pattern, ready to meet the Prussians and terrified lest that day should ever arrive. The invaders had fully-fledged warships filled with cannons and professional soldiers. Verne had no idea what his little yacht and its single gun could be expected to do against such an attack. Flee, probably.

In an odd way, though, the change of routine was a welcome balm for his writing life. Leaving the scrawny veterans in charge of the patrol, Verne could retreat to the captain's cabin with his notebooks and journals – and he was able to write. During those tedious months he completed several new novels in longhand, though they would have to wait for publication until the end of the war and a return to peace and prosperity.

Pierre-Jules Hetzel had been trapped in Paris during the worsening siege. The publisher was forced to continue a correspondence with his author through "Vernian" means – sending letters via balloon or carrier pigeon.

Verne did not think much about the political turmoil, which seemed so far away in Paris. He was here on his boat, which he loved . . . on the ocean, which he also loved . . . listening to the sound of waves and feeling the gentle sway of the currents. He was able to concentrate on his stories without the incessant interruptions of family life, without social responsibilities, without the noises of unruly Michel (who had already been dubbed "the terror of Le Crotoy" in the short time Verne had lived in the small port city).

As he sat back now, deep in thought at his small writing desk, Verne pondered a new novel about an enormous ocean liner so large that he titled the book *A Floating City*. He relished the quiet and solitude.

Until the loud clang of the *Saint Michel*'s warning bell shattered the late afternoon silence.

One of the white-haired soldiers hollered from the bow, and Verne heard the thump of running feet on deck. Someone retrieved the three flintlock weapons from the locker. Ragged voices issued orders, while others countermanded them.

Verne groaned. With a heavy sigh, he imagined it must be another false sighting. He closed his notebook and left his cabin, striding up to the main deck just in time to see two old veterans fiddling with the tiny cannon. They lit the fuse. Verne raised his hand, demanding to know what they were doing, but it was too late.

The small gun fired its two-pound ball with a sound like a child's oversized popgun. The men cheered and raised their fists into the air, hurling obscenities and insults across the water. They pointed and danced and waved their hands.

Then Verne looked into the gathering dusk to see a three-masted enemy warship approaching, its gun ports open and full-sized cannons emerging. Prussian navy men swarmed about like ants on the deck, preparing to capture or destroy the *Saint Michel*.

And his men had fired the tiny cannon in defiance.

"What have you done?" Verne gasped in horror. "You fools!"

The Prussian warship launched a broadside at them. All the cannons on its starboard hull blazed orange spitfire. Though the range was still great, cannonballs rained like meteorites into the water between the two ships. The warship adjusted her sails and bore down on Verne's minuscule yacht.

"Turn us about, men," he said. "Turn us about! Run for the shore."

One of the wrinkled veterans pulled out his flintlock to fire a wild shot at the enemy, but others quickly realized the rashness of their action. The small yacht turned toward the haven of the shore, which was merely a misty blur in the distance . . . much too far away. Verne shouted orders, but these men were not sailors, and responded with less speed and efficiency than a captain would expect on a true war vessel.

"We are doomed," Verne muttered.

As the *Saint Michel* began to flee, the Prussian warship closed the gap. Within an hour, the enemy vessel had approached close enough that the Prussians let loose another volley of cannon fire. The terrible balls struck closer, splashing all around the yacht. Miraculously, they did no more damage than splintering one of the yacht's top deck rails.

Next time, the cannonballs would probably sink them.

"We will have to surrender," Verne said, groaning in despair. "Raise our white flag."

"But Captain Verne, we are defending the French coast!"

Verne's voice cracked in abject panic. "We can do nothing against that monstrous vessel. Just look at all of her cannon!"

"Oh."

Even as they hoisted the white rag, hoping for mercy from the enemy captain, the big warship turned about, bringing her port-side cannons to bear.

Verne stared, appalled. There was nothing he could do, no means of escape. Even if he should dive overboard, he could never swim all the way to shore in the cold winter ocean.

He was about to die.

Then, as he faced the oncoming battleship, he saw a golden glow in the sea behind the Prussian vessel – the luminous yellow eyes of a deep-sea leviathan rising to the surface as it picked up speed.

Verne put a hand over his mouth and saw the great armored vessel breach the surface just enough so that its razor ridge of reinforced steel cut a vicious wake like a shark's fin. The *Nautilus*.

The veterans on-board the *Saint Michel* were appalled. "It's a monster!" At the bow, Verne gripped the side of his yacht close to the tiny cannon and shook his head, unable to believe his eyes.

The men aboard the Prussian battleship gave brusque orders to ready the cannon – just as he heard the growl and hum of the submarine boat. The armored vessel leaped forward at top ramming speed and crashed into the warship. Too late, the Prussian cannons fired, intending to sink the *Saint Michel*. But with their aim thrown off, the weapons blasted harmlessly into the sky.

Verne watched, stunned, as the *Nautilus* plowed through the lower hull of the Prussian vessel with a rending crunch. The sailing ship canted to one side, taking in huge amounts of water.

Sparks from the cannon torches ignited black powder that had spilled onto the decks. Enemy sailors ran about, trying to escape from the unexpected attack by the submarine vessel. Then the warship exploded.

Verne's heart pounded in his chest, and he found himself short of breath. He couldn't believe Nemo's timely appearance. "Old friend, you always did manage to defeat impossible odds."

"We did it, Monsieur Captain Verne," one of the old veterans said, grabbing his arm with joy. "We have sunk that Prussian ship!"

Verne scowled at the ancient soldier. The other eleven men jabbered amongst themselves, not sure what had just happened. The dusk had deepened enough to make details in the water uncertain.

"What if the sea monster attacks us next?" another one said.

"It won't," Verne answered, leaning over the side of the boat and searching the waters. "*He* won't."

As the Prussian vessel collapsed into a sinking mass of broken debris and flaming timbers, Verne wondered if he should take the *Saint Michel* over and rescue any survivors. He had only a small yacht, a few weapons, and just twelve crewmen. If he took aboard too many prisoners, they could easily overpower their captors – and then what would he do?

Verne had no stomach for an actual fight. He had never expected to be this close to the realities of war. He scratched his beard, struggling to reach a decision. The Prussian warship had meant to sink them without remorse, to kill him and his crew in cold blood, even after they had raised a white flag. They could all swim to shore, for all he cared.

Another wake curled up beside the *Saint Michel*, and a great metal shape appeared beneath the water. Demonic yellow eyes sent beams of light into the depths. With a hiss and trickle of shed water, the armored craft rose next to the yacht. The scrawny veterans scrambled to the opposite side of the boat, ready to jump into the cold Atlantic, if necessary.

The *Nautilus* floated like a dragon, water dripping off its hull plates. While waiting for the upper hatch to open, Verne gripped the railing of his yacht, swung himself over, and dropped onto the outer deck of the submarine vessel. The veterans gasped, marveling at their captain's bravery, wondering if he meant to kill the monster.

Verne heard movement below, footsteps on the metal ladder. The hatch opened to reveal an older-looking Nemo, his trim, dark beard etched with a few strands of gray. Nemo raised a hand. "Jules, I was surprised to find you out here. Quite a good thing I chose a course along the coast."

"I'm certainly glad you did," Verne answered. "Thank you, André."

"I cannot stop a war, but I *can* come to the aid of a friend." Nemo gestured. "Come aboard the *Nautilus*, for one last time. We need to say our goodbyes, you and I."

Without hesitation, Verne climbed down the metal rungs and once again entered the marvelous undersea boat. The old veterans could handle the *Saint Michel* for a little while; in fact, they would need some time to recover from their astonishment and the unexpected victory over the Prussian warship.

Inside the vessel, Verne stood in a daze. He recognized Cyrus Harding, the British second-in-command, and some of the other crewmen. Embarrassed, he wondered if these people were aware of his novel *20,000 Leagues Under the Sea*, in which he had adapted their activities for the sake of his fiction.

His greatest surprise, though, was to see Caroline aboard the submarine with Nemo. "Hello, Jules," she said. "I have missed you."

He froze, speechless and confused. By her expression, he knew that she had read his face, knew the pain in his heart. Nemo had no doubt rescued her from the siege of Paris, and though he wanted to be thankful that Caroline was safe, Verne could not quash his own feelings of jealousy.

Even since their younger days on Île Feydeau, Caroline had always preferred Nemo, had always wanted to be with him. She had waited for him when he was lost. Because of Nemo, she had refused to remarry, even long after Captain Hatteras had vanished at sea. Now, Verne's two friends were finally together. How could he not be happy for them?

"I'm glad that you are safe, Jules," Caroline said. "Paris is burning. I was not sure if you had managed to get out before the Prussians came. . ." She shook her head. "It is a terrible place these days. I have lost everything: the merchant offices, my accounts, my papers."

"You haven't lost everything." Nemo touched her arm and looked toward Verne. "We must bid you farewell, though – this time we will not come back. Have a glass of wine with us. I'll tell you what has happened since our last meeting . . . and then we must be on our way. The rest of the world is yours, Jules Verne. I want only my small, private part of it."

In the gathering dark, the *Nautilus* floated motionless beside the *Saint Michel*. After an awkward embrace, Nemo, Verne, and Caroline sat in the salon. It was a bittersweet reunion for three friends who had known each other most of their lives.

Nemo explained about the death of his wife and son, about his declared vendetta against ships of war, and even about Phileas Fogg's quest to travel around the world in eighty days.

"But we have had enough of such experiences with the cruelty of humans," Nemo said. He offered Verne one of his seaweed cigars. "From this point on, I will not bother with civilization. We will find a quiet place and make our own lives, live by our own rules." His heavy sigh spoke of a lifetime of struggles. "I tried my best to make the world a better place. But mankind does not wish to change."

"Is this fair to her, my friend?" Verne kept his eyes fixed on Nemo's. "Taking Caroline away from –"

"Yes," Nemo interrupted without hesitation. "More than you can ever understand, Jules."

Verne looked from Nemo to Caroline. Something in his chest constricted so tightly that he wondered if his heart might have stopped beating. "You . . . both . . . intend to stay together? Go off to some isolated, primitive place?"

"I have to, Jules," Caroline answered. "Please understand. All your life you wanted to write books and plays – and you have succeeded. Who could deny it? But all of my life *I* have dreamed of the freedom to write and play my own music, the freedom to choose." She took a deep breath. "You have not had to live with the accusations and scorn of civilized society. This is my chance, Jules." She took Nemo's hand in hers. "This is *my* choice."

Nemo looked at her, then back at Verne. "A world of adventure is waiting."

Late at night, Jules Verne took his leave of the *Nautilus*, knowing he would never see either of his old friends again. He returned to his own yacht, where the agitated veterans received him as if he were a tortured and ill-treated prisoner of war. Verne refused to answer their questions and withdrew, sick at heart. The old men asked if he wanted to fire the little cannon himself, to celebrate, but he brushed them aside.

He watched the *Nautilus* cruise away from the *Saint Michel*. With bubbles of released air, the submarine sank out of sight and sailed away beneath the seas.

VII

At last, after waiting for most of their lives, Caroline and Nemo basked in the warmth of each other's company.

They spoke little of their feelings at first, allowing themselves time to become reacquainted. They shared stories about their lives, the years they had spent apart. And as they talked, every movement, every expression or touch, communicated in a language more eloquent than words how much they cared for each other.

Their love, hidden for so long, had formed both a bond and a wall between them for most of their lives. The *Nautilus* crew, all of whom had known Nemo's wife and son at Rurapente, kept their distance, but welcomed their captain's restored spirits. Nemo's heart had been in pain for years, ever since he had learned of Auda's death,

But Caroline still did not know the fate of her husband.

Nemo guided the *Nautilus* north, beyond the coast of England and Scotland and into the Arctic Circle.

Gazing through the broad salon windows, Caroline recovered from her ordeal in the siege of Paris, nourished by a daily routine of calm and peace and rest. The lines of strain smoothed themselves from her face and, within days, she began to laugh again. To Nemo, her voice and her laughter was beautiful music aboard the submarine. Soon she even played on a wooden flute he gave her, performing some of her own melodies. Nemo vowed to obtain a pipe organ or pianoforte for her, so that she could play and play to her heart's content. Perhaps he could even install it here in the salon. . .

When they reached the frigid polar seas, the *Nautilus* dived beneath the shimmering ice pack that surrounded the North Pole, and he ordered all the *Nautilus*'s powerful front lights turned on. Nemo called for Caroline to join him at the bridge.

"This may sadden you, but you have needed to see it for many years. I have no choice. You deserve to know, and without it, you and I will never be truly free to –" He paused, at a loss for words, and then simply took her hand. "Will you gaze with me upon one more secret?"

Her blue eyes widened with concern, but she squeezed his hand. He guided the *Nautilus* down to deep outcroppings of rock. As they came around a bend, the yellow cones of light fell upon the skeleton of a ship's wooden hull like a beached whale. Caroline stiffened.

Preserved by the icy waters and the depths to which it had sunk, a wrecked sailing vessel had come to rest on the silty ocean floor. They could see the outline of its keel, the tall columns of its masts, even a few rotted shreds of sail and rigging rope.

"I'm sorry, Caroline," Nemo said.

The *Nautilus* cruised around the sunken wreck. After so much time, they could not determine exactly what had happened. Part of the hull had caved in, as if crushed in massive jaws of ice. They passed the muck-covered masthead figure, and finally drifted over the barnacle-encrusted nameplate. Under the blaze of light, letters stood out despite the stains and grime of decades: *Forward*.

"I don't know if your Captain Hatteras was close to discovering a Northwest Passage. All I know is that we found this vessel here. Perhaps it isn't the answer you had hoped for . . . but it is finally an answer."

Caroline fixed her gaze on Nemo for a long moment, avoiding the sunken hulk of Captain Hatteras's exploration ship. "It is an answer I wish I had known years ago. Then our situation . . . might have been different."

"Things can still be different," Nemo said, taking her hand again.

"Yes," she answered with a long slow sigh, a gentle smile touching the corners of her mouth. "Things can finally be different . . . between us."

The past, for both of them, now lay at a safe distance – not forgotten, but no longer a wall.

Epilogue
MOBILIS IN MOBILI

Paris, 1874

After the war, Jules Verne and his family settled into their new summer house at Amiens, but he still made regular trips to Paris to meet with his publisher. He was a famous writer, after all, and in much demand.

Verne dined with Hetzel at a well-known restaurant not far from the Louvre. Each man ordered roast herbed quail with potato-cheese soufflé and shared an expensive bottle of wine. Verne was happy to let his publisher pay for the extravagance, and he savored every bite. Though the author had plenty of money, he could not bring himself to be such a spendthrift. His father, now two years in his grave, would never have approved. . .

After the grueling siege had been lifted from Paris and the Treaty of Frankfurt ended the Franco-Prussian War, life began its painful journey back to normalcy. Following a few abortive starts, Hetzel got his publishing company running again – and Jules Verne continued to be the star performer.

Around the World in 80 Days was a smash hit, Verne's most popular "Extraordinary Voyage" so far. He was now considered an international celebrity, badgered for interviews and opinions on numerous subjects. At first the accolades had been amusing, and the bearded author had reveled in his fame . . . but now he felt bothered by it all. He wanted nothing more than quiet time to continue his writing.

He produced *A Floating City* (written on-board his yacht while patrolling the coast for Prussian warships) and *Measuring a Meridian*. Like clockwork, Verne's novels once again came out from Hetzel, first serialized in the children's magazine, then in bound volumes for the holidays. Indeed, life in France had returned to normal. . .

After their fine meal, the two men returned to Hetzel's courtyard offices on rue Jacob and spent an hour scrutinizing the galleys of a forthcoming story, the first installment in *The Fur Country*. But Hetzel was not quite as enthusiastic about the work as he'd been in previous times. "I am sorry to say this, Jules," the publisher ventured, "but we need to think ahead and consider perhaps a little more . . . variety in your subject matter."

"Variety?" Verne's mind raced. "In every extraordinary voyage I have explored different subjects and different places –"

"Yes, and with quite some success," Hetzel added, looking down his large nose as if it were an insurmountable obstacle. He gave his author a paternal smile. "But of late I have noticed a certain, shall we say, *sameness* to these journeys. What will you do when the earth has been completely mapped?"

"There will always be places to explore, always new adventures to tell." Verne gave his publisher a stubborn frown, careful to add just the right amount of indignation to his voice. Now that Nemo was indeed gone, he would have to create his own adventures, think up his own ideas. But Verne's imagination was up to the task; after all, he had exercised it enough. He pursed his lips. "What, exactly, did you have in mind?"

Hetzel's eyes brightened and then darted away. Verne could see that the older man was now approaching the subject he *really* wanted to discuss. "What if you were to consider, for instance, adding more . . . romance in your novels?"

Verne bristled and sat up across from the publisher's desk. He put his elbows on the now-ignored galleys. "Romance? What could a frivolous romance possibly have to do with my stories?"

Hetzel folded his fingers together and looked intently at his visitor. "In each novel, you have brave explorers and intelligent engineers – yet you rarely include a true love element."

Verne fumed. "But in *Journey to the Centre of the Earth*, my character is engaged to be married. He thinks of his fiancée often. Grauben . . . yes, I believe her name was Grauben."

Hetzel dismissed the defense. "She is mentioned a few times in the entire novel, and appears in the flesh but once. No, Jules, I am talking about a genuine relationship, true emotions and heartfelt desires. Let the reader see two people who love each other, not just give lip service to mutual adoration."

Verne narrowed his eyes and sniffed. He and his publisher had experienced occasional disagreements about the content of his prodigious output, and in his heart Verne knew that Hetzel was usually right, even when he dared not admit it.

"Jules, your novels are full of fascination, but empty of passion."

Now, though, the suggestion brought to mind Verne's own marriage with Honorine, and the loss of Caroline Aronnax. From childhood, he'd been convinced that Caroline was destined to be the real love of his life – and he had not let go of that fantasy. Of course, he'd never gotten around to purchasing the coral necklace either, the one he had promised her in the marketplace on Île Feydeau. By now he could have procured her a thousand of them. . .

"My tales are not about such things," Verne insisted. "They are about science and knowledge and exploration, extending our boundaries and traveling to new horizons." He felt his face warm with a flush. "A love story would only get in the way of the adventures." He looked away from his publisher and lowered his voice. "Besides, what do I know of romance?"

Hetzel sat back at his desk and took out a cigar, knowing his author well enough to see that it was fruitless to press the matter further. At least for now. "So, how goes the Robinson?" he asked, changing the subject.

The "Robinson" was Verne's long-planned desert-island book, his homage to *Robinson Crusoe* and *Swiss Family Robinson*, combined with André Nemo's real-life adventures as a castaway. "I have decided to rewrite it from the start."

The publisher puffed on his cigar and smiled. "Glad to hear it." When Hetzel had seen the first draft, he'd complained that it was a mere adventure story about survivors marooned on a desert island, with nothing original or thought-provoking. By now Verne's readers had come to expect cutting-edge science, intriguing speculation, and marvelous technological wonders . . . and the first version of the "Robinson" novel had contained none of that.

"I've had a wonderful idea about how to fix it." Verne stood up, full from the lunch and the wine. "Rest assured that when I deliver the manuscript, you'll be quite pleased. It will be my best novel since *20,000 Leagues*."

Hetzel beamed. "Well, there's a challenge for you."

Verne said a quick farewell and left. He had writing to do.

For years since the publication of *20,000 Leagues Under the Sea*, Verne's readers had continued to shower him with letters and praise, ecstatic in their adoration for the character of Captain Nemo. Even as a fictional person, Nemo still left Verne feeling envious and dissatisfied with his own accomplishments.

What is it about the man?

Upon finishing the submarine book, he had considered the story complete. He had described the *Nautilus* sinking in the terrible maelstrom off Norway, forever vanished along with its brooding captain and mysterious crew beneath the dark, cold waters.

But his readers begged to hear more of the dark genius. Nemo, Nemo! They wanted the captain's background explained, they wanted the mystery solved. Finally, dejected and trying to salvage his ambitious desert-island novel, he realized that Nemo might yet have another role to play. Verne had thought of a way to rid himself of his terrible jealousy, once and for all.

He wrote *The Mysterious Island* in three substantial volumes. Instead of using average castaways, Verne populated his massive novel with characters taken from Rurapente. An intelligent engineer, Cyrus Harding, led the group, used his ingenuity to build a magnificent house inside a granite cliff. The castaways learned how to smelt iron, domesticate wild animals, even set up a telegraph . . . all the while assisted by a secretive benefactor who came to their aid at appropriate moments, without ever revealing his identity.

At the end of the long novel, after readers had waited month after month during the serialization, they learned the truth: the guardian angel on the mysterious island was none other than an aging and bitter Captain Nemo, who had survived the sinking of the *Nautilus* and brought his damaged submarine boat to a cave beneath the volcano. . .

By now, Verne had realized his error in not showing the actual demise of Nemo in the first novel. He could not simply let the *Nautilus* disappear into the treacherous depths, where it was *presumed* destroyed. To rid himself of this burden forever, Verne depicted quite precisely the death scene of Captain Nemo, a man haunted by the tragic deaths of his wife and young son.

In the final chapters, with the castaways gathered around him on the entombed *Nautilus*, the captain died aboard his beloved submarine boat. To honor Nemo's final request, the character of Cyrus Harding operated the controls for a final time before disembarking. The castaways watched as the *Nautilus* sank slowly under the sea, bearing the body of the great Nemo, who was never to be seen again. . .

When Jules Verne completed the enormous manuscript, including the proud funeral, he at last felt free of André Nemo. He knew he would never see the man again, nor Caroline. As told by Verne, the story was not true . . . but the readers would be satisfied.

"Forgive me, my friends," he murmured. Though altered and falsified, the account would certainly make a grand story.

He set aside his pen and looked at the thick journal filled with his words. No matter what happened in real life, Verne's readers would remember Captain Nemo, and his fate, the way the author had told it.

* * *

The true ending of Nemo's story was quite different from fiction, though.

The *Nautilus* continued its voyage of discovery through the seas. Forsaking his war against war, Nemo preyed upon no ships, but instead remained content with Caroline's company. He chose the sub-marine's course carefully, setting out for his favorite spot on the ocean bottom.

He wanted to show Caroline the pinnacle of mystery and wonder he'd found beneath the waves. Standing with her on the bridge deck, Nemo felt like a romantic character in a storybook as they stared out at the turquoise-lit wonderland.

He looked over at the stiff-backed Englishman at the helm. "Mr Harding? A progress report?"

Harding consulted his charts. "We should arrive within the hour, captain."

Nemo took Caroline's arm in his. "Come with me to the salon. There is something you must see."

He led her again to the central salon, where he had cranked shut the iris plates over the wide, circular window, keeping the view hidden. Nemo poured each of them a glass of wine, then gestured for Caroline to sit in the chair beside him. While they waited, he looked into her face, studying the bright blue eyes that were so different from Auda's deep, dark gaze.

But Auda was gone, as was Caroline's husband – and the two of them no longer had any barriers to their lifelong love.

Caroline's eyes were electric with anticipation. Nemo sipped his wine, smiling as he allowed the suspense to build. He stroked her hair. Before long, he heard the thrumming engines slow. Harding's hollow-sounding voice came over the speaking tube. "We have arrived, Captain. All propellers at full stop."

"Thank you, Mr Harding."

He held out his hand to Caroline. She took it and stood, gliding gracefully with him over to the closed windows. Using a louver crank, Nemo slid back the metal plates, then turned a dial that extinguished the lamps inside the salon.

Outside, the ethereal light from the portholes hung like a diffuse halo around the *Nautilus*. He encouraged Caroline to take a step closer to the viewing window, to allow her eyes to adjust. When she gasped out loud, he knew she had seen.

"Behold . . . Atlantis."

Drowned beneath pristine waters that were turned a jewel blue by filtered sunlight lay the ruins of an ancient, long-forgotten city. Fluted Corinthian pillars towered beside a fallen arch adorned with dervish-scarves of seaweed. The collapsed buildings showed magnificent, unrivalled architecture, now appreciated only by colorful fish that flitted in and out of the awesome drowned temples.

"It is beautiful, André," Caroline said, letting out a long breath. Her face glowed with childlike delight. Nemo thought he had never seen her look more lovely.

An alabaster statue of Adonis-like perfection lay face down in the mud. Enameled urns that had tumbled to the soft ocean bed were now encrusted with coral. Green and pink sea anemones sprouted in basins and beside broken benches like an odd flower bed. Metallic-pink abalone shells had wedged themselves into the cracks of a crooked flagstone path.

Nemo whispered his next words close to her ear. "I love you, Caroline. I've loved you all of my life. There is so much more I want to share with you. The oceans of the world can be ours together. Will you marry me?"

Immense marble halls sagged under the weight of water and time. Gems, wrought-gold jewelry, and broken pottery lay strewn across the ocean floor. All traces of the original inhabitants of this place had vanished.

Caroline closed her eyes, letting the words into her heart like water into parched ground. "Of course I will, André." She opened her eyes and squeezed his hand. They didn't speak for a long time, just sharing the wonder of the world that lay before them.

"Come walk with me," Nemo invited, his voice barely above a whisper.

Caroline nodded. "Always."

Then slowly – almost shyly – they swayed toward each other, and their lips met in a kiss that held both reverence for the past and promise for the future. . .

Leaving Cyrus Harding in charge, the two suited up in undersea garments. Surrounded by warm water, they steadied their footing on the sandy bottom. Nemo reached out to clasp Caroline's gloved hand. The pair moved like fairy dancers in slow, graceful motion.

As they explored, the final barriers between them seemed to melt away. The ancient paths and their own tortured histories of loneliness, tragic mistakes, and paths not taken now merged with the present into one magical moment frozen in time.

Everything they had endured or experienced in their lives had brought them to this point. They were together *now* with the future ahead of them. Life was filled with opportunities, a story of love and adventure yet to be written. Regrets over what might have been were washed away by the warmth of the current.

Time had cast its veil of poignant splendor over this ancient place, a reminder that the past was not a thing to fear, but an essential part of the present and all that was yet to come. Walking together, they ventured through the sunken city, treading where no one had gone for centuries on end.

It was only the first of many wonders they would experience together.

ACKNOWLEDGMENTS

During the researching, writing, and editing of this novel, I have valued the insights, suggestions, and expertise of a great many people, including my agents Matt Bialer and Robert Gottlieb at the Trident Media Group, John Ordover at Pocket Books, Diane Jones and Diane Davis Herdt at WordFire, Inc., friends and/or fellow authors Erwin Bush, Steve Baxter, Piers Anthony, Harry Turtledove, Megan Lindholm, Cherie Buchheim, Carolyn Clink, Herbert R. Lottman for his superb biography of Jules Verne, and of course my wife, Rebecca Moesta Anderson.

ABOUT THE AUTHOR

Kevin J Anderson is a prolific author who has published over 100 novels, 49 of which have been national or international bestsellers. His work has been translated into 30 languages, and he has well over 20 million books in print. He often collaborates with other authors, such as Brian Herbert, Rebecca Moesta (his wife), Dean Koontz, Greg Benford, and Doug Beason. In his solo work he is best known for his seven-volume *Saga of Seven Suns* SF epic and his *Terra Incognita* sailing-ships fantasy. He is currently working on the *Hellhole* trilogy with Brian Herbert, and *The Saga of Shadows*, a new trilogy set in the *Seven Suns* universe. He has also written novels and/or comics for *Dune, Star Wars, X-Files, JSA, Titan A.E., StarCraft, Star Trek, Batman/Superman*, and many others.

WWW.WORDFIRE.COM

ANNO DRACULA
BY KIM NEWMAN

It is 1888 and Queen Victoria has remarried, taking as her new consort Vlad Tepes, the Wallachian Prince infamously known as Count Dracula. Peppered with familiar characters from Victorian history and fiction, this novel tells the story of vampire Geneviève Dieudonné and Charles Beauregard of the Diogenes Club as they strive to solve the mystery of the Ripper murders.

ISBN: 9780857680839

AVAILABLE NOW!

ALSO AVAILABLE FROM TITAN BOOKS:

The Further Adventures of Sherlock Holmes

Sir Arthur Conan Doyle's timeless creation returns in
a series of handsomely designed detective stories. The
Further Adventures series encapsulates the most varied
and thrilling cases of the world's greatest detective.

THE TITANIC TRAGEDY
William Seil

THE WEB WEAVER
Sam Siciliano

THE STAR OF INDIA
Carol Buggé

THE PEERLESS PEER
Philip José Farmer

THE ANGEL OF THE OPERA
Sam Siciliano

THE GIANT RAT OF SUMATRA
Richard L. Boyer

THE WHITECHAPEL HORRORS
Edward B. Hanna

DR. JEKYLL AND MR. HOLMES

Loren D. Estleman

SÈANCE FOR A VAMPIRE

Fred Saberhagen

THE SEVENTH BULLET

Daniel D. Victor

THE STALWART COMPANIONS

H. Paul Jeffers

THE MAN FROM HELL

Barrie Roberts

THE WAR OF THE WORLDS

Manley W. Wellman & Wade Wellman

THE SCROLL OF THE DEAD

David Stuart Davies

THE ECTOPLASMIC MAN

Daniel Stashower

THE VEILED DETECTIVE

David Stuart Davies

WWW.TITANBOOKS.COM

The Further Adventures of Sherlock Holmes

THE BREATH OF GOD
BY GUY ADAMS

A body is found crushed to death in the London snow. There are no footprints anywhere near. It is almost as if the man was killed by the air itself. This is the first in a series of attacks that sees a handful of London's most prominent occultists murdered. While pursuing the case, Holmes and Watson have to travel to Scotland to meet with the one person they have been told can help: Aleister Crowley.

ISBN: 9780857682826

COMING SOON!